THE LAND BEYOND

Also by Dana Stabenow

THE
LAND BEYOND

Book III *of* Silk and Song
by
Dana Stabenow

Gere Donovan Press
Vancouver WA

The Land Beyond. Copyright © 2015 by Dana Stabenow.

Gere Donovan Press
1220 Main Street, Suite 270
Vancouver WA 98660
www.geredonovan.com

First Printing, 2015
ISBN 978-1-62858-082-2

This one is for
Barbara Peters,
who always believed.

Acknowledgments

As always, my thanks to reference librarian Michael Cataggio, freelance editor Laura Anne Gilman, cartographer Cherie Northon, and especially to all those wonderful people down at Gere Donovan Press—Scott, Caton, Mike—and everybody who worried I was going to kill off North Wind. Tsk.

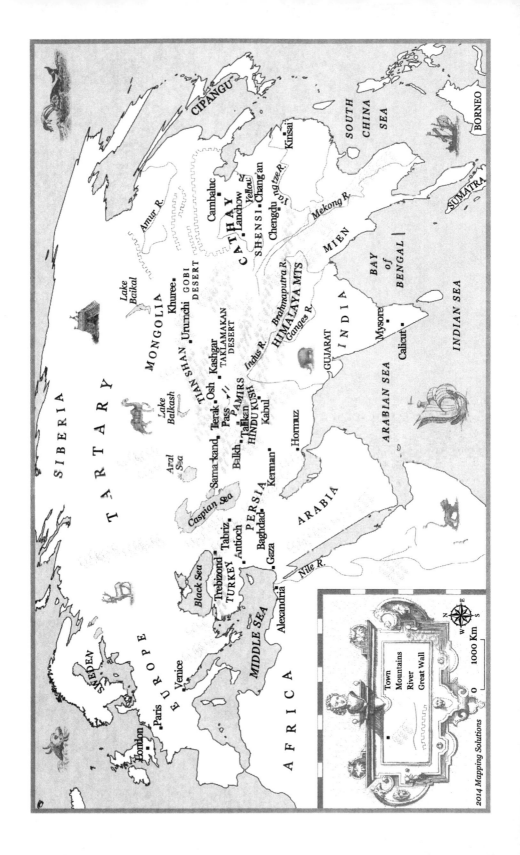

2014 Mapping Solutions

THE LAND BEYOND

· Part IV ·

· One ·

December, 1323 A.D.
Venice

⊢——⊣

The best that could be said about winter in Venice was that the colder temperatures suppressed the smell of the canals. There was, however, no known advantage to the constant fogs that lay heavily on the Laguna Veneta, ghostly tentacles of which slithered up the canals to enfold the city in a chill embrace that no hearth fire however large could ease. After nearly two years spent traveling the Road, most of the journey spent in dry desert country where a day without a hot sun glaring down just meant that night had fallen, it took some getting used to, especially in the location Johanna currently occupied.

Which was the minuscule square fronting Ca' Polo, with lesser buildings crowding the sides. She had found an alcove created by the uneven joining of two of these, bought a dark, hooded cloak that enveloped her head to foot and melted into the shadow created there, from where she observed the comings and goings of the Polo family. By the end of each day the encroaching fog had soaked her from shoulder to knee. It was a wonder she hadn't come down with inflammation of the lungs. More irritating still, watching the house had been productive of very little in the way of information. Her grandfather, Marco Polo, lay on his deathbed, but that much she had heard from the supercilious steward who had closed the door in her face the day they had arrived in Venice.

The two older Polo daughters and their husbands were the first people she identified, though she only saw them once and each couple for the exact amount of time specified by duty and no more. They arrived by private gondola, attended by personal guards, wore sumptuous clothes that shouted their worth from across the square and wooden pattens on their richly embroidered shoes to keep their feet up out of the mud. They were not noticeably grieving as they left.

She didn't see anyone who looked like the third daughter, Moreta. She didn't see the wife, Donata, either, but that was more understandable.

Summarily dismissed from the door of Ca' Polo, the second order of business on that day of their arrival in the Jewel of the Sea was to look for lodgings for the company, man and beast. Johanna found North Wind and the other horses stabling across the lagoon in Marghera, a brief boat ride away so that she could still see him and ride him every day. The farmer never raised so much as an eyebrow at Johanna's dressing in trousers and riding astride, and for that alone she would have paid him twice the silver penny he had asked for his fee.

She kept her ears open while engaged in these homely occupations, and by keeping silent learned a good deal. Venice was ruled by a Doge, one Giovanni Soranzo, eighty-three years old, a leader with the majority of the merchants of Venice solidly in his camp. This appeared to be less due to the remembrance of the martial exploits of his youth, when he conquered Caffa during the last war with Genoa, than for the rare ability to keep the peace on the Middle Sea. As every marginally competent merchant knew, peace was good for business. In the eleven years since Soranzo's ascension, Venice had made treaties with Byzantium, Sicily, Milan, Bologna, Brescia, Tunisia, Trebizond and Persia, which had greatly facilitated the movement, not to mention the security of sale goods. Doge Soranzo had also presided over the opening of trade with England and Flanders, which either inspired or was inspired by the building of a new kind of ship, called a merchant galley. It was wider and longer than existing ships, and was propelled by both sail and by 200 oarsmen. The oarsmen were free men, and armed, so that upon attack the galley could muster 200 more men to its defense. She went down to the Arsenal to see several upon the ways, and even saw one of them launched, and was impressed with the nimble way the craft took up the wind in its sails and its speed over water when it did.

Along with the rest of Venice they all spent extended periods down at the Arsenal, watching the galleys being built, and they never missed a launch. Jaufre wasted a good deal of time figuring the payload per galley, and came to the conclusion that it was roughly equivalent to that of six hundred camels. Respectable, he thought. Given a competent captain, favorable weather, and no war breaking out between any countries with coastlines, a trader could make a reasonably good living. Always supposing the ship didn't sink. Remembering the rough passage from Gaza in November, Jaufre could only imagine that they did with a frequency that would put said merchant out of business and probably into the poorhouse, if not debtor's prison.

In a month she and Jaufre and Shasha were roughly fluent in Italian, the lingua franca of the Middle Sea and Johanna practiced her fluency by sidling up to groups of Venetians and eavesdropping on their conversations. Whenever someone mentioned the name "Polo," her ears pricked up. One day a group of lawyers were trumping one another's stories of bad clients. Marco Polo had figured in several of those stories, either as claimant or defendant. It seemed that her grandfather was somewhat litigious in nature. She was smart enough during these intelligence forays not to draw attention to herself, drifting off when anyone looked her way, but gossip along with trade goods was the fuel that powered Venice, and it was amazing how much information she managed to acquire on the inmates of the Polo palazzo, or, as it was known more familiarly, Ca' Polo.

Upon his return from Cambaluc, or Cathay as the Venetians would have it, her grandfather, his father and his uncle had had some problems re-establishing themselves in Venetian society. This accomplished, chiefly by the generous giving of fabulous gifts brought with them from the East, his father and uncle resumed their positions as merchants in good standing. Marco enlisted in the Venetian war on Genoa and was captured in the Battle of Curzola.

She asked Félicien where Curzola was. A visit to the Biblioteca Marciana and he reported back. "It's an island in Dalmatia. There was a huge battle there twenty-five years ago, between Venice and Genoa. Venice lost."

Johanna nodded. That much she'd gotten. "My grandfather was taken prisoner there. It's where he wrote *Il Milione*."

"Ah."

"What?"

"He didn't write it, exactly."

"What do you mean?"

"He dictated it. A man from Pisa, name of Rustichello, shared his cell. He wrote down your grandfather's stories and published them in a book." Félicien paused. "And then about a hundred others copied it and printed it, too."

Johanna looked at him, and he held up his hands, palms out. "Don't believe me, go look for yourself. Any bookstall will have a used copy, I promise you."

Venice boasted on average one bookstore per canal, and that was just between bridges. No bridge itself was worthy of the name unless it bore at least one bookstall itself. She sampled a dozen between their lodgings and the Grand Canal and it was as Félicien had said, copies of her grandfather's *Il Milione* were readily available, some in readable condition, many not, and all, it seemed, copied by a different hand and bound by a different publisher. Oddly, as many copies seemed to have been published in French as had been in Italian. "Of course," Félicien said matter-of-factly. "French is the language of romances."

Johanna compared pages of a few of these diverse editions side by side and found very little uniformity of text between them. Some copyists appeared to have even inserted their own narrative, real or imagined, into her grandfather's.

One thing was sure: Everyone in Venice had heard of *Il Milione*. It came as a shock to Marco Polo's grand-daughter that almost everyone thought it was a fabrication from start to finish. Johanna, increasing her written Italian and French, was working her way through the fairest copy she could find of the earliest possible date of original publication, side by side with a French edition, and noted that the more fabulous of the tales her grandfather had been careful to begin with "Men say." On the facts, facts she knew to be true from her own experience, he was unassailable, what was for sale where, local craft specialties and trading practices, regional social norms, distances between cities. He wrote of gunpowder, and spectacles, and coal, and paper money, all of which she had noticed were taking hold here in Venice.

"You have to wonder," she said to Shasha that evening.

"What?"

"If my grandfather brought spectacles back with him. The recipe for gunpowder." Johanna shrugged. "All of it. Everything he wrote about."

It was a useful book for a merchant, *Il Milione*. But then, she thought, her grandfather was a merchant, after all.

And he lay dying at Ca' Polo. It was common knowledge throughout the city that his wife waited only for the drawing of his last breath before dancing in the streets.

Because of course he had married. Of course he had. The fortune with which the Polos had returned had bought him a good match with one Donata Badoèr, daughter of a wealthy merchant. The midwife Johanna had this tale from over a mug of wine in a taverna off of St. Mark's Square told her, "I delivered all three of their daughters. She told me after the birth of third one that he sold all of her dowry for himself." The midwife, a stout woman with a red face, nodded emphatically. "There was a farm, and a house, and—" She waved an expansive hand and belched. "Property," she said. "And he sold it, every bit of it. If you ask me, she never forgave him. I'd bet you a hundred ducats that she'll do everything, short of holding a pillow over his face—" Johanna flinched but the midwife, busy with her wine, didn't see it "—to see him out of this world as speedily as possible." She belched again. "Traipsing back home after twenty years' absence with a hatful of tales that would shame the devil himself. A liar, a braggart, and a fool, to think he would be believed when he came home. He probably spent the whole twenty years he was gone in Byzantium, collecting the stories of real travelers to try out on the gullible in Venice." She snorted. "Although Venetians will believe anything. As *Il Milione* well proved."

"Three daughters," Johanna said indifferently, did the midwife but know it displaying an admirable hold on her temper.

The midwife eyed her empty mug. Johanna signaled for a refill and the woman drank half of it down in a single gulp. "Three daughters, yes," she said, dabbing daintily at her mouth with the hem of her sleeve. "Fantina, Bellela, and Moreta. The first two are married."

"And the third?"

The midwife drained her mug. "Moreta? They have yet to find her a husband. She still lives at home."

Back in her shadowy corner across from the Polo residence, Johanna reviewed the information she had gleaned from a month's worth of eavesdropping and bribery, and wondered after all if she shouldn't just march up to the front door and try to force an entrance. Even being turned away a second time in ignominy would be better than standing in this thrice cursed fog. She shifted her sodden cloak in a vain attempt to find some part of it that was dry, and jumped at a noise that sounded like a muffled squeal.

She looked around to behold an urchin, her hair a mess of ink black curls clustering around a small face with a determined chin, a mouth pressed into a defiant line, and dark brown eyes, narrowed and glaring in an effort to project pugnacity and fearlessness. She couldn't quite bring it off, and Johanna wondered what her own face looked like at that moment. She straightened her expression, not without effort. She touched the purse at her waist, containing her father's book and the squared cylinder that was his bao. As always, the touch comforted her, and today it calmed her, too. "And who are you?" she said.

The chin came even more into evidence. "You're standing in my spot."

"I beg your pardon?"

"This is my spot. You can't take it. I'm here all the time, and everyone who lives on this square knows me."

And tossed her a coin from time to time, Johanna thought. Beggars the world over had their pitches. The girl's rough homespun cloak was worn and too short and her face and hands looked as if they had not seen clean water in days. "Ah," Johanna said. "My apologies. You weren't here, so I thought it was unclaimed." She didn't mention that she'd been here off and on for a month unmolested.

"It isn't."

"I see that now." Johanna paused. The girl couldn't have been more than eight years old, nine at the most. "Perhaps I could rent it from you."

The girl scowled. "Rent it?"

"Yes." Johanna searched her pockets and produced a silver coin whose place of origin she did not immediately recognize and which could have been a solidus, an aureus, a denari, a bezant, a florin or something else altogether, because making change in Venice was like that.

The girl snorted. "I take in double that most mornings."

Johanna doubted it. "I'm sure you do," she said nevertheless. "One now, and another like it at the end of the day." And then, struck with an idea, she said, "And two more like it every day, if you will stand watch here and take note of everyone who comes and goes to Ca' Polo. You know which one is Ca' Polo?"

With infinite scorn, the girl said, "I know all the palazzos in Venice."

"It is agreed, then? I will meet you here at vespers each day. You will tell me everyone who came and went through that door, and I will pay you two silver pieces."

"For how long?"

"For as long as I say." Among other advantages, having someone else watch Ca' Polo would free up enough of her time so that she could get over to see North Wind more often. Unused to being pent up in a paddock, he was already getting restive, and made his displeasure known to her by dumping her off his back at least once per visit.

The girl hesitated. "Very well." She snatched the coin from Johanna's hand and ran, her wooden soles clattering over the cobbles and the surface of the bridge as she vanished from view.

The encounter nearly caused her to miss the man who slipped out of the door opposite, but not quite.

He was short, with bowed legs. He was dressed in the fashion of Venetian men, a sleeveless tunic buttoned over a long-sleeved chemise and loose-fitting breeches, but when the hood of his cloak fell partway back from his face she caught her breath. He had a heavy brow, narrow, uptilting eyes, a short, flat nose and golden skin. A long, wispy mustache clung perilously to his upper lip and trailed down both sides of his mouth.

He was a Mongol. He had the look of Deshi the Scout, dead in the same cholera epidemic that had taken her mother that dreadful year in Cambaluc.

He pulled up his hood against the rain and hurried off. She slipped from her corner and followed.

He made several stops, one at an apothecary, one at a bookseller, and one where he walked all the way to the Rialto bridge to seek out a particular sweets seller, from whom he purchased a quantity of small, hard candies flavored with lemon.

Halfway back to the palazzo, she waited until he had drawn almost even to a small taverna and increased her pace to catch up with him. He shot her a cursory look and halted in his tracks, staring at her with eyes slowly widening, as if in recognition.

"Steppe rider," she said in Uighur, "you are far from home."

Still he stared, and made no reply.

Very well, it appeared shock tactics would best carry the day. She squared her shoulders, raised her chin, and said, "I am the daughter of Shu Ming of Cambaluc, who was the daughter of Shu Lin, also of Cambaluc, and the wife of the Venetian traveler, Marco Polo. I believe you serve my grandfather." She gestured at the taverna. "Shall we sit, sir? You must have questions. I know I do."

She gave a polite bow and stepped forward. Perforce, he fell back, and soon found himself inside a snug room where a bright, crackling fire gave at least the illusion of warmth. Johanna saw them seated at the most private table in the darkest corner of the taverna, regrettably far from the hearth, and the alewife bustled forward with a clay pitcher of mulled wine, two battered but clean pewter mugs and a plate of bread, cheese and olives. Johanna tipped her lavishly, conveying with a jerk of her head the private nature of her business. The alewife, a diplomat in coif and apron, retired behind her serving counter and never looked in their direction again.

Johanna filled their mugs. "My name is Johanna," she said. She held one of the mugs out to him.

He hesitated before accepting it. "Peter," he said eventually.

She raised an eyebrow. "Peter?"

"In Venice," he said, "I am Peter."

She wondered how old he was. In the best Mongol tradition, his face was ageless, the skin smooth, the fold of his eyelids confounding the lines at the corners that might have given her some indication. The countenance he presented was bland, but his eyes, alert and interested, gave him away.

"You recognized the name of Shu Lin," Johanna said. "Perhaps you knew her."

He said nothing.

She fortified herself with a drink. "As I said, I am her granddaughter. She was wife to Ser Polo, who served the Great Khan for twenty years. The gift of her person was a mark of the Khan's favor, or so it is told in my family."

"Is it?"

She felt a spark of anger at his evasion. "It is," she said with emphasis. "From this union came my mother, Shu Ming. She married Wu Li, a merchant of Cambaluc and a friend to Ser Polo. I am their only child."

"Wu Li," he said. "What is any respectable father about, to let you travel unescorted so far from home?"

She smiled a little. "You should talk."

"I am a man," he said, but mildly.

Her smiled widened. "You are a Mongol," she said. "You don't make the mistake of underestimating women."

He was surprised into a laugh, turned into a cough.

She let her smile fade. "My father is dead," she said. "As is my mother. I left Cambaluc to travel to the West."

"To find what family remained to you?"

It was at least in part the truth. "Yes," she said.

"Wu Li," he said, musingly. "The son of Wu Hai, perhaps?"

"Yes."

His gaze was straight and piercing. "The Honorable Wu Hai was a great friend of my master."

She felt the knot in her belly begin to ease. "Yes. He married my mother to his son, after my grandmother died."

"Ah," he said. "Shu Lin…"

"…was dead by that time. The circumstances of her death were not… pleasant."

Now she had his full attention.

"Explain," he said.

For a servant he possessed a great deal of innate authority. She told the tale without emotion, distant enough from her now that it caused her no pain.

"And Wu Hai turned his wife out of doors for the betrayal of Shu Lin and my master's daughter?"

"His entire household, except his son, my father, whom he married to Shu Ming."

There was silence as Peter the Mongol absorbed this information. "And you wish to see your grandfather."

Her heart seemed to leap into her mouth. She took a deep breath. "I do."

"What do you want from him?" he said. "He lies on his deathbed."

"So I have been told," she said. She sat back in her chair. What did she want from her grandfather? She had traveled almost two thousand leagues to find him. What now did she want to say to this storied man, this legend whose blood she carried in her veins?

"Perhaps," she said slowly, "it is what he might want from me." She met Peter's eyes. "News of his wife and daughter. The knowledge that he has a grandchild."

"He has other grandchildren," Peter said. "And if he would have wanted news of Shu Lin and Shu Ming, he could have sent for it."

She swallowed. He was brutal but he wasn't wrong. "You think he won't want to see me, then?"

"I don't know," he said, surprising her with his frankness. "He is not…" He lingered over his next words. "…himself much of the time now."

Her turn to say nothing.

"But it is possible that his daughter might wish to meet you," he said.

She looked up. "Which one?"

"Moreta," he said, and again his eyes dwelt on her face with something she recognized as fascination. "The youngest daughter, who is still at home." He smiled. "You may find you have something in common."

· TWO ·

December, 1323 A.D.
Venice

⊢——⊣

Shasha had found them a suite of rooms on the first floor of a house on the Rio del Pontego del Tedeschi, midway between the Polo mansion and the Ponte di Rialto, the bridge that crossed the Grand Canal. Jaufre was fairly certain that Shasha's major incentive for hiring these particular rooms was that each one had its own hearth. By far and away their biggest expense so far was fuel, but no one complained. They were all afflicted by the cold.

Shasha had set up a stillroom on the ground floor and was combing the various fairs and markets for herbs new and old. Soon the first floor was perfumed with the aroma of simmering herbs and spices. One thing—possibly the only thing—Venice had for sale at a reasonable price was glass vials and bottles. Shasha bought them in bulk empty and sold them full of lotions, potions and tinctures of her own devising, effective if the traffic through her stillroom was any indication. Hers was a going concern before Christmas.

She and Firas were sharing a room, which surprised no one, not after their reunion in Gaza. "Almost a honeymoon," Jaufre told Johanna, who either ignored or was oblivious to any hidden meaning in the remark. But then Johanna was gone so much of the time those first days in Venice.

Alma and Hayat shared another room, also to no one's surprise. Alma appeared determined to seek out and interrogate every human being with a claim to scholarship, however tenuous, within the authority of the Doge. Her only complaint was the lack of clear skies at night, the worse for astronomical observations. She ran into less opposition because of her sex than Jaufre would have expected. Possibly her harem-cultivated beauty was responsible but he thought that the curiosity that burned with such a genuine fire effectively negated her gender. Certainly she was unstoppable as a seeker after truth, as the philosophers of Venice deemed it to be, and she was rarely turned from their doors.

"She is determined to make up for all the time she lost in the harem," Hayat told him. Hayat's free time was spent in practice with Firas, who had commandeered the attic of their rental for his own private salle and filled it with mats and practice swords and staffs. He was insistent that the group maintain their fighting edge, honed by two years on the Road. They all had bruises, excepting only Alaric, whose Templar training was too well-learned and too long ingrained to allow for dropping his guard now.

Alaric had attached himself and his sword to the salon of an expatriate from Paris, a Messire Roland, who made a good living spanking the young Venetian whelps of wealth and privilege who harbored the laughable illusion that they could wield a sword in workmanlike fashion or, they were soon given to understand, in any fashion at all. Alaric gave lessons in the broadsword and drank his pay in a series of local tavernas, seemingly determined to betray the vows of his former order insofar as temperance and sobriety were concerned. But then the Knights Templar had been disgraced and disbanded and their leaders burned at the stake in Paris almost a decade before, so it wasn't as if he would be damned for it.

Now and then he invited Firas to join him in an exhibition and charged admission. "He is much too fond of his wine," Firas told Jaufre privately.

"I am not his mother," Jaufre said with an edge to his voice.

Firas gave him a keen look from beneath suddenly frowning brows and said no more, leaving Jaufre a little ashamed of his curt reaction.

Hari had gathered up his yellow robe and vanished behind the walls of the San Giorgio Monastery, where he had by means best known to himself become the bosom friend of the abbott. He surfaced occasionally to take tea with his companions, or to stand in rapt witness to one of the many gorgeously-costumed processions to St. Mark's Basilica. He was an object of great curiosity to the children of the city, who would trail in his saffron-clad wake and gather round in an intent and strangely ridicule-free attitude whenever Hari stopped to take speech with anyone he thought looked interesting.

"Which is almost everyone," Félicien said. "No citizen of Venice is safe from our monk." The goliard had taken himself and his lute to the largest of the local inns and was there to be heard singing songs of the Princess Padmini and the night it rained emeralds, and telling floridly embellished tales of the hedonistic life lived in Cambaluc and Kinsai. Very little exaggeration was necessary to enthrall his audience, which swelled as his fame spread. Before long he began to receive invitations for private concerts in canal-side palazzos. "Not since l'Alouette du Sud have I heard such a voice," Jaufre heard one grizzled old Frankish roué claim.

"One would think Venetians would be a little more sophisticated," Félicien told Jaufre when this was reported back to him, "but every fish bites at some bait, I suppose." And spoiled his supercilious tone with a jingling shake of his full purse and a wide grin.

"Who is l'Alouette du Sud?"

Félicien gave an airy wave. "A singer not quite as talented as myself, it would seem."

Jaufre, for his part, had watched the rest of them pursue their various interests only briefly before seeking after his own. He had thought he would do this in company with Johanna, but when he approached her she said, her mouth in a grim line, "I am going to see my grandfather." She was facing him but her gaze was fixed somewhere beyond him. "Although right now I'm going to visit North Wind."

"I could go with you," he said, but she was already out the door, her footsteps moving firmly and briskly away. It took everything in him not to pursue her, but then what would he do if he caught her? She was not someone moved easily from her purpose.

He had loved her for most of his life, this tall, slim, vibrant girl with the long bronze braid and the gray eyes that sparkled with life and the full lips so quick to smile. First their youth and then Edyk the Portuguese had kept her from seeing him as more than a friend and foster brother. But then came that moment in the yurt on the Road when he had watched her finally become aware of him as a man.

And then Gokudo and Ogodei and Sheik Mohammed had conspired to separate them for a year, and Edyk, damn his eyes, had reappeared in Gaza as they were about to take ship for Venice, and yes, he understood that there was unfinished business between them but by all the demons dwelling in the Christian hell, how long was he supposed to wait? There were other women in the world, after all.

But none like Johanna, a voice inside him said.

A voice next to him said, "Patience."

He looked around to see Shasha standing next to him. "Patience," she said again.

"I've been patient," Jaufre said through his teeth. "No one has ever been as patient as I have been." He looked away, the words wrenched out of him. "It's just that…she seems so indifferent, Shasha."

"Not indifferent, Jaufre," his foster sister said. "Just preoccupied. Until this business with her grandfather is settled, she won't have any attention to spare for anything else." She touched his arm. "It's what brought us here, after all. And we did follow her, willingly."

He took in a breath, held it, and then expended it again on a long sigh. "Patience," he said.

"Patience," she said. "For just a little longer."

After all, they both thought, by all reports the old man was dying. How long could he be about it?

"I suppose I could use the time to find us a place to sell our goods," he said. "A storefront on a short lease." He had thought that he would be about that task in company with Johanna, but he was entirely capable of doing so on his own. Entirely.

She smiled, understanding very well his unspoken words. "You could do that. You might want to get to know Venice a little better first. And the Venetians."

He began his research on the docks, watching ships arrive and load and unload. It was one thing to peruse the posted bills of lading. It was another thing to talk to the sailors and the dockhands who actually laded the cargoes. There was always some master who thought he was smarter than the merchant officers posted the length of the Grand Canal. He was almost invariably wrong, which made for amusing entertainment, but that was another story, too, one fit for one of Félicien's more picaresque stories. Jaufre wanted information, good, solid numbers and facts, and the best facts were those he could observe for himself.

Venice was a city of merchants. Everyone who lived there was a member of or made their living by association to the merchant class. If they weren't shipping, they were buying. If they weren't buying, they were selling. If they weren't selling, they were building ships to transport more goods. Even the omnipresent priests were in business for themselves, selling indulgences or pieces of the True Cross.

Venice sold lumber—what they didn't use themselves at the Arsenal building their own ships—and metal ore, and cured skins. They bought gold and silver from the mines of Germania, or did during the brief lulls between the dynastic skirmishes of the Wittelsbachs and the Hapsburgs, when the trade routes to the mines were safe to travel. They bought as much wool from England as they could and were always clamoring for more, as England, Jaufre soon learned, grew the best quality fleeces. The Venetians bought enormous quantities of fabric from Flanders in multiple weights and degree of fineness that Venetian weavers would have loved to have woven and sold themselves without recourse to a middleman, but for the scarcity of raw wool. They bought and sold at immense profit luxury items from Constantinople, the storied capital of Byzantium, everything from magnificent pieces of gold jewelry inlaid with enamel and set with gemstones to massive classical statuary that was allegedly antique. "Everything in Byzantium is for sale," one Venetian merchant told Jaufre in a rare moment of expansiveness. "For a price."

There was also, inevitably, a brisk market in slaves, brought to Venice from Gaul and Britannia to be sold to Muslim traders. Most slave auctions were held indoors, due to the inclement winter weather, with only known traders admitted. He had bribed his way into three of these and had bolted from the third auction before it was a quarter over to be sick against the wall of the auction building. He straightened, trembling, gulping in fresh air, or air as fresh as Venice could provide.

He thought he had made his peace with never seeing his mother again. His mother, captured by slavers when their caravan had been attacked on the Road between Kashgar and Yarkent when he was just ten years old. His father had been killed protecting Jaufre, and his mother, along with all the other women of the caravan had been kidnapped and sold in Kashgar. Jaufre had spent a lifetime looking for her. She would be in her forties now, if she were even still alive. She had been beautiful, he thought, although he knew a child's memories of a beloved parent were always suspect. He hoped, fervently, that they did not lie in this instance, because beauty invariably fetched a higher price in the slave market, and a higher price meant better treatment.

He suddenly wanted Johanna beside him with a ferocity that eclipsed all else. She alone understood. She alone could offer him comfort. She alone would have flayed him living for attending the slave auction in the first place.

"Are you all right, young sir?"

He turned to see an attractive young woman wearing a servant's coif and carrying a basket over her arm. Her eyes were kindly and concerned. And appreciative in spite of his condition.

Wrong woman, wrong time, wrong place. "Thank you, mistress," he said, trying to look as if he were. "Something I ate."

"Or drank?" she said, and shook her head with a smile. "There is a well around the corner, open to all. Rinse out your mouth and wash your face." She rummaged in her basket and present him with a handful of leaves. "And chew these afterward."

She went off, and he became aware of the smell of mint rising up from his hand.

He did as he was bid and then forced himself to concentrate on the rest of what was on offer on the Rialto. Venice had no land to cultivate, and so imported everything it ate and drank and wore. Vegetables, meat and grain came from Tuscany, brought daily by boat from the port of Mira. Venetians made the best bread he'd ever eaten, as evidenced by the multiple bakers' carts clustered together in St. Mark's Square, but they grew none of their own grain. A glass industry thrived on Murano, one of the other islands in the lagoon, but they exported the best of what was produced there and drank Nebbiolo imported from Valtellina in thick, heavy-bottomed mugs made of a glass so impure it was barely translucent. Shasha's vials and bottles, he remembered, were serviceable, not exemplars of the glassblowers' craft. The cloth that came in bolts from Flanders, the tailors and sempstresses of Venice labored long into the night making into richly embroidered robes for Venetian patrons. Very little of the finer cloth imported to the island city made it off the wharf again.

There appeared to be a street market somewhere in the city every day of the week, not to mention a fair celebrating either a saint's day, some of the more obscure events from the 1204 Venetian sack of Byzantium that resulted in the four bronze horses on top of St. Mark's, or the arrival of just about any ship bearing goods for sale. Jaufre thought of the Kashgar market, held at the eastern edge of the Pamir Mountains every Sunday since the birth of Mohammed, but only every Sunday. Venice was one entire city-sized market, a trading fair open every day of the week, dawn to well past dusk, including saint's days as celebrated by the local church. Indeed, the church was one of the merchants of Venice's best customers, an inexhaustible purchaser of silken vestments, gold plate, incense, and the knucklebones of saints. If Christ had had as many fingers as Jaufre had seen for sale between the Holy Land and the Grand

Canal, He would have had more arms than the Hindi goddess Durga.

He kept that last observation strictly to himself. Venice was also a city of churches, sporting on average one per canal, and everyone went to church at least on Sundays and many of them attended services once a day. Jaufre, accustomed to Persian cities dotted with mosque towers issuing forth the call to prayer five times a day, still had never encountered such a priest-ridden society. He minded his manners, and enjoined his companions to do the same. Félicien emphatically endorsed this warning, and even Alaric bestirred himself enough to say, "Best to draw no attention our way, of any kind, religious or not."

If you were not in a mood to buy or sell, a very rare occurrence in Venice, there was plenty more to keep you entertained. Along with the usual puppet shows and dancing troupes and singing groups, Jaufre saw a man juggle flaming brands while walking on tall sticks. Another man swallowed a sword, and a third put his head into a lion's mouth, although the lion had no teeth left to speak of and seemed supremely disinterested in anything but the next gobbet of meat thrown his way. There was an elephant tethered on one of the few green spaces of Venice, down by the Arsenal, upon which his owner sold rides for a bit of silver. There wasn't a line. In a large cage on the Grand Canal, near St. Mark's, you could pay to watch an enormous snake unhinge its jaws to swallow his prey, usually a stray cat someone threw into the cage. It inspired only revulsion, and a futile wish to rescue the cat.

After a week of sightseeing he went looking for a storefront. He quickly discovered that rents for commercial property in Venice were astronomical. Rooms the size of a shoebox looking out on the Grand Canal rented per month the equivalent of a round-trip passage to the Holy Land. Chastened, he readjusted his ambitions and was rewarded by a literal hole in the wall halfway between their lodgings and the Rialto bridge. Two wooden flaps comprised a wall that separated the stall from the street. The top half opened upward and was held up by a wooden pole to form a roof. The bottom half folded in half to form a counter, hinged on one side and latched on the other so he could get in and out. Both folded back into the wall and could be locked by means of a substantial wrought iron hasp. His first purchase was a bronze padlock with a key the size of his eating knife. He didn't know how effective the combination would be at keeping out burglars but it was certainly ornamental.

The street wasn't a main thoroughfare, and his new neighbors were merchants in only a small way, but there was a promising bustle to the foot traffic, and there was a taverna four doors down that offered a superior daily special, usually featuring chicken, some of Venice's excellent bread, and a variety of noodles that reminded him very little of the noodles he had eaten daily in Cambaluc but were indisputably noodles nonetheless

Empty, with his arms extended straight out he could almost touch both walls of the space. He laid one of their precious Kerman carpets on the floor, hung a few oil lamps chosen for their clear glass lenses, and filled the three walls with shelves. He spent the next two days hauling and displaying all of their trade goods.

When he was done he stood back and looked at the result with a pride tinged with regret. They had had a half a dozen camels loaded with trade goods acquired between Cambaluc and Kashgar during their time with Uncle Cheng's caravan. All but one had been lost to Sheik Mohammed's forces, who had ambushed them on the trail down from Terak Pass, with the tacit aid of that renegade Mongol general, Ogodei. Who might, from the latest reports, be knocking next at the doors of Baghdad.

He rearranged a few things on the display shelves, the better to catch the eye. When he had been healthy enough to he had acquired another half dozen camels in the Kabul livestock market and they had bought and sold from their backs from the Hindu Kush to Gaza. There were papyri, manuscripts and books bought in half a dozen cities across Persia. There were small, exquisitely made silver pocket knives from Damascus. There were strings of smooth malachite beads glowing with green and cream striations from Baghdad. There was a pile of intricately woven, brightly colored carpets from Kerman, a smaller pile than he would have liked but their quality instantly recognizable to the educated eye. Jaufre was determined to sell to none other, which was why the rugs were the most expensive items in his store. To alert shoppers to his most valuable commodity, he hung a wooden sign that jutted out at right angles from the wall that displayed a gaudy carpet with tassels on both ends, painted for him by Alma, who was enthusiastic enough with the gilt so as to make the sign very nearly glow in the dark. Jaufre was sure this was what had caused the first sign to be stolen the first night it was hung. The second sign was more restrained.

There were a few of the bright copper pots and pans left from the smiths of Kabul, those that Shasha had not given as thank-you gifts to hosts who had showed them hospitality on the Road. Jaufre regretted the loss of trade goods but never questioned Shasha's decision to do so.

He half turned, as if to say to Johanna, "Remember Bastak, the town we came to, the one after the bandits ambushed us in the pass?" And then he remembered that Johanna had not been with them during that adventure, that she had indeed been on an adventure of her own, one that resulted in a woman he barely recognized.

She wasn't here with him now, either. His lips tightened, and he deliberately turned his back on that thought. He folded his hands and smiled at the small, curious crowd that had gathered as it became evident he was about to open for business. "Good gentles, step forward, please. I am Jaufre of Cambaluc, and I bring goods to you from Damascus, from Kashgar, from beyond the fabled walls of Cambaluc itself." And with a sweep of his hand, "I am happy to answer all your questions, for truly a fascinating story lays behind every object you see here."

The story was always what put the sale over the top, and productive of stories in return, which were always useful. The more they learned about this new continent they had traveled to, the better able they would be able to navigate it in safety. "Yes, madam? Ah, that item, yes. It is a seal from ancient times. Indeed, madam, it is in truth a seal, the personal seal of a priestess of Memphis. Allow me to show you." He flattened a lump of damp clay and rolled the tiny cylinder in it, pressing firmly and allowing only one rotation. "You see? A goddess with a lamb at her feet…Yes, indeed, it is very tiny."

The woman, too vain to admit she couldn't see details that small, was convinced by the admiring murmur of her fellow shoppers. She bought the seal as a gift for her mother and went on her way rejoicing. Others immediately stepped up to take her place.

· Three ·

December, 1323 A.D.
Venice

·———·

The youngest daughter, who is still at home," Peter had said. "*You may
find you have something in common.*"

Like a face, Johanna thought.

They met at the taverna where she had met with Peter the first time.
It was convenient to both their lodgings and the alewife remained as
professionally disinterested in her clientele as she had been previously.

Moreta Polo sat across the table looking as startled as Johanna felt. The
other woman was older than she was, shorter than she was, her hair was
darker and straighter and her eyes were brown, all of which Johanna
found comforting, because otherwise any third party looking on
would have called them sisters. The same straight nose, the same high
cheekbones, the same wide mouth, the same firm chin. Moreta's skin
was pale and creamy where Johanna's was a faint gold, and Johanna's
teeth were better, but for the rest…

"No wonder you looked at me so oddly when we met," she said to Peter.

Peter was sitting back from the table with his arms folded, his
expression a carefully maintained blankness.

The other woman found her voice. "Of all my father's fabulous fables,"
she said to Peter, "of course this was the one he chose to leave out. It is

so like him."

"You believe I am who I say I am?" Johanna said.

Marco Polo's daughter looked at Marco Polo's grand-daughter again. Moreta wore a loose gray wool dress with a wide belt heavily embroidered in gilt thread with beautifully wrought flowers and leaves. Her cloak was hooded and though she drew the hood back from her face the better to see, she did not remove the hood entirely against the unlikely event someone might recognize her. She had also, Johanna noted, taken care to sit with her back to the room.

When Moreta didn't speak, Johanna said, "My name is Wu Johanna. I come from Cambaluc. Your father is my grandfather." She folded her hands on the table, sat back and waited. Almost she bristled, but not quite.

Moreta gulped, unused to such plain dealing. She fidgeted with her mug, toyed with a piece of cheese, and looked up. When she spoke, Johanna's singer's ear noticed that her voice was pitched much as Johanna's was, low for a woman but clear. "I would think that anyone looking at us would know we were somehow related." She saw Johanna's surprise, and Johanna was surprised further at the gleam of mischief she saw in Moreta's eyes. "What, did you expect me to deny you? It would be hard to do, on the face of it."

Her small joke made Johanna smile. "It would," she said.

"You are definitely a Polo," Moreta said. "There is a resemblance, even, between you and my sisters." She hesitated. In a softer voice, she said, "Is it all true, then?"

"Is what true?"

Moreta gestured. "All of it. His travels. The tales he told in his book." She shrugged. "A city of twelve thousand bridges."

Venice had only a little over three hundred. "Kinsai," Johanna said. "A city south of Cambaluc. I haven't personally counted all of its bridges myself, but it has a lot of them. Canals, too."

"Girls who dive for pearls, off the shores of some island nation in the East?"

"I have dived with them myself," Johanna said.

Moreta raised a skeptical eyebrow.

Johanna shrugged. "I dove with the pearl fishers of Cipangu. I even brought back pearls. No, before you ask, I can't prove it. You either believe me or you don't."

The other woman gave what she probably thought was a surreptitious once-over. Venice was cosmopolitan enough that Johanna was able to wear her own clothes with a cloak overall, but Moreta Polo was probably thinking that a woman in trousers who wore a knife in her belt would be capable of anything. "Dog-headed men?" she said tentatively.

"I don't know where he got that," Johanna said. "I've never seen any dog-headed men myself. I've been reading his book for the first time recently, and—"

"You hadn't read it before?"

"I didn't even know it existed until two months ago," Johanna said. "What he says he actually saw himself seems accurate. It's when he starts repeating what someone else has told him that he gets into trouble."

Moreta sipped her beer. "When he was still able to go out," she said, "people would laugh at him behind his back. Children would follow him, calling him names. 'Milione! Milione!'" She looked up. "You know what they meant?"

"A thousand lies," Johanna said. "Or something like that. A play on the title of his book. They called him that in the streets?"

Moreta nodded. "More or less." She reached for a piece of cheese and folded a piece of bread around it, concentrating on the task with all her attention. "You appear to have traveled a great deal."

"My father was a trader. My mother and I traveled the Road with him."

"The Road?"

"All the roads, east and west, north and south of Cambaluc. Or Cathay, you call it here. There are many, east to Cipangu, south to Ceylon, north to Khuree where the khans hold their summer courts. East to Kashgar. And Venice."

"And you got to go with him." There was envy in Moreta's voice. "I've never been out of Venice." She must have seen pity in Johanna's eyes, because she squared her shoulders and ate an olive. "Could you," she said, and stopped. "Would you mind telling me about your grandmother?"

Johanna raised an eyebrow. "Your father's first wife, do you mean?" she said pointedly, and then was sorry when Moreta blushed. She had dumped herself on the woman without warning, had removed her from the side of her father's deathbed, no less, and had received nothing but courtesy in return. She refilled their mugs from the jug and sat back. "I never knew her. She died when my mother was very young." She took a deep breath and let it out slowly. "She was a gift from her father to the Great Khan, Kublai Khan. The Khan in turn gave her to your father." She saw the appalled look in Moreta's eyes and said without emotion, "It was the custom once a year for the barons to send their most beautiful maidens to the Great Khan. It was a measure of how high your father stood in the Khan's favor, that he would receive such a gift. It was the greatest of honors." She drank warmed wine to moisten a mouth suddenly dry. "When he left Cathay, it was to escort a princess to her marriage with a Levantine prince. The Khan would not allow Shu Lin—"

"That was her name?"

"Yes, Shu Lin. Her daughter, my mother, was named Shu Ming. Your father was a favorite of the Khan, so the Khan held Shu Lin and Shu Ming as hostage against his return. Wu Hai, a merchant of Cambaluc, was a great friend to your father, and agreed to take them into his own house until he, Marco, could send for them."

"What happened?"

Johanna didn't look at Peter. "The Khan was ill when your father left. When he died, there was the usual scramble for power. Which always involves treachery and betrayal of some kind, which is always visited upon the most innocent of victims. Shu Lin…died. Wu Hai married Shu Ming to his own son to protect her."

Moreta digested this. "And you are their child."

"Yes."

"And my father's grandchild."

"Yes."

Moreta shredded a piece of bread into crumbs, and spoke without looking up. "Peter says you want to see him."

Johanna heart missed a beat. "I think the question is more, does he want to see me?"

Moreta sat up, as if she had made a decision. "He's very…fragile, at the moment." She hesitated. "He is as much out of his senses as he is in them, these days." Her eyes met Johanna's. "But you should see him. And he should see you." She glanced at Peter, who had sat silent throughout their conversation. "It will not be easy. My mother—"

Something shifted behind Peter's eyes.

"Yes," Moreta said, "my mother will be difficult."

Johanna mentioned nothing of the midwife's tales. "But not impossible?"

Moreta's chin firmed. "No. Not impossible."

Johanna watched Moreta and Peter vanishing into the fog that had shrouded the city in a mournful, dripping blanket, before turning to wend her way homeward herself. She was checked by a wraith the size of a half-measure of oats, who materialized out of the mist and fixed her with an accusing stare.

"Girl, you are an afreet in the flesh," Johanna said.

"I don't know what that is," the girl said, her glower melting the fog between them, "but it doesn't sound very complimentary."

"It's not," Johanna said, beginning to walk.

"I expect to be paid for today, even if you already found the people you were looking for."

"Of course." She dredged up a saying Hari had picked up in the Holy Land. "The laborer is worthy of her hire."

"What's that mean?"

"It means you labored for me, I owe you, I'll pay." Johanna dug around in her pocket and produced two silver pennies. She hesitated before dropping them into the outstretched palm. "Where do you rest tonight?"

The glower became even more pronounced. "I live at home."

"Yes."

"With my parents."

"Oh, yes?"

The girl looked away. "Well, with my father. My mother died when I was born."

"Oh."

"My father says it's my fault."

Johanna was silent, and something in the quality of her silence seemed to compel the girl to say more.

"He can't bear the sight of me."

"I'm sure that's not true."

The girl shrugged. "He tells me so often enough."

"So you sleep in the streets."

"Sometimes."

Johanna stopped in front of their lodgings. "How about tonight, you don't?"

For a wonder, everyone was home for dinner, even including Hari.

"And who is this?" Shasha said

"This is—" Johanna looked down at the girl. "What is your name?"

The girl hesitated. "Tiphaine."

"Tiphaine," Johanna said, sounding out the three syllables.

The girl nodded, looking a little sullen, as if she had only accidentally told the truth and already regretted it.

"Well then, Tiphaine, these are my companions This is Shasha, my foster sister, and Jaufre, my foster brother. Here is Alaric the Frank, and Firas the—Firas of the Alamut, and Félicien the goliard. Hari is a chughi, a priest in his own country, and here are Alma and Hayat, scholars of Persia. This is Tiphaine, everyone. She has come to share our meal."

Shasha looked at Jaufre and rolled her eyes behind Johanna's back. He grinned, but said to Tiphaine, "I hope you're hungry. Shasha always cooks enough for a cohort." He found her a bowl and a spoon, ladled in a generous helping of chicken stew thick with root vegetables and gravy, and cut her a chunk of the hearty bread still warm from the baker's oven two doors away. And then everyone pretended not to notice as the girl pretended not to wolf it down. She managed to wait until everyone else had at least gotten their spoons dirty before she looked instinctively at Shasha for permission, who smiled and nodded at the kettle. Tiphaine refilled her bowl to the brim. That disappeared a little more slowly. The third bowl she slowed down enough to actually to taste the ingredients. "Good," she said.

Shasha cut her another thick slice of bread and handed it over without comment.

In the middle of the night Johanna felt the call of nature and reached under the bed for the chamber pot. Instead she found herself clutching a handful of hair, which squealed in a distressing manner. "What—?"

There was a quivering silence, and then a small voice said crankily, "It's Tiphaine. Who else?"

Johanna realized she was still holding on to the girl's hair and let go. "I didn't hear you come in." In fact, she distinctly remembered the girl taking her leave of them after dinner. She felt for the pouch beneath her pillow. The hard shapes of her father's book and bao reassured her through the soft leather. "We locked the door behind you. How did you get back in?"

The girl snorted. "You call that a lock?" There was an ostentatious rustle as she flounced in place on the floor and began to breathe heavily through her nose.

The next morning Johanna found Tiphaine curled up in bed next to her, her face looking younger than ever beneath its layer of grime.

Everyone was poker-faced as they broke their fast the next morning, but Johanna noticed that no one left before they saw what happened next.

"How long have you lived in Venice, Tiphaine?"

The girl crammed another fistful of last night's bread into her mouth and spoke indistinctly around it. "All my life. I was born here."

"So you know it well?"

The dark eyes flashed. "There is no one who knows it better!"

"And the people who live here?"

The small but defiant chin raised. "Point to anyone on any street and I will tell you their name and the names of their parents and where they live and where their parents live and what house they look to and what they had for dinner." She met Johanna's mild look with a challenging stare.

Johanna held her gaze for a long moment, and then turned to look at Shasha, who sighed but was not entirely successful at hiding the smile tugging at the corners of her mouth. "Does the child have a home? Parents?"

"She claims a father." Johanna looked back at Tiphaine. "Well?"

The small face looked mutinous.

"If we're going to take you on as—" Johanna cast about in her mind for an appropriate job title "—courier, your father will naturally want to see that all the appropriate requirements are met."

The small brow wrinkled. "Courier?"

"Dragoman. Messenger." Tiphaine's face remained blank and Johanna said, "Page?" Although she was not entirely certain pages existed outside royal courts.

But Tiphaine's face cleared. "Page," she said. "I could be your page."

"But we cannot offer you employment without your father's permission," Johanna said.

It was one of the darker, dirtier dwellings in one of the darker, dirtier sections of Venice, near a defunct foundry off the Rio della Misericordia. Leftover slag from the foundry's workings was piled everywhere and it was impossible to walk there without collecting soot to your knees.

Tiphaine's father worked out of a storefront that made Jaufre's look palatial by comparison, located beneath the surface of the street, reached by steep, narrow steps that looked hand-hewn and which were difficult to negotiate because of the jumble of what might have been merchandise and what might have been trash piled everywhere. The one window was boarded over. The wooden door was so warped it was hard to see how it could close.

There was a front room for business and a back room for living, if you could call it that, as it consisted of a single pallet, a brazier with one broken leg propped on a cobblestone, and a saucepan that looked as if it hadn't been washed since the birth of Christ. The piles of goods continued inside, some stacked so haphazardly that they stepped warily in case of an accidental avalanche. There were bales of faded and tattered clothes, pots and pans strung together by their handles, dull knives and a box of wooden, bronze, and silver spoons thinned from years of use. One corner was devoted to remnants of what might once have been books, loose stacks of pages in a higgledy-piggledy heap. Jaufre could smell the mold coming off them from three feet away, and kept his distance. Other items were less identifiable.

Some attempt had been made to lighten the dark interior with lamps, but they were so few in number and like the saucepan had not been recently—if ever—cleaned that Johanna could barely make out the gentleman who stood inside. He said something brusquely in a language previously unknown to her, and Tiphaine answered in kind, indicating Johanna with the wave of a hand. "This is Mordecai the Jew, my father," she said, and stepped back, Jaufre thought not coincidentally out of the reach of her father's arm.

The old man, bearded and filthy and who simply could not be as old as he looked and have fathered a child Tiphaine's age, looked at Jaufre and said in roughly accented Italian, "My daughter says you wish to take her as your servant."

"I do," Johanna said.

"She is healthy and strong and not uncomely," the man said to Jaufre. "How much will you pay?"

Johanna felt Jaufre go rigid next to her and dropped a warning hand to his arm. "She is very small to be so strong," she said mildly, and named a price. This provoked the usual outrage. Fierce bidding culminated in coins exchanged, Johanna somewhat hampered with producing them by the restraining hand she must at all costs keep on Jaufre's arm. She produced a document that laid out the terms of Tiphaine's employment, on which Mordecai would not place his mark until she produced another coin, and they were done.

"Get your things," Johanna told Tiphaine.

"There is nothing here I want or need," Tiphaine said, and led the way out the door and up the stairs, as careful to kick everything off the steps on the way up as she had been careful not to kick anything off on the way down. At no time during the meeting had Mordecai looked directly at his daughter. He made no farewell to her now, nor she to him.

Halfway home she said suddenly, apparently to no one, "It would have been better if my mother had lived."

Another bridge, another canal, and she said, "It would have been different if I'd been a boy."

And that was the last word Tiphaine ever said about her family.

Scrubbed (a process Tiphaine vociferously resisted, right up until the moment Shasha picked her up bodily and deposited her into the tub), her hair ruthlessly combed (her eyes were watering by the time Shasha had judged her curls were in as much order as was possible), and clad in new skirt, tunic and belt, with a new cloak overall and sturdy, made-to-order boots on her feet, Tiphaine looked like a new and far more respectable person, but she was still dissatisfied, apparently. She fussed at the shoulder of her tunic, and looked at all their tunics one by one with a gathering frown.

"What?" Johanna said, inclined to be amused rather than annoyed.

Certainly the girl's spirit had not been broken by her unfortunate beginnings. "What are we missing here?"

Tiphaine pressed her lips together but couldn't hold it back. "You—we have no badge."

"Badge?" Johanna said, repressing a smile at the girl's quick correction.

"House badge. A—an emblem that signifies what house or company we belong to."

There was a brief silence. "She's right," Jaufre said slowly. He looked at Johanna. "Almost everyone who comes to my stall and certainly every male wears a badge of some sort sewn to their clothing."

"The Venetians only?"

He thought about it, and shook his head. "Sometimes it signifies what ship's company the wearer belongs to. The Doge's guards have uniforms, of course. A few of the nobles' servants have livery, but not all."

"It's customary," Félicien said. "Everywhere, for soldiers' companies, craft guilds, city officials."

"An identifier," Shasha said, nodding. "Something that will show the authorities we have friends, should one of us get into trouble."

Jaufre didn't look at Alaric, who would have been voted most likely of their group to get into trouble. Alaric, as usual looking a little hungover, was hunched over his morning tea as if it were his last hope of survival and was not thus far contributing to the conversation. "And it'll help us fit in," Jaufre said. "If everyone wears a badge, we should wear a badge, too."

Johanna looked at Tiphaine and smiled. "Well, you've started something now. What kind of a badge should we have?"

"Bright colors," the girl said instantly. "That you can see from across the street."

"Just colors?"

"No," she said. "There should be a shape, an animal or a—a tool."

The discussion which followed lasted over three days and was the subject of vigorous debate. Everyone had an opinion. Alaric surfaced long enough to say it should be a sword crossed on a shield. No, Félicien said, everyone would think they were a mercenary company, arms for sale. A lyre, he said, that was the thing, or a harp. Or perhaps both. Or maybe a flute, everyone recognized a flute. So they were a troupe of jongleurs now, Alaric said. He'd brush up on his tumbling.

They decided on red and yellow for colors since they were the imperial colors of Cambaluc, the pigments were easily obtained and they were bright enough to satisfy Tiphaine, who seemed to be in charge. Images suggested for the figure ranged from Alaric's sword to Félicien's harp to Shasha's suggestion of a willow leaf. "You've all been dosed with it enough times," she said. Alma suggested a quill pen, Hayat a dagger, and Johanna, of course, held out for a white horse at full gallop. Which would be fine if they were a guild of ostlers, Alaric said

"Why not a sun?" Hari said one evening. "It shines down upon us all."

"Not in Venice," Jaufre and Johanna said in the same moment. They smiled at each other.

"Ordinary," Alma said, without much feeling one way or the other.

"Universal," Hari said.

"It doesn't mean anything," Félicien said, frowning.

"Inoffensive," Hari said.

"Simple to draw," Hayat said.

"Easy to recognize at a distance," Alma said.

"And leaves the center free for any additions we might like to add later on," Shasha said thoughtfully.

"Um," Tiphaine said.

They looked at her and she flushed. "Oftentimes we are made to wear a gold star on our clothing," she said.

"A gold star?"

"Who's we?"

"Jews," Tiphaine said.

It took a moment for everyone's ideas to readjust. "And that would be bad," Jaufre said slowly.

"Jews are held to be…"

"Unclean," Alaric said, almost with relish. "They killed Christ our Lord."

Tiphaine glared at him.

Alaric bristled. "They did crucify him. It says so in the Bible, which is the word of God made manifest on this earth."

"'Away with him: Away with him: Crucify him. Pilate saith to them: shall I crucify your king?'" Félicien's voice was soft. "'The chief priests answered: We have no king but Caesar.'"

"And that makes Jews the whipping boy wherever Christ is worshipped?" Johanna said.

Félicien glanced at Tiphaine and nodded.

"Sunnis and Shias," Hayat said with a sigh. Tiphaine looked up, surprised, and Alma said, "Both of Islam, but they follow different prophets descended from Mohammed."

"Which means they can and do kill each other for any reason," Alma said.

"Or none at all," Hayat said.

"All heathens," Alaric said, but without heat.

"Does that mean—" Tiphaine hesitated. Her face was pale and she looked strained.

"What?"

The girl said up straight and firmed an already firm jaw and glared at Johanna. "Does that mean I can't stay?"

Johanna smiled at her. "Do I not hold your contract?"

Everyone looked away as the girl collected herself. She spoke first. "Very well," she said, very businesslike. "Not a sun, because it looks too much like a star. What, then?"

Johanna looked at Shasha and then at Jaufre, and they knew before she said it. "This," she said, and opened the leather purse that was always at her waist. She produced a rectangular rod half a handspan long and a small round pot, both carved from dark green jade. Alma found a scrap of vellum and Johanna uncapped the pot, revealing a red paste, a little dry and flaking after two years of disuse. She touched the end of the cylinder into the paste and pressed it against the vellum. She held up the result for everyone to see. "Three Chinese characters," she said. "My family name, and the character for trader, and the character for honest. It was my father's bao. You would say, seal." She frowned down at the imprint. Mandarin characters were not known for their simplicity or lack of flourish. "Perhaps one of the characters would be enough 'Honest,' or 'trader.'"

"Trader," Jaufre said.

It felt right to all of them, even Alaric, and Alma was put in charge of construction with Tiphaine supervising. The resulting badges were of calfskin scraped thin, cut into circles and dyed red. Alma embroidered each badge with their device in gold silk, and sewed them to everyone's outer garments. They looked good, distinctive and professional, and very shiny.

"When someone asks us who we look to, what do we say?" Tiphaine said. When no one answered she said, spacing the words out as if speaking to the very slow of wit, "What is our name? The name of our compagnia? Someone is bound to ask."

Johanna looked at her and said, "Sometimes I think I might have made a mistake, hiring you on."

The girl gave an impudent grin. "You know I'm right."

She did, unfortunately, and dreaded more days of wrangling.

"Wu Company," Jaufre said. He looked at Johanna and raised an eyebrow.

She looked at Shasha, who smiled. Johanna blinked away unexpected tears. "Wu Company it is."

Tiphaine wasn't finished. "And what does our compagnia do?"

Johanna's eyes roamed over the members of the company. Two traders, a healer and cook, an assassin, a knight, a monk, a goliard, an amateur astronomer and her, what. Assistant? Guard? Companion? Lover? All of the above. And now, a page. "Anything anyone will pay us for," she said, and smiled. "Short of robbery and murder."

· Four ·

———

Tiphaine's first task in her official capacity as Wu Company's page was to carry messages between Johanna and Moreta. She and Peter would meet as they browsed the goods in Jaufre's shop, or when Ca' Polo sent for medicinal herbs which Moreta now purchased from Shasha and had delivered by Tiphaine.

Shasha was beginning to make a modest name for herself as an herbalist, to the point that the line of people trailing down the street from their lodgings provoked a complaint from their landlord. Jaufre found her a space one canal down where she set up shop and where the line became even longer. Firas unilaterally dedicated himself Shasha's deputy and took on the task of assessing injuries and disease in order of necessity. There was a boy with a broken arm, accompanied by his mother. There was a young woman who wouldn't meet anyone's eye and who wouldn't talk to anyone except Shasha and who would only talk to her alone. There was a leper swathed in bandages and a blue robe, which failed to hide that he was in the last stages of that dread disease. There was a tall man with a wispy beard, an angry boil on his left buttock and the melancholy air of one to whom disaster and disappointment were boon companions. "He reminds me of Alaric," Shasha said to Firas.

There were also the usual tittering girls looking for love potions and the men looking for spells to curse their neighbors' crops. One woman was so insistent that Firas finally said solemnly, "They say that if a woman spits three times into the face of a frog, that she will never conceive again," and watched with some satisfaction as the woman immediately adjourned, presumably to the nearest swamp. He wished he could have followed her, just to watch.

The rest Firas purged from the line of prospective patients with smart dispatch and a pithy reminder that Shasha was a healer, not a sorcerer. The last thing they needed in Venice was a reputation for witchcraft.

He dealt with the leper more gently. "Then you cannot help me?" the leper said, his mouth hidden by the stained cloth wrapped around his face.

"No," Firas said. "Allah will decide when to call you to him, my friend. Leave that decision to Him."

"He has had little enough time to spare for me so far," the leper replied, and left on what remained of his heavily wrapped feet.

For a man with a runny nose and a cough Shasha prescribed sage leaves, rubbed and placed inside the nostrils. A housewife had cut her hand on a knife, and Shasha stopped the bleeding with an application of cobwebs.

The boy's injury was more serious. Both bones in his lower left arm were protruding through the skin, the ends fractured. The skin around them was already dark red and hot to the touch. He was in great pain, although he bore it better than his mother did. Shasha soaked a sponge in a distillation of herbs and placed it over the boy's nose. A few moments later, the strain eased from his face and he slid into unconsciousness.

His mother tried for the sponge for herself. Shasha slapped her hand away without looking up, manipulated the bones back into place, splinted the arm and bound it firmly. She measured out ground willow bark. "He will have a fever," she told his mother. She placed a hand on the boy's forehead, which already felt too warm. "Make him a clear broth and put a pinch of this into the bowl, morning, noon and night. Do not give him solid food, no meat, no bread, until the fever goes away. Only liquids, watered wine, small beer, broth. A little warmed mead in the evening, if your purse runs to it. Do you understand?" The mother nodded, but Shasha repeated her instructions once more to be sure. "If the wound begins to smell bad, if the skin of his arm turns dark, you must bring him back at once."

She and Firas stood watching the woman walk away, packet clutched in one sweaty hand and all her anxious attention on the face of the boy in her arms. "The wound is already infected," Shasha said. "That arm will very probably have to come off."

There were cripples who begged in every market place, using their lost sight or lost limbs to fill their bowls with alms. It was not a future either of them would wish on anyone, let alone the brave little boy who had just left them.

"I could use some puppy tongues," Shasha said.

Firas looked at her. "What?"

"The tongues of dogs have special properties. They heal their own wounds by licking them. Often dried puppy tongues, ground to powder and sprinkled on the wound of a man or a woman, will heal it as well."

"And am I supposed to find these puppies, kill them, and remove their tongues for you?"

"Yes," she said. She stretched the kinks out of her back. Firas kneaded her shoulders and knuckled the muscles down either side of her spine, and she groaned her relief.

"Well, then," Firas said. "Are we done raising the dead for today?"

"Mistress," a voice said.

They turned to see the tall man with the boil. He'd propped himself up against the outside wall of the house because he was unable to sit, Shasha remembered. "Ah yes, the boil," she said. Like most healers she had a tendency to call people by their afflictions. "Come inside."

He followed them inside the stall with a halting gait.

"Drop your hose," Shasha said, "and bend over."

With the air of one inured to indignity, he did so. The boil was the size of a large grape. Shasha stood well back when she lanced it, and as a result got very little of the resulting expulsion of pus on her apron. She stepped forward again to press gentle fingers against the dark, angry skin around the boil until the flow of pus and serum was replaced with good red blood.

"That hurts," the man said, more in resignation than in distress.

"I know," Shasha said. "It can't be helped." The wound drained, she applied a paste made of turmeric and a square patch of clean cloth that stuck to the paste. "Try not to dislodge the dressing, and try to keep your weight off that cheek for the next few days."

The man stood up and pulled his hose up over his buttocks in gingerly fashion. "I thank you for your care, mistress." He indicated his worn appearance. "As you might expect, I cannot pay you." He nodded at the taverna down the street. "I serve at that establishment. The owner is a woman of generous heart. May I offer you a mug?"

"Are we done?" Shasha asked Firas. He nodded.

Jaufre, home from work, met them at the door. "Where's Johanna?" he said, his inevitable greeting.

"With North Wind," was the invariable reply, and he accompanied them to the taverna. Hari, sighted on the street with his usual comet's tail of children, was hailed and joined them. It was a bustling place, a low, dark, rectangular room with a fat woman sweating in front of a large fireplace as she wielded a wooden paddle to slide round loaves of bread from a cavernous brick oven, an even fatter man dispensed enormous tankards of ale from a succession of barrels, and what was obviously their daughter. She had neither the size of her father nor the heft of her mother but had ample charms for all that, well displayed in a red gown cut low over her breasts and of a length that flirted with her ankles. She served them ale and tiny cakes made of very thin pastry layered with honey and crushed almonds. Shasha took careful note of the construction and the ingredients.

"Allow me to introduce myself," said the man, with as much dignity as he could perched half on and half off the bench. "I am Jean de Valmy, born in Provence of Alys d'Arly and Didier de Valmy. My parents died when I was very young, and I was apprenticed to the Knights Templar."

They introduced themselves, and Jaufre was niggled by the certainty that he had seen Jean de Valmy before.

"Your eyes," Jean de Valmy said hesitantly to Shasha.

"These are how eyes are made where I come from," she said.

"And where would that be?"

"Cathay."

"Cathay!" Jean de Valmy's eyes lit up. "Is it true that jewels rain from the skies in Cathay?"

"Only when the moon is full for the second time in a month," Shasha said gravely. "The next morning one must wade through emeralds ankle deep. It's a nuisance to clean up and very hard on the street sweepers, who receive an extra ration of wine that day for their trouble."

Jean de Valmy eyed her uncertainly, and she relented. "People in Cathay are born, and marry, and have children, and worship, and honor their ancestors, and visit tavernas very like this one, and eat cakes and drink wine with their friends, and grow wheat for bread, and pay taxes, and eventually die, just as the people do here," She smiled. "Our eyes are differently made." We certainly bathe more frequently, she thought but didn't say.

Jean de Valmy considered her for a moment longer, and turned to Hari. "And yourself? I see your eyes are different even from your companion's."

"Ah," Hari said, and Shasha settled back to enjoy herself as she always did when the subject of Hari's background came up, as it was never told the same way twice.

He did not disappoint her this time, either. "I was born to my mother, whose name I do not know, to a father who never knew me, many thousands of leagues distant, on the banks of the Ganges, one of the four great rivers of the world, and the spiritual home of my people."

"Who are your people?"

"We are chughi. We live long, doing little, seeing much, shunning possessions, increasing our knowledge of life so that one day we may ascend to the next level."

"The next level of what?"

"Of consciousness."

"You're awake now," Jean de Valmy pointed out.

Hari smiled again and finished his wine. "There is awake, and there is awake, my friend."

Jean de Valmy looked confused, as well he might. Heredity and inheritance was everything in his culture, and he could only dimly conceive of another to which both were shrugged off as inconsequential. "How long have you been from home?"

"Nearly five years now. And yourself?"

Jean's naturally dismal face fell into even more mournful lines. "Thirty years. My Templar master brought me on crusade." He sighed. "It wasn't as I had imagined it as a child. Few battles, little swordplay, even less opportunity to gather riches, as one is promised when one goes to war. But there were rewards. We were very busy. There was constant coming and going between the Holy Land and Paris. We sent home much gold and silver from Africa, cloth from the East, the swords and armor of Damascus, the horses of Arabia. It was a good life, certainly a profitable one, and as I can read and write, I was useful to my master, and he was pleased with me."

"What happened?"

"We were proscribed, and it became dangerous even to be who we were."

"Why?" said Shasha, exchanging looks with Jaufre. They had heard bits of the Templar story from Alaric, but another perspective on the same tale was always informative.

Jean de Valmy shrugged. "I was never told the full story. It was said that the Knights Templar were devil worshippers, that our kiss meant death, that we worshipped a black cat called Bahomet. We began to be imprisoned. Some of us were even burned at the stake. We no longer exist as a group. It is still death for a Templar to return to France."

"Yet you survived."

"Because I have not returned to France," Jean said patiently. "Although I miss it, I do. I have a great desire to visit the home of my childhood. I was very happy then. My mother was as beautiful as Helen of Troy, and my father as strong and brave as Ajax himself, and the food—" He kissed his fingers. "But such is the lot of us all, to be separated from that which makes us happy, to live out our lives as best we can in the eternal hope that upon death we will be translated unto heaven and be reunited with those we love."

"'There is no certainty in worldly matters,'" Hari quoted, nodding his agreement, "'and no perfect happiness, good is mixed with evil, and virtue with vice. One must endure, and endure with grace. That is the true test.'"

Jean's brow furrowed as he attempted to translate this into his kind of sense, Jaufre wanted to tell him not to bother. Eyeing their badges, de Valmy inquired after their provenance. "Wu Company," he said, when they had explained. "The young man, the goliard who sings. He wears such a badge, does he not?"

"Félicien?" Shasha said. "Yes. He is a member of our company."

"Ah," de Valmy said, stroking his chin. "You are a very diverse company. A goliard. A healer. A trader. A monk." He looked at Firas, turban ever on his head and short sword ever at his side, and forbore to comment further.

And then Jaufre remembered where he had seen de Valmy before. The Templar had been the old roué who had compared Félicien to a songbird after de Valmy had heard Félicien in performance.

The group parted with expressions of mutual esteem later than evening and Jaufre would have had no cause to think further on the elderly Frank until the following week, when Shasha suffered a visit from the priest of the local parish. Father Amadeo was a lean, fidgety man who wore a perpetually startled expression and spoke with all the consciousness of a man who had God and, more importantly, the church on his side and whose authority was therefore indisputable. "I have received a complaint from a member of my congregation, mistress, regarding unChristian practices taking place in your shop." Further speech revealed Father Amadeo to be a traditionalist who believed that pain and suffering were his congregation's lot in life, and that anyone who eased the pain of broken limbs or boils was regarded as suspect and their work very probably inspired by the devil.

Shasha and Firas exchanged a glance and knew in an instant the instigator of this clerical visitation. Jean de Valmy must have made a complaint in hopes of some reward. From his emaciated appearance he would likely have done so for as little as a full meal. "A broken limb or a boil isn't the work of the devil?" Shasha said. "And is it not a healer's duty to alleviate suffering if God has given her the skill to do so?"

Father Amadeo went away unsatisfied. Jaufre could practically smell the wood burning at the stake. He sent immediately for Hari, who answered the call with alacrity and marshaled his unlikely forces from the monastery. San Giorgio's infirmarian, a pleasant, rotund gentleman by the name of Brother Luca, paid Shasha a visit a week later, chaperoned of course by Hari. They enjoyed a comfortable conversation over tea that ranged from the relative efficacies of willow bark infusion taken orally over mustard seed plasters applied topically for joint pain, although Brother Luca held out for a large helping of olive oil taken internally on a daily basis and massaged into the skin weekly as the most sure relief. But then he was Italian, and in Venice olive oil was known as the mother's helper and used for everything from keeping a woman's skin young to oiling the hinges on a door. If he hadn't held out for olive oil, it would have been garlic, which he did in fact recommend for the common cold. Ingest enough of it, he told Shasha, and the smell alone would keep off even the most determined of the ill humors that assailed mankind.

Leave was taken with compliments all around and Brother Luca extended an invitation to Shasha to visit the herbarium at the monastery and make herself free of its stocks, and another invitation to Alma to meet with Brother Uberto, the monastery's precentor, who shared Alma's interest in the movement of the heavens. Nothing further was heard from Father Amadeo, and Shasha was free to pestle her herbal concoctions, tuck them into squares of parchment tied with string, and send them off to Ca' Polo or anywhere else she liked.

They congratulated themselves on their near escape from the flames of the Inquisition but Jaufre, ever cautious, made a point of attending mass at least once a week. The incense wasn't any worse than your average temple function in Cambaluc and he already had the ability to look attentive while his mind was quite elsewhere. The when to sit, stand and kneel took longer to learn. Father Amadeo looked upon his presence in the congregation with a very sour expression, which was not alleviated by the generous donation Jaufre left in the collection plate at the end of every service.

Messages from Johanna frequently accompanied Shasha's concoctions to Ca' Polo. Moreta sent messages back will less frequency, and the year had turned before Johanna got the one she most wanted.

She and Tiphaine were sitting in their lodgings, not speaking, when Shasha, Jaufre and Firas returned home.

"What news?" Jaufre said, looking from one to the other.

"Tomorrow morning," Johanna said, without meeting his eyes. "Moreta says morning is when he is at his most alert, and most himself."

There was a brief silence. "Are you sure you want to do this, Johanna?" Shasha said.

Johanna gave a laugh that was half-sob. "Want to do it?" she said. "Rather, I must."

She felt rather than saw Jaufre and Shasha exchange looks over her bent head. She held out her hands and felt each of them clasped, Jaufre's hand warm and calloused, Shasha's warm and soft from the cosmetic cream she made herself of oil and beeswax and dried lavender. "Must," she said again. "I must do this."

Peter met her at the servants' entrance. Ser Polo's house was dark and gloomy and like all Venetian palazzos belied its magnificent exterior by being disagreeably dank inside. The servants' stairway was ill lit and narrow. Johanna followed Peter on tiptoe, one hand touching the damp stone wall for reassurance. Her heart seemed to be beating unnaturally loudly in her ears.

At the top of the stair he paused, one ear to a door. The door opened inward without a squeak—she wondered if he had been busy at the hinges with olive oil that morning—and they found themselves at the end of a broad hallway, the length of which ended in a much broader stair with elaborately carved marble bannisters. Up which the invited guests were escorted, no doubt.

The hallway was wainscotted to the ceiling in some dark wood hung with varnished portraits lit by candle sconces. Already difficult to make out, they were made more so by their subjects being painted in dark clothes against dark backgrounds. They all seemed to be wearing the same dour, disapproving expression, too, and Johanna felt a most inappropriate bubble of laughter rising to the back of her throat.

Peter gave out with a delicate clearing of throat and at once one of the doors opened a crack, throwing a bar of light across the tiled floor. Johanna felt herself being taken firmly in hand and steered down the hall and through the door, which closed behind her with a thud of finality that sounded to her admittedly feverish imagination like the closing of the door to a tomb.

Moreta was standing there and the three of them stood stock still for a moment. Johanna could tell that the other two were listening hard, so she listened, too. She heard nothing.

"Did anyone see you?" Moreta said.

Peter shook his head.

Moreta seemed to relax. "Good." She looked at Johanna and attempted a smile. "I'm sorry, but if my mother sees you…"

When her voice trailed away without offering any horrible outcomes, Peter said diplomatically, "She will be displeased."

Moreta huffed out something between a snort and a laugh. "Indeed she will." She looked at Johanna. "I'm sorry. I couldn't tell him. I just…I couldn't."

There was a stir across the room. "Moreta? Daughter?"

It was an old man's voice, thready and dry. It came from a wooden bed shrouded in brocade curtains and canopy, dark blue in color. A clothes press stood in one corner, and one wall was completely covered with a set of shelves cluttered with pottery and porcelain. Johanna recognized a few blue and white bowls that had surely been made in Shinping. A small chest sat next to the bed. On it sat a candelabra, a pitcher, a squat, stemmed glass and various glass bottles. A bit of paper sat scrunched up on one corner. The container of Shasha's last potion, possibly.

Moreta went to the bed and leaned over the man lying there. "Father?"

"Ah, daughter. Some water, of your goodness. My mouth feels most dry."

Moreta poured from the pitcher and leaned over the bed with the stemmed glass in her hand. A moment of silence, and then an "ah" of satisfaction. "Thank you, daughter."

She leaned down and Johanna could hear the press of lips against cheek. "Father," Moreta said in a low voice, "there is someone here to see you."

"Who is it?" the thready voice said. "Peter?"

"Yes, Peter," Moreta said. "And someone else, too." She stood back and beckoned to them.

Peter stepped forward, Johanna following in his wake on legs whose knees felt very peculiar. They stopped at the side of the bed.

"Peter." The voice was stronger now, and Johanna looked at her grandfather's face for the first time.

His features were sunken, his beard grizzled, but his dark eyes were fixed on Peter's face with a look of pleasure. "Peter, my old friend. It is good to see you."

Moreta made as if to say something. Johanna saw Peter touch her hand briefly, and she was still again.

"It is always good to see you, master."

The old man shifted in his bed, lips tightening momentarily in what Johanna took to be discomfort. "I have been laying here thinking of the old days, Peter, in the court of the Great Khan, and on the steppes of the tribes, and in all the lands we traveled. Do you remember the unicorns, Peter? Not like horses at all, thick-snouted and short-legged and broad-bellied, with skin like leather, and two horns, Peter, two, not one as the old tales would have it."

"I remember the unicorns, master. Ugly creatures, and dangerous."

There was a snorting sound from the bed that took Johanna a moment to recognize as a laugh. "No maiden I ever met would have allowed such a creature anywhere near her lap."

He gave that snorting laugh again and this time choked and coughed. Moreta poured him some water and held the glass once more to his lips. He gulped it down and the choking subsided, although he gasped for air afterward. "Thank you, daughter."

Moreta murmured something in return, and Johanna thought she saw tears in his daughter's eyes as she turned to replace the glass on the stand.

"I did not tell half of what I saw," the old man said. "I could have written another book, and more." His fingers plucked at the sheets. "I should have. Il Milione! I'll 'Il Milione' them!" He subsided into mutterings.

There was a brief silence. "Father, there is someone else here to see you this morning."

"Oh?" The old man half-raised his head, peering through the gloom. "Make them come closer. It is so dark at this time of year."

"Here is Johanna, father," Moreta said, motioning at Johanna to come forward. She hesitated before adding, "Johanna of Cambaluc."

"What? Cambaluc?"

Johanna found she could hardly speak around the heart in her mouth. "It is true, Ser Polo."

The raspy voice strengthened. "Nonsense!"

"Indeed, I was born in Cambaluc, Ser Polo." She swallowed. I am —I have traveled many leagues to come to Venice, over roads with which you and Peter would be very familiar."

A withered hand gestured. "Come closer."

She leaned in between the bed curtains to meet the faded, watery eyes of the old man. To her surprise he seemed alert, his gaze sharp and penetrating, at least in that moment.

For a few moments neither said anything, while behind her Moreta and Peter seemed to hold their breath. After a long moment, he spoke. "Shu Lin?"

There was dead silence in the room, until Johanna managed to say, "I am her granddaughter."

The hand fell back. "Tell me." His voice was stronger and very harsh.

"Do you remember Wu Hai?"

"Of course I remember Wu Hai," the old man said testily. "The best friend a man could have. I committed Shu Lin and Shu Ming into his care when I left Cambaluc." A brief silence, into which the dying man seemed to read reproach. "The Khan would not let me take them with me when I left," he said, a little querulous, perhaps even a little pleading. "What happened, after I was gone?" When Johanna didn't answer immediately he raised his voice. "What happened?"

"Shhhh, father, shhh," Moreta whispered, glancing at the door. "Mother will hear."

The remonstration quieted him immediately, which told its own tale. "What happened to Shu Lin, Johanna of Cambaluc?"

Johanna swallowed. "She died not long after you left, Ser Polo," she said. "It doesn't matter how. Wu Hai married Shu Ming to his son, Wu Li. I am their daughter."

"But if you are Shu Ming's daughter—"

"Yes, Ser Polo. I am your granddaughter."

There was a charged silence. "Shu Lin's granddaughter," he said at last. After a moment, he said in a stronger voice, "My grand-daughter."

"Yes, Ser Polo."

The ghost of a smile flitted across his face. "I believe the proper way to address me is 'Grandfather,' young lady."

Johanna felt an answering smile, a little trembly at the corners, spread across her own face. She had not expected such instant acceptance. "Very well. Grandfather."

"Tell me of your life," the old man said.

And for the next hour Johanna did just that. She told him of her birth in Wu Li's house and of her childhood on the Road. "He took you with him?"

"He did, grandfather, myself and my mother, both of us." Before that silence became too uncomfortable she said, "We traveled to many of the places you wrote of in your book. To Kinsai, the city of many canals—"

"Canals!" the old man cried. "Hah! More canals than Venice itself! I was governor of Kinsai for three years, you know."

Johanna didn't remember that in any of the stories told to her by her paternal grandfather, but then Wu Hai had died when she was still very young. She spoke instead of the journeys south into the Indus and Mien and from there the quick trips across the water to the islands where the spices grew. He questioned her closely about the kind and quality of nutmeg, clove and cinnamon, and then, exhausting that topic, he said, on an interrogatory note, "In Mien the finest rubies are found."

Johanna smiled, and told him the story of Lundi, the man with the dhow they had met in Kinsai on her last trip with her father. She glanced at Peter and Moreta, and leaned forward to whisper in the old man's ear about the rubies that had fallen out of Lundi's turban.

He laughed again, and choked again, and was again revived with water, mixed with a little wine. Peter gave him a lemon drop and he sucked in it ruminatively. "Did you only go south, then?"

"No, grandfather, we went east, too, as far as the islands of Cipangu, the land of the Nihon. I dove with the pearl fishers there." She smiled. In this company, only he would know the pearl fishers were always women, who dove dressed only in a cloth wrapped about their loins. She thought it impolitic to say that she herself had donned this attire.

"Hah," he said, an answering smile on his face. "And the islands to the north? The ones where those large salt water weasels are so plentiful?"

"No, we did not go so far. There was no need, as the Nihon traded in them."

"Ah," he said reflectively. "Their fur makes the best coats and hats. If you could have cut out the middleman…"

"The honorable Wu Li was of much the same mind, grandfather, but we didn't have long enough in Cipangu for investigation. The Nihon's pelts were of the finest quality, and expertly cured."

"How much profit in Cambaluc?"

"Before transportation costs, almost fifty percent. The Mongols love good furs."

He grunted. "So you traveled with your father, your mother and you."

"Until he died, yes." She willed her voice not to tremble. Old griefs should never be visited upon new friends, or old friends for that matter. "My mother predeceased him by a year." She did not go into details and he did not ask. Old people were uninterested in any suffering but their own. "When he died, I left Cambaluc."

"On your own?"

"Even I am not so foolhardy, grandfather," she said. "No, I travel with friends."

"And you all came to Venice together?"

"Yes."

"To what end?"

She didn't answer.

He raised up shakily on one elbow. "What do you want, granddaughter? What do you want from me? A letter of recommendation to the merchants guild? An introduction to the Doge?" A rumble of a laugh. "I'm afraid my credit is such that neither would do you any good." A tinge of bitterness crept into his voice. "Not from Il Milione. The man of a thousand lies."

"Father—"

"Did you think I didn't know what they called me behind my back, daughter?" The old man sank back to move restlessly beneath the covers. "I did not tell half of what I saw," he said again, "for fear that I would not be believed. No, granddaughter, I see no use in my bringing you to anyone's notice in Venice." He paused and added, "Your Italian is appalling. Practice until you are fluent before you try to do business in this city." He shifted again. "I have no coin about me, but—"

"I have sufficient unto my needs, grandfather. I need nothing from you except—" here she hesitated "—except perhaps your—your regard."

"My regard, is it?" His voice was beginning to slur. "You have that, then, for what it's worth. Lean down so that I may see you once more."

She did so, tears she had not expected pricking at the back of her eyes.

"I'm sorry," he whispered. "I never tried to find out what happened. I was—I think I was afraid." He swallowed and fell back on his pillow. "And ashamed."

Well he should have been, came the unbidden thought, but again, she forbore from speaking it out loud. He was dying. What good would it do?

She felt a light touch on her elbow, and turned to see Moreta nodding toward the door, an anxious expression on her face.

Johanna straightened and took a long and what would probably be her last look at the old man, who had fallen fast asleep with the suddenness of the very ill and the very old. She had a feeling they would not meet again. "Goodbye, grandfather," she said, and followed Moreta out of the room.

In the hallway Moreta said, still in a whisper, "It's been a long time since I have seen him so alert and animated and—" she hesitated "—alive."

"And I," Peter said, his shuttered Mongol features as close as Johanna thought they might ever get to an expression of approval.

"May I come again, do you think?" Johanna said.

"Who is that!" A voice, harsh and demanding, called from the head of the stairs.

The three of them turned to behold an older woman at the head of the grand staircase, staring at them from a swarthy face which might have been attractive but for the perpetual scowl that had left deep creases between her eyes and at the corners of her mouth. "Moreta! Who is that woman?"

As if they had rehearsed it, Peter took Johanna by one arm and hustled her toward the servants' stairs. Moreta walked toward the woman, her hands held out in calming fashion.

"It's no one, mother, a—"

"Who is she? I won't ask again!" The sound of a ringing slap.

"Merely another healer, mother, who thought she might have something to ease father's joint pains—"

The sound of another slap, and as Johanna was shoved through the stair door she caught a glimpse of Moreta half-turned from her mother, one arm raised in her own defense. "I told you, we've done all we can! The Lord God visits only so much pain on us as we can endure, and endure he must, like—"

The door shut on the rant and Peter galloped Johanna down to the bottom of the stairs and shoved her out into the street. "I'll send word when there is news," he said and closed the door. Johanna walked away as fast as she could without running, the hood of her cloak drawn closely about her face in case anyone was looking out the windows of Ca' Polo.

"As well as can be expected," was Shasha's verdict.

"You're sure no one followed you when you left?" Jaufre said.

Johanna nodded. "I took care not to come directly home," she said. "I stopped for a meal on the way, and went to the market. I saw no one twice."

"Good." Jaufre sat back and crossed his arms. "Donata Polo doesn't sound like a pleasant person."

"No," Johanna said definitely. "She isn't." She remembered the black-visaged presence at the head of the grand staircase, whose rage and jealous resentment could be felt all the way down the hall as something nearly palpable. "From what Moreta has said, and what my grandfather said this morning, I think she's something of a despot, too."

"Abusive?"

She nodded.

"Murderous?" This from Jaufre.

In fact Donata Polo reminded her somewhat of Dai Fang. Selfish and vicious. "I don't know," Johanna said. "Possibly. Dangerous, certainly."

Jaufre gave Johanna a considering look. "All right," he said. "You've done what you came to do. Now what?"

She sighed. "I'll see him again, if it is possible. His wife will only be more suspicious from now forward, and he is very ill." And his wife is determined he shall stay that way, she thought.

"So, we're in Venice," Jaufre said. "You've met your grandfather."

"So now what?" Shasha said.

"Good question," Johanna said, making a face. She fiddled with a string unraveling from the hem of her tunic. "I know, this was all my idea," she said without looking up. "And you two have never tried to—to— "

"Talk you out of anything?" Shasha said, and exchanged a look with Jaufre, who laughed.

"What would be the point?" Jaufre said. "This was the destination you chose for us. We could come with you, or you would go alone."

"You make me sound like—like—"

"Foolish?"

"Stubborn?"

"Spoiled rotten?"

Johanna flapped a hand. "All that and more," she said. Her smile was crooked. "You still came with me."

"Yes, well." Jaufre looked at Shasha. "It wasn't as if we had someplace better to go."

"We don't now, either," Shasha said. "But I don't much care for the idea of staying here past the winter."

"Well," Johanna said, and cocked a brow. "We are still traders."

Jaufre shrugged. It didn't need answering, if it was even a question.

"And we haven't seen all there is to see here," she said. She felt for the square, leather-bound book in the purse at her waist. "And my father's book is not yet complete. There are new roads to see and to write down in it."

Jaufre and Shasha exchanged looks. "Obviously," Jaufre said.

"Without question," Shasha said, smiling.

Johanna felt a matching smile spread across her face. "Then I say we gather up a pack train of—asses, I suppose, as camels don't seem to have successfully crossed the Middle Sea, more's the pity, and horses are too expensive to feed to be used for pack animals. We gather as much information as possible as to the kind of goods that are most in demand to the north of Venice—"

"Spices," Shasha said.

"Small items, to pack as much as possible into as small a space as possible," Jaufre said. "Jewelry, gemstones, small antiquities."

"Seeds," Shasha said.

"Sugar?" Jaufre said.

Shasha shook her head. "Too bulky, and they cultivate honey here. Venetian glass?"

"Big pieces will be too heavy, and too breakable," Jaufre said. "Vials for potions and tinctures, perhaps." Shasha nodded. "Coral, amber, ivory, worked or unfinished. Small pieces, nothing larger than would be suitable for a belt buckle."

"And spices," Shasha said again, in case either of them hadn't heard her the first time.

Johanna looked at the two of them for a long moment. "And we leave when—"

"Spring," they said together.

Johanna nodded. "After the snow melts and the ground dries out."

"I'm told there are high mountains to the north," Jaufre said, "but also that there are hard but negotiable passes through them."

Johanna laughed, as anyone who had been through the Tien Shan would do at the mention of other, de facto inferior mountains. "No plans to stay put, then?" she said.

"No!" they said in unison, and this time all three of them laughed.

"We should acquire an agent here, though," Jaufre said thoughtfully. "If we are to continue trading, we will need a source of goods from the East, and Venice appears to be the acknowledged source of foreign goods for trade in these parts."

"May, then," Johanna said.

They looked at each other. "May," they agreed.

Later that evening Jaufre came to Johanna's room. She looked at him, and, unbidden, the tears began to gather and fall. He gathered her up in his arms and lay down with her on her bed, and held her all night. Once she said, "It's not as if I really knew him."

His heart beat strongly and steadily beneath her cheek. He stirred, and said, "It's not Ser Polo you weep for, Johanna."

"Who, then?"

His smile was barely visible in the dim glow of the embers of what was left of the fire in the little fireplace that graced her room. "You weep for Wu Li, and Shu Ming, and the life you've left behind. Ser Polo was the last link left to that old life."

She listened to the beat of his heart beneath her ear. "Do you still think of your mother, Jaufre?"

He remembered the women being stripped naked at the slave auctions down on the Grand Canal. "Always."

"I wish we could have found her for you."

"So do I."

They fell asleep then, holding each other until morning, when the watery daylight leaked through the small window high up on the wall stirred Johanna to consciousness. She stretched luxuriously, feeling a sense of well being at odds with the emotionally taxing experience of the previous day.

Jaufre stretched in turn and blinked up at her. "Good morning."

"Good morning," she said. "And thank you." Impulsively she leaned down to give him a quick kiss.

He was instantly awake, one hand behind her head and another around her waist. He rolled them over so that he was lying on top of her, one leg sliding between hers, as he deepened the kiss.

Shock kept her frozen in place for one moment, and then another, and then another, until she realized that her shock had passed and that her hands were moving up his back, kneading the warm, firm flesh beneath the rough nap of his tunic. His lips moved across her cheek and down her throat and she gasped when he pulled her nightshirt down her shoulder, exposing her breast. Her nipple hardened instantly and his lips were there, suckling, rubbing with his tongue.

She heard breathless, whimpering, mewling sounds and realized that came from her. Her body was arched from head to toe, she had one leg wrapped around him and she was rubbing up against the hard ridge of flesh between his legs with a need she only dimly remembered from the time by the lake with Edyk. This need seemed far more urgent, more— more necessary.

He raised his head. His blue eyes were narrowed, his golden hair tumbled. "Johanna," he said, his voice rougher than she'd ever heard it.

"Jaufre," she said, in—disbelief? Wonder?

"Johanna," he said, this time in unmistakable satisfaction, and felt for the drawstring at her waist.

The door to the room opened. "Johanna, you must come—oh."

The door closed again. After a moment came a knock, and Shasha's subdued voice from behind it, "Johanna, Peter is here and asking for you. You'd better come." A brief pause. "I'm sorry." Footsteps moving away.

Johanna stared up at Jaufre. "I'm sorry," she whispered in her turn.

Jaufre was the son of one ex-soldier and the friend of two others, and he had lived his entire life within earshot of muleteers, camel handlers, grooms and ostlers. These were not people known for moderation in language, and every curse he had learned was on display and at full volume as he extricated himself from Johanna's bed and fumbled his clothing into place.

Her face heated when she saw that his trousers were halfway down his legs and that it was she who must have made that happen.

He looked up and saw her expression and snarled, "Say 'I'm sorry' one more time, do!" He yanked his trousers up and stormed out.

She gaped after him. "Jaufre," she said. "Jaufre!"

He did not return.

She stood up and stared around the room as if she'd never seen it before. And then she got dressed and went out into the common room, where Peter sat, his face ravaged with grief.

He looked up at her and said, "He's dead. Early this morning." He swallowed. "He wasn't in pain and he wasn't alone. He just—left."

· Five ·

Spring, 1324 A.D.
Venice

⊢——⊣

The effects were barely noticeable, at first. Through January and February custom at Jaufre's stall began to fall, but no more than his fellow stallholders on the street. At first he thought it was due to the usual drop-off of business after the Christian festivities in December, during which a great deal of money had been spent by the citizens of Venice not only at his stall but at every vendor in the city, large and small. By March, when the rise in temperature and increase in daylight brought more custom to the stalls around him and less and less to him, he began to wonder.

When he mentioned it at dinner that night Firas and Alaric exchanged glances. "What?"

"Master Roland told us he's been having trouble selling tickets to the next exhibition," Alaric said.

Jaufre frowned. "The last time I was there for practice, he told me that the salle was too full during the afternoon to accommodate non-paying guests. He told me morning hours would be best."

"Morning hours being when there are fewest people there."

Firas looked at Shasha. "And Shasha has had little call on her for potions and tinctures of late."

"Custom has been falling off since late January," she said, troubled.

"Well," Félicien said lightly, setting aside a bowl of stew he had barely touched, "not to chime in on this tale of woe, but I have been—uninvited—from performing at the Inn of the Four Horses."

"What!"

"Why?"

"You draw more of a crowd than any other performer in Venice!"

"That's not all, I'm sorry to say," he said, glancing at Shasha. "I'm afraid Father Amadeo has been inveigling against the devil again."

"In Shasha's name?" Firas said, his voice hard.

"No," Félicien said. "Not yet. Just generally expounding on the notion that man is born to suffer, and that anything that interferes with that suffering is the work of Satan himself and should be shunned by all true faithful." He glanced at Hari and added, a little mockingly, "However much we stand in the favor of the abbot at the monastery of San Giorgio, it appears we shall not, after all, be impervious to the scourge of Father Amadeo's tongue."

"I have heard nothing of this during my visits there," Hari said, looking troubled.

"January," Jaufre said, looking at Johanna. "I don't know. What happened in January?"

No one except Shasha knew for sure why Johanna blushed to the roots of her hair, although they all had their suspicions. "My grandfather died in January," she said, willing her color to subside. Her eyes widened and she looked at Shasha. "And Peter came to tell us so." She thought for a moment, and looked at Tiphaine. "Will you take a message to Ca' Polo for me?"

The girl bounced up. Between the new clothes and the regular food, she looked a handspan taller than when Johanna had first brought her home. "Of course," she said briskly.

"Delivered directly into Moreta's hands if possible, and if not, Peter's. No one else."

"Certainly."

It took three days for a reply. "She will meet you at the taverna at none."

Alas, perhaps blinded by his grief, it appeared that Peter had not been as careful as Johanna had been in seeing that she was not followed when she left Ca' Polo. "My mother," Moreta said, and grimaced. "My mother," she said again, and stopped again.

Johanna thought of the frighteningly enraged woman standing at the top of the stairs at the end of the corridor when they had come out of Ser Polo's room. "It's all right," she said.

Moreta's head came up and she said hotly, "No. It isn't. She had Paolo follow Peter to your lodgings when I sent him to you with news of Father's passing. Then she wouldn't rest until she knew everything about you."

"Does she know—"

"Yes," Moreta said. "I don't know how, because Peter didn't tell her, and she hasn't said a word to me about you, and I'm the only other one who knows." Her brow creased. "I can't understand why."

"Can't you?" a voice said, and startled, both of them turned to see Donata Polo standing there in her luxurious dark robes with not a fold out of place. She was attended on her right by a serving woman who looked every bit as censorious as her mistress and on her left by the man who had shut the door so decisively in Johanna's face on the day of her arrival in Venice. He looked very pleased with himself.

The three of them bore a distinct resemblance to the statues on the temple walls she had seen in Mien as a child, glaring of eye, thunderous of brow, prepared to smite the unworthy. Although with fewer arms.

The taverna's keeper, yet again proving her worth, became absorbed in the examination of her stock of pitchers and mugs, one at a time, inspecting them for flaws.

"Can't you?" Moreta's mother repeated, looking from her daughter's face to Johanna's and back again. "I see. I see, indeed. A bastard of your father's, looking for largesse. Well, we know how to deal with your kind."

The temple statues of Mien had frightened her. This woman did not, perhaps because she had known another woman very like her in a prior life. Johanna rose to her feet, shaking Moreta's hand from her sleeve. "A granddaughter, certainly," she said, stepping forward and perforce causing Serra Polo to step back, which didn't please her. Unfortunately, Johanna was taller than she was and she couldn't glare down her nose at the younger woman. "I ask nothing of you, Serra Polo. I want nothing from you. I came a long way to meet my grandfather, and I merely wished—"

Serra Polo looked at her daughter. "I had not thought to suffer such disloyalty in my own house."

Moreta closed her eyes for a moment. "He was pleased to see her, Mother."

"Pleased! Pleased! I will say what pleased your father and what did not! You thought to bring this stranger, this—this adventurer, this pretender to the house of Ca' Polo, and make your father's last days on this earth a living misery!"

"He was pleased to see her, Mother, and to hear news of the—" she hesitated and cast Johanna a quick look of apology "—friends he had left behind."

"Friends," Serra Polo said with awful sarcasm, and swept Johanna with a look from head to toe that was far from complimentary. "Friends, indeed."

Johanna allowed a smile to cross her face. She ignored another desperate tug at her sleeve and said, "Obviously a great deal more than friends."

Serra Polo was quick to hear the deliberate mockery in Johanna's voice, and anger stiffened into outrage. Before she could say anything else, Moreta got to her feet. "It's time we went home, Mother."

"But before you do," Johanna said, "call off your dogs. I am no threat to you." She raised an eyebrow. "Or to your inheritance."

"I know nothing of dogs," Donata Polo said inaccurately, and swept out of the establishment, followed by her minions, everyone satisfied at having the last word.

Tomorrow, Moreta mouthed at Johanna, pointing at their table, and followed.

Johanna turned to look at Peter, who had had sat still and unperturbed through the encounter. "Well?"

His eyes held the hint of a smile. "My master left me well provided for in his will. I dance to no one's tune but my own, now."

She sat back down and gestured at the taverna keeper, who miraculously remembered she had customers. She bustled over with a new pitcher of small beer and whisked away Moreta's mug so there was no sad remembrance of absent friends. "What will you do now?" she said.

His shoulders lifted in the merest shrug. "It depends on what she does next." She remained unidentified but not unknown. "Moreta was the only member of that household who had any value for my master. If she needs me, I will stay."

If he was allowed to, Johanna thought. "Will you go home, otherwise? Do you miss the wind on the steppes so much?"

She couldn't be sure but she thought he might almost have smiled, if he didn't have a racial reputation for stoicism to live up to. "What is home to me now," he said with a sigh.

It wasn't a question, so she didn't try to answer. "Lacking other options…" She hesitated. "You could join Wu Company."

He surprised her with a laugh, a deep, rumbling sound pleasant to the ears. His eyes positively twinkled and he said, "I don't know that I have it in me to chase another Polo halfway around the world, mistress."

She grinned at him. "All I can promise is that it won't be dull."

He looked at her for a long moment. "I will think on it."

"Your very existence is an affront to her," Moreta said the next day. They had met at the taverna and Moreta had said that since there were no more secrets left from the Grand Canal to the Rialto Bridge they might as well go to Johanna's lodgings. Shasha made them comfortable with hot tea and sweet biscuits and settled down in a corner with mortar and pestle, there to grind ingredients and eavesdrop.

"Your mother appears to be harboring what seems to us to be a disproportionate amount of rage," Johanna said. "And is occupying herself in venting it all on us."

"My mother is a very angry woman. She's been an angry woman all my life, and she is better at holding a grudge than anyone I've ever met. Paolo spends all his time ferreting out information for her, I believe just to fuel more slights and grievances. It is a way of life for them both, now." Moreta sipped her tea. "This is wonderful," she told Shasha.

She bit into one of the biscuits, and Shasha held up a hand. "Not as wonderful, I know," she said ruefully. "My friend the baker turned me from his door before he taught me all his secrets."

"It's simple," Moreta said, "double the butter."

Shasha was pleased. "Thank you, lady."

"Moreta, please."

"But we have given her no call to hold a grudge," Johanna said.

Félicien was teaching Tiphaine how to finger chords on his lute, with Hayat and Alma interested auditors. Jaufre and Firas were attending to the ongoing conversation, thus far taking no part in it. Hari was as yet persona grata at the monastery and Alaric was out, probably drinking somewhere in a taverna. He wasn't going to be able to afford it for very much longer if Donata Polo did not soon relent. One of the potential benefits of her enmity, Johanna thought.

"She needs no reason," Moreta said. "My father offended her by spending her dowry the first year of their marriage." She paused, and added meditatively, "I really think she might have killed all three of her children in the womb in revenge, could she have found a way."

A discordant jangle of lute strings, and Johanna looked around to see that Tiphaine was realizing that there were worse things in the world to be than a motherless child.

"My sisters married as soon as my father could arrange dowries for them. I…" She sighed. "I didn't want to leave him."

"Will you have to live with your mother now?" Alma said, exchanging an appalled look with Hayat. The harem was looking better to them all the time, Johanna saw.

Moreta's smile was grim. "Yes, but in his will my father settled my dowry upon me, for my own use. I have already an apartment set aside at Ca' Polo, and I have my own friends. I shouldn't have to see more of her than I can bear." She drank tea. "But you."

"Yes?"

Moreta looked around the room. "You must leave Venice. All of you."

"We always meant to," Johanna said. "It was never our intent to settle here."

"Yes, but—" Jaufre said.

"What?"

He spoke to Shasha. "I'm having difficulties acquiring an agent for us, and even more difficulty in acquiring sales goods. Not to mention which…" He looked at Firas.

"No one will sell us pack animals," Firas said. "I've been down to the livestock market and the merchants are all very pleasant, some even cordial, but all of their stock is spoken for." He stroked his beard. "They say they can sell us none for fear that this year's gray cloaks will go unprovisioned."

Translating "gray cloaks" to "pilgrims," Johanna said, "But that's nonsense! There are all the donkeys in the world at Gaza, and Jerusalem." Moreta was shaking her head. "Is your mother's influence so strong in Venice, then? She doesn't sound like a friend who would be that welcome on anyone's doorstep."

Jaufre snorted out a laugh but his head was turned away when Johanna looked at him. She knew a flicker of temper, then. She hadn't meant she was sorry, she couldn't ever make love with him. She'd only meant she was sorry they'd been interrupted (and she had been, teeth-grindingly sorry, ready to kill Shasha sorry). But try as she would she had been unable to corner him alone anytime these past two months to say so. He seemed to positively enjoy nursing his grudge and feeding its flame wherever possible. Donata Polo could take lessons.

The thought made an involuntary smile cross her face, which of course he turned his head at the last moment to see. He looked suspicious immediately, because of course she had to be laughing at him, didn't she, even if he was sitting there doing nothing. She hid a sigh and turned back to Moreta.

"She doesn't have to be friends with anyone to have influence, Johanna," Moreta said. "She just needs to be born into the right family, one that has lived here forever and is related by blood and marriage to all the other right families. Since the day Paolo reported back to her, she has been spreading the word, palazzo by palazzo, canal by canal. Your morals are suspect, your faith nonexistent—"

"I go to Mass every Sunday!" Jaufre said, sounding aggrieved. His regular attendance to Father Amadeo's services certainly wasn't for pleasure.

"—and worst of all, your coin is not to be trusted. Venetians will do well to neither sell to nor buy from you, to avoid socializing with you, indeed, better they should turn aside rather than touch shoulders if they meet you on the street." She nodded at the badge on Johanna's shoulder. "You made yourselves so easily identifiable with your compagnia insignia, too. She didn't even have to describe you individually. No member of Wu Company may trade in Venice."

There was an edge to Johanna's voice. "And because Donata Polo says it, it must be so?"

"Well." Moreta drank tea. "It's not quite the law." She looked up from her cup. "Yet."

It was silent in the room as Moreta held out her cup for a refill. "That really is marvelous tea, Shasha. Where did you get it?"

"We brought it with us," Shasha said. "I have seen none for sale here in Venice."

"What a pity."

"We have our living to make," Johanna said. "We are traders by profession. Where else can we buy goods to sell, if not in Venice?"

"And how do we get those goods anywhere," Firas said, "if we can buy no pack animals?"

"Especially if they decide to burn us at the stake first," Félicien said.

Moreta sat back, her cup filled. She did not look as downcast as the rest of them did, Johanna noted, or as indignant as Johanna felt. "You have an idea," she said.

Moreta sipped her tea. "Perhaps." She looked at Johanna. "What you said to my father that day." She hesitated, looking at the others. "About the pearl fishers of Cipangu."

"Yes?" Johanna said, mystified.

"Is it true, what you told me? That you dove with the pearl fishers?"

"Yes," Johanna said.

"You dove, and brought back oysters, with pearls in them? So you have the knack of finding small objects at depth?"

"Moreta—"

"The Wedding to the Sea!"

Moreta nodded at Tiphaine. "That is my thought."

Everyone in the room who was not Venetian looked askance at one another. Tiphaine bounced to her feet, black curls flying, all eagerness to explain, and Moreta waved a hand for her to be about it. "It's an annual holiday, the Feast of the Ascension! The Patriarch blesses a golden ring, and then there is a grand procession of boats from the Basilica of St. Mark to the Church of San Nicolò on the Lido, with the Doge and the Patriarch and all the nobles dressed in their finest silks and velvets. And there is music, and jugglers, and stilt walkers, and dancers, and acrobats—"

"Any horse racing?" Johanna said, sitting up straight.

"Horse racing?" Tiphaine frowned. "No. I don't think so. I've never heard of any."

"Oh." Johanna slumped, losing interest. She had a large bruise on her right hip from the expression of North Wind's continuing displeasure the previous day. If horses could talk, he would have heartily endorsed any idea that got them back on the Road as soon as possible.

"But oh, it is such a fine sight to see, the costumes are so beautiful, and they throw coins—" She caught herself, and added haughtily, "For the street urchins to catch, you understand. Not for respectable citizens."

"Of course not," Johanna said, to an accompanying murmur around the room.

"Then the Doge on el Bucintoro—"

"El Bucintoro?"

"His barge, oh, wait till you see it, it is the most magnificent boat ever built, all gilded with gold! It is from el Bucintoro's deck that the Doge throws the blessed ring into the sea, so that La Serenissima renews her vows once again to the sea that gives us our livelihood." She clasped her hands and stood in rapt silence.

"Yes, well," Johanna said, a little at sea herself, "that sounds most romantic, and, ah, a spectacle to behold. But I don't quite see what—"

"The instant the ring goes into the sea, Johanna," Moreta said, "Venetians strip off their clothes and dive after it."

"What?" Johanna thought of the filth she saw every day in the canals, of the opaque green of the waters. "By all the Mongol gods, why?"

Moreta smiled. "Because whoever recovers the ring lives tax free in Venice for the next year."

The silence that followed this statement was profound.

"I dove with the pearl fishers, too," Jaufre said.

"I dove deeper and brought back more pearls," Johanna said.

"That is true," Shasha said, a little reluctantly, and later Johanna would take her to task for that.

"Shasha, that was Cipangu, where all the ama are women."

"Because they're better at it than the men!"

"But this," Jaufre said, glaring at Johanna, "is Venice, where women doing anything but having babies and minding their homes and going to church is frowned on. You think Serra Donata has them whipped up against us now! I can only imagine what they're going to say when you strip down on the side of the Grand Canal to dive in!"

"But with two divers, our odds of recovering the ring increase," Shasha said, stepping in neatly to avert the imminent conflagration. She looked at Jaufre. "The waters of Venice are not exactly the waters of Izu, which

I remember as clear right down to the bottom. I doubt the bottom of a Venetian canal has been seen in a thousand years."

Johanna and Jaufre subsided, seeing the sense of this. "When is this feast day?" Johanna said.

"May," Moreta and Tiphaine said together.

"Two months," Johanna said. "Can your mother starve us out by then?"

Moreta smiled. "Probably not. And you can always take the ferry to the mainland to buy foodstuffs, if you have to. But you have to stay in Venice, because only those resident in Venice on the day itself may dive for the ring." She set down her cup. "And you will need a sponsor, someone from one of the first families, because only such are eligible to dive. That I cannot help you with." She grimaced. "In fact, if my mother got wind of it, she would make it her new mission in life to see that you never acquired such a sponsor."

Johanna and Jaufre looked at each other, animosity forgotten, for the moment. "Gradenigo," they said at the same time.

"Which one?" Moreta said.

"Giovanni Gradenigo," Jaufre said. "He was the captain of the ship that brought us here from Gaza. He told us, very grandly, that he was a great-nephew of a doge of the same name."

"Gradenigo," Moreta said thoughtfully. "I haven't met this Giovanni, but a Gradenigo was our last doge but one, memorable chiefly because he got Venice excommunicated again."

"Again?"

"Unfortunately. The family's influence lessened somewhat after his death, but there is a younger one of the house named Bartolomeo who is known as a coming man. Yes, the Gradenigos might do, so long as there is no association between our families of which I am unaware. Will he do it?"

"From his conversation I think he would welcome the opportunity."

Jaufre grinned, and Johanna watched, fascinated, as the dimples creased his cheeks. It seemed like years since she'd seen them. "So long as he gets to wet his snout."

"Ask him," Moreta said. "And soon."

· Six ·

←⎯⎯

A re you all right?" Shasha said in a low voice.

"I'm fine. I just wish they'd get on with it."

It was late May, forty days after Easter Sunday. The air was warmed by a sun in a pale blue sky for a change unobscured by clouds, but Johanna couldn't stop shivering.

From the size of the crowds on the quay and the amount of boats in the Grand Canal there wasn't a Venetian left at home that morning. The cathedral of St. Mark's held a crowd whose overflow packed the piazza in front of it. From the loggia above the portico the four great bronze horses that Venice had looted from Byzantium a hundred years before reminded everyone of Venice's might and reach. Johanna never saw them but she was reminded of Uncle Cheng's observation that everything worth looking at in Byzantium was now in Venice.

She sighed, and shivered again. Almost two years and so many leagues away, that infinitely warmer evening in Kashgar. Where was Uncle Cheng now? En route somewhere, no doubt. If the rumors about Ogodei settling west of Terak were true, if the renegade Mongol general had decided himself satisfied with the territory he had overrun to date, Uncle Cheng could be arriving in Kashgar itself, selling silk and buying bronze. Mongols, however acquisitive of territory, never underestimated the necessity and profitability of trade, and whatever else Ogodei did to gather territory beneath his banner, he would do nothing to obstruct the free passage of goods and merchants. Uncle Chang and his livelihood would be safe.

The sound of thousands of Venetians on holiday forcibly returned her attention back to the present. Impossibly the great buzz of shouts and laughter increased in volume when the massive doors of the cathedral finally opened wide to disgorge the Patriarch, the Doge, the Senate, the heads of all the guilds, the legate from Avignon and the ambassador from Paris walking together as if joined at the hip, any noble with rank enough to squeeze themselves inside for the service. Everyone was wearing every necklace, tiara, and ring they possessed. The cumulative glitter was painful to behold.

In contrast, Johanna and Jaufre wore belted robes of brown fustian that muffled them from head to toe. They looked, she thought, like something you might find down the privy hole after a harsh winter on short rations.

Fortunately, no one was paying them any attention. "The cloth of gold times the nobili in this procession would provide enough sail for five sea-going vessels," Giovanni Gradenigo said irreverently.

"There's a song in that," Félicien said promptly, and for all Johanna knew set about writing one in his head that minute. He'd been on the nearest street corner earlier, playing his lute and singing songs about farting peasants, lovelorn knights and cuckolded husbands, to the sniggering delight of a gathering crowd. His smooth soprano was as mellow as ever, a voice that never broke or missed a note, to which the growing pile of coins in the hat on the cobblestones in front of him could attest.

Hymns sung loud if untunefully, accompanied by drums and trumpets, were drowned out by the bells of St. Mark's, which by themselves were loud enough to jar the teeth from your head. The procession from the church was preceded by banners and crosses and the teeth and toe bones of saints in gilt boxes held high on elaborately decorated litters, and was followed by a crush of Venetian citizens following behind, all determined to miss no detail of this day when Venice once again tied the very sea herself to the city in holy matrimony.

"Impressive," Jaufre said, sounding amused, and Johanna knew he was remembering the processions of Cambaluc, which for richness of regalia and self-importance of its dignitaries outshone this one by a mile.

Tiphaine snorted. "This is nothing," she said grandly. "You should see Corpus Christi Day. All the reliquaries are out on Corpus Christi Day."

The procession made its stately way across the piazza to the Grand Canal, where el Bucintoro waited, heavy with paint and gilt and silken hangings and golden figurehead. Unconsciously Johanna held her breath as the highest were shown tenderly on board and settled themselves into luxurious seats, and the gilt ship sank in the water beneath the accumulated weight of all that might and majesty. When they were all aboard if the water did not quite overlap the gunnels it certainly nibbled at them. If it hadn't been flat calm, if there had been even the slightest chop, Johanna would have had every expectation that el Bucintoro would have swamped before they were an arm's length from the dock.

The sailing master barked orders, lines were loosed and the golden vessel separated from the quay in the stately fashion befitting its august cargo. Both lines of oars sliced into the water at precisely the same moment. A mighty shout went up from the quayside and from boats large and small crowding the waterway, whose number Johanna estimated in the hundreds.

"All right, it's time, get in," Gradenigo said, and Johanna turned to scramble into the nimble craft tied next to them, Jaufre right behind her. Shasha and Firas were left on the wharf, Shasha anxious and Firas as enigmatic as ever. Alaric, looking painfully sober, stood next to them, with Alma and Hayat, hands clasped and looking concerned. Even Hari had deemed this occasion worthy of an absence from the monastery. He smiled benignly, to see their comrades set forth on a mission as foolhardy as it was unquestionably futile. Certainly no one cheered as Gradenigo pushed them off. Their new badges flashed in the sunlight, bearing the flamboyant, full-sailed ship of the Gradenigo Azienda. Tiphaine had objected most vehemently to Wu Company's badge being removed, however temporarily, for the remainder of their stay in Venice.

Johanna suspected that the girl wanted any glory to be reflected back to its proper source. If any glory there was to be had.

"Where's Tiphaine?" Johanna said suddenly. A movement caused her to look around. "Tiphaine! I told you to stay on the quay!"

A small face with a mutinous expression looked back at her from the stern and said nothing. A muffled sound was heard and Johanna said dangerously, "Jaufre, don't you dare laugh."

"Wouldn't think of it." Jaufre stared off in the middle distance with a bland expression on his face.

Gradenigo and a short, wiry man Johanna recognized from the voyage from Gaza wielded an oar each as they joined the grand procession of what looked like anything that had a reasonable chance of floating, from a bathtub on up to a cog. Most of them were oar-driven but Johanna saw a few small skiffs rigged with jibs darting recklessly before, between and behind the much larger vessels that made up the bulk of this unwieldy fleet, and giving rise to not a few curses bellowed as only sailors can, especially when the big ships stole the wind and the sailboats became momentarily becalmed between two fast-approaching and much larger hulls.

Their own vessel was made of cedar planed suicidally thin and formed into an open, narrow shell with two thwarts inside to sit on and two oar-locks in which to rest the oars, and that was all. The draft was so shallow that with all five of them inside it rode low enough to sink if anyone so much as inhaled. The three passengers were enveloped in a fine spray raised by the oars but she had to admit that the little boat skimmed over the water like a bird in flight, overtaking and passing laboring craft as if they had been frozen in place, passing so close to others that you couldn't have inserted a feather between them, shifting course so rapidly that they shipped water over first the port side and then the starboard and then the port side again, until they were close, too close if the shouts from above were any indication, on el Bucintoro's stern. There Gradenigo laid off a few lengths and used his oar only enough to maintain their position.

"There," he said with evident satisfaction. He saw Johanna's expression, mistook it for admiration, and sent her a cocky grin.

Johanna blew out a breath and looked at Jaufre, who was also grinning. Over her shoulder she heard Tiphaine laugh out loud. She wiped her face on her sleeve and forbore to comment.

"Don't do that," Jaufre said, catching her hand. "You'll wipe it off."

The procession came to a halt, or as much of a halt as the tides and currents would allow. The flotilla came together in a cluster about the Doge's barge. Gradenigo fended off a couple of pretenders to their position, vigorously enough to cause said pretenders to hastily right their craft before they went under. A larger craft tried to muscle its way in but Gradenigo held his ground, Johanna thought by sheer force of will, because this wooden leaf they were barely floating in certainly had no tonnage capable of offering any threat. The current hymn, rising from the ships at sea and the crowds on shore, came to a ragged, triumphant crescendo and broke off, and in the following breathless silence the Doge rose to his feet and made his way to the side. They weren't more than a couple of arms lengths from the hull of el Bucintoro and she could see his lined face clearly. He was smiling.

"Get ready," Gradenigo said.

"Are we too close?" Jaufre said in a low voice, rising to his feet, hands at the tie of his robe.

"He's an old man, how far can he throw?" Gradenigo said.

The old man's arm raised and Johanna saw the tiny gold ring in his hand, illuminated for just an instant by the rays of the morning sun. She stood, the little craft rocking beneath her feet, and shed her robe next to Jaufre. Everywhere she looked men were tearing at their clothes, on boats, on shore.

Her robe fell next to Jaufre's in the bottom of their boat. They were attired in tunic and trousers and slippers, white for better visibility underwater and wound close to their bodies in strips more white cloth covered with a thick layer of grease. Johanna's hair was caught back in a long braid and it too was slicked over with a layer of grease, as was every exposed bit of her skin. Shasha had rendered the fat of two sheep for enough to encase her and Jaufre both during their dive.

A tiny gold object sailed over the gathered flotilla, actually bouncing off the grasping hand of a young grandee attired in velvet, who leaned too far out of his boat and toppled into the water a moment after the ring hit the surface.

"Go, go, go!" Gradenigo said, a moment before a mighty shout went up from the assemblage.

Johanna, who had been taking deep, whistling breaths from the moment they had stopped moving, brought her hands over her head and dove over the side, conscious of Jaufre's slicing into the water next to her only a second later. Even with all the practice dives they had made over the past month, it was gaspingly cold. Johanna blinked her eyes to clear them, pulled her head down and kicked hard and pulled harder with her arms, heading for her best guess as to where she might find the ring.

Something grabbed at her foot and she kicked hard, half-turning to see a bearded man in shirtwaist and hose hanging off her ankle. He was grinning, or he was until Jaufre took a handful of his hair and yanked, hard. An explosion of bubbles from his mouth and Johanna's ankle was free. She felt someone else take hold of her braid and yank and she was momentarily arrested in her dive, until a moment later Jaufre was on him. Her attacker's fingers were already slipping from the greased braid but Jaufre shoved two brutal fingers up his nose and a cloud of blood obscured his face. He screamed and air bubbled out of his mouth and he struck for the surface.

Jaufre pointed, and she followed the direction of his hand and took a precious second to reorient herself. Was that a flash of gold? She pulled herself down with all of the strength in her shoulders and arms, putting all the muscle in her hips and legs behind her kick. The deeper the water, the darker it was. If the ring fell below a certain level she'd never see it. If it reached the bottom she would never find it. The pressure was building on her ears and in her lungs and she began to let out air, one tiny bubble at a time, in measured beats. The water became colder still, almost paralyzingly cold the further down she dove, the farther behind she left the weak spring sun.

There! A flash, and she kicked and reached out, and, disbelieving it even as it happened, her hand closed around something hard and tiny and round. She pulled up and someone grabbed her braid but again, Jaufre was there and this time he didn't bother with nostrils, he grabbed between the man's legs. The man tried to scream, there another explosion of bubbles, and Johanna was free. She kicked for the surface, her lungs burning now, it was too long since she'd done this, she was out of practice, but she could not inhale, who knew the filth that she would bring into her body, and then there was the drowning, no, and then yes! She broke the surface, the force of her kick propelling her out of the water as far as her waist, and Gradenigo was there and he had her arm, the one with the fist clenched tight around the ring that would make all their fortunes.

Another shout went up, this one loud enough to be heard at the doors of Everything Under the Heavens itself, although this might have been partly due to the fact that Venice realized that a woman had retrieved the ring this year.

She collapsed on the bottom of their tiny eggshell of a boat and used the rest of the air in her lungs to blow out her nose and gasp, "Jaufre?"

There was a splash and a gasp and a sleek head surfaced. Gradenigo and his crew grabbed him by the hair and the seat of his trousers and lifted him on board, although Tiphaine went over in the process. Gradenigo grabbed the back of her tunic, lifted her out of the water, shook her vigorously and tossed her into the stern.

"Did you get it?" Gradenigo said to Johanna.

"Did you get it?" Jaufre said.

"Did you get it?" Tiphaine said, pushing her soaking curls out of her eyes.

"Did you get it!" the crowd bellowed.

"Quick," Gradenigo said, "your robes."

When they were decently swathed once again in brown fustian, Johanna's braid tucked inside, Gradenigo helped her to her feet. She kept her knees loose so as to keep her balance in the rocking boat. She did not want to go back into that cold, dirty water, not ever again. Above her, a row of heads crowded the side of el Bucintoro, one of them, she saw fleetingly, belonging to the Doge himself.

She rolled the ring forward to hold it between thumb and forefinger, and then, her fingers cold and numb she almost dropped it, to the accompanying, deliciously horrified gasp of everyone watching. But the grease on her hands was so thick the ring stuck to her fingers. She raised her hand over her head, and the sun, which seemed to have increased in strength and brightness in the moments she had been gone from it made the golden hoop glitter like the finest diamond ever pulled from the sands of Nubia.

This time the shriek was loud enough to be heard at the door of Heaven itself.

There was some grumbling about the winning diver's sex and nationality, not to mention the unfair advantage of the grease. Gradenigo, backed by his family's name and especially by the vocal and public support of his cousin Bartolomeo, his family's coming man, overbore it. He could indeed conduct business in Venice tax free, for a year beginning from the day of the Wedding to the Sea. "He wants to meet you, by the way."

"Meet who?"

"All of you," Gradenigo said, "but especially Johanna." He winked. "He admired your diving costume. As did all of Venice."

"I assume he admired mine as well," Jaufre said in a silken voice.

"All of you," Gradenigo said hastily, "the entire Wu Company is bidden to dinner at Ca' Gradenigo on Saturday next. Bring your best stories, because he will expect you to sing for your supper. But now." He smacked his hands together. "Let us construe." He cocked an eyebrow. "How would you feel about leading a shipment of goods to Lyon?"

"Where is Lyon?" Shasha said.

"And what's there?" Jaufre said.

"A city in France about a hundred and seventy leagues west of Venice," Gradenigo said, "and a trading fair in France where the House of Gradenigo has a permit to buy and sell."

"Who trades there?" Johanna said.

Gradenigo smiled. "Everyone."

Firas raised an eyebrow in Shasha's direction. "That certainly sounds comprehensive," she said, and Johanna hid a smile.

It was as well that the dinner with Gradenigo's cousin didn't take place until the following Saturday, as it took that long to get all the grease off.

On Monday they met again with Gradenigo on the Grand Canal. "You will be coming with us to Lyon?" Jaufre said.

"Are you mad?" Gradenigo looked horrified. "The first sailing of pilgrims takes place next week, and besides, I am building my own merchant galley down on the Arsenal and I'll want to be here when she launches. You will be on your own, my friends."

Johanna and Jaufre exchanged glances. They preferred it that way, but— "And you'll trust us with your cargo? You may never see us or it again."

Gradenigo grinned. "Considering that I don't have to share a year's worth of profit with the Doge? You could plunge over the edge of Mount Genevre and I'd never miss the income. Enough of this now, come with me."

They followed him to a large warehouse of solid construction secured by a padlock the size of a newborn babe. Venice liked its locks large. Gradenigo led the way inside. "What will you have? Greek antiques from Rhodes? This is said to be the head of Athena by no less than

Praxiteles."

"Definitely not," Jaufre said, and Johanna said firmly, "Much too bulky."

Gradenigo shrugged. "Ah well, if I can't sell it here, it will go with the rest of the marble to Rome and be burned into lime. Sponges from Calymnos, then? Olive oil from Kerkyra? A Gozurate mat, perhaps? See the leather, both red and blue, and the birds and beast embroidered in gold. A fine piece, worthy of any lady's bower."

Johanna caught sight of a bundle of cloth and caught it up. "Silk from Chinangli! Where did you come by this, when the roads to the East are overrun by the armies of Barka Khan and Hulaku and Ogodei?"

The Venetian smiled. "If there is a market for such a thing, a way will be found to supply it."

Gradenigo led them deeper into a labyrinth that appeared to contain a sample of all the riches of the known world, cloth from Flanders, silk from Lucca in Italy, leather from Spain and North Africa, furs from Germany, spices, wax, sugar, alum, lacquer again from the East, grain, wine, dyes, cotton, flax from Egypt. In the stables behind the warehouse Gradenigo housed horses and livestock from Gaul to Africa. In one small room, reinforced, this one locked three times over and heavily guarded, he kept gold and precious stones.

"Anything anyone could ever want," Johanna said.

He looked at Johanna, fingering his beard. It was clear that he wondered at her lack of awe. She looked down at the hems of her trousers and repressed a smile.

The arrangements were straightforward. Gradenigo drew up a commenda, which set out the details. The investor, Gradenigo, would supply the goods and take three-quarters of the profit. The merchants, Johanna and Jaufre, would put up the other quarter, take possession of the goods for trade, and do the transportation and selling.

Reading it, Jaufre said, "We have a free hand, then."

"Yes," Gradenigo said. "It is up to you what you do with the goods and where you go to sell them. When you return, however, you will note that you must make a detailed and fair statement of profit and loss."

"And if we didn't?"

Paolo smiled. "Surely it's obvious. If you wish to continue in trade, you must cultivate a good reputation among the investors. If you do not, if you are suspected of dishonesty, trickery or thievery, no investor will ever back you again."

"I suppose you investors talk to each other." Jaufre didn't make it a question.

Gradenigo's smile widened. "Of the honesty and dependability of merchants, most certainly. Of the trade itself..." There was no need to complete the sentence.

"Spices," Shasha said, ignoring Johanna's grin. "Pepper, and nutmeg."

Gradenigo grimaced. "I'm low on spices. See Tomasso on the Street of Spices, tell him I sent you and that I expect his very best price or I send you to Enzo instead."

"Paper?" Jaufre said doubtfully.

Johanna shook her head. "Too bulky, too heavy, too subject to damp."

"But it fetches an excellent price in Lyon," Gradenigo said, and waved off their protests. "Don't discount it immediately, is all I ask. Perfume?"

They settled on spices, perfume, glass vials always in demand for oils, potions, unguents and tinctures, pearls and such other gemstones as Gradenigo had in stock, and since they agreed on oil in spite of its weight and the bulk of its jars they decided they might as well include paper in their trading stock, after all.

"What do you want us to bring back?

"Wool," Gradenigo said. "And if you run across any gold or silver ingots going cheap..." He laughed at their expressions. "Wool," he said. "I'll be happy if you bring back nothing but packs and packs of wool, preferably English wool." He stroked his beard. "When my new ship comes off the ways, I may look for a route to bring English wool to directly to market in Venice, without having to pay out extortionate fees to all those overland middlemen." His eyes gleamed. "I could start my own house, independent of my family."

Johanna and Jaufre and Shasha managed to spare a few moments to lay in their own goods. Jaufre, from his experience on the Rialto, specialized in jewelry for the discriminating—and wealthy—buyer, along with his usual store of manuscripts, scrolls, and books, too, in spite of the space they took up. Johanna found a dealer in antiquities down on the Grand Canal who had never heard of the Polos and was happy—for a price—to help her lay in a good stock of curiosities, including two chess sets made from ebony and ivory, one fashioned after the court of Genghis Khan and complete with long mustaches, the other made in the image of a Persian court, with the pawns made in the forms of dancing girls, which Hayat examined critically. "The maker of this set hadn't been within a league of a harem."

While the three of them were stocking their pack train, Hayat, Alma, Hari and Félicien took the opportunity to visit Padua, where Alma had heard there were some fine frescoes. They returned aglow with discovery, or at least Alma did, and Félicien was busy writing a song about the experience so Johanna assumed he was aglow, too. "Giotto, he's the artist, we wanted to meet him," Alma said. "But he was away in Assisi, alas."

Behind her back, Hayat rolled her eyes.

Alma looked at Johanna imploringly. "Are you sure you don't want to go to Rome? There are many examples of classical architecture there that I would like to see."

"You didn't see enough Roman ruins in Palestine?" Jaufre said, remembering his time as a pilgrim guard with a shudder.

In two weeks they were ready. Their last night they held a farewell dinner in their lodgings, to which they invited Moreta and Peter. "It's good you are leaving," Moreta said. "My mother is so angry that you managed to circumvent her ban that I think she might be thinking of hiring assassins."

Johanna shrugged. "That's all right, we've got one of our own."

Firas sighed. "So discreet, young miss, as always."

They ate well, drank well, and sang road songs, and were generally happy to be once again on the move. "All of you?" Moreta said, her eyes lingering on Tiphaine, who scowled back.

"I'm going with them," she said fiercely. "She bought me. She has to take me."

Johanna raised her hands helplessly at Moreta's look.

Moreta looked at Alma and Hayat, who sat close together on the bench the other side of the table. "And yourselves?"

Alma smiled. "I was too long held in one place I am not done moving yet."

"Where she goes, I go," Hayat said.

"And you, boy," Moreta said to Félicien. "You have quite a following in Venice. You could make a good living here, in spite of my mother. Especially now that you stand in Gradenigo's favor."

"I have learned all the songs I can in Venice, lady," Félicien said.

And you, sir knight?"

"I, too, am a Frank, lady, and have been long gone from home." Alaric burped.

"And you go with them," Moreta said to Shasha, and to Firas, "And you go with her." She smiled.

"And we go wearing our own company's badge," Tiphaine said, proudly displaying hers, which had once more replaced the Gradenigo ship.

Johanna looked at Peter, who sat a little back from the rest. "And you, Peter? Now that your master is dead? Will you be leaving Venice?"

"I will, young miss," Peter said, and acknowledged the shadow of sadness that passed briefly over Moreta's face. "But not north. I will be going east, with Captain Gradenigo's next shipload of pilgrims. I have a wish to die with the wind of the steppes once again in my ears."

"The latest news says that Ogodei still holds much of the area west of the Terak," Johanna said.

"He is a Mongol," Peter said. "I am a Mongol. He will let me pass."

She felt for the lump at her waist, the jade cylinder of her father's bao, the square solidity of his book. They were the only things left to anchor her to her beginnings.

"I will hate to leave you behind," she said.

He smiled. "Look forward, young miss," he said. "Your grandfather always did."

They took two boats over to the mainland at dawn the next morning, where their pack train awaited. Johanna heard a piercing whinny and a demanding stamp of hoofs, and ran to North Wind to bury her face in his mane. First he leaned against her, and then he tried to step on her foot. It had been a trying winter for both of them.

"Here," Jaufre said, cupping a hand. She placed her foot in it and he tossed her into the saddle. To him her smile was as radiant as the sun just breaking over the horizon. He couldn't stop the answering smile from spreading across his face.

Impulsively, she stretched out her hand. He caught it in his own, and they stared into each other's eyes. Or they did until North Wind did a combined hop-skip-and-jump, skittering like a foal, and broke into a trot. Johanna leaned forward to pat him on the neck. "On the Road again, North Wind!"

His stride lengthened into a smooth canter. She looked over her shoulder, laughing. "Well? Come on, everyone! Let's go!"

· Seven ·

Summer, 1324 A.D.
Lombardy

—

They soon discovered that travel in Europe was nothing like travel in Cathay, or in Persia for that matter. The Road was marked by steles built by the Great Khan. Each of the cities along its many routes had clean, well-maintained caravansaries for travelers and their livestock, or at the very least campsites, all of which came under the protection of the cities who built them and, not coincidentally, charged fees for their usage.

Here there were few roads worthy of the name, even fewer of which were signposted and of those few almost none were reliable. Lodging was a free-for all of inns, all of them independent businesses and most of them verminous. There was no oversight from the various cities next to whose walls they were built, and there was no oversight from the city fathers, which left travelers prey to assault, robbery, and sometimes even murder.

On the other hand, the string of cities from Venice to Milan presented multiple opportunities for trade. Wu Company neglected none of them.

Verona boasted forty-eight towers and a ruler of martial temperament who was constantly at war with his neighbors. But he was also vitally interested in his fellow man and no sooner had word arrived in his court of visitors from storied Cathay than members of Wu Company one and all were summoned before him. They washed off the dust of the road and arrayed themselves in their finest clothes and sallied off to entertain as best they could the honorable Cangrande della Scala, ruler of Verona and various surrounding subjugated cities as well. He had a lantern jaw, intelligent eyes and was of medium height, with the broad shoulders and muscled arms of a man more comfortable with a sword in his hand than a scepter. They had been required to leave their weapons in the outer chamber but one of his aides whispered in della Scala's ear and his eyes lit up. "Let us see these swords of yours, my friends."

These were sent for forthwith and a great deal of time was spent examining and discussing the weapons. Della Scala was a little disappointed in Jaufre's smiling insistence that he was a trader first and a warrior only at necessity. Della Scala and Alaric got on much better, especially after he sent for wine and other refreshments for his guests. He did have a few questions about Cathay and even more about Ogodei when they let fall that they knew the Mongol warrior. He stroked his beard as he listened to Johanna describe in flat, unemotional terms the siege and ultimately the utter destruction of Talikan as she had witnessed it the year before.

"A man to be reckoned with," della Scala said, some moments after she had finished.

"My lord," Johanna said, and hesitated.

"Speak freely, and without fear," he said. "You are my guests."

Having been steeped in the history of the eternally treacherous battles of the court of Everything Under the Heavens from birth, she doubted that meant much.

But Alma spoke up. "Mongols are not to be reckoned with, my lord," she said. "An opponent has two options. Submit, or die to the last man, woman and child. If a city resists his forces, when the Mongol wins, and he almost always does win, my lord, he will then send in teams of men to kill every last living survivor. Those few he allows to remain alive are usually soldiers he conscripts into his army." She paused, and glanced at Hayat. "My friend and I were citizens of Talikan, and we saw these same things with my own eyes, so I know them to be true."

There was a brief, appalled silence, and then Jaufre said smoothly, "Of course it is not a decision that any Western ruler would have to face, my lord. Ogodei and the Mongols are thousands of leagues to the east, with many strong nations and an entire sea between."

"Of course," della Scala said, a twinkle in his eye. "You have a singer of songs among you, I am told."

"We do, my lord," Jaufre said, effacing himself, and Félicien came forward, lute in hand. Della Scala motioned for a stool to be brought and the goliard disposed himself to play a tune involving a farmer, his wife and a traveling monk that had the court roaring their appreciation.

When Félicien finished his impromptu concert della Scala said, "I understand you have a magnificent white stallion in your train."

"We do, my lord," Johanna said.

"I would like very much to see him," the lord said, Johanna perforce went to fetch North Wind from the inn outside the city walls. Della Scala's eyes lit up, as so many pairs of eyes had lit up before during their travels. He ran his hands over the stallion's back and legs, Johanna keeping North Wind on a very short rein for fear he might nip the royal buttock for its owner's presumption.

"Some scarring of the legs, I see," the lord of Verona said.

Johanna thought of the weeks in the mountains of the Hindu Kush. "We have ridden some rough trails together, my lord."

He stood back and gave the stallion a critical examination, nose to tail. "Is he fast?"

She said blandly, "He has won a few races, my lord."

Della Scala looked at Johanna, a question obvious in his eyes, and she said, hurriedly, "Alas, my lord, North Wind suffers no one on his back but me."

The royal eyebrow raised. "You? A woman?"

She forced a smile and shortened the rein even more when North Wind moved restlessly. "Even so, my lord. We formed an attachment when he was very young."

North Wind snorted and tossed his head, shortened rein be damned.

Della Scala grinned. "I daren't risk my own dignity," he said conspiratorially, "but…" He cast an eye around the courtyard. "Piero! Come here. Try out this fine steed's paces."

Piero, a young noble in a velvet tunic lavishly embroidered with gold thread and silken hose, swaggered into the center of the courtyard. "Of course, my lord."

Johanna felt the tension on the rein slack as North Wind went very still.

Every member of Wu Company stepped as far back as they could without actually leaving the courtyard. The courtiers and their ladies, in their innocence, pressed forward for a better view. Johanna took a deep breath, exchanged a pregnant glance with Jaufre, and offered an arm to della Scala. "The sun is very hot this morning, is it not, my lord? Allow me to find you a bit of shade."

The corners of the royal mouth quirked but he took her arm and she urged him to a place where the city wall cast the most shade and was coincidentally as far from the action as she could put him, halfway up a flight of stairs leading to the top of the wall. "Your view would be best from here, my lord." She kept the sentence as much as possible to a suggestion and not a plea.

The lines around his eyes crinkled, but he said solemnly enough, "It would indeed. I'm obliged to you for your courtesy, Serra Johanna."

She watched long enough to see him gain a stair higher than North Wind could kick and hurried back to the stallion. Jaufre relinquished the reins, his face preternaturally sober, and didn't need her nod to remove himself from the area forthwith.

"Ser Piero," she said. The young man looked fit enough beneath his pomaded locks, and she gave a mental shrug and handed over the reins.

North Wind's nearside ear flickered once. Other than that, he remained motionless.

Piero eyed North Wind's broad back. "It is a style of saddle with which I am unfamiliar." He shrugged. "Ah well." He grabbed a handful of North Wind's mane and vaulted up onto the stallion's back.

Johanna took a few quick steps away. There was a still, silent moment when the world seemed to hold its breath, including North Wind. He remained motionless for just long enough for the young lord to gather in the reins and kick the stallion in the sides.

It wasn't a kick really, more of nudge, the merest hint even, perhaps, but North Wind had been confined for six months on a farmer's paddock and he had not just regained his rightful rider and his rightful place on the Road to put up with this sort of nonsense. He reared on his hind legs, standing almost upright, and not bothering to break a sweat over it, either. Piero let out a startled yelp, almost lost the saddle but managed to hold on with his legs. North Wind came down on his front feet, hard. Piero managed not to be pitched over the stallion's head, just. North Wind kicked up with his rear legs, so high that Johanna, alarmed, thought for a moment the stallion will allow himself to tumble over into a somersault. Piero held on through that, too, although he lost a stirrup.

North Wind huffed out an impatient breath and without further ado lay down and rolled over. Amid a cloud of curses Piero got his leg up and out of the way just in time. Credit where credit was due, he tried to hang on to the reins but when the stallion began rubbing his back in the dirt like a dog, hooves in the air, he threw up his hands and retreated to a chorus of catcalls and jeers.

Johanna looked around and found della Scala next to her, tears of laughter in his eyes. "Your North Wind has run some races, you say?"

"A few," Johanna said demurely.

Jaufre, hearing this, said to Shasha, "So, not leaving tomorrow morning after all."

The lord arranged a race for two days later. North Wind looked over his competitors with manifest contempt and would have humiliated them all if Johanna hadn't held him back a little. When they crossed the finish line to the roar of the crowd at a gait a little too close to a trot, she brought him to pass before the lord's viewing stand, where she caught a satisfactorily heavy purse, and bowed her thanks.

She raised her head to see him speak to Piero, standing at her elbow, and was ready when the young lord came to their lodgings that evening. They remained in Verona for another week while North Wind serviced two of the lord's favorite mares at a fee which included board and room that even Jaufre said was handsome.

From Verona they travelled to Brescia, still recovering from the siege of 1311 by Henry VII, now Holy Roman Emperor, and Bergamo, which city either was or was not currently under the jurisdiction of Milan, it was never made quite clear. They found nothing to delay them in either place and so pressed on to Milan. There, after fifty years of Visconti rule, the city seemed more stable than warlike Verona or subjugated Bergamo, and much more prosperous. The guilds were thriving, particularly the craft guilds. Of those, the weavers held sway, and Jaufre and Johanna spent as much time as they could observing the weavers at work, or such work as the proprietary guilds would allow. The first question they were asked everywhere was "Do you trade in wool?" When they were asked where they were going, the first comment was always, "Write to us if you get as far as England. I'm in the market for as much of the finest wool as I can get. The best prices, I promise you."

The seemingly endless dynastic struggles between France and England, Jaufre learned, had the wool trade in a constant state of flux, frustrating grangers in England as much as it did weavers in Milan, and putting a high demand—and a higher price—on fleeces of every grade. He began a running tally of names and places, just in case. No wonder Gradenigo was thinking of testing the wool trade by water.

When they identified themselves as being from Cambaluc, there were similar questions about the availability of silk in commercial quantities, but none like so urgent as the inquiries over wool. "They get all the silk they need from Lucca and Florence," Johanna said. "And Venice. Venice has been cultivating the worm for two centuries now."

Jaufre nodded. "The consensus seems to be that the finest wool comes from England."

She looked at him. "Are we specializing?"

He shrugged. "I wouldn't mind seeing where my father was born."

She smiled. "Then we should go there."

She turned on her heel and walked off down the street. He ran to catch up. "I didn't mean this very minute."

She laughed over her shoulder. "No, this very minute I mean to see that all is well with North Wind."

He followed her to the stables of the large inn. North Wind had his head over his stall door, looking in her direction every bit as much as if he'd been expecting her, and not waiting too patiently, either. Johanna let herself in his stall and crooned to him, offering an apple in recompense for the horrors of solitude the great stallion had had to endure during their hours apart. She found his brush and began to curry his already perfect coat. He whickered out a long, pleased sigh.

Jaufre hitched the door closed and leaned against the wall, arms folded. Johanna looked around and saw him watching. "What?" she said, smiling.

Deliberately, he pushed himself off the wall and stepped forward to stand in front of her, keeping his gaze locked with hers. He heard her breath hitch and was glad of it. The horse was too close for her to back away and he was glad of that, too. "I was just thinking," he said, raising a hand to brush back a curl that had escaped from her braid.

"What? She sounded breathless. "What were you thinking?"

Both hands came up to cup her face. "That I was jealous of the horse."

He lowered his face to hers.

"Oh," was all she had time to say before he kissed her.

It was like this every time, he thought somewhere in the dim recesses of his mind where rational thought still held marginal sway. He touched her and it was as if he'd been enveloped in flame. One touch and he had to, he must fill his hands with every curve of her flesh, trace every hollow with his lips, sometimes he felt he would be satisfied by nothing less than eating her alive. All the finesse of North Wind at stud, that was as close as he could come to describing it.

It wasn't as if she was struggling, some part of his mind noted. Somehow they had found themselves up against the stall and her legs were wrapped around his waist and when he managed to pull enough of her tunic down to find her breast her back arched and she whimpered. Her hands raked at his back, one slipped between them. Her hand closed around him and he groaned and raised his head to kiss her again.

They should do this someplace else, he thought as he reached for the drawstring of her trousers. She deserved better than being tumbled in the straw of a stall. Of North Wind's stall.

He raised his head. "If we do this is that bedamned horse going to take exception?"

"I'll risk it."

He gave a half laugh and then groaned again, but this time because they heard voices approaching the stable. A moment later they heard Shasha say, "The stallion is just down here, my lords."

When the group arrived at North Wind's stall Johanna was currying him as if her life depended on it and Jaufre was raking straw in much the same manner. Shasha took one look at the both of them and turned to the half dozen nobles with an affable smile. "This, good gentles, is North Wind, of whom you have heard so much, and his owner, Johanna of Wu Company and Cambaluc."

Johanna paused long enough to give a slight bow in their direction.

"North Wind can be, shall we say, a little temperamental—"

Johanna nudged the stallion and he woke up enough from his pleasurable doze to whinny loudly and snap his teeth.

"—so perhaps we could adjourn to the public room of the inn to discuss matters further? Thank you, thank you, yes, just across the courtyard, and his owner will join us there."

When the voices had faded they looked at each other. Jaufre thought Johanna looked most marvelously disheveled, and Johanna thought Jaufre looked seriously disgruntled. "I'm sorry," she said helplessly, and then gulped, remembering the last time she apologized to him. They stared at each other for a long moment, and then Johanna couldn't help it, a tiny giggle erupted, another, and then they were both laughing so hard they could only stand by leaning against the stall. North Wind, indignant at this lack of sangfroid, or perhaps hoping for another apple, gave Johanna a vigorous nudge with his nose, and she staggered forward into Jaufre's arms again.

"I didn't mean I was sorry," she said, when she could speak again. "Then or now."

"I know," he said, resting his forehead against hers. "I was feeling—interrupted."

"So was I, and that was what I was sorry for," Johanna said, with feeling

He raised his head. Blue eyes met hazel. "I can wait."

"I can't," she said.

In an heroic act of self-sacrifice, he pushed her a little away. "Go talk to the lords."

She took a step away and then as if in the grip of some irresistible force stepped back. A little shyly she laid her hands on his chest and looked at him. "This thing, it is going to happen between us."

"Yes," he said. "Yes, it is. Thank all the gods."

"This is what you've always wanted? Even so long ago as Cambaluc?"

"Yes."

She looked at her hands, flat against his tunic, and looked up again. "I didn't know. Until that time in the yurt, after Kuche, I didn't even—how could I not have known."

It wasn't a question so he didn't attempt to answer it, but in truth he had no idea how she could not have known. He had known, almost from the moment that he had fallen asleep behind her on her camel, his arms around her waist, his head on her shoulder. Well, perhaps not that soon, she was only ten years old at the time, but it was difficult now to remember a time when he did not love her.

She could not sustain the intensity of his gaze for any longer and dropped her eyes again to his tunic. "Could we—I don't—it's not that—" She huffed out a laugh. "I seem to have lost my ability to put words together and have them make sense." She met his eyes, if fleetingly. "With Edyk, I was saying goodbye. I knew—well, I thought I would never see him again. I'd known him my whole life, longer even than you. I loved him, and I wanted him, and I couldn't leave him without—without—"

"I understand," he said, not without effort.

"Do you?" Another fleeting glance. "With you, it's different, it's less—less—" She cast about for the right word. "Friendly."

Unbelievably, he found the ability to laugh. "Good."

"Truly? Because we are friends, too, Jaufre. Wu Li took you in and made you my foster brother. I have always loved you that way. Friends, and, and...comrades." She was silent for a moment, and then said with difficulty, "This—what I feel now is different."

"Friendship is how it begins, sometimes," he said. He cupped her face in his hands. "We'll take this however you want to, Johanna, but understand me now. I love you, and I want you in all the ways a man wants a woman."

She flushed. "I want you in all those ways, too."

His heart thudded in his ears. "Good," he heard someone say hoarsely, and swallowed hard. "Good." With every ounce of self-control he possessed, he dropped his hands and stepped back. "The gentlemen are waiting. You had better go talk to them before Shasha comes looking for you."

She looked the same way he felt, hungry and impatient, but she knew he was right. "Later, then," she said around the lump in her throat.

He smiled. "Later."

The Milanese nobles found North Wind's owner a little distracted, and later they congratulated each other on the very favorable stud fee they had been able to negotiate. That was not North Wind's owner's reputation. Shasha, when she heard of it, was less than complimentary.

Alaric was waiting for Jaufre when he returned from the stables to their rooms on the first floor, intent on seeking out the landlord to see if there was an additional room available. If there wasn't he would find one in another inn, and he was dwelling on the possible and protracted activity to take place within when Alaric, annoyed, spoke his name in a louder voice. "What?" he said. "Oh. Alaric. I'm sorry, I wasn't paying attention."

"You certainly weren't," Alaric said severely. "I must speak with you."

"Is it important? I—"

"It is very important," Alaric said, and waved him into their private common room, small but comfortably appointed. "Sit down."

Alaric himself did not sit, taking up a stance in front of the fireplace, hands clasped behind his back. Coming out of his romantically-inspired fugue state, Jaufre noticed that the Templar looked remarkably sober. Thinking back, he realized that Alaric had been so since their last days in Venice.

"There is someone I want you to meet," Alaric said.

"Fine," Jaufre said. "Invite him to dinner. Shasha always cooks enough for—"

"—for a cohort," Alaric said. "Yes, yes, I know. We must go to him."

"Why?"

"He is cloistered."

"A monk? Where?"

"In Butrio."

"And Butrio is—?"

"About seventy leagues south of Milan."

"Seventy leagues," Jaufre said. He only hoped it hadn't come out as a scream. "That's three or four days travel. Each way."

"This from the man who came all the way from Cambaluc."

Jaufre reddened beneath Alaric's disbelieving eye. It wasn't the distance, it was that he'd had other plans for how he would be spending the next four nights and they hadn't involved sleeping rough with Alaric.

"He knew your father," Alaric said.

That, unfortunately, did get his attention. "This monk?"

"He was a Templar, in our company. When we were disbanded, he took his vows and retired to the monastery in Butrio." Alaric stared off into the distance.

"Was he with you at the fall of Ruad?" Jaufre said.

To his surprise, Alaric's expression darkened. "Yes," he said, and stood abruptly. "North Wind will be busy in Milan for the next week, which will give us time to get there and back again before Wu Company departs for Susa. Will you come or not?"

Every part and fiber of his being was screaming no. "I'll be ready in an hour," he said, and sought out Johanna and lay the matter before her.

"No," she said instantly, brow darkening, and then she said, "This monk knew your father?"

"Alaric says so."

"And he brings this to you only now?"

He reached for her hands and pulled her close, some part of him marveling that he finally, at long last, after what felt like forever, had the right to do so. "It's only a week."

"But—"

He kissed her. "You could spend the time finding a yurt," he said. "One just big enough for the both of us. For when we're between inns."

She relented a little. "I suppose I could do that."

He kissed her then, and she kissed him, and neither of them gave a thought to holding anything back. When they finally broke apart they were both trembling. "Does Alaric know if this monk is even still alive?" she said, her voice so rough he hardly recognized it.

He hadn't asked. "He seemed certain."

She took a deep, shaky breath. "Go, then," she said. She even laughed.

"What?"

"Just that I find it extremely annoying that North Wind's love life is better than my own."

His response to that left her certain that he'd broken at least two of her ribs. "Go," she said, breathless, half laughing, half crying. "And Jaufre?"

"What?"

"Ride fast."

Jaufre forced himself to let go of her. In the courtyard he said to Alaric, "Let's get out of here before Hari finds out we're going to a monastery."

For speed, they took two of the Arabians that Firas and Johanna had liberated from Sheik Mohammed's stables during her escape from Talikan. Jaufre pushed the horses hard enough that Alaric complained. Jaufre's only response was to press on even harder.

Félicien complained, too, but he was uninvited and so ignored by both Jaufre and Alaric. He'd returned to the inn in time to see them saddling the horses, inquired as to why, and volunteered himself as the third member of their party. Jaufre didn't care, all his intent focussed on getting there and back again as quickly as possible, and though Alaric huffed and puffed he made no serious objection. Félicien dashed into the inn for his kit and into the stable for a mount and was now riding in their train on a rented nag, gitar slung over his shoulder. Whenever a hill slowed down their passage he brought out a wooden flute he had acquired in Venice and practiced. It's plaintive wail did seem to calm the horses.

They passed through a fertile plain where flourishing farms and manors jostled for place with dense alders and tall elms, an occasional poplar and willow, grove after grove of olive trees, and a deciduous tree with a straight trunk and dark green leaves that Jaufre recognized as an ironwood tree, common in Everything Under the Heavens. Alaric called it a hornbeam and dismissed it as of no consequence. They splashed through innumerable rills, streams and rivers, all of them seeming to flow south and east. "They flow to the Po," Alaric said. "All the water here does."

They clattered into the village that was neighbor to the hermitage just before dark on the third day. Their steaming mounts were led away by an ostler, all agog at this unheralded visitation by two knights accompanied by their own minstrel. Jaufre managed not to laugh when he was so addressed but Alaric straightened up as if he'd heard a trumpet fanfare and paraded into the common room, hand on the hilt of his sword and looking loftily down the length of what was after all a very long nose.

The innkeeper, a man of some dignity himself, was deferential without being obsequious. He bowed Alaric to the best table, flapping his apron at the two men who already occupied it, who gratified him by springing to their feet and finding another table without comment or complaint. Félicien's gitar might have had something to do with that, because after a meal of hearty stew, bread and an excellent cheese, one of them approached the table and asked humbly if the lord's minstrel might favor them with a song or a story.

Jaufre looked around and saw that the word had gone forth. There were no longer any empty seats and there were more people leaning against the walls. Ah well, country folk must find their entertainment where they could, and the hermitage, so far as he could tell as they had approached it at dusk, was in an isolated spot that could not have seen much traffic.

"I don't expect there will be many coins in my cap from this crowd," Félicien said in an undertone.

"Be kind," Jaufre said. "It's not every day one has the privilege to hear the song of a young goliard who has traveled all the way to Cathay and back again. Especially in a town this size, this far off any main road."

The room was dimly lit by a few fat candles in sconces and the light of the fire on the hearth, but he thought the boy blushed. He wondered again if Félicien had even been out of swaddling clothes when he left home. Other than admitting to being a Frank, the goliard had steadily ignored any other questions as to his life before he had joined their campfire and company one evening somewhere between Chang'an and Dunhuang. Or possibly Dunhuang and Turfan. "Sing," Jaufre said. "They may not have much to give, but you do. And they will talk of this night for years to come."

The goliard struck a chord and did as he was bid, and before long a bashful young man appeared with a small drum to beat out the time. A tonsured monk brought a wooden flute to play high while Félicien sang middle and the gitar sang low. There were songs of the Road, marching songs and marrying songs. Songs of love lost and love found, songs of battles lost and won. Many Jaufre recognized and many more he did not, but then the goliard had the gift of the true entertainer, the ability to divine what his audience wanted to hear and to give it to them in a key they could hum along to.

The next morning they were up with the dawn, or Jaufre was, the need to be back in Milano at Johanna's side riding him hard. Félicien didn't stir but Alaric followed him downstairs to break their fast in the common room, the site of last night's concert. "Enough!" Jaufre said, cutting the knight's grumbling short. "You wanted to make this journey and you wanted me to meet your friend. Let's go meet him and be about our business."

They presented themselves at the door of the monastery, an imposing edifice built of square blocks of local stone. There was an arcade surmounted by a second story with a row of rectangular windows, a church with a vaulted ceiling supported by pointed arches and painted with luminous frescoes, and a low dormitory attached to the main building. There was a thriving garden and an orchard filled with fruit trees.

The knight had rung the bell hanging outside the main door. It was answered by the same tonsured monk who had accompanied Félicien on the flute the night before. Jaufre had thought that the purpose of a monastery was for its inmates to be sequestered from public life but the ways of Christianity were still a mystery to him and he made no comment. The monk, who introduced himself as Fra Lamberto, greeted them with enthusiasm, heard out Alaric's request, and shook his head. "I will ask," he said, "but Brother Donizo rarely speaks to anyone these days." He saw Alaric's look and shook his head. "No, no, he is well, at least in body." His brow creased. "It is his spirit which suffers, and nothing I nor Father Matteo say can ease him." He cast a shrewd glance over the two of them. "Perhaps you can," he said thoughtfully. "Oblige me by waiting a moment, do."

He rustled away and returned shortly. "Come with me."

They followed him down the arcaded passageway, each of the column's capitals carved with fearsome animals or human figures writhing in the worst the Devil could do to them, a sight guaranteed to keep you at your prayers. They entered the long, low building and proceeded down a corridor of many doors, entering the last one on the right. "Brother Donizo? Brother Donizo, I have here two visitors for you." He stepped inside and motioned the others to follow.

It was a tiny room, scrupulously clean and sparsely furnished with a cot and a niche in the wall with a statue Jaufre recognized as the most prevalent Christian saint, the woman in blue with the child in her arms. The statue was delicately made and really beautifully colored, perhaps by the same hand that had created the frescoes in the church. Before it knelt a man clad in the same rough spun brown robes as Fra Lamberto. His hands were clasped in front of his face and his eyes were closed and his lips moved soundlessly.

"Brother Donizo?"

The man on his knees looked up finally, blinking, as if the light from the eastward-facing window hurt his eyes. They were a light blue, so light that for a moment Jaufre thought his was blind. But those blue eyes looked first at Fra Lamberto and then traveled to the knight standing at his shoulder, and widened. "Alaric?" The monk stumbled to his feet and had to be caught by Fra Lamberto before he fell. "Alaric!" He reached out, weeping, to grasp Alaric's hands in his own. "Alaric! You came! You came at last!"

They sat outside in the sun, Fra Lamberto fetching watered wine and a plate of bread and olives and then tactfully leaving them alone. Jaufre sat a little apart, watching the other two men. Brother Donizo had stopped crying but he was still incapable of complete sentences. "Alaric. After all this time, I—When we parted, you—I never expected—It's been so long—"

Alaric patted his arm and muttered soothing nothings and plied Brother Donizo with watered wine. After what felt like a very long time to Jaufre the monk pulled himself together and attempted a smile. "And who is your companion, Alaric? I'm sorry, my boy," he said belatedly. "I am a little overcome. It has been so very long since I saw Alaric, you see."

"You know his face, Gilbert," Alaric said, watching the monk closely.

"No, I—" The blue eyes widened. "No! Robert? But how can this be? He left us when—"

"Yes, he left us," Alaric said, interrupting the monk. "He married afterward, Gilbert. This is his son."

"His son!" There was a long moment of profound silence as Brother Donizo, or Gilbert, stared at Jaufre. "He saved us. He saved us both. And how we repaid him, Alaric. How we repaid him."

"He didn't want it, Gilbert. He didn't want any part of it."

The monk made a gesture of repugnance. "I know, but—"

"What did you do with it, Gilbert?" Alaric said softly.

"What's 'it'?" Jaufre said, his head whirling at the thought that here was someone else who had known his father. "What are you talking about?"

Gilbert sought Alaric's eyes. The two older men looked at each other for a long moment. "He is truly Robert's son?" the monk said.

"Show him your sword," Alaric told Jaufre.

Jaufre pulled his sword from the sheath he wore on his back, and handed it to the monk, who received it reverently. His grip was sure and practiced, for a monk. "It is Robert's, of course," he said, his awed voice barely above a murmur.

"Yes, it belonged to my father," Jaufre said, losing patience. "What of it?"

"You didn't tell him?" Gilbert said.

Alaric's face was like iron. "Some of it. Not all."

In that moment both men looked considerably older than their years.

· Eight ·

Summer, 1324 A.D.
Lombardy

—

There had been four of them after the fall of Ruad. Alaric and Robert, Jaufre's father, yes, but also Gilbert, a Frank like Alaric and now the man known to them as Brother Donizo, and a fourth man, Wilmot of Bavaria. The son of a wealthy mason with social ambitions, his father had bought Wilmot his knighthood. "Like Robert, it was what he could do, not what he wanted to do," Gilbert said, sounding rueful.

Ruad, the island redoubt of the last of the Crusader outposts in the Levant, had been given to the Templars by the Pope in 1301, who would hold it until it was overrun by the Mamluks two years later. The ordinary troops had been slaughtered to a man and the surviving knights shipped off to prison in Egypt, where most of them starved to death.

"It was Robert," Gilbert said. "The four of us would have been caught, too, but for Robert." He gave Jaufre a sober look. "I owe your father my life." He looked at Alaric. "We all do."

"Why?" Jaufre said. "How?"

Gilbert looked at Alaric and sighed. "Robert was much more long-sighted and realistic about the future of the Templars in the East."

"About the future of the Templars, period," Alaric said.

"That, too," Gilbert said.

Confusion is rampant at the end of any sack, they told him, which he already knew from Johanna's account of the fall of Talikan. Confusion at the fall of Ruad was compounded by Ruad's location. "An island," Gilbert said. "And we were hopelessly outnumbered. In 1301, when Ghazan didn't come when he said he would—"

Alaric spat. "Mongols," he said, the word itself an epithet. "Never trust them."

Jaufre thought of the Mongol Baron Ogodei, and didn't disagree.

"Yes, well, when the Mongols didn't come, Robert told us it was over." His smile was wry. "We didn't believe him, of course."

"Wilmot did," Alaric said.

"But you and I didn't," Gilbert said. "Our faith was still strong. We believed in the righteousness of our cause, that the Holy Land was meant to be under Christian rule, that we would triumph over the Saracen savages and that that God Himself would appear in our vanguard to lead us with flaming sword back to Jerusalem." He closed his eyes and shook his head.

Jaufre let the silence linger for just as long as he could bear it and no more. "But my father..."

Gilbert opened his eyes, looking upon the flourishing garden as if uncertain how he'd come there. "I think he was planning our escape from the moment Ghazan's forces retreated. The week before Ruad fell, he went up to the walls to look over the situation and when he came down he gathered the four of us together and told us that we had to leave. By that time, none of us needed much convincing." He looked again at Alaric. "I'm going to tell him. All of it."

"Confession is good for the soul," Alaric said.

"So they say," Gilbert said. "At any rate, I have never confessed this to anyone else, but I am going to now, to Robert's son." He turned to Jaufre and straightened where he sat. Clad in rough homespun, his hair tonsured, he nevertheless somehow had the faint air of the knight he had once been, with all the strength and pride that came with the oath and the office. "There was a room," he said, "where they kept what remained of our treasury."

Jaufre stiffened. Gilbert noticed, and gave a wry smile. "Yes. The structure of our lives was crumbling, and all we had to hold us together was Robert's determination that we would survive. How, we asked ourselves, we who had always had our meals and roofs and clothes and armor and weapons provided for us, how were we to live?" He sighed. "But I won't make excuses. Alaric and I decided to help ourselves to some of it before we left. In all the confusion we thought it would never be missed, that we would never be noticed." A short laugh. "Our mistake. There were others, equally interested in the remnants of the Templars' treasure." He glanced again at Alaric. "Alaric was wounded in the escape. Wilmot would have left him behind, I think, but Robert insisted."

Jaufre tried to imagine it, the noise, the shouting, men wounded and dying, the boats landing on the beaches, the walls breached, the enemy pouring in.

"The fort was burning by the time he got us down to the beach. He'd hidden a small boat among the rocks. We buried our mantles and armor in those same rocks and got in the boat and pushed off. Halfway to shore we were seen and capsized. God, I have never seen such a hail of arrows. They might be heathens but the Saracens are excellent shots. I can only attribute to the protective hand of God Himself that only I was hit." Gilbert put a hand to his leg, massaging the memory of an old wound. "Wilmot took me and Robert took Alaric and they managed to get us ashore and into hiding. He found us food and medicines and tended us until we were well enough to travel."

"And the treasure?"

Gilbert laughed shortly. "We should have drowned with the weight of gold and silver we were carrying with us, Alaric and I. Wilmot and Robert would have killed us both when they discovered it, if we hadn't needed it so badly, to pay for the food and medicines."

"And afterward?"

Gilbert shrugged. "Robert and Alaric went to Antioch to seek work as caravan guards. Wilmot and I went to Byzantium and took ship for Venice. I came here." He glanced at Alaric. "It was what I had always wanted."

"You talked about it enough," Alaric said.

"Yes, I suppose I did. I imagine that is how you knew where to find me?" Alaric nodded, and Gilbert sighed. "Wilmot left me here and went north, he said to seek work as a mason at Chartres. They're building a cathedral there."

"They've been building it for a hundred years," Alaric said sourly.

"Then Wilmot should have been successful," Gilbert said. "I have seen or heard nothing of him since."

There was a weighted moment, and then Alaric, as though the words were forced from him, said, "Where is it?"

Gilbert looked up. "Where is what?" he said blankly.

"The rest of the treasure. Where is it?"

"Where is—" Gilbert's face cleared and he turned a look composed equal parts of realization and sympathy on the man who had once been his brother in arms, his co-conspirator, his fellow thief. "It is here, Alaric," he said gently.

"Where?" Alaric looked around the garden. "Is it buried somewhere?"

Gilbert sighed. "Come with me," he said, rising to his feet.

They followed him about the monastery until the bells rang for vespers. There was a great deal to see, the handsome church and the arcaded cloister they had seen before, a chapter room large enough to accommodate all the community at Sant' Alberto's, lay and clerical. There was a many-roomed novitiate, spare and scrupulously clean, a library of well-filled shelves that made Jaufre's palms itch, and a scriptorium with cunningly arranged skylights that introduced much-needed light on the work of monks laboriously copying out more manuscripts. There was a large kitchen, an infirmary, two guesthouses, one for men and one for women, and a large and well-tended herb garden that Jaufre wished Shasha could see. The vegetable garden and the orchard they had already seen. "There is also a leper's hospital," Gilbert said, with a wave of his hand that indicated the hills in back of the monastery.

Alaric had followed Gilbert on this tour of Sant' Alberto's facilities with a steadily decaying patience. Now he said, "Where is it, Gilbert?"

Gilbert met his eyes with a slight smile. "I told you, Alaric. It is here."

"You gave it to the monastery," Jaufre said, a grin spreading across his face.

"What!"

Gilbert smiled again. What with his confession to Jaufre of the truth of their escape from Ruad and his confession to Alaric of what had happened to the rest of the Templar treasure, he was looking years and years younger. "Yes," he said happily. "I put it to work here. It seemed best."

Alaric seemed unable to speak. When he did he was barely coherent. "I— we trusted you! How could you—you—you false friend! You thief!"

"You could have taken your share with you when you went east with my father," Jaufre said. "Why didn't you?"

Gilbert chuckled. "Because he was following Robert and Robert wouldn't have countenanced it."

Alaric shouted something incomprehensible to the sky and stamped off into the orchard, scattering monks as he went.

He seemed to have calmed down by the time they gathered in the refectory for dinner. Jaufre thought he detected what might even have been a trace of pride in the eyes that appraised the long, well-polished oak table and the finely woven tapestries that warmed the stone walls.

And later that evening, when the other two supposed him asleep in his blankets, he heard the low-voiced conversation. "You are weary, and heartsore, Alaric," Gilbert said. "You could stay here. You should stay here. I won't guarantee you will find peace here. I haven't." A brief pause. "Although perhaps the possibility of it, now. We could use a good blacksmith. You were always handy around a forge."

Alaric grunted, and Jaufre wondered if he would be returning to Milano alone.

But then Alaric said, slowly, "No. Perhaps, one day. But no, not now. Not yet."

"What are you looking for, Alaric, that you can't find here?"

"Goodnight, Gilbert," Alaric said. "We'll say our goodbyes in the morning."

"Alaric. Why did you come seeking the treasure? Why now, after all these years?"

A loud snore.

A sigh, the light of the candle snuffed, and the slap of the monk's sandals as he let himself out of the guesthouse.

As promised the next morning Gilbert stood at their stirrups to wish them goodbye and godspeed. "Thank you, my boy," he said to Jaufre. "I am glad that Robert went on to have some happiness in his life. Your mother sounds like a fine woman, and I can see for myself that they had a fine son."

"Thank you, Brother Donizo."

The monk took courteous leave of Félicien, and moved to Alaric. He reached up a hand and they clasped arms for a long moment. "I hope to see you again in this life, Alaric."

"As God wills." Alaric smiled. "Brother Donizo."

A league or so onwards Jaufre motioned to Félicien to drop a little way behind and said to Alaric, "You've never struck me as one who hankered after riches, Alaric. Why seek out Gilbert and the treasure now?"

They rode in silence for a few moments. "Because," Alaric said. He swallowed and turned to look Jaufre full in the face. He looked miserable, and ashamed. "Because it was all I could do to provide for Robert's son." He faced forward again. "And it turned out I couldn't even do that much."

He kicked his mount into a canter and moved ahead, leaving Jaufre staring after him, mouth open.

They traveled as quickly back as they had come, wringing the last ray of sunlight out of the day before stopping for the night. The closer they came to Milano, the more Jaufre became preoccupied with thoughts of Johanna, and of all the wonderful things they would do together, some of them even with their clothes on. For the first time he wondered where they would settle, where a home that would suit them both could be found, and then all he could think about was the house they would live in, and the room that would be theirs, and the bed in that room. Would they marry? In what faith? Children. Shasha would stay with them, and Shasha staying meant Firas would stay, too. Firas was a fine man, a good fighter, loyal, intelligent, able. He could wish for no better brother-in-law.

The others? He didn't know. After the revelations of Sant' Alberto, he couldn't predict what Alaric would do. Tiphaine was with them for the duration, that was certain. He grinned to himself. She might even be their first child.

They stopped to water their mounts at the ford of a small stream. Jaufre was just pulling at the reins of his horse to keep him from drinking too much when movement caught the corner of his eye. He looked up and they were surrounded at spear's point by a company of ten men, mounted. He reached for his father's sword and found his hand knocked away, replaced by the point of a sharp point pressing into his neck. He went very still, his empty hands raising in surrender. He heard an oath and a thud and turned his head to see Alaric on the ground, glaring up at his attacker.

"Yes, yes," said his attacker, very brisk, "suffice it to say we are outlaws and villains, but we have no interest in you and will take none if you give us what we want without resistance, after which we will be on our way and you on yours."

Alaric used his horse's stirrup to pull himself to his feet, his face red with rage. "You would leave us disarmed, on foot, on a road where—"

"We don't want your weapons or your horses, good sir," said the knight, as the circlet around his helm indicated he must be. He raised his head and smiled at Félicien.

Something in the quality of the goliard's silence made both Jaufre and Alaric turn to look at him. He was still astride his horse, sitting very still, his face whiter than Jaufre had ever seen it. "Don't harm them, my lord," he said. "Please."

"That, my dear Félicienne, is entirely up to you."

Félicienne? There was something odd in the pronunciation of the goliard's name. Jaufre looked at Alaric and saw dawning revelation, succeeded by furious anger. "Félicienne! Félicienne?"

Their attacker was politely incredulous. "You didn't know?" He looked from Alaric to Jaufre and back again. "Truly? You didn't know?" He threw back his head and laughed so hard he seemed in danger of loosing his seat. "Oh my dear Félicienne! You have fallen in with fools!"

The goliard waited for the knight to stop laughing, and met his eyes with a calm that seemed to Jaufre to be very hard won. "How did you find me?" he said again.

"Oh, my very dear." The knight laughed again. "If you will persist in singing where people can hear you, eventually someone will recognize the dulcet tones of l'Alouette du Sud, famed all over Provins for her voice, and her poetry." He looked over his shoulder. "And sooner or later, that someone will remember the very generous gifts waiting for anyone who could lead me to her."

Jaufre saw Alaric follow his gaze, and did the same. An older man dressed in bright new clothes lurked behind the spearmen. "Jean de Valmy!" Alaric spat out the name.

Not since l'Alouette du Sud have I heard such a voice. Later followed on closer and Jaufre was certain deliberate acquaintance by the oh so casual comment, *The young man, the goliard who sings.* He had no very certain idea of what was happening here, but he knew one thing. "You treacherous, sarding whoreson," he said.

The older man reddened and looked away.

"I hope your new hose are easier on your boiled ass than your old ones were," Alaric said. "Betrayal must pay well."

The knight kicked his horse until it was alongside Félicien's rented nag. "That is a very unworthy mount for you, my lady wife. Allow me." He stretched out an arm.

Wife?

Félicienne didn't move. "If you don't harm them, I will submit to you, willingly."

"By God, you will. I seem to remember missing out on my wedding night." This last was said with an odd twist, and Jaufre saw a flicker of revulsion cross Félicien's face.

"I give you my word, here and now, witnessed by your men, that I will not run away again, that I will share your bed, that I will bear your children without complaint." Jaufre, watching her, thought she might be sick over her saddle there and then, but she was not, and continued to speak in a strong, steady voice. "I will do all these things. But you must let them live."

The knight laughed. "Do you imagine you have a choice?"

Something like pride flickered in Félicien's dark eyes. "I escaped from you once before, if you remember, my lord."

"I do remember," the lord said silkily. "I don't make the same mistake twice, be sure, lady wife."

Félicienne raised her chin, but Jaufre could see her hands trembling on her reins. "You have to sleep sometime, my lord."

The lord stared at her for a long moment, and then burst out laughing again. A merry gentleman, indeed. "Florian!" he said, still laughing. "Call off the dogs and go on ahead. I will follow."

"My lord—"

"God's balls! Do you think I can't manage a green boy who can't even get his sword out of its sheath in time to use it and an old man long past his prime who should be dreaming by his fire? I, Ambroise de L'Arête?"

"No, my lord."

"Very well, then. Get you gone."

The point pressing against Jaufre's neck disappeared. Something warm trickled into his collar. There was some signal unseen by Jaufre, and the troop wheeled its mounts as one and moved down the road at an orderly trot, with L'Arête's lieutenant leading and Jean de Valmy falling in behind, head sunk beneath his shoulders. Jaufre only wanted the opportunity to strike it off.

"Well, my dear?"

Her eyes sought Jaufre's. "Tell Johanna and Shasha and Hari—tell all of them goodbye for me."

"It's true then?" he said, disbelieving. "You're a woman? And this man's wife?"

A tremulous smile. "And my thanks to them, from the bottom of my heart. And to you, Jaufre."

She grasped the knight's arm and was hoisted behind him. With the loose end of his reins he lashed at the two loose horses and sent them crashing through the undergrowth in different directions. Jaufre's mount neighed and sidled and made an abortive attempt at rearing.

"My lord—"

"My very dear lady, they are fortunate I don't kill them both for having traveled in your company unchaperoned." The knight nodded in their direction. "Gentles. We should not meet again." His smile was thin, and there was a wealth of meaning in the way he sheathed his sword. "Really. We should not."

He kicked his destrier into a trot and then into a canter, and Jaufre and Alaric watched as they disappeared in the wake of the troop of spearmen.

· Part V ·

· Nine ·

Fall, 1324 A.D.
Milano

—

Félicien is a girl?" Tiphaine said.

"Not just a girl, a married woman," Alaric said, who appeared not just surprised but outraged at the revelation.

"No beard," Jaufre said. He'd been thinking about it all the way to Milano. "I kept thinking he was just too young to shave."

"I never saw him shit," Alaric said, toasting the room with his wine and drinking deep. "Should have known right then. Unnatural, a man never shits."

"He never removed that awful robe," Alma said, her nose wrinkling. "I offered once to wash it for him and he thanked me but said he preferred to wash his own garments."

"Dirt can be a useful disguise," Hari said. "People do not care to look too closely at the unwashed."

"He never said much, either," Alaric said. "Except when he was singing."

"Didn't want to draw attention," Hayat said. She looked at Alma. They knew what that was like.

"He looked so young," Jaufre said again. "I kept thinking he must have left home at ten."

"Félicien's a girl?" Tiphaine said.

"I don't understand how we didn't know this," Johanna said. "He—she was with us for almost two years. How could we not know this?"

"Well," Shasha said, and exchanged a meaningful look with Firas, and Hari cleared his throat and refolded a section of his orange robe into an elaborate pleat.

Johanna stared at the three of them. "You knew? The three of you knew and you said nothing?"

"It was her business," Shasha said.

"It was our business, too," Jaufre said with, "especially when she's got some crazed lord for a husband chasing after her. He could have killed us both." And would have, if she hadn't traded herself for them. The memory seared him like a burning brand.

"Why did she run from him, would be more to the point," Shasha said. "He was so young. She. She was so young. She couldn't have been more than a child when she was married to him. Obviously she disliked her situation enough to run as far and as long from it as she did." She looked around the room. "And what are we going to do about it?"

Alaric choked over his wine. "Do? Do? He's—she's his wife! You don't interfere between a man and his wife!"

"He was with us almost since we left Cambaluc," Shasha said, eyes on Johanna.

"She lied to us!" Alaric said. "We owe her nothing!"

"Alaric!" Jaufre's voice cracked like a whip. "She bargained herself for us, traded herself for our freedom. There was nothing to stop him from killing us and burying us there. No one would ever have known."

Alaric's gaze dropped and a tinge of color might have crept up the back of his neck. Still, he said, "We don't even know where he took her."

"We have a name," Jaufre said. "Ambroise de L'Arête."

Alaric fired up again. "And they're nobility! You saw the circlet he wore on his helmet!"

Shasha, startled, said, "Is this true?"

"And they were my lord and my ladying it all over the place," Alaric said, triumphant.

Jaufre's face was hard. "It doesn't matter. She sacrificed her freedom for our own. She didn't want to go with him, Alaric. Surely you saw that for yourself."

"She's his wife," Alaric said. "She has no choice in the matter."

Johanna took a deep breath and let it out slowly. "We have other obligations."

Jaufre whirled around. "By all the Mongol gods! That we do, and first among them is—"

"First among them, Jaufre, is our obligation as merchant traders to carry the goods in our care to the trade fairs in Lyon, as we contracted with Ser Gradenigo to do."

He stopped short, breathing hard.

"Further," she said, as calmly as she was able, "Lyon is the crossroads for commerce in this part of the world. Everyone who buys and sells goes through Lyon, which means—"

"—news of everyone," Shasha said, jumping in because Johanna was right and she didn't want her to have to take all of Jaufre's fire when he realized it. "Our best hope for finding news of Félicien is to go to the place where the most news circulates."

Jaufre's breathing, loud in that silent room, began to slow down.

Firas stepped in. "Do we stick to our planned route?"

"I think so, yes," Shasha said. "Perhaps we move more quickly now." She looked around. "Does anyone have any other comments or observations?"

Alma exchanged glances with Hayat, and said, "We'll revisit this discussion in Lyon, yes?"

Alaric snorted.

"Of course," Shasha said before Jaufre could say something that this time would alienate everyone in the room instead of only five or six of them.

"North Wind had his last appointment in the duke's stables this morning," Johanna said. "I have accepted no more offers."

This time Jaufre snorted, and followed that by leaving the room. The door did not quite slam behind him.

"Wait," Shasha said, when Johanna would have gone after him. "Give him time to cool down."

"I didn't know he cared so much for Félicien," Johanna said.

"I don't know that he did, or does, young miss," Hari said. "What I believe he objects to most is the way she left us." He gave a faint smile. "Suppose it had been you? Or Shasha?"

"Or even yourself," Firas said.

"Or even my unworthy self," Hari said, unperturbed by the mocking note in the assassin's voice. "It would be unwise to be too quick to judge. Like so many travelers before her—" his eye excluded no one in the room "—the young woman evidently had reasons to be far from her native land."

There was a brief, freighted silence.

"Then why did she return here with us? She must have known the risk." Johanna paused. "Alaric? What was it you said that man—her husband called her? The Songbird of the South?"

"The Lark of the South," Alaric said, his voice soft now. He repeated it in French. "L'alouette du Sud."

"You come from the south," Jaufre said. "Are you familiar with this name?"

Alaric drank drained his mug and refilled it from the pitcher on the table. "I've been in the East for so long, home might as well be a foreign country to me. I have heard all the same news that you have heard of my homeland, and in none of it was there mention of this—lark." He drank and gave the hearth a malevolent stare. "Old man sitting beside a fire," he muttered. "Who's past his prime?"

"Félicien's a girl?" Tiphaine said.

Johanna paused outside the room Jaufre shared with Hari and Alaric. The room they had shared with Félicien. She raised a hand as if to knock, and let it fall again.

She slept alone that night in the room she had acquired for the two of them. The next morning she found him in the stable yard, where he already had their pack animals assembled. He was evidently prepared to drive all of them single-handedly to the warehouse where their goods were stored and load each of them himself. "Jaufre."

He spared her a glance. "What?"

"We should probably lay in a few supplies for the trip," she said, trying to keep her voice reasonable. "There are very few towns of any size between here and Lyon and we still have to get over the Alps."

"I sent Shasha out at daybreak. She knows what we need."

"Jaufre." She caught his arm as he finished tacking up one donkey, only to have him pull free and move on to the next. "Jaufre, we'll never be able to leave today."

He yanked hard on a cinch, and the donkey gave a bray of protest. "We are leaving today."

"Jaufre—"

He rounded on her so ferociously she actually backed up a step. "We will leave today, Johanna. Or I will, alone."

He wasn't interested in comfort, only action. She waited until he'd turned back to the donkey, and then stepped forward to begin tacking up the next one.

By noon Shasha was back, trailed by a dozen street urchins Tiphaine had each bribed into carrying back a mountain of supplies. Everyone helped, even Alaric. They were loaded by sext and an hour later they were on the road west.

Jaufre set the pace and the plain of Lombardy seemed to roll away beneath them of its own volition. They found campsites near water sources, living as much as possible off their own supplies, showing arms and attitude when they thought a display of force advisable. "I don't want any trouble," Jaufre said, "but by Mohammed's hairy ass I want to look like we could cause a lot of it if needs be."

Alaric's eye brightened at the prospect, but they were for the most part left to themselves. They saw more pilgrims than any other kind of traveler, gray-robed and en route for Venice and Jerusalem. Dame Joan was still vivid in their memories and they all expressed their silent gratitude to whomever might be listening that these pilgrims were going in the opposite direction.

Les Alpes rose steadily before them, tall and sharp-edged and snow-capped. The pass through them was called Moncensio in Lombardy and as they would discover, Mont Cenis on the other side. The trail switchbacked suicidally up from the plains but when they achieved the pass Johanna said to Shasha, "Not quite Terak, is it?"

Jaufre heard her. "Let's just hope there are no surprises waiting for us on the other side."

"Always with the cheerful prospect in view," Firas said, but he said it for Shasha's ears alone.

The pass was quite beautiful, ringed with white peaks and blue lakes. Going down, the trail felt less likely to fling them from the side of the mountain into the ravine beneath. It was August by then, with the bright, pitiless sun leeching the blue from the sky. The temperature rose as the elevation fell and made everyone snappish. Firas, scouting ahead, found a campsite near a trickle of water barely large enough to suit their needs. They picketed the livestock, and Johanna led North Wind downstream and let the cool water trickle over his hooves. He nudged her, and she produced a bit of apple. He munched contentedly.

A splash behind her and she turned her head. "Jaufre." Her heart rose at the thought he might have followed them.

"Don't go too far way from the others," he said. "It might not be safe."

North Wind nosed at her pocket and she smiled a little. "I think I'm safe enough."

"Don't forget, I've seen a time when even North Wind wasn't enough to keep you from harm."

"Jaufre," she said when he turned. She splashed over to put her hands, a little shyly, on his shoulders. "Jaufre," she said again. She leaned in to kiss him.

She felt a flash of undeniable awareness go through him, felt an instant of yielding, felt his hands on her arms tighten for a moment. And then he used them to push her away. Not roughly, but firmly, and with finality. "Not now, Johanna," he said. "I can't think of anything until Félicien is safe again."

She stood for a long time, the water gurgling around her feet, staring before her at nothing in particular. Then North Wind snorted and she went to lean up against his vast, comforting bulk, before he nudged her again and she remembered she had a curry comb.

The inchoate jumble of city-states and personal fiefdoms and royal dominions that formed the chain of mostly Frankish states stretched from the Middle Sea north to wherever the Holy Roman Empire began.

Mostly they spoke French, albeit with regional accents that tested everyone's polyglot abilities to the maximum. It was fifty leagues from Mont Cenis to Lyon. The first half of it was mountainous, but they made up the distance on the rolling plan that succeeded the mountains and were taking the ferry across the Rhône three days later. Wu Company had about five minutes to appreciate the setting, a city crowded between two rivers and two hills, prosperous and bustling and ready to do business with anyone regardless of race, color, creed, nationality, gender or diet, before Jaufre called them together, his voice pitched low so as not to be overheard.

"Shasha, find us a place to stay. Firas, a place to stable the livestock. Johanna, find the Gradenigo agent. Alaric, you're with me."

"And where are you going?" Johanna said it but they were all thinking it.

"I want to see the inside of every inn and tavern and tour every market inside and outside the city walls. I want to know what people are saying. I want every scrap of news and gossip going. The rest of you keep your eyes and ears open. If you see two men talking to each other on a street corner, I want to know what they were saying. Drop Ambroise de L'Arête and l'Alouette du Sud into the conversation whenever you think you safely can, but don't let it come back on us. I don't want him to know we are coming."

He and Alaric, his expression indicating he was anticipating the taverns, vanished into the crowds of people moving through the eastern gate.

"Good thing this seems like a nice place," Johanna said, in not quite a growl.

Shasha raised an eyebrow at Firas.

"He is certainly focussed," he said, and shrugged. "At least it's warmer and drier than Venice."

Alma was gazing at an edifice on a hill. "I wonder if that's a university?"

Hari, standing next to her and gazing likewise, said, "Or perhaps a church?"

Tiphaine, who had disappeared from their train when they arrived at the outskirts of the city, came trotting up. "Did we want to stay inside or outside the walls?"

"Outside, I think," Shasha said. She looked again at Firas. "I imagine our lord and master would not like to be locked behind gates if he wanted to leave in a hurry."

Firas laughed.

"Very well," Tiphaine said, impatient, "there is a large inn called The Sign of the Black Lion this side of the south gate. It is large enough for our party and it is spoken well of in the city. There is a stable nearby. I don't know if it's large enough for our needs. We'll have to go see."

"Is it indeed?" Firas said. "Very well, young miss, let us seek out this inn." They went off, Tiphaine marching importantly at the assassin's side.

Johanna slipped from North Wind's back. "Evidently I'm off to find one Phillippe Imbert, Ser Gradenigo's agent in Lyon. As I have been bid." She tossed the reins to Shasha. "Don't let him bite anyone."

"Johanna."

She looked over her shoulder, her jaw very tight.

"Try for some understanding."

"Oh, I do understand," Johanna said, and departed.

"Of course you do," Shasha said, and warned Gradenigo's stallieres to mind the pack animals and their merchandise carefully in this throng of people, and issued a dire warning as to what would happen if any of them slipped off to the Lyonnaise fleshpots before they were given leave to do so.

Phillippe Imbert was a smooth-talking Frank, his robes made from the finest fabrics in the richest colors and his beard clipped in the latest fashion. He had an eye for the ladies and he certainly had an eye for Johanna. It took a while to convince him that Gradenigo of Venice would send a woman to deal for him, even with Gradenigo's letter in hand as evidence. "Ser Imbert," Johanna had to say at last.

"No, no, Sieur Imbert on this side of Les Alpes," he said, laughing.

"Sieur Imbert," she said through her teeth, "while I'm flattered by your attentions, as what woman with blood in her veins wouldn't be—" and fluttered her lashes, because after all it was nice when someone demonstrated appreciation for her feminine charms, even the wrong someone "—I speak truly when I say my companions and I are come to Lyon this day with goods new even to the wharves of Venice. Of course, if you are too busy—"

He was merchant enough to react immediately to the implied threat. "No, no, dear lady, heaven forfend, never too busy—"

But he didn't entirely believe her until he met her the next morning at the warehouse Shasha and Firas had managed to secure for storage space. The quality and variety of the goods was wholeheartedly approved of. Sieur Imbert was anxious to receive the goods and since Johanna, but especially Jaufre, was anxious to be rid of them, matters proceeded apace. Afterward Jaufre said, "We should pay off the stallieres and send them home, and sell the pack animals."

Johanna looked at him in surprise. "But Jaufre—"

"We don't know how long we'll be gone, once we go," he said. "There's no point in paying for five men and fifty beasts to sit around and eat their heads off."

"We're not returning to Venice, then," she said.

"No, we're going after Félicien. How many times do I have to say so?"

She stared at him, eyes narrowing. "Only one more time," she said very gently, and turned and walked away.

Shasha, watching, saw him take a step after her and visibly make the decision not to. Instead he turned on his heel, collected Alaric, and headed back into the city. "I could kill them both with my bare hands," she said meditatively.

Firas chuckled. "I'll bury the bodies."

"Done."

Johanna and Shasha wrote out a statement of profit and loss for Gradenigo, to be left with Sieur Imbert along with the earnings they had accumulated along the way. Sieur Imbert made himself of further use by recommending a farmer a league from Lyon who would be willing to stable North Wind and the other Arabians, and Johanna worked off some of her temper by moving the horses there that afternoon. North Wind's general magnificence had already raised some comment in Lyon and the sooner he was out of sight the better.

"L'Arête is a château fifty-five leagues south of here," Firas said.

"Blade is what l'arête means in French," Alaric said. "Or edge."

They were in their sitting room at The Sign of the Black Lion, surrounded by the remnants of dinner. Their voices were pitched low in what Johanna thought an excess of caution. The noise from the common room downstairs was muted, and footsteps could be heard occasionally in the passage outside the door, but it was a solid door and Lyon was a town that took a group like theirs in stride.

"It's also what the Château L'Arête looks like," Alma said. "In the library at the monastery, where Sister Eliane was kind enough to grant me entrance, there is a map of the region. I made a copy." She produced a roll of vellum very much in the manner of a conjuror pulling a coin from an urchin's ear, and it was greeted with the same kind of acclaim now. She unrolled it with a flourish and they weighted the corners and perused it with attention. Johanna felt instinctively for her father's book, opened it to its furthest written page and began to scribble on the page after Lyon.

"It's rudimentary, as you can see," said Alma, "but here is Lyon and it is in the north—see the indicator here, that says that Paris is in this direction—which means that everything this way is south. Here is Le Puy, and Pradelles. Florac. Avignon where their grand imam lives. And here, east of Avignon, is L'Arête."

They followed her finger as it traced the journey. "The river," Jaufre said. "It goes almost all the way. We could hire a boat here in Lyon."

"And get off in Avignon," Shasha said, tapping her finger on the city.

"And walk the rest of the way," Alaric said with a grimace.

"Easier to hide from view without horses," Firas said.

"Look here," Alma said. "These illustrations around the edges? They show the major cities and castles in the area of the map. This one? This one is L'Aréte."

The drawing was the size of Johanna's palm, and it was clear that Alma had spent the most time on it of all the drawings. It showed an abrupt, skyward thrust of rock capped with towers and walls made of the same rock. One tiny road crept backwards and forwards up one side and the rest was given to sheer vertical cliff. "And how do we get inside that?" she said.

"It doesn't show," Alma said, "but Sister Eliane, who comes from Provins, says there is a village at the top, a village outside the castle walls."

"So we could get that far," Firas said. "And then, perhaps, reconnoiter."

Be best if we didn't get ourselves killed in the interim, Johanna thought. She glanced at Jaufre and left the thought unspoken.

"How far?" Jaufre said. His face looked hollowed out, almost haunted. "How far from Avignon?"

"As you can see, many of the distances are not marked, so I asked Sister Eliane." Alma looked up and around at the circle of faces. "She said not more than seven leagues."

Jaufre pored over the map. "It does not look to be rough country."

"The Blade will be sure to make it rough enough if he catches us on his ground," Alaric said.

"He won't hurt Félicien, will he?" Tiphaine said in a small voice.

Shasha gave her a smile that she hoped was more reassuring than she felt. "No."

"Why?"

"Because he needs her." Shasha looked at Johanna.

"She's the daughter of the last lord of L'Arête," Johanna said. "Who was improvident enough not to have a son, and so when Ambroise started making incursions onto L'Arête lands the old lord bowed to the inevitable and married him to his daughter, his heir. The old lord died almost immediately thereafter. Some say naturally, some say by Ambroise's design." She shrugged. "But then his reputation is so bad, they would say almost anything."

"You didn't see him," Jaufre said.

"And the daughter?" Shasha said quickly.

"Disappeared the day of the wedding."

"How did she manage that?"

"There are a lot of stories," Johanna said. "The one I liked best was that she escaped in the company of a band of troubadours who had been summoned to L'Arête to help celebrate the day."

They all thought about that in silence for a few moments, remembering the slim young goliard in his rusty black robe, sitting cross-legged by a campfire, head thrown back in lusty song, his flat black cap open side up on the ground in front of him. He'd gone home coins to the good most nights. He could write songs as well as sing them, and accompany himself on almost any instrument that came to hand, lute, gitar, flute, hautboy, even the morin khuur, that odd instrument so loved by the Mongols, strung with horsehair and played by dragging more horsehair strung on a bow across the strings. It had always sounded like a cat in heat to Johanna.

"What was her name?" This from Alma. "The daughter's?"

"Aceline Eléonor." Johanna paused. "Félicienne." She sighed. "Aceline Eléonor Félicienne de L'Arête."

"It's true then," Hayat said, and at a look from Jaufre, added, "You have to admit, Jaufre, it is a tale fanciful enough to keep a sultan's interest."

He couldn't deny it. Instead he said, "Ambroise?"

"He calls himself The Blade, which tells its own tale." Firas' lip curled. A man was frightening in and of oneself, and no fanciful name, no matter how exaggerated, would make him more so.

"His reputation with the church is bad as can be," Hari said. "The priest of his church is one of his own choosing, and the monks say he is no priest, either. None of his people are obliged to attend services, and he, ah, redirects the church tithes into his own coffers." He paused. "Which I must say is what they find most objectionable about him, although they say also that no woman's virtue is safe within his borders, and any man's life is forfeit. It is rumored that for fun he shoves people who have displeased him off the castle wall to see if they can fly." He paused again. "One of the monks called Ambroise the devil on earth."

There was a momentary silence, not untinged with respect. When these faith-ridden people called someone a devil, it was not a condemnation to be taken lightly.

"All right." Jaufre stood up and began to pace back and forth. "Back to Ambroise. We know what he looks like, we know where he lives, we know he thinks he is a khan on the order of Ogodei."

"What's a khan?" Tiphaine said.

"A king," Shasha said.

"A tyrant," Jaufre said. "We can't attack in force because we don't have a force, so stealth is our only option."

"There is some news lately from the south," Hayat said. "In spite of the fact that people don't like to talk about him, it is said in the marketplace that he has found his runaway wife—and the heir to L'Arête—and brought her home in triumph."

"It is also said in the marketplace that the Lark of the South sings no more," Tiphaine said.

There was a brief silence.

"People don't mind so much talking about her," Tiphaine said, with a cautious look at Jaufre, "at least about her before she married the Blade. She was famous for her beautiful voice. Her father hosted a great celebration of jongleurs and troubadours and minstrels every year at L'Arête, and she would sing with them."

"There is a long and noble tradition of chansons de geste in Provins," Alaric said, who had an eye on Jaufre himself, "going back before Queen Eleanor. Her son, Richard the Lionheart himself, wrote songs. I remember songs by a duke in Aquitaine, more by a countess in Die."

"At any rate, our Félicien is definitely this same Aceline Eléonor Félicienne de L'Arête," Jaufre said. "And is our friend and companion, and requires our help." He removed the weights and rolled up the map. "I'm going down to the waterfront to find us a boat going south."

· Ten ·

October, 1325 A.D.
Provins

⊢——⊣

North Wind can't come," Jaufre said that evening. "He will draw attention. He always does."

"The farm where they are now will suffice. I'll ask Phillippe to keep an eye on them." Johanna only hoped the big stallion wouldn't come after her if he decided she'd been gone too long. It wasn't as if he hadn't done it before. "What about a boat?"

"I found one that will give us deck passage," Jaufre said.

"For how many?" Firas said.

"What do you mean, how many?"

"Exactly what I said," Firas said, unperturbed. "Alaric?"

"Certainly," Alaric said with hauteur. "I would not allow my companions to travel into danger alone."

"So three of us. Who else?"

"Me," Shasha said.

Hayat and Alma exchanged long looks. "We're going," Hayat said.

"I don't know how much use I will be, but I believe I must witness this story through to its end," Hari said.

"You will have to put off your chughi robe, Hari. We need to draw as little attention as possible."

Hari nodded agreeably. "Of course, young master."

"I'm going," Tiphaine said.

"No, you most certainly are not," Johanna said.

Tiphaine glowered. "I most certainly am, and there is nothing you can do to stop me."

"You think not?"

"I know not! If you leave me behind, I will follow you, and I will help rescue Félicien! She's not just my friend, she's a member of my compagnia! She wears my token!" Tiphaine pulled at her tunic to display the insignia of Wu Company on her right shoulder, brave in red and gold.

"Yes," Johanna said. "Yes, of course she does." She looked up to meet Jaufre's eyes. "It's unanimous, then. Nine passengers, then."

But later, when the others had dispersed about various tasks and they were alone, Johanna said to Shasha, "What are we doing, Shasha? We're not warriors, we're merchant traders."

Shasha looked at her with a serious expression. "You would leave your friend in such hands?"

"No, but marching into the middle her husband's army wouldn't be my first reaction, either."

"We don't know that he has an army."

"We know he has a company of mounted spearmen. Some of us are going to get hurt, Shasha. Some of us may die."

"And if it was you? It was you, in fact, and not so long ago, either."

Their eyes met. Shasha had sent Firas for Johanna when Johanna was a prisoner in Talikan. She might not have escaped Gokudo if Firas had not come for her. She might now be prisoner in her stepmother's house in Cambaluc, subject to mistreatment no less degrading and humiliating than what Félicien was no doubt experiencing right now. She had not been angry to see Firas, she had been ecstatic.

All the tension that had existed between her and Jaufre since his return from Sant' Alberto fountained up and something inside her seemed to break beneath the pressure.

Shasha saw it in her face. "Here now," she said, drawing Johanna down to a cushion by the hearth and pulling her into a comforting embrace. "Here, now." She rocked them both back and forward, and made no mention of the hot tears soaking her shoulder.

"I never thanked you for sending Firas after me, Shasha," Johanna said, snuffling miserably into her foster sister's tunic. "I am the most selfish and ungrateful person who ever lived."

"Nonsense." Shasha patted her and continued to rock. "It's not that you don't want to save Félicien, Johanna," she said. "It's that you'd rather Jaufre didn't want to save her quite so badly."

Johanna didn't deny it. How could she, when it was true?

They reduced their belongings to the bare minimum, storing the excess with the ever resourceful Sieur Imbert, and at dawn boarded the barge on which Firas had procured them deck passage. It was a long, wide boat with a nearly flat bottom, made for ferrying goods up and down the Rhône from Genéve to the shores of the Middle Sea.

"There's no sail," Johanna said, and then subsided when the boatmen tied their bowline to the stern of another barge almost exactly like it, which was in turn tied to the barge ahead of it, and so on for a total of six. The lead barge was harnessed to a team of horses on shore, as was a spring line from each of the other barges. A boy who looked younger than Tiphaine had the lead horse on a rein and led them down a well-worn path on the edge of the river bank. The lines took up the slack between horse and barge, the horses strained briefly against their harness, and they began to move slowly down the river. "It's been a dry summer," Firas said. "The barge captain says that normally there is enough current that they can float down in good time, but not this year."

Each barge was piled high with goods, and each carried deck passengers as well. There were two horses in one of the barges, and Johanna tried hard not to be resentful at leaving North Wind behind. North Wind was an army in and of himself. Besides, she already missed him.

The water lapped contentedly at the hull and the landscape passed slowly by. Here, it was mostly tall grass interrupted by the occasional drainage ditch. They passed fields with the harvest grouped together in shocks, waiting to be winnowed, other fields where serfs were already beating the grain against cloths spread on the ground. A high, thin layer of clouds muted the usual ferocity of the southern sun, and an unusual air of peace and tranquility settled upon the company. It was the first moment of inaction they had experienced since Jaufre and Alaric's return from Sant' Alberto.

"I've been thinking about how we get into L'Arête," Johanna said.

Most of them had made comfortable nests against and among the bales and bundles on deck, but this statement brought everyone into an upright, attentive position.

She smiled a little. "It's not that startling," she said. "Alaric has told us that troubadours are a tradition in Provins. What could be more natural than for a group of troubadours to be traveling there?"

"The Lark of the South escaped the first time with a band of troubadours, we've been told," Alaric said dryly. "I don't think the Blade is going to look too kindly on the breed. Besides, I can't sing."

"You don't have to," Johanna said. "I can, and so can Shasha, Hayat and Firas. Hari can hum. Alma can play a flute."

"Not very well," Alma said. "I haven't practiced since Talikan. I don't even have a flute with me."

"We'll buy you one in Avignon," Johanna said. "It'll come back to you."

"I can sing, and kept a decent beat on a tambour, too," Jaufre said.

They all gaped at him. "What?" he said, a little defensively.

He really didn't know, Johanna thought, marveling.

"Jaufre, you can't go," Shasha said when it became clear that Johanna wasn't going to.

"What! Why not?"

"Because Ambroise has seen you, Jaufre," Firas said, "and in Félicien's company, too. He will know you again. You and Alaric, neither one of you may go with us to L'Arête. It would probably be best if both of you waited for us in Avignon. In fact, I'm not at all sure we shouldn't put the both of you off at the last stop before Avignon." He paused. "Or perhaps you should stay on board until the next stop after Avignon. The last thing we need is for someone to describe you to de L'Arête or any of the twenty of his men who have also seen you."

They were still arguing about it five days later when they docked at Avignon. "I can dye my hair and my skin," Jaufre said. "I could give myself a tonsure and dress in a habit."

"Yes, a Christian monk would be traveling with a troupe of troubadours," Shasha said.

"Why not?" Jaufre said. "We've already got a Buddhist one."

"So far," Firas said, "we've got one good idea on how to get into L'Arête. We haven't talked about how we're going to get out again."

They were speaking in low voices, crowded into the only room they'd been able to find in the most flea-ridden inn farthest from the city gates. Not that the inn wasn't noisy enough to drown out any conversation. Their door looked out onto the kitchen, which abutted a yard where the cook pitched out excess offal and left it to be fought over by stray dogs. The only way to breathe without vomiting was to keep the door closed, which made the room almost unbearably stuffy. And to Shasha's indignation they were paying more for a night there than they had for a week anywhere else on their entire journey from Venice.

Avignon was the seat of the Christian Popes, and the city overflowed with papal officials, petitioners noble and common, ambitious priests and prelates from England to Venice looking for advancement, servants, flunkeys, sycophants, bootlickers and hangers-on. Perched on a hill on the edge of the Rhône, the massive stone wall that surrounded the city seemed barely strong enough to contain the many towers that sprouted from inside it. They were all topped with banners and standards and pennons standing straight out in the harsh wind blowing out of the south that the locals called the mistrau. The banner flying from the tallest towers on the tallest hill of the city bore the crowned keys of the Pope himself.

The nobles were the worst, of course, as they never traveled alone and their enormous entourages were each determined to prove how much more important their liege was than anyone else's. That afternoon, in the time it took to find shelter for the night, Johanna saw three street fights between servants dressed in different liveries.

"Young men with swords," Shasha had said with a sigh.

Scarcely were the words out of her mouth when a young man with, yes, a short sword at his waist shouldered past her, followed by three of his fellows, all four clad in similar blue and green livery. The last to shove past her jostled her with enough force that she was knocked off balance. Firas caught her and set her back on her feet.

"Watch where you're going," this gentleman said over his shoulder.

"Watch yourself!" Johanna said.

As if she had rung a bell the four swerved around and came back to array themselves in a line in front of Johanna and the others. "Did I hear a mouse squeak?" one said, wriggling a finger in his ear. His friends laughed heartily at this sally.

Another stepped forward and had the temerity to flick the badge on Johanna's shoulder. "And to whom might you belong, my pretty?"

"Myself," Johanna said.

He had a spotty face with dark eyes and a full head of dark hair. "Oh ho, this one has teeth," he said, evidently vastly amused. He snaked an arm around her waist. "And how does your master let you out alone, my pretty?"

"I have no master," Johanna said. She even smiled when she said it.

Jaufre stepped up and by a feat of legerdemain managed to insinuate himself between them. He smiled down at the gentleman from his superior height and said, "We littles aren't worth the trouble, my lord."

The gentleman wasn't a lord and if they hadn't known that before they would have known it soon afterward by the whistling and stomping and catcalls of his companions. When the commotion died down enough to be heard Jaufre said, "We're but lowly merchants, my lords—" including them all in a deferential bow "—grubbing about with buying and selling. No one you could wish to dirty your hands on."

It was obvious the four of them were greatly tempted to give Wu Company a drubbing just on general principals. Then again, eyeing this oddly well-armed company, some instinct for self-preservation told them to live to fight another day. When they had achieved a safe distance they called a few insults concerning merchants and traders and took to their heels, disappearing into the crowd, which had barely taken notice of the entire encounter.

After which Jaufre rounded on Johanna. "Unnoticed and if possible, barely seen," he said in an infuriated whisper. "Did I not make myself clear?"

Remembering it now, Johanna allowed her gaze to dwell on him, pacing back and forth between them and the single, tiny window placed high up on the wall of their stuffy little room. Even on the barge he had been constantly in motion, bow to stern and back again, earning more than one reproof from the crew, who offered to set him ashore where he could walk behind the horses. On occasion he took them up on it. Once she had accompanied him, pacing beside him, saying nothing. It was the only comfort thus far that he would accept.

There was a fumbling at the door and Johanna was halfway to her feet, hand on her knife, in company with almost everyone else in the room, when Tiphaine tumbled into the room. "He's here!" she said, eyes bright, breast heaving.

Shasha put her finger to her lips and Johanna said in a low voice, "Who's here?"

"Him!"

"Him who?"

Tiphaine all but stamped her foot. "Ambroise! The Blade! The man who stole Félicien!"

In two strides Jaufre had Tiphaine by both elbows. "Are you sure? How do you know it's him?"

She wrestled free and this time she did stamp her foot. "It's the talk in all the markets! He's here to petition the Pope about something, I couldn't find out what, but he's got a company of ten men with him."

Jaufre spun around, his face lit with a fierce excitement. "That's ten men not at L'Arête," he said.

"We need more information," Firas said, a warning note in his voice. "How long will it take him to get his audience with this Pope of theirs? As you can plainly see, there are many in line in front of him."

"Lines!" Jaufre stared at him incredulously. "You think this is about lines, about who got here first! It's about whoever offers up the most coin! We saw that in Venice!"

We saw that in Cambaluc, Johanna thought. It was the same the world over, evidently.

"By the sheerest of luck," Jaufre said, "we have been given an opportunity here, Firas. We must take it. We leave tonight."

His force of will nearly had them all trooping for the door, until Alaric spoke. "Wait," he said.

He'd been sitting in the darkest corner, wrapped in his cloak, a pitcher of something cradled protectively in his lap. Now he set the pitcher carefully to one side and rose to his feet. It was easy to dismiss this man as negligible, to define him by his sour attitude and the drink ever to hand. But in this moment, as he rose to his full and not inconsiderable height, Johanna was faintly surprised at the presence and the authority he managed to gather around him.

"We have followed you on this ridiculous quest to rescue your lady fair," he said to Jaufre, "even though I warned you how it would be from the beginning. She is his legal wife, in the eyes of God and under the law of the land. She has been with him long enough that the marriage has undoubtedly been consummated. She could even by now be with child."

He stepped out of his corner and into a stray ray of the day's last light fell on his face. He looked most stern.

"Now you want us to follow you into L'Arête itself, which is by all the accounts one of the most inaccessible châteaux in Provins. A place with one small road traversing the face of a sheer, vertical cliff face some furlongs in height. The same cliff face, I would point out, that surrounds the entire castle. There is one gate, we are told barely large enough to admit one man at a time, and that man must be walking, not riding. It is unassailable, Jaufre, possibly even impregnable, and since we don't muster an army at our backs, we are not capable of settling in for a prolonged siege. I have no intention of allowing you to lead us recklessly to our deaths in a quest that is hopeless, not to mention unlawful, to begin with. And we don't even know if she wants rescuing." When Jaufre would have spoken he held up a hand. "I know, I was there. She did not want to go with him, but in this world, Jaufre, this world to which she willingly returned, I might add, she had no choice. She is his wife. She lives on his sufferance and under his authority. And she knows it, Jaufre, if you don't."

It was as many words as Alaric had ever put together in one speech without slurring them or burping an interruption. Sheer astonishment held them speechless for a long moment.

"I agree," Shasha said, breaking the silence. She met Jaufre's furious and somewhat wounded look without flinching. "For one thing, we should try to discover if Félicien is here with him."

Jaufre opened his mouth, and closed it again. It was clear he hadn't thought of that, but then none of them had.

Tiphaine frowned. "I heard no word of her."

"We must be sure," Shasha said. "There is no point in racing off to L'Arête to rescue Félicien if she isn't there."

"Agreed," Firas said in his calm way. "Alaric, Jaufre, you will remain here tomorrow, out of sight of Ambroise and his men. The rest of us will go into the city when the gates open and glean what information we can. We will meet back here at nightfall to take stock." He held up an admonitory figure. "Remember not to get caught inside the gates. If you do and we decide to leave tomorrow night, you will be left behind."

The next morning Johanna headed straight for the palace, a massive stone edifice with multiple towers, many doors including the main, columned portico, and staircases large and small that led up or down labyrinthine passages. A bell that she was certain could be heard in Lyon clanged every quarter hour and brought everything to a momentary, wincing halt.

She ordered a cup of small beer from one of the many taverns scattered around the edges of the palace and disposed herself at a table tucked into an alcove that had an excellent view of the palace's front door, which appeared to accommodate most of the traffic. A discreet bribe to the host and she was left alone.

The Place des Papes was teeming with people of every station, although the crowd was dominated by religious. They were all dressed head to toe in black, which must have been stifling on such a hot day. The higher prelates were easily identified, their garments were of the finest quality fabric, fit the best and were for the most part the cleanest. None of them could take a step without a citizen, lord or commoner, catching their sleeve and whispering in their ear. This was almost invariably followed by something passing by hand from one pocket to another, and the cleric taking himself a few more steps down the Place, there to repeat the experience.

A lucrative business, religion.

There were many carts selling foodstuffs and religious souvenirs. More than one cart was upset by groups of young men engaging other groups of young men dressed in differing livery, a repetition of the scene they had witnessed outside the city the day before. In all instances the vendor was left to pick up the pieces and reassemble his business as best he could, with no assistance, no recompense and no apology. It didn't seem to discourage any of them, or their customers, who waited at a distance until the young hooligans had swaggered on, and then gathered again around the resurrected cart.

A lucrative business, but a labor-intensive one.

The bell in the tower thundered out one o'clock and when her bones stopped vibrating Johanna ordered a plate of bread and cheese and another cup of small beer. The bread was fresh baked and hearty and the cheese a kind she had never seen before, hard with blue striations. It was several steps above the Mongol byaslag she was used to, and she was settling in to enjoy it when another commotion drew her attention. She was vastly unsurprised to see two groups of young men scuffling together, to encouraging shouts from the crowd and heartfelt curses from the vendors. One dressed in silver and black threw another dressed in red and blue against a cart selling roasted hazelnuts. The cart went over and the brazier scattered coals and nuts, causing everyone nearby to dance out of the way. The hapless vendor bleated his distress and scrambled after his goods.

This time a priest came forward, a man whose lack of height was more than compensated for by the bulk of his brawn. He reached into the welter of flailing limbs for an ear each and banged their heads together, hard enough to have Johanna cringe just a little in sympathy. He then stood them on their feet, not letting go of their ears, and looked around the circle of staring faces. "I'm sure all you good Christians have something better to do with your time than stand around watching a couple of foolish boys—" he banged their heads together again for emphasis "—beat up on each other for no good reason other than the colors they wear."

Such was the priest's authority that the crowd found something better to do immediately, and the priest let the two boys go and strode off, followed by many an admiring glance, not least Johanna's. When she looked again for the two heroes, still staggering, she found the one in black and silver had been helped tenderly to a table in the very tavern at which she was sitting, and had been joined by his fellows.

They were all four of them handsome young lads, not a day over twelve, fair of face and form, dark of eye and hair, with fresh complexions and erect carriages. They were almost similar enough to have passed for brothers. Johanna wondered if they'd been chosen for their looks, a matched set to enhance their lord's consequence.

The table was also near enough that their conversation was clearly audible to her, and whose first words held her transfixed. "My lord Ambroise will not be best pleased if he gets to hear of this. He told us to mind our manners in Avignon."

"At least until he gets what he wants from John," another said.

"God's balls," the third said, "we'll be here until Christmas."

"What does he want from the Pope, anyway?" the fourth said, and found his already abused ear soundly boxed by the first. "Ouch! What did you do that for, Bernart?"

"Because, Guilham, my lord does not want his business bruited about the streets," Bernart said, looking around, and Johanna made sure her face was over her plate when he looked her way. "If you cannot learn discretion, perhaps you do not belong in his service."

Guilham, his face red with anger, lurched to his feet and stumbled away. Most fortuitously, he stumbled in Johanna's direction, and more fortuitously still he tripped over a stool and fell face forward on her table, knocking over her cup of small beer and breaking the cheese plate.

She sprang to her feet with an exclamation of dismay. "Sir! Are you hurt?" She picked him up and set him on his feet again, where he stayed, none too steadily. "Here, let me help you." She made a show of brushing the bread crumbs from his tunic, waiting for him to raise his head. When he did, she gave him her best smile. "Are you well?" she said. "Perhaps a drink to refresh yourself." She contrived to sit him on a stool, the very one he had tripped over, and motioned to the host, who arrived posthaste with a pitcher this time of small beer and another, larger plate of bread and cheese. She poured the boy a cup, broke off some of the blue-veined cheese and put it on a piece of bread and served him so, with yet another smile as an appetizer. He was still blinking from the first one.

"What, Guilham, and who is your new friend?"

Johanna looked up with all the surprise she could muster showing on her face. "Gentlemen?" She took in their livery with an awed glance, and looked at Guilham. "Ah, I see. You are comrades. Please, join us."

They did, Bernart looking her over very frankly. She knew what he saw, a young woman dressed for the road in well-made clothes who didn't look hungry enough to sell herself by the hour. She did wear insignia, the characters of Wu Company, on her shoulder, which meant she was not without protection. Still, she was alone, and this led him into error. "A professional lady, is it? Perhaps you can find time to, ah, fit all of us in," he said, elbowing one of the others, who sniggered dutifully.

"Sir," she said, in a voice she copied from one of the khan's wives at Cambaluc, chill enough to freeze the small beer pouring out of the pitcher, "you labor under a misapprehension. I am trader, a merchant, in fact, and my company even now sets up our stalls in the marketplace."

Bernart wasn't quite convinced—after all, no respectable woman went about in public without at least one servant to lend her consequence— but he was willing to play along. "Where are you from?" he said.

She looked him in the eye and said firmly, "Cathay."

He laughed. She did not. The other three boys leaned forward. "Cathay? Truly?"

She produced another dazzling smile, directed this time impartially around the table of eager faces, not neglecting Bernart. "Truly."

After that all she had to do was simper, and tell some of the more sensational tales from her grandfather's book. She ordered more small beer and two more platters of food, because food was a guaranteed way into the confidence of boys of this age. In combination with the admiring attention of an attractive older woman, it proved irresistible. "Where are you gentlemen from?" she said, refilling their mugs with a generous hand.

They responded with names of four different Frankish-sounding places. She eyed their uniforms. "Yet you all wear the same livery."

"We are in service to the Lord of L'Arête," Guilham said.

She produced a look of abject admiration. Her mouth might even have dropped open. "Truly? You serve at a noble court?"

They preened as only boys on the verge of manhood can. "Indeed," Bernart said, with what he imagined was just the right amount of hauteur. He was so very young. They all were.

"Imagine!" she said. She dropped her eyes and said modestly, "I'm merely a trader, a traveling merchant, you know. I've never even been inside a nobleman's house." She paused to let the difference in their stations sink in, and then said, with hushed reverence, "Is L'Arête a, well, a castle? No, really?"

She had learned a great deal indeed by the time the bell sounded vespers and a shadow darkened their table. They looked up, to behold an older man wearing their colors in richer fabrics, a man with a strong, hard face and heavy gold around his neck and on his fingers. "So, gentlemen," he said, "you have found a friend. How nice."

Johanna looked at Guilham, and saw his face had gone white.

"I believe we were to have met before none in the Rue Peyrollerie," their lord said. There was a leather whip coiled at his waist, and he allowed one hand to toy with its end, which had more than one tail. "And yet I find you not there, but here." He affected a slight bow toward Johanna, his eyes flickering over her person, noting the quality of her clothing and her badge and then dismissing her in the next moment. "In charming company. Which would no doubt provide its own excuse. For some other, less demanding lord."

Such was the paralyzing force of Ambroise's tongue that Johanna thought for a moment none of the four boys were ever going to be able to move again. She wasn't all that sure about herself.

"Gentlemen," he said. "With me. Now."

The last word cracked like the whip at his side would have, and there was a clattering scramble that knocked over all four stools and a babble of apologies, directed not at her but at their lord. They were really afraid of him, Johanna saw, and it was manifestly obvious that the lord Ambroise enjoyed their fear.

At that moment another quarrel broke out on the other side of the square and everyone turned involuntarily to look. She took advantage of the confusion to slip away into the dusk and was so late she nearly got her robe caught in the city gate as it closed behind her. There she was pounced on by an infuriated Shasha. "Where have you been all day?"

"Gathering information," Johanna said airily. She grinned. "And meeting the lord of L'Arête."

"What!"

They gathered back at the inn, crowding into the cramped room and speaking only so loud as to be able to hear themselves over the roistering going on in the common room next door. Someone had foraged for better food than could be had from their landlord and they sat in a circle around a roast chicken and a rice and shrimp dish seasoned with saffron, and apples and cheese to follow, talking as they ate. When they were done Shasha passed around a damp cloth for them to wipe their hands and faces.

"So," Johanna said, summing up. "Félicien isn't with them. She was left at home, I would imagine under close guard of those of his personal guard he didn't bring with him. Ten of them, according to the boys."

"And how long does he remain here in Avignon?"

"The boys don't know. One of them said they'll stay as long as it takes to get what Ambroise wants from Pope John."

"Do they know what he wants?"

Johanna gave an impatient shrug, but said, "They think it's something to do with his wife. He married her for L'Arête, but it sounds as if their church has to formally invest lordship in Ambroise. Because she's the heir. Something like that, I didn't really understand all of it, and I couldn't ask too many questions or they would have become suspicious."

"Perhaps this Pope was named in Félicien's father's will," Alaric said. "He might have stood as her guardian, should she be yet unmarried at the time of her father's death."

"But she was."

Alaric shrugged. "Lords tend to secure their succession by soliciting the endorsement of the marriage of their heirs by the most powerful lord of the land. In these parts, that's the Pope." He shook his head. "L'Arête sounds like a rich property, and Provins is a rich region. Any liege lord would want the allegiance of the lord of L'Arête, if only to be able to tax its profits."

"The point is that Félicien is in L'Arête, and right now, this minute the lord isn't," Jaufre said. He sounded as if his patience was fraying.

"Under heavy guard," Alaric said, without much hope.

"Those boys?" Johanna said. "They are terrified of him." She raised her eyes to look at Jaufre, and knew the same thought was in their minds. And if the lord of L'Arête gave his pages cause to be terrified of him, how much more cause would he give his runaway wife? "There used to be five of them. Five pages. I gather one of them died recently."

Jaufre made an impatient gesture. "Sad, if true, but what has that to do with us?"

Firas was quicker. "Did Ambroise give him flying lessons?"

"They wouldn't say specifically, just that he died." She paused. "They are terrified of him," she said again. "I've never seen such fear."

"And if L'Arête has left orders from its lord not to admit troubadours?"

"The boys did not say so. And Ambroise isn't home."

"But how will we get out again?" Alaric said, a little querulously.

"We can't know that until we see the place," Firas said

"I've found someone who knows the way and is willing to guide us," Jaufre said.

"Someone trustworthy, I hope?" Alaric said.

"Someone for hire," Jaufre said. "He has a boat and will bring us across the river and then guide us to L'Arête." He looked around at their faces. "We leave tonight. And Alaric and I will be accompanying you to L'Arête."

"What!"

"By the round-eyed Christian god—"

"Jaufre—"

"Jaufre, please be reasonable."

"You'll get us all killed!"

"Wait," he said. "They won't know us. Trust me."

His smile was thin but it was the first smile any of them had seen on his face since Sant' Alberto, and it was enough to silence them long enough to listen to what he had to say.

· Eleven ·

October, 1325 A.D.
Provins

—————

When the bells rang lauds they donned packs filled with the bare minimum of food and necessities and crept out of their room, picked through the offal-strewn yard and down to the river's edge where a small, open boat waited for them. "This is Pascau," Jaufre said in a low voice.

The boatman, of middle age and wary mien, gave a curt nod and motioned them into the boat without further delay. They were almost too much of a load for it, and Johanna was sure they were all thinking of how many boats they'd almost swamped to date during their journey west, and if this was going to be the last one. Pascau stood in the stern, wielding a single oar with an offhand competence that was marginally reassuring.

Their passage across the river was swift and silent and unwitnessed so far as they could tell. The current left them considerably downstream on the opposite shore, but there was a neat moorage which hid the boat beneath a dense thicket of willow that argued steady usage.

There was a small clearing up the bank beneath more willows. "Sleep here," Pascau said. "Leave at first light."

They wrapped themselves in their cloaks and made themselves as comfortable as they could on the bare ground. At dawn they broke their fast with bread and cheese and were off across a flat landscape of stubbled fields lined with tall plane trees. The day was gray, with a mist that hung low to the ground. They kept to the shadows and slept rough the next night, too. The second morning found them approaching a collection of rock piers in fantastic shapes.

Pascau gestured at the rocks. "The Valley of Hell."

"Cheery," Hayat said.

"Welcoming," Johanna said.

Pascau's face, set in uncommunicable lines, didn't change. "No sense of humor," Hayat said.

Rosemary, thyme and lavender grew in thickets from every available crevice, perfuming the air with their scents, long limbs grasping at the carelessly-placed boot. Shasha walked in a permanent crouch, rubbing leaves here, plucking branches there. The plane trees had given way to cypress, and here and there olives trees had scratched together enough dirt to make a living. All the trees were stunted and twisted and leaning southeast beneath the eternal abuse of the mistrau, and rocks, herbs and trees clustered so thickly together as to make the way very difficult. From the brief glimpses they caught of it, the trail would have made their journey a little easier, but not so much that they dared risk encountering other travelers by taking it. The mist had lifted and the late autumn sun blazed down without mercy and everyone's clothes were damp with sweat and grimed with dust. Altogether an unprepossessing group, Johanna thought, looking them over. No self-respecting castle would let them in the door.

At mid-afternoon Pascau came scrambling back down a rocky incline and motioned to Jaufre. They held a brief, hurried consultation. "He says L'Arête is over this rise," Jaufre said. "He says we must go carefully if we don't want to be seen."

"I don't want to go at all," Alaric said, but it was the barest grumble and easily ignored.

"He's found a spot on the ridge covered with rosemary grown very tall," Jaufre said. "We are to crawl into it and be very careful not to crawl out the other side."

When they had climbed and crawled and slithered into place, they could understand Pascau's caution.

"In truth, a very blade," Firas said, after a long, awed moment of silence.

A massive stone of brilliant white, the southern end pointed, the northern end squared off, L'Arête appeared to have debarked from the mountains behind it to set sail on the flat plain below. Its sides were one continuous face, so smooth they looked planed by the same giant hand. Wave-like curls of vegetation clustered thickly all around its base, through which a single narrow road crept back and forth. Anyone on the road would have a sheer and certainly injurious, if not fatal drop on one side of them going and coming.

"They must have water up there," Firas said. "They could never withstand a siege otherwise."

"There is a small river in the valley below," Alaric said, craning his neck.

"If they were under siege they would never be able to get to it," Hayat said. "And it would be easy to poison." Johanna knew she was thinking about the river upon which Talikan had been built. Ogodei's first action had been to poison it.

"How high is the rock, do you think?" Shasha said.

"Five times the height of the towers of St. Mark's, and that's just the rock," Firas said.

Everyone's eyes raised to what grew from the top of the rock.

On a ledge close to the summit many tiny houses had been carved from the white rock of the precipice and roofed with orange tiles. Above them was the castle.

Johanna swallowed.

It increased the height of the freestanding ridge by a third. There were a dozen towers of varying sizes and shapes, sides pierced with multiple arrow slits. The towers were connected by a thick, high wall, built from more white rock. The wall was topped with a battlement defended by a parapet. Even at this distance she could see movement through the crenellations in the parapet. Guards. Ten spearmen that they knew of, but how many more?

Inside the wall roofs of buildings could be glimpsed, including a large square keep. Another wall ran around the village to connect with the castle wall on either side. Because of the differences in elevation the doors into both were easy to identify. Neither looked welcoming.

L'Arête wasn't just impregnable. It was unassailable. All its defenders had to do was lock the doors and rain down death on their enemies with mangonels, one of which was in plain view on the south end of the prominence.

They slid back down and gathered in a circle beneath a clump of cypress. Even Jaufre looked shaken.

"How are we going to get in there?" Alma said.

"How are we going to get out again?" Alaric said.

Jaufre squared his shoulders. "We go with Johanna's plan. We're an itinerant band of troubadours, looking for a place to sing for our suppers."

"And if the Blade discovers our presence?" Alaric said.

"He's not here," Jaufre said.

"And we'd best be gone before he returns," Firas said. He nodded at Pascau, who was sitting apart from them, an expression stolid indifference on his face. "Have you paid him yet?" By prior arrangement they spoke only Persian among themselves.

"No," Jaufre said, affronted. "He gets paid when we return safely to the Avignon side of the river."

"Is he coming with us?"

"No. He says he'll wait here."

"Tell him you'll double his fee if he comes with us," Firas said.

"Firas—"

The assassin shrugged. "It's the only way to be sure he won't hotfoot back to Avignon and sell us out to Ambroise."

"He could sell us out to them instead," Alaric said, jerking his head in the direction of L'Arête.

"They'd kill him, too, and he knows that," Firas said, and looked at Jaufre. "Either he comes with us or someone stays here to see that he doesn't run off. I nominate you and Alaric."

Jaufre looked back in the direction of the castle. "We'll wait till morning. Come around this ridge in plain view like we have nothing to hide and nothing to fear." He looked at Tiphaine. "How is your juggling coming along?"

The guards at the gate were bored. The cloudless morning promised another blistering day in this unusually warm fall, and since the lord was away their attention to their duties was not perhaps quite what it ought to have been. They flirted with the village girls, opined on the past excellent harvest with the villagers, and speculated on how the war was going in the Low Countries, or was it Bavaria? At any rate, a war somewhere they weren't, where soldiers other than themselves reaped the spoils of battle in gold plate and jewels and women willing or unwilling, it mattered not.

They didn't hear the flute at first, and when the beat of the tambourine registered they didn't rush to the gate, which stood wide open to facilitate what little breeze there was. It wasn't until Tiphaine, dark curls caught up in one of Alma's gauzy, glittering scarfs, strolled through the gate, juggling three rag balls as if she'd been born to it, that they realized the defenses of L'Arête had been penetrated. Before they could sound the alarm the invading force resolved itself into a small troupe of traveling troubadours. They relaxed, although the sergeant of the guard, when summoned, looked apprehensive and muttered something about the lord not liking it.

"He's not here, is he?" one of the guards said. They'd all heard the story about the lord's lady eloping with a different group of troubadours on her wedding day, but she was back, wasn't she? The reputation of the Lord of L'Arête was so fearsome that they saw little enough in the way of travelers. They hated Ambroise as much as they feared him, especially after that poor little tyke had been thrown from the wall. The half of Ambroise's personal guard who had remained behind when their lord went to Avignon had left the day before to inform the boy's parents of his death, although be sure they wouldn't tell them how he had died, or why. However the parents reacted, the show of force would keep them in line. It wasn't the first time they had performed such a task, and it never failed of effect. It would also occupy them for at minimum four days including travel time.

So they were bored, and feeling a little rebellious while not under their lord's eye. "Come on, sergeant, have a heart," one of them said, eyeing Alma, who smiled at him and put a little extra into the sway of her hips. "One night. What can it hurt?"

Tiphaine melted the sergeant's heart by tossing him her balls one after the other, and darting in to catch the one he dropped before it hit the ground, neatly catching the other two when he tossed them back and returning all three into a simple fountain. The sergeant laughed and the guards applauded, and the townsfolk came out of the houses lining the tiny street that wound uphill to the square, situated, very conveniently, directly outside the gate into the castle. There, Johanna and Jaufre came forward and with a graceful bow to the assembly launched into a spirited rendition of one of the very first songs they'd ever heard Félicien sing.

O wandering clerks
You go to Chartres
To learn the arts
O wandering clerks
By the Tyrrhenian

You study Aesclepion
O wandering clerks
Toledo teaches
Alchemy and sleight-of-hand

O wandering clerks
You learn the arts
Medicine and magic
O wandering clerks
Nowhere learn
Manners or morals
O wandering clerks!

It scanned and rhymed in French, thank goodness, even Provencal French, and their voices blended together well, and if they sang a trifle loudly, why, they had their way to make in the world and could be pardoned for a hearty sell. Besides, the song went over so well that by the middle of the last verse everyone was chanting along, the last "O wandering clerks!" bellowed out by guards, villagers and soldiers peering through the crenellations from the castle parapet above.

Johanna bowed again, and fell back, deferring to Jaufre, who stepped up. His hands and face had been stained a deep brown with walnut juice and his blond hair was hidden beneath a long dark scarf knotted elaborately in the way of the Tuareg. Alaric's skin was likewise stained and he had condescended, at Jaufre's insistence and not without the inevitable grumbling, to leave his sword behind and to be dressed in yeoman's clothing. When he remembered he stooped to disguise his height. She only hoped it would do.

"Good gentles, thank you for your kind attention and applause for our humble offering," Jaufre said, pitching his voice to be heard over the castle walls. Indeed, the people standing in front of the crowd fell back a little from the force of it. "We are Jerome's Jongleurs, late of Venice, Jerusalem and Persia—" he let his voice drop dramatically on that last "—and with your kind permission we will entertain you with a show this evening beginning at dusk, here in your beautiful place de la cité." He flourished another bow, Johanna feared to the imminent hazard of his headdress, but by some miracle it remained upon his head. "I am that selfsame Jerome, and here—" indicating Johanna "—is the lovely Jeanne of the East, who will sing you stories of the wonders of Cathay, the mirrored roofs of Cambaluc, of the Great Khan himself, and of Princess Padmini, and of the night it rained emeralds." He winked.

An anticipatory murmur ran around the crowd.

"Mohammed of Alamut, student of the Old Man of the Mountain Himself, will dazzle you with tricks of the sword!"

Firas stepped forward, too dignified to bow to people so infinitely beneath him. They had of course left all their long weapons behind in Lyon, but they all wore short swords, although the women wore theirs in light scabbards strapped to their backs beneath their clothes. The sword Firas wore was slightly curved, not quite a scimitar but similarly shaped, and he drew it now and tossed it up into the air, where it spun three times and fell hilt first neatly into his hand. There was a rumble of appreciation from the guards.

"Zubadiyah, late of the harem of the Sultan of Bagdad and valued student of Giotto of Firenze will draw your likeness in charcoal!" Alma insinuated herself forward, hips rolling in the best harem-approved manner, to the point that one goggle-eyed man had his head thumped by his indignant wife and was subsequently towed home by his ear. A charcoal sketch on a piece of vellum that had been scraped so many times the sun shone through the illustration it bore was held high in her hands as she circled the square, although when asked later hardly anyone and certainly none of the men could have said what the illustration was.

"And the lovely Umayma will tell your fortunes as they are written in the secret stones of Damascus," Jaufre said, dropping his voice again as Hayat stalked out and fixed the crowd with a bleak and intimidating eye. She had been the hardest to convince of her role when they had planned this mad scheme on the journey from Lyon to Avignon, and she was privately terrified that the first fortune she told would get them all killed. She didn't know that her demeanor alone convinced everyone with a penny in their pocket that some austere and unforgiving deity had blessed the intimidating Umayma with the seeing eye, and all of them determined on the spot to have their fortunes told that evening.

There was a bit of applause following Hayat's introduction and into the middle of it tumbled Tiphaine, regaining her feet with ease and commencing a fountain with three apples the fruit vendor had not known were missing until Tiphaine caught them all, bowed, and strolled over to return them to him. Charmed, or perhaps mindful of the ripple of laughter from his fellow villagers, he gave her one, and she winked at him and bit into it with gusto.

Born to the part, Johanna thought.

"We meet again at dusk, good gentles," Jaufre said, bowing again. The crowd began to disperse, chattering eagerly—L'Arête with the master it had, diversions were probably rare, something Johanna had counted on when she made her plan—and the headman and the sergeant of the guard stepped up to begin negotiations. Non-resident duties, a tax one paid to reside inside the gates for a night, and stallage, the right to offer one's wares, or as in this case a performance within that city were both reasonable, as both gentlemen planned on attending the evening's entertainment. Inquiry brought the information that the lord was not in residence. "How sad that we shall not be able to entertain him," Jaufre said, trying his best to seem so.

The sergeant, mistaking his meaning, grinned and clouted him on the shoulder. "Never fear, good Jerome! Entertainment such as you provide is not easily come by in L'Arête. The people here will reward you well."

"His family is with him?" Jaufre said casually. "His knights and their ladies?"

The sergeant's bonhomie dimmed. "There is only his wife remaining, and I doubt she will attend," he said dryly.

"A pity." Jaufre bowed and effaced himself to rejoin his companions. "She's here," he said in a low voice. "The sergeant confirms it."

They refreshed themselves at the communal fountain in the center of the square and retired to an unoccupied corner out of the sun. They piled their bedrolls and packs and Alma and Hayat went off to see what could be had in L'Arête in the way of charcoal and scraps of paper, parchment or vellum. A sullen Pascau subsided beneath a large plane tree, attended by a vigilant Alaric and an ever-smiling Hari, who maintained a constant flow of gentle conversation. Pascau did not look to be greatly attending.

Tiphaine went off with them and returned before they did, looking as if she would burst if she couldn't speak. Jaufre and Johanna retired with her to a shadowy corner.

"Ambroise's personal guards are gone off somewhere!"

"Quietly," Johanna said, smiling over Tiphaine's head at a curious housewife.

"The spearmen, Johanna, they're gone, off to some manor east of here." Tiphaine's eyes were blazing. "They won't be back for at least three days and perhaps as long as a week."

Johanna looked at Jaufre and saw that his eyes were blazing, too. "Our luck is in," she said, "but we stick to the plan."

Tiphaine looked up at the wall of unbroken white rock stretching above them. "Do you think she heard us?"

"Someone will tell her," Jaufre said, with more confidence than he felt.

"Will she know it's us?"

"She wrote the song we sang, Tiphaine," Johanna said. It was the only way they had been able to think of to get word to Félicien of their presence. She only hoped it worked.

No one contacted them during the afternoon, but they hadn't expected it. Even if Félicien was free to move about the castle, even if her close guard had been raised, she would most probably have a servant with her at all times, and that servant was in the pay of Ambroise. She had given Ambroise her word not to leave again but that didn't mean he believed her.

Félicien had to find her way out of the castle, because otherwise they were going to have to find their way in, and then find Félicien's room, and somehow get in and out of the room, castle, castle gate, village, village gate, down the precipitous path without being either stabbed, shot by the castle archers or pulverized by the mangonel.

But first she had to know they were there. Johanna looked up at the wall and saw faces peering at them over the parapet, but not the face they most wanted to see.

People began filtering back to the square well before dusk, blankets and cushions in hand along with food and drink. Jaufre had marked off a half circle of space next to the castle gate, where normally nothing was allowed, the gate remaining clear of detritus at all times as a matter of security. But for this special occasion, with the master away, the sergeant of the guard had allowed himself to be persuaded. He had also been persuaded to allow a couple of rough tables to be set up and their legs lashed together to provide a rudimentary stage.

Jaufre and Johanna with Shasha, Alma, Alaric and Hari started off with what had brought them their crowd, a repeat of Félicien's wandering clerks song. That went over well, some of the village folk were even joining in the chorus. Johanna only hoped that Félicien heard it the second time if she hadn't the first. They followed it with a drinking song.

When I see wine into the clear glass slip
How I long to be matched with it;
My heart sings gay at the thought of it:
This song wants drink!
I thirst for a sup; come circle the cup:
This song wants drink!

The last line was more shout than song and from that moment the audience was theirs to do with what they would. After a dozen songs the musicians rested while Tiphaine juggled and tumbled and was impudent to the audience and Alma drew portraits for anyone with a penny to pay. This was very popular and the coins in the little bowl passed by Tiphaine while small in denomination were large in number. The sergeant, who had commandeered a seat in the very front, gave Jaufre a gratified nod, and Jaufre bowed in acknowledgment. Alma took up her flute and accompanied Shasha on a song about a traveling artist and a farmer's wife, which went over as well as any song about a farmer's wife and a traveling anyone did.

The others retired, leaving Johanna the stage. She sang a song of strange things culled from her grandfather's writings, of the stones that burned, of the tribe with tails. She sang of Aijuruc, daughter of Caidu, a warrior of the Bright Moon who refused to marry anyone who could not defeat her, and lived unmarried to the end of her life in her father's kingdom far beyond the mountains of Salamander. She sang of Ferlec, where the first thing they saw in the morning they worshipped for the rest of the day, and the resulting disasters this odd custom caused. She sang of the pearl fishers of Cipangu, and the enchanters of Tebet, and of the monks of India, who caused ropes to climb to the sky and then climbed them to vanish into the air. Her voice had never been able to reach as high as Félicien's but she could write songs every bit as well, and she had not spent all that time reading the different versions of her grandfather's book in vain. Her audience showed their appreciation with generous applause and much coin.

For the second interval Hayat, adorned by an elaborate turban made from one of Alma's spangled harem scarves, of which she apparently kept an infinite number wound about her person beneath her clothes, settled onto a rug and told fortunes with the storied Secret Stones of Damascus. The Secret Stones of Damascus were a handful of smooth agates recovered from a tiny beach between Lyon and Avignon, one dark in color, the rest light. On the river they'd all worked with Hayat to come up with a plausible set of stories that could be altered to fit anyone. Her fierce and forbidding aspect led everyone to regard her with some trepidation, and added that much more weight to the fortunes she told. It helped that, in Hayat's fortunes, every man's crop or business would prosper, every married woman would bear a male child next, and every maiden would marry a man both handsome and kind.

In the break after Hayat's fortune telling Johanna noticed two women standing just inside the gate to the right of the stage. One was dressed in gray, the other in black. Both wore cloaks in spite of the warm evening, their hoods pulled forward so as to shadow their faces.

She nudged Firas, who was nearest. "I saw," he said, his lips barely moving. He drifted off to stand near Jaufre, who was doing his best to look everywhere but at the gate. If you didn't know him, perhaps you might not notice, Johanna thought. Perhaps.

By now the audience was in an excellent mood, beating time in a body to a trio of marching songs that evoked the spirit of the Road. Johanna sang in her mellow contralto of Princess Padmini and Ala-ud-din, and women wept. She sang another about the night it rained emeralds on the steps of the palace in Everything Under the Heavens, and men sighed with envy. What they could do with a fistful of emeralds.

Their last song was the plum tree song, the first song Jaufre had ever heard sung by the Wu family, with Wu Li keeping time on a small skin drum, Shu Ming plucking out the tune on a lap harp, their voices melding with Johanna's and Shasha's and Deshi the Scout's.

White petals, soft scent
Friend of winter, summoner of spring
You leave us too soon.

The lyrics, which were not at all or not only about a plum tree, had as powerful an effect translated into French and performed before this audience of villagers and castle guards as it had had on Jaufre in the caravansary in Kashgar so long ago. They had taught it to Félicien, who had sung it with them over a thousand leagues of Road and more, and who was standing now just inside the castle gate, close enough to them to join in. She didn't.

He found himself swallowing back tears, and felt Johanna's touch, gentle and fleeting on his hand. He turned his head to look at her, really look at her for the first time since Milano. The moon had risen and flooded the square with light, and she looked so beautiful to him in that moment that she seemed almost not of the same world he inhabited.

Their eyes held for a long moment of absolute stillness, that ultimate accolade of the professional performer, and then she smiled, and applause crashed over them, shouts and whistles and clapping of hands and stamping of feet. Before it had quite ebbed the troupe launched once more into "O Wandering Clerks," this time everyone joining in, Jaufre, Johanna, Shasha, Firas, Alma, Hayat, Hari, Alaric, and of course Tiphaine, who sang louder than any of them. By then almost everyone in the audience was letter-perfect in the chorus, if not the lyrics.

The bowl Tiphaine passed during the last chorus came back gratifyingly full. The villagers dispersed and the castle folk returned to their lodgings or duties and the troupe gathered in a tight knot in their shadowy corner, ostensibly to refresh themselves and take their own rest before departing the following morning.

"Did you see the two women standing inside the gate?" Tiphaine said.

They all had. Jaufre tore off a chunk of bread and ate it mechanically.

"They left just after the plum tree song," Shasha said, her voice low.

"The sergeant will never consent to us staying another night," Alaric said.

"And he would be right not to," Hari said. "Ambroise could return at any time."

"The spearmen he left behind could return at any time, too."

"She has to come to us," Johanna said.

Jaufre shot her a look but said nothing.

There were still some villagers moving around the square, extinguishing braziers and packing up vending carts for the night. Several of them drifted over to offer thanks for the show. A slight woman in gray hovered in the background until the rest had left. She kept casting nervous glances at the guards, as if the moment they looked her way they would arrest her just on general principles. "Alma," Johanna said in a low voice. "Hayat."

Hayat picked up a jug of watered wine and Alma four cups and they sauntered over to the gate and engaged the two guards in conversation. The massive wooden gates were closed now, and undoubtedly barred from the inside. There was a smaller door, sized for one person, in one of the larger doors, but no one could use it without being challenged by the guards, two more of which were very probably stationed on the inside.

The woman in gray came closer, her manner tentative, if not outright terrified. The hood of her cloak was pushed back enough that they could see her face. Her features were fine but lined and drawn, her figure thin to the point of emaciation. "Who is the one called Jaufre?" she said in a voice barely above a whisper.

No one could move or say anything for a moment, and then Jaufre began to surge to his feet. Firas' hand on his shoulder pressed him firmly back down. "And who asks, milady?"

The woman cast another look over her shoulder and stepped forward to speak rapidly in so low a voice she could barely be heard. "It is not safe for you here. The lord is expected back at any moment. You must go." She half-turned, as if to leave.

"Who says this, lady?" Jaufre said, straining against Firas' hand.

She cast another glance at the gate. All the guards' attention was on Hayat and Alma. She turned back to Jaufre and spoke quickly. "The one who wrote your song. You are in grave danger. You must go."

"Lady, tell us only this. Does she truly wish to stay? In her own heart?" Alaric stirred and Jaufre quelled him with a single, ferocious glare. "Please speak truly. We have come a great distance to see to her well-being."

"You must go," the woman said. "You must go, and she must stay. It is the way of things."

"Tell her," Jaufre said, "tell her that we won't leave without her." He shove Firas' hand off his shoulder and came to his feet, the better position from which to issue edicts. "She must come with us when we leave tomorrow morning."

"If she doesn't come, we won't leave, and then we will all die here together," Johanna said. She met Jaufre's glare without flinching. "Tell her that, milady."

"I must return before someone notices I'm gone," the woman said, a panicked look on her face.

"Return?" Firas said. "How? The gates are locked and barred for the night."

Johanna looked at the gates dwarfing the figures of Alma and Hayat and the guards. "Milady? Is there another way out of the castle?"

The morning dawned bright and a little chilly, a welcome relief from the heat of the day before, but it wouldn't last. From the heights of L'Arête one could see a layer of insubstantial mist collecting in the hills and hollows of the mountains west and north of the castle, making the weird shapes of the rocky spires look horrifyingly animate and inherently evil. The farmlands to the east disappeared into an accumulating haze.

The troupe, packs shouldered, had arrived at the gate just as it opened and were taken fond leave of by the guard stationed there. One pulled Jaufre aside and confided a new joke that might make it into the next show, and he laughed and slapped the fellow's back and slid a penny into his hand. He hailed the other guard and retold the joke, with embellishments, and the three of them roared with more laughter.

The two guards did not notice that the troupe had increased by one, a slender figure wrapped in a gray cloak emerging from the morning shadows to mingle with them as they passed through the last gate. Hayat slipped an arm around her waist and pretended to be whispering something in her ear. Tiphaine skipped along on her other side, juggling her rag balls, and the rest of them moved back and forth, changing places continuously to create a confusion to the eyes. Alaric took the lead with Pascau firmly in tow, so the boatman noticed nothing untoward, not at first.

They moved down the little road that switched back and forth across the face of the mountain. "More slowly, if you please," Firas said, waving over his shoulder at a group of children hanging over the village wall. Everyone tried to but it was difficult not to break into a run. The lack of cover made them imagine arrows trained on their backs from every direction. It was a positive relief when they reached the top of the hill across the valley and turned to wave their goodbyes for the last time before disappearing around a corner and down the other side.

"Félicien, what—"

"Not now!"

"She's right," Shasha said. "To the river as fast as ever we can."

"Who is that?" Pascau said, noticing for the first time that they were now eleven, not ten.

"It doesn't matter," Jaufre said. "Lead us back to the boat and get us across to Avignon."

Pascau looked alarmed, as one who lived seven leagues from L'Aréte might well be. "A gold florin over and above your pay and you'll never see us again," Firas said.

The mention of gold was enough to soothe the boatman's anxiety, at least for the moment, but Johanna thought that the sooner they were out of Avignon the better.

They force marched all that day and all of that night, again keeping to the shadows beneath the trees, this time in fear of meeting Ambroise on the road coming back. They stopped only to eat of their remaining meager rations and relieve themselves, and reached the river before noon the next day. Pascau, possibly motivated by the thought of the gold florin that waited for him on the other side, possibly just wanting to be well rid of these dangerous passengers, rowed them across with a will.

"Find us a boat going upriver," Jaufre said. "Preferably one leaving today." Tiphaine, Firas and Alaric scattered. The rest of them repaired to an inn with a common room large enough to lose themselves in and ate the first hot meal they'd had in days. Johanna, eyes adjusting from the blazing sun to the cool darkness, saw the servants bustling round with laden trays and slopping pitchers through a faint veil of incredulity. They'd done it. They had penetrated the defenses of L'Arête itself and come off scathless. She turned her head to look at Félicien. And they had rescued their comrade.

Félicien leaned back against the wall, the gray hood drooping around her face. Johanna thought she had her eyes closed but couldn't be sure. Everyone else was looking at Félicien, too. Félicien had yet to say how she had come to join them and they had no idea how soon the alarm would be raised in L'Arête. Perhaps it already had been. Perhaps a guard was even now galloping for Avignon with the news for his lord.

Meanwhile, they were back in Avignon, and in a room full of loud conversation they were an oasis of silence. It was occasioning a few looks. Johanna cleared her throat and smiled. "This is good bread, isn't it," she said, tearing into a piece with her teeth. "And excellent small beer."

"I, uh, don't know when I've tasted better," Hayat said.

"We should ask for the name of their brewer," Hari said, a man who to Johanna's certain knowledge had never touched alcohol of any kind.

"Do you think it will rain tomorrow?" Alma said brightly.

It was Tiphaine, of course, who found them a boat going in the right direction, departing the following morning. They took a room and spent a tense night during which no one got any sleep.

Ambroise de L'Arête was still in Avignon. "He's staying in a house near the palace," Tiphaine said. "On the rue Pey—" She stumbled over the word.

"The Rue Peyrollerie," Johanna said.

"That's right," Tiphaine said, surprised. "How did you know?"

"He mentioned it," Johanna said. "When he came for the boys."

"You've seen him, then," Félicien said. She was curled in a corner, as much apart from the rest of them as possible in the cramped space. It was the first time she had spoken since they had left L'Arête.

"Yes," Johanna said. "Here, in Avignon, before we left for L'Arête. I, uh, met his pages, and I was still with them when he came for them."

Félicien gave a sound that was nothing like the lighthearted laugh they were used to hear from her. "Pages," she said.

"Yes," Johanna said slowly. "The four boys who wear his livery. Guilham. Bernart. I don't remember the names of the other two."

She waited, they all did, but Félicien said nothing more.

The next morning they waited in their room until there was just enough time to get from the inn to the quayside before debarking, and slipped outside in twos and threes so as to attract less attention. It was a market day and the streets were already crowded with carts and stalls and it seemed the entire city of Avignon had come outside the walls, determined to enjoy the unseasonal weather while it lasted. All the better to be lost in a crowd, Johanna thought.

They had reverted to their travel clothes, tucking away all vestiges of the troubadours who had entertained L'Arête so well. They moved at a slow, steady pace, determined to avoid attention and keeping their eyes on the ground except when necessary to navigation.

Which was why they almost walked straight into Ambroise de L'Arête. Walking with Jaufre and Félicien, all the warning Johanna got was a glimpse of black and silver. She stopped dead in her tracks. The bullish body dressed in incongruously elegant attire, topped by that leonine head, moved through a crowd that knew instinctively to give way before it. The four pages followed, towed irresistibly in his wake, but Johanna wasn't looking at them. She was looking at Pascau, whose arm was grasped firmly in Ambroise's hand, and who looked like already regretting his bargain.

They were headed in the direction of the quay. Johanna caught the arms of her companions and began to steer them around Ambroise's route and on toward their destination.

"What?" Jaufre said. He'd felt the tension in her grasp.

"Ambroise," she said, breathing the name through stiff lips.

Félicien started, but she said nothing and she didn't faint.

They made their way forward, the crowd thinning as they reached the wharf, not daring to look behind them, although there was a spot between Johanna's shoulder blades that had commenced a furious itching, one she was sure that both her companions were experiencing, too. She wondered where the others were and if they'd seen Ambroise. So far of them he knew only Jaufre, Alaric, Félicien and, perhaps, Johanna herself, although she had effaced herself that day in the Place des Papes as soon as humanly possible. But Pascau knew them all. Her step quickened in spite of herself. She had no desire for flying lessons from the Lord of L'Arête.

"There," Jaufre said, and she looked and to see the mast that Tiphaine had told them to look for. She was a little river freighter, with a broad, shallow hold and a single mast. The square brown sail was being hauled up as they approached, and she saw with relief Shasha's face peering anxiously over the rail, Firas at her shoulder. They allowed their pace to quicken. When they got to the boat they didn't bother with the ladder, Jaufre caught up Félicien and tossed her up into Firas' waiting arms. Johanna was already halfway up the ladder when Firas was setting Félicien on her feet, with Jaufre close behind her.

As they achieved the deck a rotund, authoritative individual cracked out orders, lines were loosed and they slipped from the quay into the current.

"This way," Shasha said, and led the way forward to the bow. The rest of their companions were already there. No one, wisely, was hanging over the gunnel to see if Ambroise was in sight on the dock.

Félicien subsided to the deck with her back to the mast. She kept her head down and her face covered by her hood.

"Félicien—" Jaufre said.

"Not now," she said, and such was the urgency in her voice that they left her alone.

"Give her time," Shasha said, patting Jaufre's shoulder.

The sail luffed and then caught the mistrau and billowed out with a crack, to be quickly close-hauled by the crew. Downriver traffic adhered to the western side of the river, leaving the center and the eastern side to the upriver traffic. Their course was a series of short tacks, a continual back and forth against the wind. The ship's crew was kept constantly on the hop, and Wu Company stayed in the bow and kept out of their way.

Between the current and the mistrau, their speed upriver was kept to not much more than their speed downriver had been, but they were away, blessedly out of Ambroise's reach. With the relaxation of tension they were overtaken by a sense of extreme fatigue and spent most of that first day dozing with their heads pillowed on their packs. Except to relieve herself in the half barrel provided for deck passengers, Félicien kept to her position at the mast. No one had much to say. Alaric sat facing forward in the bow, his back to the rest of them, stiff with disapproval.

"But at least we could count on him when we needed to," Shasha said to Firas. It was late the third evening.

Firas grunted. They were laying on her cloak and wrapped in his, looking up at the stars in the night sky. Night showed fall's true colors with a considerable drop in temperature and everyone was wearing all the clothes they had brought with them.

Someone moved and Shasha raised her head. "It's Félicien."

"Shasha—"

She patted his arm and followed the girl. Alaric had rolled himself into his bedroll and was snoring slightly. Félicien was standing in his place in the bow. Shasha came up to stand behind her. "Félicien."

"Shasha."

So hard and cold was her voice that Shasha was at something of a loss as what to say next. "Are you well?"

A brittle laugh. "As well as can be expected." A pause. "Why did you come?"

Shasha smiled a little. She could smile, now that they had satisfied Jaufre's mad obsession, and now that they were all safe. "Jaufre would not allow us to rest until you were free once more."

"The fool!" Félician whispered. "All of you, such rash and reckless fools!" She turned and put back her head, and the same moon that had shone down on them in the courtyard before the castle of L'Arête shone down on her face now. She looked as if she had aged twenty years in the months they had been apart. "I traded myself for you, Shasha. For all of you. The only thing that kept me in L'Arête was the thought that you were free."

"He understood that, Félicien. But he could not accept it. And neither could we."

"He will come for me," Félicien said, and then she gave that humorless laugh. "Ambroise. He will come for it."

"And we will deal with that when it happens," Shasha said.

"Fools," Félicien whispered. "You are all fools. And soon to be dead fools."

"How did you get out?"

Félicien sighed. "The same way I did before. There is a secret passage from a place hidden near the kitchen. It exits in the shrubbery near the outer gate, very close to where I joined you. My father said it was built by his grandfather. Ambroise knows nothing of it."

"It's how you joined the troubadours?"

"I didn't leave with them. I just left at the same time they did. I hoped Ambroise would think to follow them instead of looking for me."

Shasha wondered what had happened to the troubadours. "And the woman who came to us?"

"Laloun? She is my maid. She was still at L'Arête when I—when I returned. I tried to make her come with me but she said where the guards might not notice one, they would be sure to notice two. She's pretending to be me, keeping to my room until someone discovers her."

Shasha thought of the thin, terrified woman in the courtyard of L'Arête. "She must love you very much."

Félicien made no reply.

"I see that you have need to relieve yourself quite often, and that you have been sick over the side, more than once," Shasha said. "Are you with child?"

Félicien shuddered. "Laloun believes so," she said, the hard, cold note back in her voice. She looked at Shasha, eyes black as the night around them. "Can you get rid of it for me?"

Shasha was silent for a moment, and not because the question was unexpected. "There are certain herbs," she said. "They are very dangerous, and they don't always work."

"I don't care if they kill me," Félicien said. "I want this devil's spawn out of my body as soon as ever you can help me to do so. Or I want to be dead." That cold, bitter laugh again. "Either will do, and perhaps the one is more attractive than the other."

There was nothing to be said to that, at least not at present. "The pages," Shasha said. "What did you mean when you spoke of them in that way?"

"Ambroise doesn't like women but he needs an heir to secure his position as lord of L'Arête," Félicien said. "He likes boys. Little boys. His pages are all chosen for looks and age. The instant one turns thirteen he is dismissed back to his family with a handsome reward."

She choked and clapped her hand to her mouth. She turned abruptly to face forward again, taking in deep, cleansing breaths of air. Behind them, Shasha sensed an alertness in the company, although they neither moved nor spoke. Alaric had stopped snoring. They were all awake, and listening. It was as well, because Shasha didn't think Félicien could have told her story twice.

"He couldn't—he could barely—he had to bring in one of the boys and—God, I hate him. I hated him touching me. It makes me ill. The very thought of it disgusts me. It always has. I don't know how any woman can bear it."

"You could have become a nun," Alaric said.

"Or I could have had myself locked in a dungeon for life and been done with it!" Félicien said, almost shouting.

Prudently, no one else offered commentary.

Félicien bent forward from the waist and was suddenly and comprehensively sick over the side. Shasha rubbed her back until she straightened, wiping her mouth on a corner of her cloak. "Afterward, the boy vomited, and Ambroise took him outside to see if he could fly. Do you know what that means? Do you, Shasha?"

"Yes, we know."

"Their parents must have heard something," Félicien said. She sounded exhausted now. "A messenger came from them, demanding the return of their son. It's why Audouard took the rest of the troop to their château, why they were gone when you came, why the guard was so lax." She began to laugh, half hysterical. "Little Roubin died so I could escape. Isn't that funny, Shasha? Isn't it?"

Shasha moved forward to take Félicien in a secure embrace that ignored every effort to throw it off. "Sit down, Félicien. Sit down here, and take comfort. You are with us now. Free once again to determine the course of your own life."

"I won't be free until you rid me of this incubus in my belly."

Félicien spoke no more, her confidences at an end. Soon she dozed off, jerking and whimpering now and then in her sleep. Shasha went back to her place at Firas' side and was grateful for the warmth of his body to take the chill from her flesh.

Johanna could not sleep, eyes wide and staring blindly up at the starry sky.

By his breathing, Jaufre lay wakeful, too, throughout all of that very long night.

· Twelve ·

Late fall, 1325 A.D.
Lyon and environs

———

They debarked at Lyon with due haste and went directly to Sieur Imbert's. He came forward to kiss Johanna's hand and smile warmly into her eyes.

Sieur Imbert," she said, allowing it. "Well met."

"Sieur Imbert? Surely it was Phillippe the last time we met?"

She had the grace to blush. "Phillippe then. Forgive our manners, but we are in something of a hurry."

"You are returning to Venice?"

They had discussed this thoroughly on the boat. Félicien—she would not answer to any other pronunciation—had told them, and repeated herself with bitter emphasis. "He is coming. He is right behind us. He won't stop. He wants this—" she clenched her fist and struck herself in the belly, not gently "—he needs it to reinforce his title to L'Arête, and he won't stop until he has possession of it again." Her face twisted. "And he won't want to have to go through a second time what he went through to get it the first."

She had paused, and then turned abruptly and was sick over the side. Other than a little water she had been unable to keep anything down, and she seemed to grow thinner and paler with every passing hour. She wiped her mouth on the hem of her cloak. "He is coming." She looked at Jaufre and said angrily, "I traded myself for you! And look how you treated the gift of your lives!"

Jaufre opened his mouth to respond but Firas said, "Did Ambroise travel to Avignon with only the ten spearmen?"

Félicien frowned, her near hysteria arrested by the assassin's calm manner. "I don't—no. He took Florian. And the four pages, of course." Her lips twisted. "John likes his vassals to put on a bit of a show."

It took a moment for them to realize that she meant Pope John.

"With Ambroise, that makes twelve armed, experienced men." Firas was silent for a moment, hands on his belt, a calculating look in his eyes. Presently he said, "I believe Félicien is correct. Ambroise will be coming, and he won't be coming alone." He looked around with a slight smile. "Well, we are not exactly toothless ourselves, and he won't expect any of the women to be able with arms, so we may even have a slight advantage."

"I know something else he won't be expecting," Johanna said.

Alma and Hayat looked at her, and then at each other. "No," Hayat said. "No, he won't."

Firas looked at Johanna. "Oh. Ah. Yes. I had forgotten. Very well. We need a plan."

"We can't go back to Venice," Johanna said. "This trouble started there and followed us here." She paused. "What happened to Jean de Valmy? Did anyone see him at L'Arête? Or in Avignon?"

"Ambroise killed him just after we left you, rather than pay him the rest of his Judas price," Félicien said drearily. "They dragged his body into the woods and left him for carrion."

It might be the one action taken by Ambroise de L'Arête that they could all approve of. Johanna wondered what had happened to Pascau. "We can't return to Venice," she said again. "This trouble could follow us back to Gradenigo. We owe him too much to take the chance."

"There are merchant fairs north of Paris," Firas said. "I have heard people speaking of them."

"We have nothing to trade at present," Johanna said.

"Chartres," Alaric said.

"Where is Chartres?" someone said, and someone else said, "Why Chartres?"

"A hundred leagues, maybe a little more," Alaric said. "North and west of here. And because I have a friend there who may be able to advise us."

Jaufre glanced at him but held his peace. From the conversation between Alaric and Gilbert, he wouldn't have thought that Alaric and Wilmot would have much to say to each other, or that a stonemason would be especially able to advise them on matters of trade. "Everyone I've talked to since we stepped ashore in Venice wants wool," he said. "By all accounts the best wool comes from the north. Let's go look for wool."

Afterward, Jaufre wondered at the spark of satisfaction he saw in Alaric's eyes when the group decided on Chartres. Much later, he wondered if Alaric's irritation at riding to Félicien's rescue might have been less because he disapproved of their violating the sanctified bond of marriage than because they were riding in the wrong direction.

"Ambroise will come," Félicien said in a hopeless voice. "He will kill you all."

"No," Johanna said. "No, Félicien, he won't." She leaned forward and grasped Félicien's hand. "He won't. Trust me, Félicien. Trust us. Firas? Let's work on that plan."

"Indeed, young miss," Firas said. "Let's."

Here in the present, in Lyon, Johanna smiled at Gradenigo's agent and said, "No, Phillippe, not Venice. We thought we'd try our luck in the north."

Firas, Jaufre and Alaric retrieved their weapons from Sieur Imbert's warehouse and spent a day giving everything in their armory a new and sharper edge, in case the plan went awry. Shasha scoured the markets for supplies. Alma and Hayat returned to the convent to inquire after maps apropos to this journey. Hari went to the cathedral to insinuate himself into the bosom of the clergy there and perhaps acquire some names of brother clergy in Chartres who might look kindly on visitors from Outremer.

The next morning Johanna and Tiphaine walked to the farm where their mounts were stabled, some two leagues south of town. North Wind caught Johanna's scent on the mistrau and they heard him trumpeting half a league away. Dusty, hungry and thirsty, Johanna broke into a trot, bypassed the farmhouse and went straight for the paddock in which the great white stallion was stamping up and down. The fenceposts around him were made from sawn lengths of tree trunks buried deep in the ground, which explained why he was still inside them. Johanna undid the latch on the gate and North Wind thundered up and whickered and whiffed down her neck and back and sides and around her waist and between her legs and under her arms until, laughing uncontrollably, partly from relief that he was still here, she caught a handful of his mane in one hand and vaulted astride. He went from a standstill to a full gallop and she wound her hands in his mane and flattened herself against his neck and let him go. Behind them she could hear Tiphaine whooping and shouting. Her eyes blurred with tears, not all generated from the wind forceful enough to blow the braid out of her hair. Félicien was free, none of their company had died in L'Arête, and she was on North Wind's back again. In this moment it was more than enough.

After what felt like a league at a full gallop she judged it safe enough to pull North Wind into a canter and turn him back toward the farm. As she approached she saw the farmer and his wife and two children gathered outside the front door of their farmhouse. Tiphaine was perched on top of a fencepost, waving her scarf over her head. The farmer was grinning, but his wife and children looked as if they'd bolt inside at the first opportunity.

Johanna stopped at a safe distance, or as safe as North Wind would ever be, swung her right leg over and slid to the ground on legs that trembled just a little. Her smile trembled just a little, too.

"That big one, he thinks he is so tough," the farmer said, coming forward, "but he missed you. He pined for you, I swear it."

"I pined for him, too, Glaude."

He grinned again. "He would have been all the better for a gallop every day, but no one had the courage to try to get on his back."

She stepped back and ran her hands down the stallion's flanks and legs. "He looks well, very well indeed. I am grateful for your care of him."

Glaude shrugged. "*C'est normal.*"

"And the others?"

Glaude shrugged again. "Eating their heads off." He cocked his head. "One of my mares came fresh while you were away. I put the black to her."

Her turn to shrug. "You had my permission." Her turn to cock her head. "Not North Wind?"

He shook his head. "She is small, my Celestine. I would not burden her with a too-large foal." He jerked his head at North Wind. "He could smell her. He wasn't happy."

Johanna laughed. "I can imagine."

The wife came forward, a little fluttery, one wary eye on North Wind. "Please, come in and refresh yourselves."

They adjourned to the farmhouse, which was old even in these parts, and small, snug and immaculate. A sharp word and both children scurried to lay the long table in front of the hearth with bread and cheese and olives and a pitcher of water. "The water is good," she said, "we have our own spring," and took a drink to prove it. Everyone sat down and ate heartily. At last Johanna sat back with a sigh. "That was wonderful, Magali. Thank you."

The housewife beamed, and cuffed her son, who was pinching his sister.

"Outside, the pair of you, and feed the chickens." She refilled Johanna's cup and her husband's, and bustled about setting her kitchen to rights.

"Glaude, I wonder if you have room here somewhere for ten of us. Perhaps tonight, and definitely tomorrow night and perhaps for a third night, but that would be all."

He considered. "We have not beds enough—" a wave of his hand indicated the farmhouse, which was not large "—but there is a loft in the barn. It is clean, and there is hay to make your beds. And you may use the spring, of course."

Johanna smiled. "Hay beds are a luxury for the likes of us. Can you feed us, too? We will be happy to pay."

They agreed on a price, and Johanna spent the afternoon going over the horses and their tack, which was in better repair than when she had left it behind. She remonstrated with Glaude, who waved a hand and said again, "C'est normal."

Perhaps rendering kindness to strangers was normal in this part of the world, Johanna thought. She was immeasurably soothed by the notion. No one joined them that evening and after a hearty dinner of pottage and bread Johanna sang and Tiphaine taught "the children" (as she referred to them) how to do a basic fountain, which she did not see fit to tell them she herself had only learned how to do not three weeks before. Everyone went to bed pleased with themselves.

The rest of Wu Company arrived in good order the next day at mid-afternoon. Félicien had new clothes in unrelieved black, tunic and trousers and cloak, and tough new boots. When her hood fell back Johanna could see that she looked far from well, and as soon as she dismounted she went to the edge of the trees and was sick.

Jaufre was watching her with a worried expression. "She's been continually ill," Shasha said. "I don't know how far or how fast she is going to be able to travel."

"Is this normal for pregnant women?"

"Not to this extent, nor of this violence, not in my experience. She has diarrhea, too."

"What?" Johanna said, when Shasha seemed reluctant to say more.

Shasha drew Johanna to one side and lowered her voice. "I consulted a midwife in Lyon. She says there are cases, very rare, of pregnant women who suffer excessive, constant vomiting and diarrhea throughout the first months. It frequently leads to miscarriage."

They looked at Félicien, still standing at the edge of the trees, bent over, shoulders heaving. Jaufre approached and said something they couldn't hear. They did hear Félicien tell him to go away, and so did everyone else.

"Miscarriage?" Johanna said.

"Yes," Shasha said. "Even, in extreme cases, the death of the mother as well."

"Is there nothing you can do?"

"The only thing that might help would be to confine her to bed. She would want to know why."

Their eyes met. Johanna said nothing. There was nothing to be said. They had to leave very soon, whether Félicien could travel or not, and if Shasha told Félicien what might happen, Félicien would be the first of them on a horse.

They stayed two nights at the farm and woke the morning of their departure in the hour before dawn and were riding out of the farmyard before the family had woken. Johanna left a pouch filled with coin on the sill of the window next to the door, and sent a silent wish for good fortune to follow Glaude and Magali and their children always.

There was a well-traveled road near Glaude's farm that ran north to Paris but they had decided to keep clear of the road and so struck out through the forest, made up of mature trees with broad canopies of leaves turning gold and orange and red. There was little undergrowth, certainly nothing like the choked countryside around L'Arête, and the horses had no trouble picking their way.

It was a cool morning beneath clear skies, and after so many days without rain the ground was hard as iron. They kept to a brisk walk and gradually the land began to rise. Firas was riding ahead and Alaric behind, and both came cantering up when the party emerged on a knoll covered in sweet grass and a tiny spring bubbling up out of the ground. The sun was well up by now and they dismounted to break their fast.

And that of course was when Ambroise sprung his trap, catching them out of the saddle, weapons sheathed, food in hand.

They emerged out of the tree line, the lord of L'Arête, Florian, ten mounted spearmen and four boys who rode two to a horse and looked cold, tired, and terrified. The men held spears at the ready. No one had bothered with bows, Johanna noted, probably because arrows occasionally went anywhere and the count's lady was among them.

Ambroise was dressed in the same black and silver Johanna had seen him in in Avignon, with additions. The sword at his side did not look the least bit ornamental and his neck, shoulders and arms were thick with muscle, statement enough that he knew how to use it. He wore a round helm with a nose guard and a cuirass, both of black steel polished to a dull gleam. He rode an immense black destrier who was curried to a fare-thee-well, tacked up in black leather and whose hooves looked oiled that morning.

Together they formed a single weapon that gave every appearance of being unstoppable, invincible, ultimately lethal. It was a first blow struck before the battle had even begun.

A veritable Prince of Darkness, Johanna thought, an appearance deliberately designed to intimidate and if possible frighten.

North Wind snorted and sidled and she realized that her hands had tightened on his reins. Her heart was thumping in her chest hard enough to escape and run away on its own, and she didn't seem to be able to catch her breath.

Yes. It was possible.

She took a deep breath and walked forward to stand next to Félicien. Behind her North Wind stamped his displeasure.

Jaufre had his sword out before Alaric and Firas, but only just. Johanna, Alma and Hayat did not reach for theirs.

"I'll go with him," Félicien said. She sounded tired.

They ignored her, spreading into a half circle that would have looked rehearsed to anyone paying attention. Johanna and Félicien hung back. Alma, Hayat and Hari scattered to the sides of the clearing but did not go so far as to disappear into the trees.

"My dear Féliciennc, you most certainly will go with me, but it will avail your companions nothing," Ambroise said. "You gave me your word, you broke it, and I, as you well know, always pay my debts in full." Ambroise pulled his sword and nudged his mount forward "In fact it will give me very great pleasure to dispatch them one by one myself, while you watch."

Jaufre stepped into his path and his sword was dealt a contemptuous blow that had it flying from his hand. He tumbled back just out of the reach of Ambroise's sword. Firas fell back into a guard stance and was similarly dealt with, and Alaric as well, although this was the part of the plan they had had the most trouble getting Alaric to agree to. "You never learn, old man," Ambroise said.

Alaric regained his feet and glowered.

Now Ambroise was facing Félicien, and Johanna.

Johanna said, she hoped clearly over the thundering of her heart, "You may not have her, Ambroise."

"Ah yes, the lady in the Place des Papes," Ambroise said. His smile bared his teeth and no more. "You made only one mistake. Well, two, actually. You stayed around long enough for me to notice you, and you wore the same sigil as your friends there." He gestured at Wu Company's badge. "It wasn't difficult to find word of that sigil, and of you, in Lyon, which led me directly to Sieur Imbert." His smile was thin. "He was persuaded to tell us all he knew very quickly indeed."

Johanna knew a pang of remorse and then a flare of anger. "You may not take Félicien again," she said again and stepped forward, well within reach of Ambroise's sword.

"Johanna—" Jaufre said.

The count laughed. "Too little, too late, boy. Your lady friend appears eager to go to her death." He drew back his sword to strike with an almost lazy gesture. Johanna dodged the edge of the blade, just, tumbling forward to come perilously close to the destrier's front hooves. She screamed. She screamed very loudly and very impressively. The destrier, uneasy, began to dance. A hoof struck and pain flashed up her arm. She screamed again, this time in good earnest, and kept rolling forward so that she was directly beneath the black war horse. She kicked out at his legs, connecting about half the time. The destrier stumbled and Ambroise cursed. Johanna kept screaming.

North Wind had had a trying few months. He had been force marched over the Alps from Milano to Lyon with no chance to stretch his legs in a race. In Lyon he had been imprisoned on a farm, where, to add insult to injury, when a mare came into season no one had availed themselves of his superior services. His human had gone away and left him for an unconscionable amount of time, the longest they had been separated since leaving Cambaluc. Behind a fence even he couldn't break down and it wasn't for lack of trying.

He'd just got her back, and now she was screaming. He'd just gotten her back and someone or something was trying to hurt her.

Enough.

Before Florian or the spearmen or the boys or Ambroise himself could react, North Wind yanked up his picket, which had been knocked only loosely into the ground to begin with, and sounded a thunderous challenge. Anyone who had ever seen him race would have recognized the standing start that was his signature. One moment he was standing still, looking half asleep, and the next he was charging forward at full speed. He roared a challenge that could have been heard back in Lyon, terrifying the rest of the horses, theirs and Ambroise's alike. It didn't help that none of Ambroise's men, or indeed Ambroise himself expected any resistance from a bunch of money-grubbing traders. This was supposed to be a simple slaughter and a reclaiming of property.

Instead the horses plunged, reared, plunged, neighed, and plunged again, bucking and twisting, their instinctive desire to get away, to get right away right now, as far as they could get as fast as they could go. Two of the boys fell off. One of the spearmen nearly did. Two of the spearmen's mounts got their bits firmly between their teeth, yanked the reins from their riders' hands and crashed through the trees to disappear. The rest of them were fully occupied in trying to bring their terrorized mounts under control.

Johanna waited until the very last moment, trading a few more kicks with the destrier, and scrambled from beneath the destrier's belly and rolled clear. The others of her company were following suit with promptness and agility. North Wind thundered down on Ambroise, who raised his totally inadequate sword in a pitiful semblance of defense before the great white stallion slammed into the black destrier and knocked him completely off his feet. He fell heavily on his side with a thump that shook the ground and set a few branches swaying. He lay there, wheezing his astonishment.

Ambroise barely got his leg up out of the way in time and stagger to his feet. He raised his sword to the great white stallion rearing before him. North Wind treated this puny defiance with the contempt it deserved, and broke Ambroise's sword arm with his left front hoof and cracked Ambroise's breastbone with his right front hoof. Ambroise's sword fell from a suddenly numb hand. Ambroise fell on top of it.

North Wind dropped to all fours and did something Johanna had seen him do only once before, in a little campsite south of Talikan when two men had thought to take advantage of three unarmed women. He hopped. He hopped straight up into the air and came down on all four feet, landing directly on Ambroise. One hoof missed altogether, one sheared off an ear, the remaining two landed directly on his chest. The sound of cracking ribs echoed around the clearing.

North Wind hopped again, bellowing his outrage. This time his rear hooves landed on Ambroise's pelvis. Ambroise screamed, louder even than Johanna had.

Possibly affronted by a noise made by someone else other than himself, North Wind hopped a third time. Both front hooves landed on Ambroise's face. There was a crack and a sort of a splash and his skull split and his brains and blood splattered across the grass, to lay glistening red and gray in the morning sun.

The lord of L'Arête's screams stopped.

North Wind snorted and turned to find Johanna. Finding her, he sniffed her all over. She smelled like herself, although she was pulling rather hard at his mane to hold herself up. No matter. She was well, which meant all was well in North Wind's world. He raised his head and bugled his triumph, terrifying all the other horses a second time. Satisfied, he dropped his head and nudged Johanna to scratch behind his ears. She did so, noticing in some dazed part of her mind that her hand was shaking. She did not look down at his hooves. She looked up instead, to see Tiphaine peering from behind the trunk of a tree at the edge of the clearing, her dark eyes enormous. Johanna fought to bring a smile to her lips but they were trembling, too.

Ambroise's men got their horses back under control and stared at the broken mess that had been their leader with white faces. "You—you did that on purpose," one of them said.

Jaufre, like Firas and Alaric back on his feet, sword at the ready, said baldly, "Yes." He recognized the man as Florian, Ambroise's lieutenant.

"We will kill you all," Florian said.

"You can," Firas said, stepping forward. "But we won't go easily."

"And we'll be sure to take some of you with us," Hayat said. She was flanked by Alma and by Johanna, who stepped around North Wind to stand with them, all three with swords drawn. L'Arête's men looked at them askance. They were only women, of course, but one similarly trained couldn't help but notice the easy assurance with which they held their weapons. They appeared, incredibly, to have had some past experience, and if there was one thing a soldier disliked, it was unknowns in battle. It was the unknowns that would get you killed. These women looked like they knew how.

"But why should it come to that?" Hari said soothingly, coming forward and smiling his warm smile at the lieutenant. "You're Florian, aren't you?"

Such was Ambroise's reputation that Florian had not seen this much naked steel arrayed against him in a long time. He had forgotten how the edges gleamed in the sun. He felt the sudden uncertainty in the men at his back. "Yes," he said.

"You were the lord's second in command?"

"Yes?"

"And…" When Florian said nothing Hari tut-tutted, and said kindly, as one explaining something to a child, "And there is no one left in L'Arête above you in rank?"

Realization dawned on Florian's face. "No," he said. "No. There isn't." He hesitated, and looked at Félicien.

"You must press your claim without me," she said. "I will never return to L'Arête. In this company, before these witnesses, I renounce all claims to L'Arête and its attendant properties." The finality in her voice convinced them all, even Florian. "One thing, however."

"What?"

"What happened to Laloun, my maid? She put herself in my place so that I could escape."

"She is locked in the dungeon, awaiting my lord's return."

Félicien gave a thin smile. "There will be no flying lessons for her, Florian. Let her go."

He stared at her.

"That is my price," she said. "Let her go, and you will never see me again. I will never contest with you for the title of L'Arête. It is yours. Do with it what you will. All I ask is that you let Laloun go."

He wavered visibly. Hari pressed Félicien's words home, even walking forward to stand within weapon's reach and staring up into the lieutenant's face, his expression calm and serene and wholly without fear. "Go directly back to L'Arête and see things secure there. Then go to the Pope and demand title by right of conquest. If you go to him first, he can then give it away to anyone he wants, so don't give him the opportunity. Take L'Arête and hold it for yourself, and then ask for his blessing."

There was a brief silence where no one moved.

"If you're going to do so, you'd better do it now," Jaufre said.

"Indeed," Firas said, and went so far as to sheathe his scimitar and tuck his thumbs into his belt. "Who knows what has happened in L'Arête in your absence? Another man could be thinking the same thing." He glanced at the pages. "There are those with motive enough."

Florian followed his gaze to the boys, and his mouth set in a grim line.

"Let Laloun go," Félicien said again. "Give her a horse and money and tell her to make for Lyon and Sieur Imbert." She hesitated. "You didn't kill him, did you?"

Florian gave a short laugh. "There was no need. He told us everything we wanted to know almost without our asking."

"As we told him to do," Jaufre said, determined that the Blade's men understand that this morning had been a trap into which they had ridden all unknowing.

When they were working out the details of their plan, Firas had said, "Ambroise will not consider us a threat. We will use that arrogance to our advantage." They had waited to be sure that Ambroise had had enough time in Lyon to track down Sieur Ambert, who had instructions to give them up as soon as he was asked. Firas and Alaric had scouted ahead to find the most suitable place to be ambushed in, and had withdrawn back to the farm, there to wait another night so that Ambroise and his men could set their trap, all unknowing that a different trap had already been set, for them.

"What if they decide to take us at the farm?" Johanna said.

Firas had shaken his head. "This isn't his territory. Remember Sant' Alberto. He chose to ambush Félicien somewhere without witnesses. He will do the same here."

"I don't want Glaude and his family hurt," she said.

"They won't be," Alaric said. "Firas is right, Ambroise will wish to draw as little attention as possible to the fact that he lost his wife a second time." He looked at Johanna. "Are you sure North Wind will react as you say?"

Johanna, Firas, Alma and Hayat had only smiled.

Now, Florian flushed darkly, and Jaufre was satisfied. "Then let us go our separate ways in peace."

Florian hesitated for a moment longer, but only a moment. "Audouard! Retrieve Ambroise's body and find something to wrap it in."

What was left of L'Arête was rolled into in one of the spearmen's bedroll and tied across this saddle. Bits and pieces persisted in falling off until they tied both ends of the bedroll with strips of hide. The lieutenant tied the reins of the destrier to his saddle and, with a long, last look at the members of Wu Company, Hari smiling benignly, the rest grim and determined, moved out. The two unhorsed boys scrambled back on their mounts and kicked them into a trot. The last Johanna saw of them as they disappeared into the trees was Guilham's astonished face as he twisted round in his seat behind.

"What happens to them?" she said.

"If Florian really wishes to hold L'Arête, he'll send them back to their parents," Alaric said. "Otherwise he will have in his keeping four excellent excuses for sieges. Especially if their parents are at all ambitious."

"I expect they'll be glad to go," Johanna said.

His gaze was somber. "I expect so."

· Thirteen ·

Winter, 1325-1326 A.D.
Chartres

⊢——⟶

The fine weather broke the next day. The heavens opened up and it rained day and night. Their clothes were wet, their bedrolls were wet, their horses were so wet they steamed. Every inn they came to was already packed to the rafters with people seeking shelter and they slept outside more often than not. They all had colds, and Félicien was still sick all day every day and throughout most of her nights.

The terrain was easy enough and the road well marked for a change, but the hundred leagues to Chartres felt like a thousand. They were twelve days in transit, and of course the rain started to taper off their last day en route. The next morning dawned, if not clear then at least with high clouds and blessedly no rain. The forest had given way to rolling fields of stubbled grain. At noon Shasha said, "What's that?" and they followed her pointing finger to the massive stone spires rising up from the horizon, as if to knock at the very doors of heaven itself.

"That would be the cathedral," Alaric said, spurring up from the rear. Firas returned from scouting ahead to confirm that they had, indeed, reached their destination. A feeling of mild exhilaration swept over the company, even Jaufre, who had spent the journey with his chin on his shoulder, could relax a little. He didn't trust Florian to keep his word. Félicien was too great a prize.

"Are we Wu Company again," Tiphaine said, "or are we still Jerome's

Jongleurs?"

"Wu Company, I beg you," Alaric said in a tone so dry it surprised a laugh out of the rest of them. The farther north they traveled, the lighter of heart Alaric seemed to become. It was a pleasant change.

Chartres was a small, prosperous town clustered around its crowning glory, the cathedral, an immense and awe-inspiring edifice of stone surrounded by flying buttresses and surmounted with two towers in two different styles. The town around it bustled with inns and taverns, and shops selling everything from cockleshells to shards of the True Cross. One busy agent was organizing pilgrimages north to Notre Dame in Paris and south to Santiago de Compostela in Galicia, with a sideline in same to Jerusalem, via Venice.

"I feel right at home," Johanna said.

They found a comfortable, commodious inn with excellent stabling and settled in with a sense of relief. Jaufre investigated the state of his trouser hem and went off to find a gem dealer who might be interested in purchasing a ruby, since Chartres was too busy a town for cheap lodgings. Shasha disappeared for the entire day and returned that evening with an elderly woman with a severely curved spine who walked with the assistance of two sticks. She had wise eyes and a quiet, calm manner. They vanished upstairs for an hour and then the old woman came down alone and left, the sound of her sticks on stones tapping off into the distance.

Johanna went softly up the stairs and down the hall and knocked on the door. "Shasha? It's Johanna."

"Come in." Félicien turned her head on the pillow and gave a weak smile. Shasha was lifting a covered chamber pot in preparation for emptying it outside. "I'll be right back," she said with a smile. As she brushed by Johanna, she murmured, "See if you can get her to talk."

Johanna shut the door behind her and brought a stool next to the bed. Sitting down, she said lightly, "I won't ask how you're feeling."

"Please. Don't."

There was a touch of ruefulness in the reply that sounded more like the old Félicien. Encouraged, Johanna smiled. "What do you want? Peace? I can go away again."

Félicien reached for her hand. "No. No, please stay." Her eyes were sunken, her face white and drawn. The skin of her hand felt hot and dry to the touch.

Johanna looked at the tray of food on the table next to the bed. "Haven't managed to eat anything?"

"I can't keep it down. Most annoying."

"I would imagine."

They sat in silence for a few moments. Félicien kept hold of Johanna's hand. "I can't believe you came for me." For the first time in speaking of it, her voice held wonder and gratitude.

"It was Jaufre," Johanna said. "He knew the right thing to do from the beginning."

"I was fond of him, you know."

Johanna blinked. "Jaufre?"

A faint smile. "Yes, Jaufre. The man so in love with you that other women might as well not exist." She shifted and winced a little. "Especially women dressed as men."

"I thought—"

"What, that I didn't like men? Well, I didn't, then. Until I met him. He is just as all the songs say. 'A parfit gentil knight.'"

Johanna had thought of Jaufre in many ways but as a knight was not one of them. "I didn't know."

"No, and nor does he, and don't tell him." The bed creaked as she shifted again. A drumming began on the roof. "Rain, again. I'm glad we're inside and dry."

"So am I," Johanna said with feeling.

"You have a lovely singing voice, Johanna."

"Thank you. So do you." She hesitated. "When we were asking after you, we heard you had a nickname."

Félicien smiled. "L'Alouette du Sud," she said.

"Yes."

"My father said I was born singing. My mother died when I was born, and I was all he had, and my voice pleased him very much. He hired many teachers for me, from Avignon, Lyon, Nice, one all the way from Paris. And when I was growing up, every troubadour and jongleur and minstrel and poet passing within a hundred leagues of L'Arête knew they could find a meal and a bed there. All my father asked was that they sing for me, and to let me sing with them." Her eyes closed and she swallowed hard and breathed deeply several times. "One of them gave me that name."

"It…sounds like a good childhood."

"The best." Félicien sighed and opened her eyes again, the nausea passing for the moment. "And then I grew up, and my father decided I must marry."

"Why Ambroise?"

"He was strong enough to keep me safe, or so my father thought." A soundless laugh. "He was looking forward to grandchildren. And then he died, and I tried to break the betrothal. Ambroise showed up with his troop, forced me in front of a priest. I ran." She was silent for a moment. "At least he's dead. He won't hurt anyone ever again."

She looked at Johanna. "You know what I'd like?"

"What?"

"For you to find a lute or a gitar for me. I'd like to teach you some songs."

Their eyes met.

"All right," Johanna said in a low voice.

She met Shasha on the landing, and it was a good thing she did because her eyes were filled with tears and she tripped on the top step. Her foster sister caught her before she fell down the stairs. "Johanna! Be careful! I don't want to have two patients on my hands." She took a closer look at Johanna's face and put down the chamber pot. "What is it?"

Johanna took a long, shaken breath. "Félicien thinks she's dying, Shasha. Is she?"

Shasha folded her hands and frowned down at them. "I don't know." She raised her eyes. "She isn't improving, certainly."

"What did the old beldame say?"

Shasha hesitated. "She said," she said at last, "she said that she had known only a very few women who suffered this badly during pregnancy. And that all of them had died."

Johanna swallowed. "She wants me to bring her an instrument, and let her teach me songs."

Shasha's face cleared a little. "Good. If she takes an interest in something other than her condition, perhaps it will help."

Johanna was a little shocked. "Shasha! She has been most grievously hurt!"

"Well, and so have others been hurt, and hurt worse," Shasha said, a trace of anger in her voice. "And recovered, and gone on to live useful lives. So could she."

"Could she?"

Shasha pressed her lips together. "Perhaps. I don't know."

"Can you not...help her?"

"If by help you mean help her abort her child, I fear that at this stage anything I did would only make things worse." She sighed. "I told her so, and she told me she'd rather be dead than carry what she persists in referring to as 'it' to term."

The next day Johanna went out into the town and found a music shop that sold instruments, and spent far too much on a beautiful lute made of walnut polished to a rich gleam, inlaid with mother of pearl. She bore it back to the inn, and her first lesson commenced that evening. Félicien, propped up by many bolsters and rolled blankets, sat up, her back to the headboard, and cradled the lute in her lap. "Well, now, what first, I wonder. The dawn song, perhaps. It's always been my favorite. Yes, the dawn song."

Every day Johanna attended Félicien in her room and learned all of the songs the goliard had in her repertoire, joined by other members of the company or not. Some songs Johanna had heard many times, like "O Wandering Clerks." Others were completely new to her, and she could only marvel at Félicien's capacity to remember each note and every word of what appeared to be every song she'd ever heard, and be capable of retrieving them at will.

"Where did you learn all these? You couldn't have learned them all sitting at home in L'Arête no matter how many troubadours your father imported for you."

The goliard's smile was reminiscent. "I picked up some Latin from a defrocked priest I traveled with for a time, and I read everything I could get my hands on."

"Such as?"

Félicien shrugged. "Forgotten scrolls in a letterless lord's solar." She strummed a few plaintive notes. "An illuminated manuscript at a monastery where we spent the night." This time the lute sounded like a monk's chant. "A good jongleur can memorize three hundred lines of poetry after only three hearings. I don't know that I ever got that good, but the more I memorized, the more easily rhyme came to me. Almost everything is written in rhyme, you know, religious tracts, scrolls on the cultivation of wheat, a chatty little pamphlet on how to get and keep a husband. All in rhyme. Paper is so scarce."

It wasn't in Cambaluc. Not for the first time, Johanna deeply regretted not learning the art of paper making before they had left. She didn't trust that her memory would be as good as Félicien's. "Where else did you find songs?"

In Montpelier Félicien had met Beatrix, the lady of the local castellan, whose husband went on crusade. "'If I had gone with him, I would have been only a wife,' she told me over a fine dinner," Félicien said. "'Here,' she said, 'I am castellan of my own keep.'"

"I have heard of this Beatrix," Alaric said, disapproving. "She disinherited her son in favor of her daughter and granddaughter."

"Good for her," Shasha said, earning an indignant look from the Templar.

"It was Beatrix who first showed me Geoffrey of Monmouth's *History of the Kings of Great Britain*. I promptly wrote a song of Igerna's rape by Uther and she was horrified. She said Igerna was willing, that Geoffrey of Monmouth made that very clear." Félicien's lips twisted. "Of course, Geoffrey of Monmouth was a man."

No one said anything.

Félicien took a deep breath and struck a presentation chord. "And then at the puys, the gatherings when all the jongleurs come together, we would all sing our songs and learn each other's. I've borrowed from Polyhister stories of people who sacrificed to Apollo by dancing barefoot over hot coals, of pythons that grew long and fat by feeding from the udders of milk cows, of lynxes who urinated topazes, of the dog-headed Simeans of Ethiopia, ruled by a Dog-King."

She laughed, a little guilty, her cheeks flushed with real color for the first time in days. "Once, a local priest denounced me for singing a song of romantic love between a knight and his lady, what he condemned as pagan practices, 'fit only for the ears of the devil himself.'"

"What did you do?"

Félicien's smile was sly. "I substituted the Virgin Mary's name for the name of the lady in the song, and all was well."

Alaric actually laughed. "You should have been burned at birth, my lady." Alone among all of them, he refused to revert to calling her Félicien.

"Then," Félicien said, "there was a tale of a knight who pretended to be deaf and dumb so his lady would be assured of his discretion and take him into her bed." This time she laughed with them, and then her face went white and Johanna got the night jar up in position just in time. She washed Félicien's face with the damp cloth always at the ready. No one said anything. They were all too used to it by now.

"The songs I liked best were the ones the jongleurs wrote about themselves," Félicien said, her eyes closed. "Ottar the Black made the mistake of dedicating a poem to the daughter of King Olaf, was condemned to death for his presumption, and gained his reprieve by singing the king's praises on the way to his execution. 'A song without music is a mill without water,' he was quoted as saying, and troubadours from the Danube to the Nile promptly acquired that line for songs of their own. They are great thieves, the jongleurs and the troubadours; they steal lines, verses, entire songs without fear and without shame."

Félicien's eyes opened. "It is a great honor, you know. It means the other singer likes the work." She smiled. "Besides, you know the story. Why did God make thieves thieves and jongleurs jongleurs?"

"The thieves had first choice," Johanna replied by rote, and smiled back at her friend, though her heart was breaking.

Félicien insisted that Johanna teach her her songs, too. "There isn't much point," Johanna said. "When I sing of China, such tales are treated as fine fables, though hardly true."

"It's only because your songs dare to imply that the Chinese culture is far more advanced and superior to the European," Félicien said, and Johanna laughed.

More months passed, December, January, February. In the beginning Félicien was well able to reach and strum all the chords, but as winter progressed she was reduced to plucking out individual notes. Her flesh shrank, as her belly grew incongruously in contrast, a hard, firm lump beneath the bedclothes that if nothing else provided a good platform for her instrument. She could no longer rise from her bed unaided, and the company formed the habit of spending their evenings in her room. Alaric and Firas brought tack in to be mended and swords and knives to be sharpened, Shasha mixed dried herbs and put them in packets, Alma painted. Hayat had bought a lap loom and was weaving a scarf of blue silk and green wool, a lovely thing. She had refused to have anything to do with weaving since they had left Talikan, as it was too much a reminder of endless tedium of the harem. It seemed she had decided it was time to take it up again.

Tiphaine roamed the town for delicacies to tempt Félicien's appetite, and when Félicien couldn't eat them ate them herself. Jaufre looked in, but could never bear to stay for long. Félicien's eyes no longer followed him from the room. Mostly she looked out the window.

One evening when they had left Félicien to try to sleep, Shasha said, "The infant hasn't moved in days. I think it has starved to death."

Johanna thought of the skin and bones that were all that was left of Félicien's body and wasn't surprised. "Could that help Félicien? Now that she only has herself to nourish?"

Shasha leaned against the wall and shook her head. "If it had happened sooner, perhaps."

"Shasha? Is she truly going to die?"

Shasha's face twisted. "I should have helped her as she wished me to."

Johanna put her arms around her foster sister. "And if she had died, you would never have forgiven yourself." She felt hot tears soak into her tunic. Her turn to comfort now.

Hari took up permanent residence in Félicien's room, violating his chughi rules to spend his nights with a woman. They teased him about it, gently, which he took with a smile, and remained where he was. Sometimes he and Félicien spoke through the night. Sometimes they simply shared the silence.

One day Johanna came to the door of the room. It stood ajar, and she paused when she heard the voices inside. "Peace comes from within, young goliard," Hari was saying. "Do not seek it from without."

"I don't, truly I don't, Hari. I found my peace in freedom, and I lost it again because I didn't want to leave the company of people who had become my friends. Who had become more family to me than my own."

"Do you wish, then, that you had not met us on the Road?"

There was a long pause, but then Félicien said, "No. No, I don't."

"Good. Happiness never decreases by being shared."

"Hari?"

"Yes?"

"What happens? Afterward?" What might have been a sob. "I have never been what one could call religious, but I am afraid I have sinned greatly, and that I will be punished for it."

"Do you wish for a priest, young goliard? There is a parish church here, with a priest I find to be kindly and intelligent. I could—"

"No, he will only make me confess, and I don't want to confess to a stranger. And I don't need to be forgiven by any man."

"If it would give you ease—"

"It wouldn't."

A long silence. "Buddha says that even death is not to be feared by one who has lived wisely."

A choked laugh. "There are many who would say I have not lived wisely, not at all."

"Yourself included?"

Another long silence. "No, Hari. No. At the very least, I have lived, and I would not have been able to do so had I remained at home." Johanna could hear the smile in her voice. "I would not have met you. The man who now shares my nights."

In March the days lightened, and lengthened, and came one evening when it was warm enough to leave the window uncovered, when the scent of new grass was in the air, when birds returned from the southern reaches filled the room with song, when Félicien said to Johanna, "Wear your robe tonight."

The robe in question had belonged to Johanna's mother, a robe that she had packed carefully and brought with her all the way from Cambaluc, her most precious possession. It was called the Robe of a Thousand Larks and it was made of heavy gold silk, with wide sleeves and a wide skirt that, after Johanna had unpicked the hem and let it down, just reached to her feet. It was embroidered in silk thread with a thousand larks in all their yellow, orange, red, green and black glory. In between the larks wound brilliant flowers on green vines and black branches.

It was a glorious example of the spinner and the weaver's art, and Johanna looked glorious in it. Félicien stared at her from her emaciated face with its sunken eyes and cheeks. Her hair had begun to fall out and Shasha had taken to wrapping her head in one of Alma's harem scarves, the only color about her now.

Shasha had summoned them all to attend Félicien that evening and they had all obeyed that summons, Firas, Alma, Hayat, Hari, Alaric, Tiphaine, even Jaufre, who stood in a corner, his arms crossed, his face in shadow.

"Sing the dawn song," Félicien whispered.

Johanna struck a chord, and the sadness of lovers about to be parted was repeated in the features of her face, the gleam of her hair in a last stray beam from the setting sun, and above all in the husky contralto tones of her voice.

Ah, would to God that never night must end,
Nor this my lover far from me should wend,
Nor watcher day nor dawning ever send!
Ah God, ah God, the dawn! how it comes soon.

The glittering of the brilliants sewn on the Robe of a Thousand Blossoms captured the little light in the room and threw it back tenfold, so that amethyst lilies and ruby roses seemed to sway in a gentle breeze, and nightingales' wings flickered in flight.

Sweet lover come, renew our lovemaking
Within the garden where the light birds sing,
Until the watcher sound the severing.
Ah God, ah God, the dawn! it comes how soon.

She looked up from the lute to see Félicien's drowsy smile, saw her eyes close, heard the rattle of breath in her breast. She handed the lute blindly to someone and kneeled to take her hand. Shasha came to kneel at Félicien's other side, and the rest of them gathered round, as Félicien the goliard, also known as Aceline Eléonor Félicienne de L'Arête, also known as l'Alouette du Sud, slipped from her earthly vessel, and left it, and them, behind.

· Fourteen ·

Spring, 1326 A.D.
Chartres

┝━━━┥

The day after they buried Félicien, Johanna stood in the yard of the inn and closed her eyes in repugnance against the brightness of the day. The sun felt warm on someone else's skin, not hers. She felt numb and oh so tired, and beneath it all there was a tiny core of molten anger, anger at Ambroise, at Florian for abetting Ambroise, at Shasha for not being able to cure Félicien, at Félicien for dying. That anger was encased for now in a hard layer of ice but its distant warmth was at present her only comfort. One day soon it would perhaps break free of its icy shroud. One day.

She heard North Wind give an inquiring whinny. Soon, she would take him out for gallop. Soon. This afternoon, perhaps. Tomorrow. Next week.

She felt the others assembling around her, and opened her eyes to see that they were all there, gathered around Hari.

Hari had been an exemplary member of their group since Johanna had rescued him from a potentially fatal beating before the gates of Kashgar, where he had been arrested for preaching without a license. He never again forced his religious beliefs on an unsuspecting populace, or at least not in a manner that rebounded adversely on their company. Upon their arrival in any city, his first action was to seek out the religious community and disappear for days. Imams and priests, rabbis and patriarchs, monks and nuns, scholars and pedagogues, all were of abiding interest to Hari, and evidently none were proof against the chughi's air of mild inquiry, which was all he ever displayed. When Johanna had asked him what he was doing, he smiled and said, "Listening." Once when Jaufre asked him where he was going he had replied only, "Forward."

He had put off or covered up his yellow robes with clothing more suited to the current climate, but there was no hiding the yellow skin that clung so closely to the high cheekbones, or the tilted eyes, or the shaven head. He would always be other, so long as he stayed in the West, but he seemed unconscious of the second and third looks cast his way, and none of them could deny the air of gentle authority he exercised. People did what he told them to as a matter of course. Not excluding themselves.

And so here they were this morning, emerging pupa-like from their winter cocoon, burdened with heavy grief at the loss of their comrade, and for the first time in all their time together uncertain of where they were going, or even why.

"Come with me," Hari said.

They followed him, dispirited and unquestioning, through the winding streets of the town and up to the cathedral. It was after morning services but before the line of pilgrims had begun to form see the holy relic, and they passed unhindered and unchallenged between the two towers, under the royal portal and down the center aisle. There were a few people at their prayers and someone cleaning the candleholders on the altar, but for that they were alone. Any scrape of the sole or whisper floated up and was magnified by the impossibly high, vaulted ceilings, carved with fantastical shapes and painted with bright colors.

"Stand here," Hari said. They stood, nine abreast where there should have been ten. They had passed rapidly from light into dark and they closed their eyes to let them adjust.

It was the first time Johanna had been in the cathedral itself, although she had been to its Christmas fair, looking for something, anything to cheer Félicien this past December. What had she bought? A puppet, she remembered, and she and Tiphaine had made it dance on the bedspread, and Félicien had laughed, back when she could muster up enough energy to laugh—

"Look up," Hari said. "Look up, now."

Obediently they opened their their eyes and looked up, and were assaulted by a blaze of colored light shining through windows that on every side reached for the sky, for the heavens, for the stars themselves. Crowned figures royal and religious, common folk wielding axe and saw and scythe, burghers making and merchants selling, saints ascending unto heaven and angels on outspread wings, mother and babe, mother and man, mother and sacrificial son. Green vines like emeralds and roses like rubies and borders like amber and stars like diamonds twined about the figures, creating a jeweled setting for an already almost blindingly dazzling display.

Dumbstruck, they drifted in ones and twos from window to window, necks craned, eyes straining. Only Alaric and perhaps Hari understood half of what they were looking at, but somehow they knew that they were reading a book, a book that could tell them the history of the culture of the land in which they now stood. Of course, Johanna thought, of course, in a land where so few people could read, of course the church must have a way to imprint its legends on the lay folk, who after all could not spend all of their time listening to sermons. Here was their story, all their stories, written in light and color, for everyone to see and remember. But it was more than just a book of the church, it was a book of the people as well, kings to commoners. You knew where you were in society, who you were when you came here. Here there was certainty. Here there was clarity. Here there was comfort in the regular order of things.

She found herself standing next to Jaufre, and glanced at him. He, too, was staring up, absorbed, this time in a tall, slender column of glass showing a tree springing from one man's groin in the bottom panel and ending at the top in another man crowned with seven doves. "Their Christ?" he said.

"Yes," she said, in an equally hushed tone. "It's almost enough to make me believe."

He shook his head. "They're barely civilized enough not to shit in their own drinking water, and then they build something like this."

Alaric had come to stand by them. "You know why they built it, don't you? To bring in pilgrims to spend money in the town. It's why all cathedrals are built."

Jaufre looked at him. "You don't even believe that yourself." A thought struck him. "Wilmot. I completely forgot. Is your friend here?"

Alaric shook his head. "I've asked. If he was here, it was only briefly, not long enough to make an impression on any of the residents. No one remembers him."

It was past noon when they emerged again, feeling half-drunk on the wonders within, to find pilgrims lining up to view the Sancta Camisia, allegedly the tunic Mary wore when she gave birth to Christ and the cathedral's most precious relic. Behind the pilgrims a man was perched on the edge of a fountain, a bound trunk on the ground below, open to reveal a sheaf of forms. Another man displayed a writ of some kind upon a red velvet cushion. Even at a distance they could see that the writ was most wonderfully decorated with great scrolls and flourishes, and the cushion was no less wonderfully decorated with elaborate embroidery in gold thread and gold tassels. It was very gaudy.

To one side a flock of men in clerical black stood with their hands folded piously beneath their cassocks, crucifixes gleaming upon their breasts. Behind them a huge wooden cross had been raised and draped with a banner.

Alaric caught his breath and crossed himself.

"What is it?" Jaufre asked in a low voice.

"That banner is the banner of the Holy Father himself," Alaric said, murmuring a prayer and crossing himself again.

"Of Pope John in Avignon?"

"The same."

"What's going on?"

"I don't know."

Everyone appeared to be waiting for the bells in the tower to stop ringing. When they did, the crowd surged forward, hands held out, usually with coins displayed in them.

"I have here your passport to Paradise!" the man on the fountain cried. "One quarter florin saves you seven years of penance! Have you committed the mortal sin of carnal knowledge of your mother or your sister? Poor Christian soul! Step up, place your coin in the bowl of the Holy Father! You will receive a letter of remission of your sin, and if the Holy Father forgive it, then God must also. Step up! Did your father die unshriven? Poor Christian soul! As soon as the coin rings in the bowl, that soul will fly straight from Purgatory to Heaven! Step up!"

They stepped up in a body, crowding around, fighting for place. Even a few pilgrims broke rank, perhaps tired of waiting for Mary's attention. A third man counted the money as it dropped into the bowl with one hand, and handed out forms from the chest with the other.

"I thought you said you had to confess your sins to a priest," Johanna said to Alaric. "That was why they wouldn't let us bury Félicien in one of their graveyards."

"And that you couldn't be forgiven your sins until you had done penance for them," Shasha said.

"Usually on your knees in church," Jaufre said.

Alaric's mouth was a thin line of disapproval.

"Is it not said, 'Who fears not, God, Thy gifts to take and then Thy ten commandments break, lacks that true love which should be his salvation?'" Hari quoted piously.

"Amen," Jaufre said heartily, and was seconded by a chorus.

Alaric scowled. "Let's get out of this crowd."

They let him lead the way home because none of them could keep their faces straight.

Life was not all tragedy, Johanna thought, and people were not all of them evil. For every Ambroise there was a Hari and a Firas and a Jaufre and yes, even an Alaric. For every Chartres Cathedral built to the great glory of church and state by the hand of man, there was a man offering you an opportunity to buy your way into heaven.

No, not all tragedy. Johanna felt the numbness that had enveloped her upon Félicien's death begin to ease, and when she next drew breath the scents of spring were rich in her nostrils.

And Félicien?

She was unaware she had said the words out loud until Jaufre answered her. "Félicien would have written a song about it," he said.

She looked at him and saw that he was smiling. "And not a nice one."

Even Alaric smiled.

That night Shasha conspired with their landlady, with whom they were by now on quite good terms, and produced a feast of roast chicken and a heaping bowl of root vegetables mashed with butter and herbs, and another bowl of fresh-picked strawberries for dessert. Johanna couldn't remember the last time she had eaten anything that tasted as good.

They cleared away the debris and returned the dishes to the scullery, and came to roost on the fenced paddock that currently housed North Wind. He trotted directly up to Johanna and nosed her so impatiently that she nearly fell off the rail. She climbed back up and produced a wizened excuse of an apple excavated from their landlady's cellar. North Wind snorted down the front of her tunic and after a little fake dissembling deigned to accept the tribute.

He ambled away, munching, as the other three Arabians and the rest of their mounts fell in a respectful distance behind. He still had that scar on his right foreleg from that time in the Hindu Kush, when they ran from Gokudo until they caught him. There was another on his left hindquarter, a rope burn suffered from one of Sheik Mohammed's men.

She looked around at her human companions. They were all scarred in one way or another, too.

"So," Shasha said. "What do we do next?"

It so happened that they were facing north. Johanna saw Jaufre raise his head and stare off at the horizon. "I'd still like to find a good source of wool," he said. "Good quality fleece would fetch a fine price both in Lyon and in Venice."

Alaric was picking at his teeth with a twig. "They do say," he said, "that the best wool comes from England."

"Do they," Shasha said, eying Alaric narrowly. There had been something suspiciously studied in his statement.

He returned a glance of limpid innocence and spread his hands. "So I have heard. I've never been there myself, of course."

Johanna wondered what wool cost in England. It had been an expensive winter. She herself was down to two rubies, one sewn into the hem of each leg of her trousers, the last of her patrimony, the last gift she would ever receive from her father. As for coin, there was precious little left of that left in any of their pockets.

"Then perhaps we should go to England," Jaufre said.

Alma and Hayat exchanged glances. "What?" Jaufre said.

"Well," Hayat said. "Where is it?"

"North," Alaric said. "And west. And we'll have to cross La Manche."

"The channel? What channel?"

"It's what they call where the ocean travels between Normandy and England." He looked at their blank faces, and added kindly, "Normandy is also north."

"There's a university in the town," Alma said to Hayat.

"And where there is a school, there will be a library," Hayat said, with resignation.

"And where there is a library, there will be maps," Alma said, with satisfaction.

"How far to this channel?" Firas said.

Alaric shrugged. "Fifty leagues, perhaps?"

Johanna looked at him, at his purposely diffident air, and thought that he knew down to the rod how far it was to the channel.

"And how long a voyage to cross it?"

"If the weather is fine, a day or less."

Their last voyage, a storm-ridden journey across the Middle Sea, was strong enough in everyone's memory to be relieved to hear it, even if they didn't quite believe that any sea voyage could be quite that easy. Tiphaine, never having been on a ship, was enchanted at the notion and bounced on top of the fence, to the imminent danger of them and the railing they were sitting on. "When do we leave?"

"As soon as possible," Alaric said.

"Why?"

"It's spring. In two months' time, or when the ground dries out, whichever comes first, armies will begin to march. It would be best to be gone before that happened."

"Which armies?"

"All of them. Did you think all those ships were being built in Venice only for trade?" Alaric grimaced. "The English kings have been fighting with the French kings ever since Henry II died. All this—" he waved an inclusive hand "—or much of it once belonged to the English, by marriage portion of Eleanor of Aquitaine. They've been losing it a piece at a time to the French ever since, but they're very tenacious, the English. There is nothing they love so much as a vain hope, and they are more than willing to sacrifice any number of lives to it."

That last came out a little acidly. "You know them well, in spite of never having been there," Shasha said.

"There were many English among the Knights Templar." He nodded at Jaufre. "His father was only one of them. My suggestion is that we sail from Harfleur. It's a smaller port than Calais, with fewer ships to choose from, but it's closer to us. And farther from the Low Countries."

"The Low Countries?"

"Someone is always fighting over or fighting with the Low Countries," Alaric said. "They are very rich, and so present tempting targets to anyone with a large enough army. We would be much safer avoiding them altogether, even though it will be a longer sail from Harfleur."

"Fifty leagues," Shasha said, sliding to the ground. "Say a week's travel— what is the way like? Should we go supplied, or will food be readily available for purchase on the journey?"

"We begin practice again every morning," Firas said. "If we are going where armies march—"

"Armies march everywhere, all the time, Firas," Alaric said. "And we are not an army, in and of ourselves."

"Nevertheless—"

"A ship! We're going on a ship!"

They moved off, chatting animatedly. Johanna found herself alone with Jaufre for the first time in months. She hesitated, looking at him.

"What?" he said.

"Is looking for wool the real reason you wanted to go to England?"

"Oh, well…" He looked a little self-conscious, which was better than the open, gaping wound that had been living with them lately. "I suppose I would like to see the land my father came from."

"Will you look for his family? Your family?"

He shook his head, more definitely this time. "No. They are nothing to me." He looked at her. "Johanna."

Something in his expression made her heart skip a beat. "What?"

"I'm sorry." He took in a breath and blew it back out again. "It's late to say it, and if you have a shred of self-respect you won't accept it, but I am truly sorry."

She didn't pretend not to understand. She surprised them both when she said baldly, "Did you love her?"

He looked first surprised and then confused. "What?"

"Did you love her? Félicien? I thought you—I thought we—" She couldn't go on, her throat closing over the words. She looked away, unable to bear the sight of his face when he said "Yes."

"Johanna. Johanna, look at me." A large hand raised her chin and she willed back the tears to meet his eyes. They were so blue, and so dear. "Of course I loved her," he said, and her heart plummeted. "No. Listen. Listen to the rest. Listen to all of it." He put his hands on her shoulders and pulled her towards him. She went, step by hesitant step. "Of course I loved her, as I love them all—" he jerked his head at the group now entering the inn. "—the whole annoying, irritating, infuriating bunch of them. They are my comrades, as Félicien was my comrade."

"But she was more than that," she said.

He squeezed her shoulders. "I lost my mother the same way, Johanna."

She looked up, startled, and he smiled. "I didn't think I'd have to explain this to you of all people. My mother was kidnapped and sold into slavery when I was ten. I never saw her again, but I never stopped looking for her." He raised his head and stared into the distance with blind eyes. "I went to the slave auctions in Venice, Johanna. I watched women being stripped to their skins, their mouths forced open to show their teeth, filthy, grinning old doctors produced to attest to their virginity."

He gave a shaky sigh. "I was sick. Worse than Félicien on the worst day of her illness. I barely made it outside." He looked back at her, his eyes very bright. "I swore to myself, then and there, that I was done looking for my mother. I swore to accept the fact that she had gone beyond my reach. That my memories of her were all I would have. All these years of looking for her, and I finally realized. I wasn't ever going to find her. I wasn't ever going to rescue her. The last word I would have from her, the last sight of her I would see would be from that morning on the Road, three days from Kashgar. When we woke, and broke our fast with tea and dried fruit, and she made a joke when I brought in a bag of dried camel dung for that night's fire."

She felt tears sting her eyes. "It's not a bad last memory." She thought of her own mother's death. But she had been there, holding her mother's hand as she died. She hadn't seen her mother disappearing around a street corner in every city between Cambaluc and Venice for the last ten years.

She looked at Jaufre. "And then Félicien was taken."

"Yes, and it was my mother all over again. She was taken, and I could do nothing to stop it. I might as well have been that ten-year old boy again, utterly useless, utterly ineffectual. I couldn't let it go, Johanna. I couldn't let her go." He searched her face. "Do you understand?"

She thought back to those days and weeks following Félicien's taking, when Jaufre had seemed so maniacally focussed on getting Félicien back, allowing nothing and no one, not even his friends and comrades' doubts and fears to get in his way. "We could have been killed, Jaufre," she said. "All of us, not just Félicien."

He gave a short, explosive laugh. "Don't I know it! Looking back I can't believe I did that. But I had to." He looked at her again. "We had to. We had to rescue her, because we could. We could not have left her there, with him."

She thought of Félicien, laying on the bed in the room upstairs in the inn, wasting away to a skeleton, her hands growing ever more frail on the strings of her lute. How much more terrible would those days have been, had they been spent in L'Arête? "No," she said. "No, we could not."

He looked relieved, and then doubtful. "Does everyone feel the way you do?"

She pushed him away gently. "That is something you must talk to them about. Each and every one of them, Jaufre, from Hari to Tiphaine. Make your peace with them, or it will blight us all going forward."

He drew close again. "And us?" he said. "Did I blight us, too? Did I lose what we could have been, too?"

She gave a sudden, blinding smile. "You don't get rid of me that easily, Jaufre of Cambaluc." She kissed him swiftly on the corner of his mouth. "Félicien died free, and she died among friends, among people who loved her." She drew back and looked at him with steady eyes. "All that we did, all that we endured, all that we dared. It was worth it."

She ran after the others.

He watched her go, the lithe girl with the bronze braid and the golden skin, running easily across the yard to disappear inside the inn.

One thing he hadn't told her, one thing he might never tell her, was what he had felt when she tumbled beneath the belly of Ambroise de L'Arête's destrier, to deliberately place herself within range of the dangerous hooves of a trained war horse. A terror greater than any he had ever felt seized him and for a moment he couldn't move, he couldn't speak, he could do nothing but watch to see if the destrier trampled her to death. Such was his concern to keep Félicien free of Ambroise that when they had made their plan, when Johanna had insisted it was the only way to provoke North Wind into action, he had not thought what it would mean.

She could have been injured. She could have died. Surely she knew that, and much sooner than he had. And she had done it anyway.

He looked about himself with new eyes. Their world over the winter had slowly contracted to the room in which Félicien lay dying. But here, outside that room, there was sun, and blue sky, and trees and shrubs going from bare limb to fat buds overnight, and pollen gathering in yellow drifts on roadsides, and farmers laboring in the fields, and calves and lambs mastering insubstantial legs to totter in search of mother's milk. He saw gray-cloaked pilgrims on the road, eyes fixed on the towers of the cathedral, burning with the hope that the Holy Mother would grant their wish for a son, a cure, forgiveness, grace.

Inside the inn his friends waited.

And then he closed his eyes and gave devout thanks to whomever was listening for the luck of a fool such as he.

· Fifteen ·

Summer, 1326 A.D.
England

⊢——⊣

They were away three days later and at the coast of Normandy a week after that. The route was well signed, the roads were dry, the weather was delightful, the inns were plentiful and welcoming, and, refreshingly, no one they met was trying to kill them. Jaufre spent time riding with each of them, making his peace. Alaric was acerbic, Firas calm and might even have been a little amused, and Shasha read Jaufre a lecture about reckless behavior, notwithstanding for how worthy the cause.

"We could do nothing less for a friend who wished to be free of the harem," Alma said, and Hayat nodded her agreement.

"'Friendship is the only cure for hatred, the only guarantee of peace,'" Hari said, and smiled his wonderful smile.

"Did you hear when North Wind landed on Ambroise's head?" Tiphaine said. "Crack! Squish! That'll teach him to mess with Wu Company."

They crossed the river Seine at Tancarville and followed it down to its mouth, where the town of Harfleur presented a bustling picture of energy and industry. "They're starting a merchants' association here," Tiphaine said, returning to the inn where they had procured rooms for the night. "Perhaps Wu Company should make ourselves known to them."

"Perhaps," Jaufre said, looking at Alaric, just entering the common room. The Templar had been dispatched to find them passage across the Channel, and from the sour expression on his face he had not been successful. He sat down and called for a pitcher of wine but it was seen that he drank abstemiously, at least for him, and ate heartily of bread and cheese and a heavenly bean stew flavored with bits of chicken and sausage and a lot of garlic.

The inn was close to the waterfront and catered to a clientele of merchants, traders and ship's captains. The conversation was certainly animated but it never got too loud and bargaining for freight and rates was conducted briskly and professionally. Like the city itself, the inn appeared to exist to do business.

Alaric pushed back his plate and refilled his cup. "I have not found us a ship," he said. "It appears that Edward's wife is cuckolding him with one of his lords, and she has betrothed their son to the daughter of Hainault. She's brought him over to meet the girl. A smart man's money is on Isabella's primary purpose being to use the daughter's dowry to finance a rebellion against him." He saw blank looks surrounding him. "Edward, king of England. Isabella, his wife. Edward, their son. Hainault, one of the Low Countries everyone is always fighting over. And I'm sure," he said, staring glumly into his wine, "that ineffectual bastard Charles probably has an incompetent hand in this somewhere." He saw their looks again. "Charles IV, king of France."

"You speak of these great people with great familiarity," Firas said.

Alaric snorted. "I do, don't I."

"More to the point, what does this have to do with being unable to find transportation to England?" Jaufre said.

Alaric sighed. "All the Harfleur ships are in Calais, looking for work in transporting the royal party across this summer. Invasions are good for the transportation business. You can charge anything you like and they have to pay."

"Not all the ships, surely," Shasha said.

Alaric studied Johanna. "I assume we need a ship big enough to bring along the livestock?"

"You are correct in that assumption," she said.

"Well, then." He raised his hands in a gesture of defeat, and let them drop again. "There is one possibility I have yet to explore."

"What?" they said in a chorus.

"I'd rather not say. I'll leave tomorrow at first light. I should be back by nightfall. If not, the day after."

They looked for him the next day, and the day after. On the third day he rode into the stable yard as they were assembling in the common room for dinner. He had a glorious black eye and he chewed as if some of his teeth were loose.

Nobody said anything until they were finished. Alaric poured a cup of wine, filled his mouth and held his head on one side for a moment.

Shasha cleared her throat delicately. "I don't know that that will do any good."

Alaric swallowed. "I don't, either." He put both arms on the table and leaned on them. "Jaufre."

"Yes, Alaric."

"You remember I told you about my sister."

"Your what? Oh." One night he had sat on the wall of Bastak and watched the moon travel across the sky as Alaric told him about Jaufre's father. Not all, as it turned out, but some, and some of Alaric's own history as well. "Your sister," he said. "The one who, uh, convinced the guard to let you go when your father betrayed you."

"You never asked what happened to her."

"No." Not that he hadn't wondered.

"We were…separated after the escape." Alaric swished the wine around in his cup. "She came here."

"Here? To Harfleur?"

"Yes." Alaric sat up and drained his cup. "She has a ship, big enough for us and the horses, too."

Jaufre looked at Johanna, who looked at Shasha. "And will she take us to England?" Shasha said.

Alaric felt tenderly of his jaw, and winced. "For a price," he said. "For a price. She'll be landing us in one of the smaller ports. She doesn't—" He thought for a moment, and then said, "She has no charter for any of the larger ports."

Johanna might have seen the suspicion of a smile hovering around his mouth for a moment, and then it was gone, too soon for her to be sure.

They paid their charges at the inn the next morning and were off with a clatter of hooves, turning right out of the yard and trotting down the road that ran next to the river. The river widened and the trees of the high ground became marshlands covered with tall reeds, but the path stayed hard and dry. They reached their destination by sext, the sun high in the sky. By then the other side of the river was lost in the fine mist rising from the surface of the river.

It was a good-sized village clustered around a single dock stretching out into the water. Moored on either side were two ships. Both had single masts with square sails rigged between mast and boom. The hulk was round-hulled, the cog flat-bottomed. The hulk had a round stern and a side rudder. The cog had a square stern with decking built on the inside around three sides, and a center rudder controlled by a capstan.

A woman stood in the stern of the cog, watching them come. As they approached, Jaufre saw that she was tall and thin, long of face, with dark hair and eyes. The similarity was unmistakable, but unlike Alaric the lady crackled with energy. "Are these yours?" she said.

"They are," Alaric said.

"Well, get them aboard before we miss the tide."

Introductions were deferred until the horses were loaded into the hold, where stalls had been created by boards bolted to the hull. Posts formed a center aisle. "Hobble them," the captain said, peering down from the deck. "I don't want one of them to take a notion to kick holes into my hull in mid-channel."

The horses were duly hobbled and backed into their stalls. North Wind's indignant trumpeting could probably have been heard in Harfleur. He knew all too well from his only other sea passage how uncomfortable being under sail could be, and he did not take kindly to the feel of a deck rising and falling beneath his hooves again. Johanna held his head and soothed him while more boards were slotted in to form gates. They went further and ran a line over the horses' backs, in case they took it into their heads to rear. A couple of bales of hay were tossed between the two ranks of stalls. North Wind calmed and deigned to lip at it.

Johanna gave him a last reassuring pat and went up on deck. The lines had already been loosed and the downriver current was parting them rapidly from the dock. Gulls screamed overhead and Johanna saw a pod of porpoises surface and blow and dive off their bow, backs gleaming wetly in the sun. At mid-river the captain said, "Set sail!" The large square of canvas raised and shook itself out and bellied gently before the offshore breeze. Through it all the sunlight on the river was bright enough to blind, and it was warm even out here on the water. In her ear Jaufre murmured, "It can't be this easy, surely?"

She laughed and turned, leaning on the rail. "Hush. The gods will hear, and make us suffer."

They stood like that, smiling at each other, for a good long while, and then in mutual unspoken agreement turned and watched as they left the mouth of the river and Normandy behind. "So," he said finally, "what do you reckon? A pirate?"

She looked over her shoulder at the captain, who stood, arms folded, behind the helmsman at the capstan, legs spread in a stance that took the small swell beneath their hull with ease. She was dressed much as they were, in tunic and trousers, a wide sash of some dark red material wrapped twice around her waist.

As they watched Alaric approached the stern, and the captain's arms dropped and she advanced to the steps he was approaching, where she planted her hands on her hips and glared down at him. He halted immediately and returned to where the rest of the company was gathered amidships. "I don't think they parted well," she said thoughtfully.

"No," Jaufre agreed.

"What do you think happened?"

"Nothing he's proud of," he said, keeping Alaric's confidence. "Or he wouldn't have let her give him that black eye."

The downstream current and the outgoing tide took them out into the Channel, and there a nice strong offshore wind took over. The swell was minimal, with no chop at all. The cog slipped through the water like North Wind down a race track, leaving a wake of frothing foam behind them.

The captain spoke to the helmsman and took to the deck in a single bound. Jaufre and Johanna joined the others as she reached them. "All right," she said briskly, "if the wind doesn't change we might make landfall before dark. Alaric told you that you will be set ashore in Cornwall? The south of England," she amended when she saw their blank expressions. Her language was cultured and refined, its timbre and accent much like her brother's. "It's a rocky, barren coast but the harbor is good, if small, and well sheltered, and there is a place for you to stay the night. Not an inn, but I—do business with the owner there. He's a genial soul and welcomes travelers. The agreement was half up front, half upon delivery, and I will expect payment in full before we land you." She nodded and marched back to the helm.

They ate bread and cheese and last year's pears for lunch, and then Jaufre took his courage in his hands and ventured to approach the aft deck. "Captain?"

She turned her head and saw him standing at the foot of the stairs. She hesitated, and then nodded permission. "Yes?" she said.

He smiled the smile that the ladies of Cambaluc had considered his secret weapon. The captain did not visibly melt. "I wondered how often you made this passage," he said.

"As often as I have paying customers," she said. "Why?"

He cast an appraising glance over her craft. "I make the length to be some sixteen rods?"

"Seventeen," she said.

"And the beam, one and a half?"

"One and three-quarters."

"Making your payload —"

"Four thousand hundredweight."

"Very nice," he said. "Big enough to make a good living, not big enough to be too enticing a target, and fast enough—" he glanced at their wake "—to outrun all but the most serious trouble."

She smiled, he thought reluctantly, but she did smile. "What is your interest in my *Faucon*?"

Falcon, he thought. An apt name, as falcons were swift and elusive. Also predatory, but he preferred not to dwell on that at the moment. "I'm a trader," he said. "I'm always interested in the means of transporting goods."

She eyed the hilt of the sword looming over his shoulder. "A trader."

"Yes, a trader," Jaufre said firmly. "Where you are landing us, do you call there on a regular basis?"

This time she laughed. "Say rather, on an irregular basis," she said.

"Do you ship fleeces?" he said. "Wool?"

"Often," she said.

"And land them at your village?"

"It's not my village," she said, "and no, I land English goods at Harfleur. There is no point in unloading my cargo at the village and then paying someone to haul it all the way to a buyer, now, is there?" Her voice was mocking.

"None at all," he said. "How do the Harfleur wool merchants find the quality of your fleeces?"

"English wool is much prized by merchants all over the continent," she said.

"I know," he said, "I've heard nothing else since Venice. English wool seems to be universally regarded as the finest wool there is." He meditated for a moment. "If an ambitious trader—"

"Such as yourself," she said, a faint smile lifting one corner of her mouth.

"Such as myself," he said, returning her smile, "if such a trader, new to the ways of England, was desirous of buying and exporting wool, how would he go about it?"

Still smiling that faint smile, she shook her head. "Don't even think it, young sir. The fees will be astronomical. You'll need a charter from your local lord to do business. Every shire and city you pass through will levy a tax. There will be export fees, and the port fees—" She shook her head again. "No, young sir. For a stranger, a man new to England, one with no connections, such a thing cannot be arranged."

He was somewhat dashed by the certainty in her voice, and then rallied. "And how would one avoid some, or all, of those obstacles, captain?"

She smiled warmly. "Why, however would I know that, young sir?"

When she laughed he laughed with her.

When he rejoined the others, Johanna raised an eyebrow at him. "We were discussing the wool trade," he said. "What can I say? It's been months since I bought or sold anything that wasn't for our own consumption. Time to start thinking like a trader again."

They rolled up together in his cloak and fell asleep, protected by the gunnels from the sharper sea wind, comforted by the warmth of last rays of the setting sun, lulled to sleep by the gentle swell of the ocean.

It was dark when they woke. Jaufre sat up and Alaric said immediately, as if he'd been waiting for him, "The wind changed. It took longer to get here than the captain estimated. We'll land at first light. Go back to sleep."

Instead, Jaufre got up and went to stand next to Alaric, who was leaning on the rail. "How did she end up here?"

Maybe the concealing dark inspired in Alaric the urge to confide, as it had that night in Bastak. "Angelique got me out of the dungeon, but we were pursued. Her horse went lame. I panicked and left her behind." When Jaufre would have spoken he held up a hand. "Don't. There is nothing you can call me that I haven't called myself over the years. There is no word, no epithet, no curse bad enough." He gave a laugh that was more like a groan. "If Robert had known, he would have called me all of them and invented some new ones, too."

Memories of his father were so dim and far off now. Jaufre knew he looked like him, height, hair, build, eyes. He remember a deep voice and a rich laugh, and large, calloused hands over his on the hilt of the sword he now carried. But he liked the man Alaric spoke of. The man who would never leave a comrade behind, let alone a sister.

Water lapped at the sides of the cog. Jaufre thought he could see the dim outlines of land off the beam. They appeared to be standing off a coast. "How did she end up here?" he said. "And how did you know where she was?"

Alaric sighed. "When we were in Avignon, I sent a message home. What was my home. To our old priest, who was always a good friend to the two of us. He was the one who got us our horses." He took a deep breath.

"I didn't know if he would reply, but he did. In not very kind terms. Oh, nothing less than I deserved, and I knew it. But he did tell me to look for Angelique in Harfleur, as the captain of a ship, and her own ship, no less." His voice was rueful. "Our father disowned her when her part in my escape was learned, but she had a lover, a Dane, a ship's captain— this ship. She eloped with him, and she sailed with him. He died four years later, after which the crew accepted her as their new captain. She settled in Harfleur, and eventually wrote to Father Étienne that she was alive and well."

"Is she a pirate?"

"What? No! What makes you think that?"

There was a smile in Jaufre's voice. "She is so far as I can see unattached to any guild or association. She moors in a small village inconvenient to offloading merchandise in Harfleur, but very convenient to hide any cargo she cares to ship from prying eyes. She lands in a foreign port so small—" he gestured to where he could hear the surf hissing against the shore "—it is completely dark at night."

Alaric sighed. "You are entirely too observant, and in that, young Jaufre, you are very like your father, indeed." He paused. "Not a pirate, no, but a smuggler, I fear."

"And used to using her fists in a fight?"

"Indeed, and able to use them to give me a proper welcome. Now get some sleep. It will be dawn soon."

· Sixteen ·

Summer, 1326 A.D.
England

———

T he dawn broke on clouds gathering over a steep coast, colored sullen orange to deep red. They were reflected against the oily, steadily increasing swell beneath the *Faucon*'s hull. "Yes," the captain said, "let's get docked now."

She brought the ship in close enough to what looked like an uninterrupted shoal that her passengers held their collective breath, and then a ray of sun broke through the clouds to illuminate a narrow channel. The *Faucon* threaded it with easy confidence.

Inside the reef was a small, half-moon bay, with a narrow edging of golden sand on the left and an outcropping of rock on the right that formed a natural breakwater. There was a man-made rock pier, patiently chipped to a broad level surface just long enough to dock one ship the size of the *Faucon*. The shore dropped so steeply here that there was room and to spare for the ship's draft at any tide, and there were men waiting to catch their lines.

A gangplank was laid of deckboards and the horses led up from the hold in short order. There was a stable with a small paddock halfway up the bluff into which the horses were turned, while the passengers followed the captain up a twisting path to a large building that backed against the cliff. It was square and solid and made of the same black rock as the pier. Johanna, looking over her shoulder, saw the *Faucon*'s crew lading bundles and boxes to the end of the dock and vanishing around a corner. She wondered if she'd missed a warehouse built at the water's edge.

The heavy wooden double doors of the keep opened at their approach, and the captain took two strides and embraced the man standing in the opening. He was half a head shorter than she was and an arm's length broader but she nearly raised him off his feet. He let out a booming laugh and pulled her down into a loud, smacking kiss. Jaufre nudged Johanna and they looked on, grinning, as Alaric looked at first startled, then revolted, and finally resigned.

They trooped inside, where the first floor of the stone keep was taken up by one enormous room. A set of stairs climbed the back, north-facing wall, in which a great stone fireplace was set with a stack of logs that burned with a welcome warmth. Next to the fireplace a door opened out the back, through which wafted the enticing scent of baking pastry. Two long tables had been set up in the center of the room, benches on either side and a chair at the head of one of them. "Sit!" their host boomed, his deep voice echoing off the stone walls. "Sit and break your fast." His French was rough but perfectly understandable. He sat in the chair and had the captain sit on his right. "And who are all these lost waifs seeking shelter from the storm?"

As if in counterpoint thunder cracked in the distance. "Me, for one," the captain said dryly. Her crew pattered inside and closed the doors behind them before taking their places at the second table. At some unseen signal servants entered from the door at the back bearing platters of large, crescent-shaped pastries stuffed with minced onion, root vegetables and some kind of meat, well spiced—Johanna watched Shasha take a bite and immediately begin cataloguing the ingredients— and pottery mugs of small beer.

"So? Who are these people eating at my table? Or is it a mystery again?" Their host winked.

"It is not a mystery, so far as I know," the captain said, "but first I should perhaps introduce you to them, Hugh. Allow me to make known to you one Hugh Tregloyne, the master of this keep." She made a graceful gesture with one hand. "Your guests may introduce themselves."

One by one they went around the table and did so. Alma and Hayat were examined pretty thoroughly and Tiphaine would have been chucked under the chin if she had been within arm's reach. If Tregloyne's gaze rested on Alaric's face a little longer than on the rest of their faces, and if he looked backed forth between Alaric and Angelique, and if he drew any conclusions, he was tactful enough to say nothing. Oddly, his gaze lingered longest on Jaufre.

"So," he said when they were done. Lightning flashed outside the back door, thunder rumbled again, and rain followed immediately, an instantaneous deluge that stopped almost as soon as it started. "All the way from distant Cathay. Welcome to Glynnow." His voice mocked without being offensive. "What would such world travelers want with Cornwall, then?"

They looked at each other. "Well, sir," Jaufre said, "we are interested in wool."

Tregloyne stroked his chin. "Buying or selling?" He heard Jaufre out, and at the end shook his head, much as the captain had. "The tax will eat you alive, young Jaufre. Every city and town you travel through will levy a charge, and the ports!" He threw up his hands.

"How do the graziers feel about all these taxes?" Jaufre said.

Tregloyne snorted. "How do you think? And the local merchants and traders as well. But there is no other way to get their goods to market."

"What if we camped between towns?" Jaufre said. He looked at Angelique. "And what if we shipped from a small port, with whom we had negotiated a reasonable shipping and lading tax, hired locally for lading, and contracted a favorable rate with a single ship to transport goods?" He let them think about that for a few minutes. "It would remain a small business, obviously. Although I know a Venetian trader with his own ship who might be able to find his way to Harfleur, the wind and gods providing."

The captain sat up. "Who would that be?"

"Giovanni Gradenigo, of the family Gradenigo," Jaufre said.

"I have heard the name," the captain said. She looked at Jaufre with growing respect. "A sea route to the wool markets in Venice, avoiding the overland fees and expenses, would greatly increase your profit. Always supposing this Gradenigo's price for transporting it could be kept to a reasonable amount."

"I believe it could," Jaufre said. "Captain Gradenigo has a wish to build his own business, apart from his family's." He thought of their crossing of the Middle Sea. "And he is a fearless sailor."

"Better an old sailor than a fearless one," the captain said dryly.

They sat in silence for a few moments. "A business small enough not to attract attention," Tregloyne said.

"Obviously," Jaufre said with a smile. "A place called the Shropshires has the best wool, or so I'm told. How far is it from here to there, and how bad are the roads?"

Tregloyne sat forward, his interest now fully engaged. "The condition of the roads I can't tell you," he said. "I've stayed close to home these last few years. The road used to be good from Exeter on, but the royals have been very busy trying to stab each other in the back and they're not particular about trampling who gets in their way betimes. I can give you a few names, though, if you wanted to look for yourself." He thought, frowning. "You would want to make for Ludlow," he said at last. "It's in the heart of the Shropshires, about seventy leagues from Launceston, the nearest market town, which is eight leagues from Glynnow. Before making any firm plans, I would recommend that you travel the route, and talk to such graziers as might be interested, and examine the quality of their wool. Do you know anything about wool?"

"I know where it can be sold at a profit," Jaufre said. He smiled at Shasha and Johanna. "And I know all the ways it can be fiddled to seem to weigh more than it does."

Tregloyne let out his booming laugh. "I'll just bet you do, young Jaufre of Cambaluc." He saw Jaufre's look and said, "Yes? What is it?"

Jaufre hesitated and glanced at Alaric. "I just wondered if perhaps you had heard of a family called de Beauville."

"De Beauville," Tregloyne said, eyes fixed on Jaufre's face in a disconcertingly intent stare. "De Beauville. There was a family of that name. Expatriate Normans, granted land by Henry III, or perhaps it was John Lackland. The property was outside Launceston, I believe."

Jaufre swallowed, his mouth suddenly dry. "'Was?'"

"There were four sons, as I recall," Tregloyne said, matter of fact. "One of them was shipped off to the Templars." He glanced at Alaric. "The first died at Stirling. The second died at Methven. The third died at home of the bloody flux." He shrugged. "All died without issue. Their father made some effort to find the fourth son and return him home to take up his father's estate and provide it with heirs. It came to nothing, unfortunately, and he died soon afterward. The estate reverted to the crown."

Jaufre let out a breath he hadn't known he'd been holding. "Did you know them? Any of them?"

Tregloyne shrugged. "The elder son, to nod to on market days. He was a short, fierce fellow, dark-featured and very bellicose." His eye again wandered over to Alaric. "Much like his father, and two of his brothers. The fourth son was tall and fair. Were they some relation to you, young Jaufre?"

A hand slid into his, and Jaufre felt Johanna's presence warm and solid next to him. "Possibly. It doesn't matter now," he said, a wry twist to his mouth. "Not if they're all dead."

"If you could prove your parentage," Tregloyne said, "the estate—"

Jaufre cut off the words. "I couldn't, and I wouldn't. And besides, I'd rather attract as little official attention as possible."

"Oh? Is there something I should know?"

Jaufre smiled. "No, sir, I do assure you. We have left behind no unpaid debts, and no enemies." He looked around the table. Everyone stared soberly back. No living ones, that was. Except perhaps for Dai Fang, and one could not imagine Wu Li's widow ever leaving Cambaluc, and certainly her reach would never extend as far as England. "It's just that any business is better conducted as far from the official eye as possible. It won't be possible forever, of course, we will require our own charter eventually, but I'd like to keep as many hands out of our pockets as possible."

"Understood," Tregloyne said. "And, young Jaufre, if you manage to put together enough of a supply chain to fill a ship the size of, oh, say the *Faucon*—" He grinned at Angelique "—Glynnow would be a port willing to keep its lading tax—what did you call it—reasonable."

Calling a one-ship dock a port was something of a stretch, Jaufre thought, but they would see what the numbers added up to before they made any firm decisions. Still, he liked Tregloyne, and Angelique felt like someone they could do business with. Wu Company could do much worse.

That evening they gathered around the fireplace and sang and played for their host, to such effect that he was moved to enthusiasm. "God's teeth, are you sure you're merchants? You sound like professional minstrels!"

"We learned from the best," Alma said.

"The best taught you well," Tregloyne said. "Now let's have that drinking song again," and he beat time on his thigh from first verse to last. "You know," he said, when they were done and everyone was quenching their well-earned thirst with watered wine, "a group of traveling minstrels is welcome everywhere."

He met Jaufre's eyes and nodded. "Every village and town and city, every manor and castle. In the towns, you could time your performances to market days, when all the farmers and graziers come in to trade. A man is always eager to pass the time of day with travelers. It's the only way to get the news."

They digested this in silence for a moment. Jaufre, looking around the table, saw no serious objection to the idea, although Alaric did cast up his eyes.

Next to him, Johanna stirred. "Tell me, sir," she said, "do the English race horses?"

Their host and the captain retired up the stairs, Alaric averting his eyes from the spectacle. "Well?" said Jaufre. "What do you think?"

"If we go in telling the truth, we should be prepared to be hung at the first crossroads we come to," Firas said.

Shasha nodded. "There will be strong, entrenched interests vested in keeping things the way they are. Our plan will be money out of their pockets, and they won't like it."

"Perhaps…"

"What, Hayat?"

"Tregloyne said we'd be welcome at manors and castles, too. If we could gain the sponsorship of a lord—"

"But then he'd want his share of the profit," Jaufre said.

"So will Tregloyne, and so will Captain Angelique," Hayat said.

"But they'll earn their share." Jaufre scrubbed both hands through his hair. "It's like being nibbled to death by ducks."

"We don't own a ship," Firas said, "and even if we did we don't know how to sail it. We don't own a port, on either side of the Channel. We were never going to be able to do this alone."

Jaufre made a rueful face. "No." He looked at Hayat. "We'll travel to this Ludlow, by way of Launceston. We'll keep our eyes and ears open, and if we see someone who might help us—"

"And who we think won't hurt us," Alaric said.

"Then we'll see." Jaufre shook his head and gave a short laugh. "It's a good idea, Hayat. It's just that we've been independent for so long, with no ties."

"Gradenigo—"

"He had no power over us beyond our contract," Johanna said. "Accepting a lord's protection would be different."

"Especially when he finds out we can sing," Tiphaine said, yawning.

Jaufre ruffled her hair. "And that you can juggle."

They bedded down around the hearth, but Jaufre found himself too restless to sleep. He got up and went to the back door, whose bar was more easily raised than the immense oak beam across the front doors, and slipped outside.

The square house had been built on the right side of a swift-running stream set between steep banks. A footpath led up the side of the stream. He followed it and in a very short time gained the top of the cliff that ringed the little bay. The moon was nearly full and the sky was cloudless now and the sea calm, so that he could see every slab, every pillar and pinnacle of rock as it rose out of the water, the tiny white ruffles of foam on the rocks, and the sand of the little beach. The bare mast of the *Faucon* barely bobbed as the ship sat sedately next to the rocky pier. From here, in the moonlight, it was easy to see the channel between the two rocky pillars the captain had guided their ship so confidently and competently through that morning.

In this light, from this angle…he squinted. Those two rocky pillars looked almost manmade, or rather as if their original forms had been at least in part deliberately shaped by the hand of man. He wondered how long Tregloyne's people had been living at Glynnow, and how long ships had been landing goods here.

There was mostly grass and a few shrubs on the cliff. Too much wind for trees, perhaps. Farther up the stream he saw a clump of houses clustered on both sides of it, and some turned earth beyond them. Where Tregloyne's people lived, probably.

There was a sound behind him and he turned to behold Johanna standing before him. She had undone her braid, leaving her hair a mane of ripples and curls, each one kissed by moonlight. She was carrying their blankets over her arm.

His heart began to thud against his ribs.

She smiled, and turned to shake the blankets out and lay one neatly on top of the other. She turned back to him, waiting.

He stepped forward to slide his hands around her face. "Johanna."

"Jaufre."

"Are you sure?"

"I am," she said, and raised her face.

He kissed her, sliding his arms around her and pulling her in so tightly that she uttered a slight protest. He loosened his hold immediately. "I'm sorry," he said. His head dropped back, his eyes closed, his blood pounding in his ears. "I have wanted you for so long. Loved you for so long."

"I know that now," she said, tracing his lips with a fingertip. "I'm sorry I was so silly."

"I should have said something sooner."

"I should have known."

"It almost killed me when you went to Edyk."

She raised her head at that. "I'm not sorry I went to him, Jaufre. I won't ever be sorry. I loved him, too. If he had wanted me to, I would have been with him again in Gaza."

"I know." And he had known, and it had nearly killed him to say nothing then, too. "I wanted you to come to me."

"And now I have."

His heart seemed to have lodged somewhere up in his throat. He was so hard he couldn't bear the touch of clothing against his skin. "I don't know if I can go slowly."

She smiled. "We'll go slowly," she said. "Later."

She stepped back and her hands went to her girdle. It fell, and so did her tunic, and her trousers. She stood naked before him, proud, perhaps a little shy.

He couldn't get out of his clothes fast enough, and then finally they were laying together on the blankets, skin to skin, and he finally had his hands on her, on the golden skin turned silver in the moonlight, on the breasts like apples, on the curve of her belly, on the curls between her legs. He knew her so well, had known her most of his life, and still there were mysteries to be found. The creamy taste of her skin on his tongue. The velvet of her nipples. The sweet curve of her hip. The length of her legs, thigh, knee, calf, down to her ankles and back up again, lingering, savoring, feasting.

She was moving restlessly beneath him now, reaching for him. He caught her hand and held it down, and slid his fingers between and up. She was ready for him, hot, wet, clutching at him, trying to draw him in. He exulted in it, wanted to shout it from the top of the cliff. Oh yes, she was ready.

She would be more so. He found the place and rubbed, gently but firmly, with the tips of his fingers. He heard her gasp and he looked up and saw her head raised, watching him. She saw him watching her, and arched her back and opened her legs more.

Johanna exulted in the feel of Jaufre's hands on her where she had imagined them to be ever since that yurt in Kuche. She couldn't catch her breath. She raised her hips and pushed against his hand. "Harder," she said, and she could hardly recognize her own voice. "Harder, faster, oh, Jaufre, oh—" Her hips thrust, raising her body into a bow of flesh and bone straining toward that one glorious end.

She fell back, panting, and he settled in between her legs. "Take me in your hand," he said, and she could hardly recognize his voice, either.

She reached between them and closed her hand around the hard, hot length of him. She had watched, covertly, from time to time, curious, trying to imagine what lay beneath his clothing, if he was like Edyk, or different. He was both, she discovered now, like and different, and he was Jaufre, which made him something else altogether, something more. She tightened her grip and it was his turn to throw back his head, eyes closed, mouth tight. He was wet at the tip and she rubbed it with her thumb, and his breath hissed out. "Johanna," he said, and she shivered at the sound.

She rubbed the tip of him against her, up and down, up to the place that was the seat of all this frenzy of need, down to where he would come inside her, up again, down.

"Johanna!"

"Jaufre," she said, but it was almost more of a growl, and she brought him down again and inside her. He held very still, weight on his elbows, looking at her. She could feel him inside her belly, inside her veins, inside the blood pumping through them. She felt hot all over and cold all over and hot all over again. She wanted more. There was more and she would have it. She raised her legs and wrapped them around his waist, and catching and keeping his eyes, she raised her hips, driving him all the way inside. She pulled back, slowly, agonizingly, and he groaned and closed his eyes. "Johanna. Don't. Don't—"

She grabbed his hair in both fists and said, "Look at me. Look at me!" She pulled him inside her again, and now he took up the motion, slowly, steadily, watching her, wallowing in her, rejoicing as she reached for her pleasure.

"Wait," he said.

"You wait," she said.

"Not yet," he said, "no, Johanna, not yet, not yet—"

He thrust forward for what he was afraid would be the last time and felt her clamp down on him and arch beneath him and heard her cry out his name, and for the very brief space of time granted to him before he followed, he thrilled to the knowledge that it was him giving her that much pleasure.

She felt the base of her spine melt in a burning rush and heard him call her name in a half-shout, half-groan, and felt a rush of power that he had wanted her so much and had waited so long and that it was so very good for both of them.

They lay together, a messy, sweaty tangle of repletion, and watched the moon travel a little farther across the night sky, as the sea chuckled and gurgled against the rocks below, as if nothing special had happened here on this little patch of grass. She smiled to herself.

When he got his breath back he raised his head to look at her. Her eyes were closed and there was a smile on her face. "All good?"

Her smile widened and she opened her eyes and looked at him, a goddess in the moonlight. "All great."

He dropped back with a relieved sigh. "I was afraid I was going to have all the finesse of North Wind at stud."

"You didn't," she said, "but we can work on that."

The next morning Shasha took one look at them and brewed Johanna a cup of her special tea, the same tea she had served her when Johanna went to Edyk. "It's not a guarantee, you understand," she said, "but it works with most women most of the time." When Johanna only smiled she said anxiously, "You understand that what you're doing is what makes babies, don't you, Johanna?"

Johanna burst out laughing.

· Seventeen ·

Summer, 1326 A.D.
England

⟨———⟩

It was a golden summer. Everywhere they travelled in England, people remarked on it. At every village and town, people paused from their work to stand and bask in the sun, as if they were afraid that it would wink out in the next moment. "Forty years of wet misery had we," one Devonshire farmer told them. His broad face was creased with an almost personal resentment. "Bad harvests. No harvests. People eating each other they be so hungry. The winter snow bury the county for months, and the summers the rain come down like it be poured out of a pitcher that never emptied." He closed his eyes and raised his face again to the sunshine. "This be back now. For a while now, maybe. We be enjoying it while we can."

When they weren't drinking in the rays of the resurrected sun the English were toiling in their fields, sowing grain and corn, pruning and espaliering fruit trees, working night soil between rows of vegetables and across fallow fields, pitching every spare scrap of food to the pigs and the chickens, frantic to make up for the previous hungry years, and constantly terrified that the sun would leave again and the rain return and all their work go for naught.

The halcyon weather was of far more interest than the royal to-ing and fro-ing across the Channel and the countryside, but one thing was abundantly clear across all levels of society. The English felt they had been taxed beyond endurance, and what was worse, to no purpose.

Such careful inquiries as to more profitable markets for wool that Jaufre felt safe enough to make were greeted everywhere with interest, if not outright enthusiasm. Further, many of the people he spoke to lay blame for a generation's worth of drought, flood and famine squarely on the doorstep of the ruling family, whose fraternal disorder since the reign of Edward Longshanks had clearly roused the wrath of God Himself. God had visited His displeasure upon the English with forty years of drought, flood, blizzards and famine, and defeat after defeat in the continual war with the Scots culminating in the shameful battle of Bannockburn. Everyone, it seemed, had a brother or a son or a nephew killed at Bannockburn, and what had they died for, indeed, when ever since the bloody Scots raided the border at their whim?

The eating away of Plantagenet properties on the continent by the French was also an issue. Everyone knew how vastly inferior the French forces were to the English. There could be no other explanation than God's personal displeasure. To be taxed for war was duty owed to the king, this was understood. But to be taxed for losing foreign wars on every border and front (and now those thrice bedamned Glendowers were stirring in Wales), to be taxed for wars the English lords were fighting against each other, domestic disputes that led only to more domestic disputes and to the turning of good English fields into abattoirs, this was not so well understood, or so well tolerated. It was in many cases resented enough to create discontent among even the lowest laborers in the fields. It was as yet only a rumble, as examples of rumbling rotted in cages hung from every city gate and castle wall and crossroads post, but it was there if you listened for it. The royal family and the noble families clearly did not bother to listen, and that unconcern caused equal discontent.

But, meanwhile, the sun shone down, and the rain fell in plentiful amounts it seemed only after nightfall, and seemed always to end before dawn. Given this kind of encouragement it was no wonder the land responded. Never had Wu Company seen such a lushly growing countryside, such greenly growing fields, such a profusion of wildflowers. Every ewe had a lamb and often two, every cow a calf, and the amount of chicks in every farm yard was a hazard to navigation. Nor were they alone in marveling at the pastoral scene set before them, because there were English adults living who had seen nothing like it before in their lives, and who could not help but gaze about themselves in wonder.

Jaufre was aware that his own happiness at loving and being loved by the object of his affections colored his perception of everything he looked at, but he tried, he truly tried to look at his surroundings with a merchant trader's clear, practical eye. Was it his fault that all of England looked as if it had been dusted with gilt?

They made love everywhere they could find a moment to themselves, in a hayloft, behind a barn, one memorable time in a lord's solar, on the lord's very bed, while the rest of the troupe entertained the lord and his household in the great hall below. "We could probably be beheaded for this," Johanna said, flushed and scrambling into her clothes.

"Only if we get caught," Jaufre said, snatching a kiss.

Tregloyne had been correct in that a troupe of traveling minstrels would be welcome everywhere. No farmer was so anxious over his crops in this extraordinary year that he could not bring his family into the village for an evening's entertainment. No city burgher was so concerned over the price of pepper that he would allow his neighbors and fellow merchants to attend such an event without him, and possibly from his absence infer that his business was so fragile it required his constant presence. The ladies of the wealthy and the nobility heard their servants speak of the wonderful singing troupe, some members of which had come from as far away as Cathay and Persia, and summoned them for command performances in their halls. Firas with his scimitar, Shasha with her tip-tilted eyes, Hari in his yellow robes, Alma and Hayat with their groomed beauty, Tiphaine with her tumbling curls and juggling fountains, even tall, spare, aloof Alaric, these would all have been oddities had they been traveling on their own, to be regarded with circumspection and treated with caution. In company with Jaufre and Johanna, the young lovers, they were romantic and mysterious but not dangerous.

The one snag was the languages, which seemed to change by the league. Even their facile ears and nimble tongues were put to the test in the battle between Cornish and Devon and Welsh and whatever it was they spoke on the English side of the Welsh border, where even Johanna admitted defeat. Fortunately, almost everyone spoke French in some fashion, from baron to freeman and even a few villeins, and on the rare occasion when they did meet with total incomprehension a translator could always be found.

And, Johanna discovered to her and North Wind's immense gratification, not only were the English vitally interested in horse racing, there seemed to be a racetrack outside every major town. The stallion took on all challengers with enthusiasm. He hadn't raced since Milano and he was eager to stretch his legs and show these inferior English nags the speed a horse with his august lineage considered a winning pace. Gentlemen arrived in groups to inspect him, and to arrange more races for him, and to make appointments for their mares. Some of the mighty were so enraptured that they might have been inclined to exercise *droit du cheval*, had Johanna not been so very obliging about renting him out to stud, and had North Wind not himself held such decided opinions on allowing anyone other than Johanna on his back.

They traveled first to Launceston, where they held their first performance at the livestock fair. From there they went east to Exeter, where they were lucky enough to encounter a fair whose grounds had a stage for rent. From Exeter they went north to Bristol, a seaport with as much bustle as Venice, which boasted a healthy shipbuilding industry and an energetic wool trade, and where the amount and variety of seafood outran their experience even of Venice. "Our competition," Firas said, from where they stood watching the loading and unloading of ships at very nearly a run, with more ships lined up in the channel waiting for their turn.

Jaufre grinned. "No. Pretty soon we'll be their competition."

North of Bristol they detoured around Berkeley, where they had heard the castle was being sacked by one of the Despensers, a king's favorite. This detour brought them deep into the Cotswolds, a farming shire whose cottages were built of a uniform golden stone cut into perfectly square blocks. When they saw the first one Alaric murmur something to himself and went forward to examine the wall of the cottage.

They dismounted. "What is it, Alaric?" Jaufre said.

"Wilmot's father did work like this," the Templar said, running his fingers down the impossibly straight lines and angled corners of the stones. "There is no mortar, do you see? It would take a mangonel to break down this wall."

A farmwife came to the door, her children peering from behind her skirts, but when she saw the party had women in it she relaxed. She spoke enough French to invite them to water their mounts at the horse trough that was a feature of every farmhouse they passed and asked if they would like a meal of bread and cheese and radishes, with fresh fruit to follow. It was late in the day and soon her husband and her eldest son came in from the fields and they were invited to camp near the house. His name was John and hers was Mary and they were happy to share their dinner pottage, and in gratitude for their hospitality Johanna staged an impromptu performance, signaling Tiphaine to bring out her rag balls. Alma produced her charcoal and a precious piece of her stock of parchment to make a sketch of the entire family which was much admired. Firas and Alaric staged a fierce mock duel and of course then the eldest son had to hold the sword of the victor, which of course required instruction, and then Hayat gave the children a ride on the Arabian she had been riding since they'd stolen him out of Sheik Mohammed's stables.

They were seen off with thanks the following morning, and they rejoined the road at Tewkesbury, where they tarried for a week at the behest of the local lord, who had taken a fancy to having every mare in his stables who might be even peripherally interested topped by North Wind, and then left for Birmingham, which rivaled Bristol for size and was a city of artisans and craftsmen, boasting products from the hands of the finest wood workers any of them had ever seen. Jaufre was tempted to switch cargoes, but as Shasha pointed out, fleeces could be folded flat and bound together many to a bundle, whereas chairs and chests manifestly could not.

From there they went west, deep into a verdant country of forested hills and rolling farmland, where every second person they met was a grazier, a farmer of sheep. Jaufre's knowledge about wool grew exponentially, and he bored everyone at dinner on the best breeds to produce the finest fleece to be spun into the best wool fabrics. They avoided Ludlow, Shropshire's largest town, as it belonged to the Mortimers and Roger Mortimer was reputed to be Queen Isabella's lover and about to aid her in invading England. The Despenser sacking Berkeley could easily make Ludlow Castle his next stop. The members of Wu Company did wonder if the impending civil upset would interfere in a major way with commerce, but after forty years of internecine warfare the English themselves were inured to the prospect. "They always be fighting," one grazier said with a dismissive wave of his hand, "but they always be needing clothes to wear and food to eat, too, and I don't see no fine lady milking her own cow or no fine lord tending his own sheep."

Thus far they had avoided any encounters with the warring factions, although there was rumor and conjecture on every tongue. Alaric especially was avid for all the news he could get. All knew that Queen Isabella and Roger Mortimer, in company with her son, Edward, the Duke of Aquitaine and the heir to the throne had gathered together on the shores of Holland, together with a group of Dutch and German mercenaries, prefatory to invading England and wresting the crown from the king's head. Another rumor had it that Charles of France was mustering his own invasion force from Normandy, although Alaric let out a mighty snort when he heard that. Throughout the summer one force or the other was held to be landing at, alternatively, Portsmouth, Hastings, and Dover, with a critical minority holding out for London itself.

As to which of the factions should win, no one would commit themselves, high or low, city or country. It was agreed that Edward had been an ineffectual king with a dangerous predilection for all the wrong friends. However, no one thought—or said out loud—that Isabella and Mortimer could manage the kingdom any better. "They be taking the coin out of the land as fast as ever they could, whoever they be," said a farmer outside of Worcester, "and putting none of it back in again. It make no matter to us which royal ass sits on a throne in London." There were grave nods from his friends, one of whom went so far as to spit and say, "Most of them know not even which way is west," which raised a laugh.

There was a faint hope that Edward's heir, the duke of Aquitaine, might be an improvement over either, but he was only a boy, thirteen or fourteen, wasn't it? He would be surrounded by those same lords who had bankrupted the nation with their petty jealousies and revenges until his majority, or until he gathered together enough powerful lords of his own to oust the old ones, and then it all started over again.

"These folk hold no illusions about their overlords," Firas said one evening.

Alaric opened his mouth to say something, and closed it again. Johanna saw, and wondered what he had been about to say, and why he had thought better of it.

They reached Bristol again in mid-September, and were still there when they heard that Isabella and Mortimer's forces had landed at Orwell in Suffolk. They had intended to move on the next day to Glynnow by way of Plymouth this time, but they waited instead to hear the news. A few days later it came with a group of men under arms, who told them that London and many of the larger cities were in a state of anarchy, everyone in a panic and no one in authority. The king was said to be in flight into the west before the march of Isabella's army, much enlarged by English nobles defecting to Isabella's side. He was expected momentarily in Bristol itself, and the troop of men stationed here, led by one Lord Dundry, were king's men, and were there to meet him.

Shasha began packing immediately, but even all of them working together couldn't outpace a king in full flight and they were coming up on Bristol's south gate just as the royal party clattered through. The heavy wooden gates shut behind them and the bars thudded into their brackets with finality.

The royal party was a pitifully small group of men. The king rode at their center, barely visible over the heads and shoulders of the rest of them, but the roar of the crowd said he was there. Jaufre swore beneath his breath. Johanna squeezed his hand. "It's all right," she said in a low voice. "We don't know any of these people, we'll just—"

"Wilmot!"

It was Alaric, shouting out the name.

A stocky man in full armor, mounted on a destrier, swiveled his head as much as he could. "Alaric? God's nightgown, Alaric is that you?"

Alaric bounded forward and practically yanked the man from his saddle, and then they were both pounding each other on the back, tears streaming down their cheeks.

"Wilmot," Alaric said, choking over his and still pounding his friend on the back, although the other man's armor must have hurt his hand. "I saw Gilbert in Sant' Alberto. He said you were in Chartres. I looked for you there."

"I was there," Wilmot said, disengaging himself and giving a hitch to his cuirass. He looked around and waved at someone in the men surrounding the king. They clattered on without him, and Alaric led the way back to their inn, where Shasha was just in time to reclaim their room.

They commandeered the largest table in the common room and ordered food and drink. "Why did you leave Chartres?" Alaric said. "Gilbert said that you intended to go there and take up your father's trade."

"I went there," Wilmot said, and paused. He was a stocky man with a thick neck and heavily muscled arms that tested the sleeves of his tunic. "I went to the cathedral, and prayed."

Jaufre was watching Alaric, who was wholly enthralled, intent on Wilmot's every word. "Yes?"

"A voice came to me, and told me that I was a soldier, and that I must not yet put up my sword. I must find a worthy cause, and fight for it."

At that Alaric did raise a brow. "Edward?"

Wilmot flushed a little. "It wasn't Edward exactly. It was Robert." He met Alaric's eyes squarely. "Robert saved our lives after Ruad. Robert was English. So I came to England and offered my sword to the king." He refilled his cup and drank deeply, and set it down again with an explosive thump. "Well, God's bones, Alaric. You've been to Chartres.

You've seen the cathedral. If anyone was ever going to hear voices, that would be the place."

They both laughed.

"And you?" Wilmot said.

Alaric glanced at the other table. "I went home, and I was not made welcome, so I returned to the East and offered my services to a much less exalted personage, but he paid well and on time." He gestured. "That's where I met my friends."

Wilmot looked at the circle of interested faces. He blinked at Alma and Hayat, indisputably women but dressed and, God above, armed like men. Hari with his thin, ascetic face and his yellow robe. Firas, unmistakably a warrior, if most certainly not a Christian one. Shasha, with her foreign features set in such a bland expression that one could express no surprise or aversion. Johanna, who earned an appreciative look. Tiphaine, an urchin with curly black hair who had no place at this table. His gaze came to rest on Jaufre, who made no effort to hide his curiosity. Wilmot's eyes widened, and Johanna saw his hand tighten on his cup.

"No, Wilmot," Alaric said. "Your eyes do not deceive you. This is Jaufre. Robert's son."

Wilmot stumbled to his feet, staring. Jaufre, not knowing what else to do, stood up, too.

"I knew your father, boy," Wilmot said.

"I know," Jaufre said. "I've heard the story."

A wintry smile. "All of it?"

Jaufre glanced at Alaric. "I've met Gilbert, too."

"Ah." Wilmot took a deep breath and let it out on a long sigh, and sat down again. His eyes saw something over Jaufre's shoulder. "By the great good lord, boy, is that your father's sword?"

The great sword was leaning against the wall, since it was so long Jaufre couldn't sit properly with it. "It is."

"He gave it to you?"

"He—" Jaufre hesitated. "He died in the East. He left it to me."

"Damn," Wilmot said, with feeling. "I'm sorry to hear that, boy."

"Jaufre," Jaufre said. It had been a long time since he'd let anyone call him boy.

A trace of amusement crossed Wilmot's face. He jerked his chin at the sword. "Do you know how to use it?"

"Yes," Jaufre said. "Not very well, though."

Wilmot shook his head and exchanged a glance with Alaric. "Do you know who gave it to your father?"

"No," Jaufre said. "Who?"

"Wilmot—" Alaric said.

"Your grandfather," Wilmot said. "Before he sent your father off to join the Templars."

"Oh." Jaufre thought of the story that Tregloyne had told him of his paternal relatives. They hadn't sounded like the kind to give a disposable son so costly a gift. "That was kind of him."

Wilmot gave a crack of laughter. "Aye, that it was, boy. And if you're not very good at using it, you should get better." His face set in grim lines. "As soon as possible."

"I'm not a soldier," Jaufre said, meeting his eyes steadily. "I'm a trader. I'm about to go into wool."

"Then give up that sword to someone who can use it," Wilmot said, frowning.

"No," Jaufre said. "It's all I have left of my father. It stays with me. If I have to use it, I will."

Wilmot refilled his mug and sat back. "Is that what you've been doing, Alaric? Setting up as a wool merchant with this—this—"

"We are Wu Company," Tiphaine said. She thrust a thumb beneath her badge and pushed it out. "As you can plainly see by our badge."

Wilmot, nonplussed, stared at the Chinese character. "Oh." He cleared his throat. "Yes. Plainly."

"Furthermore," Tiphaine said, nose in the air, "we are also minstrels. We have performed in some of the highest houses in the west of England, and all of the villages and towns." She thought. "And most of the fairs, too."

"I see." Wilmot stroked his chin. "Are you any good?"

Tiphaine bristled. "We are very good indeed, sir."

"Well. In that case, you had better come and perform before the king after his evening meal."

Everyone sat up with a jerk. "I don't think—" Jaufre said.

"We're not really—" Johanna said.

"It's a great honor, of course, but—"

Wilmot stood up. "Excellent. His majesty's troubles are many. He could use a little distraction. I'll send for you this evening, then."

· Eighteen ·

Fall, 1326 A.D.
England

┣━━━┫

T hey had no occasion to see Bristol Castle on their way north other than as a menacing outline against the sky. It was perched on a hill on the edge of the river Avon, with a moat fed by the river. A formidable curtain wall ran inside the moat and was interrupted by towers. Inside the curtain wall was a massive keep guarded by two sets of doors which had to be challenged and opened sequentially and the entrants inspected by a host of nervous guards in various liveries who looked as if they'd rather not admit anyone at all. They were ushered into a great hall, a large, rectangular room with tapestry-covered walls and tables and benches ranging around three sides. The longest table stood on a platform at the far end of the room.

Wilmot came forward to meet them. "Excellent," he said. "His Majesty was most pleased to hear of the evening's entertainment. The past few days have been an anxious time for him." He gestured and a few stools were brought and set far too close to the king's table for Wu Company's comfort.

Close up, the king was seen to be tall and spare, with blue eyes and thinning fair hair, and looked oddly familiar to Jaufre, although he couldn't think why. His gaze was a little vague, and Jaufre wondered if he were shortsighted. He had deep pouches beneath those eyes, due to worry or drink or both. Probably more of the latter, Jaufre thought, as the royal nose was a little swollen and red-veined. Well, he was about to lose his throne, or so it seemed. Reason enough to drink.

His attendant lords and retainers looked collectively strained, edgy, almost on tiptoe, as if the next loud noise would have them either reaching for their swords or bolting for the stables. From their demeanor, Johanna thought that the stables would be the preference for most of them.

"You have his majesty's permission to sit in his presence," Wilmot said, and retired to lean his shoulders against an ill-executed tapestry depicting Vincent at work with his pickaxe digging the Bristol Channel while his brother Goram slept in his chair.

The king condescended to address them directly. "Yes, indeed, sit and play something..." He hesitated. "Play something lively for us."

They arranged themselves before him, Johanna on a stool with Félicien's gitar, Jaufre standing behind her with a tambour, Alma next to her with a flute, Hari with a lap harp he had learned to play that summer from a Welsh harper they had encountered in Oswestry. Shasha, Firas, Hayat and Alaric stood behind them and Tiphaine, who was developing a rather nice alto, stood next to Hari. Johanna struck the opening chords without consulting her fellow minstrels but they had all known what their first song would be from the moment the king had spoken.

O wandering clerks
You learn the arts
Medicine and magic
O wandering clerks
Nowhere learn
Manners or morals
O wandering clerks!

After a summer of command performances, they had learned to meld their voices together into a mellifluous whole in which the lyrics were clear and understandable to the farthest ear, accompanied by music that intensified the rich emotion they brought to each song. They had learned to stay in a chord that suited their collective reach. They had learned that they had a gift for comedy, as manifested now. Even the king was chuckling when they came to the last line, and before the last note died away Johanna launched into the drinking song they had sung at L'Arête, and again in Glynnow, the one Tregloyne had so enjoyed the night they landed in England.

When I see wine into the clear glass slip
How I long to be matched with it;
My heart sings gay at the thought of it:
 This song wants drink!
I thirst for a sup; come circle the cup:
 This song wants drink!

The king laughed outright at the end of the song and thumped the table with his tankard. They followed this with half a dozen more songs, and by then the tension that had been so clearly felt on their arrival had as clearly eased. The king leaned forward and said, "Our good Wilmot has said that some of you are from the East. Is this so?"

Jaufre looked around and saw that he had been chosen as spokesman. He rose and bowed low. "It is, sire. I am Jaufre, the foster son of Wu Li of Cambaluc of Cathay. This is Johanna, daughter to Wu Li, and Shasha, his foster daughter. Hari is a chughi from the Hindu Kush. Firas—" probably best not to say the word "assassin" in this company "—is a Saracen warrior of Alamut. Alma and Hayat are Persian scholars." Because, well, they were, or Alma was, and he didn't want to go into the whole harem topic in this company of men who were used to getting anything they wanted by just reaching for it. "Alaric—"

Unexpectedly, Alaric stepped forward and made obeisance. "Sire, I am Alaric de Claret. My father was Regnault de Claret. We were presented to your father in Marseille in 1270 by Blaise of Agnois, who was our liege lord."

The king looked a little appalled. "A nobleman's son, and a sworn man? How came you to be a member of this company?"

Alaric, amazingly, did not blush for shame. "I was a member of the Knights Templar, sire. When they…ended, I was still in the East and had to make my way home. I met my friends in Kabul, and we have traveled together ever since."

The king shook his head disapprovingly. "It has ever been our thought that our brother, Philip the Fair, by God's grace the ruler of France while he still lived, was, er, over-enthusiastic in his persecution of the Templars. Our sympathies are with you, Alaric de Claret."

Alaric bent his head. "I thank you, sire," he said. "May I also make known to you the son of a fellow Templar, Jaufre de Beauville."

"De Beauville?" The king frowned. "I thought he said his name was Camelot."

Jaufre, ears burning, inwardly forming the intention to kill Alaric stone dead at his very first opportunity, rose to his feet, tried to hide the tambour, and executed a clumsy bow. "Cambaluc—" he sounded out the syllables "— is where I spent my formative years, your majesty."

"Your father was a Templar, too?"

"He was, my lord. He died in the East some years ago."

"De Beauville," the king said ruminatively. "De Beauville. There is something familiar about the name." He waved a hand. "It will come to me. Now, one more song, I pray you, and then we should all seek our beds this night." He smiled wanly at the man sitting next to him, a stocky, dark-browed man younger than he was. "I doubt few easy nights will be vouchsafed any of us in future."

None of the men in the king's party looked appreciative of this reminder that the king's wife's forces were even now bearing down on them from the east.

"The dawn song," Johanna said, trying to relax the spine that had gone rigid at Alaric's introduction. Royalty was notorious for bestowing favor or blame at its slightest whim. It was much better and far healthier to avoid either. She was furious with Alaric. She plucked a string with fingers she willed not to shake, and sang alone, accompanied only by instruments. There was a moment of silence when she finished, and then the king led the applause. "You have a lovely voice, my dear," he said.

Johanna bent her head. "Thank you, your majesty."

The king sighed, his eyes wandering around the room. "I only wish there were more of mine to hear it, but alas, I believe Isabella landed with so few men because all the support she needed was already here."

That was awkward however you looked at it, and no one knew quite how to reply.

The king smiled. "But that is melancholy talk, after such wonderful entertainment as you have lightened our cares with this evening. I thank you. Wilmot! A purse for, er, Wu Company."

This surprised them all, but they bowed their thanks and backed out of the great hall. As they left, Johanna thought that Edward's eyes followed Jaufre, but it might have been her imagination. She fervently hoped it was.

Firas tossed the purse to Shasha, who weighed it appreciatively in one hand. "Generous of the gentleman. I wouldn't have thought he had coin to spare, especially in his situation."

"Who was that black-browed man sitting next to him, who scowled at us so ferociously?" Hayat unconsciously reaching for the short sword that usually hung at her side. It was forbidden to carry arms into the presence of the king.

"Not a music lover, I fear," Hari said.

"The current favorite, the younger Despenser, I would imagine," Alaric said. "The eldest did not seem to be in evidence."

Johanna managed to fall a little behind with Alaric on the way back to their inn. "Did you mean that to happen?" she said.

"What to happen?" he said.

"All of it," she said. "You have been pushing us north ever since Avignon. Did you always mean to meet with the king? And to bring Jaufre to his notice?"

"It doesn't seem to have harmed him any," he said.

"Kings and princes are omnipotent and capricious," she said. "It's a bad combination, and it's never wise to draw their attention. Don't do it again, Alaric."

Wilmot met them at the inn a little later, and he and Alaric took a seat by the hearth in the common room, talking well into the night.

The next morning they woke before dawn, packed, saddled their horses and led them down to the south gate. There had been some apprehension that with Edward in residence and hostile forces approaching that the gates would remain locked, but they opened at dawn as usual. Wu Company was first out and proceeded south at a fast trot. At the top of the first hill, Alaric reined in and looked back at the castle, the royal standard flying defiantly from the tallest tower. "'The sins of my youth and my ignorances do not remember,'" he said. "'According to thy mercy remember thou me: for thy goodness' sake, O Lord.'"

He crossed himself and sat with his head bent for a moment, and then with a grim expression kicked his mount back into a trot and caught up with the others.

They clattered south as fast as they could without damage to the horses, and the first week of October were welcomed by Tregloyne with open arms, and, a few days later with more restrained enthusiasm by Captain Angelique. "It will be my last trip for a while," she said. "The Channel becomes even more unfriendly than usual at this time of year."

They sat down to a council of war. Jaufre recounted all the information he had gathered from the graziers he had spoken with and the interest he had received in an alternative method of shipping and selling their fleeces. Enough were willing to take a chance on the unknown—and the possibly illegal—to fill the *Faucon's* hold many times over.

"This is what I propose," Jaufre said at last, looking at Tregloyne. "I would build a house and a warehouse here on your property, for the purpose of running a summer caravan between Glynnow and the Shropshires. We would keep to the smaller villages. This can be done, as the villages are never very far off the main roads. There would still be fees and taxes, of course, but much lower fees and taxes than if we went city fair to city fair as the other merchants do. We would transport the fleeces here, and ship them to Harfleur on the Faucon."

He looked at Angelique. "I will write to Captain Gradenigo. When last we spoke, he had the intention of trying to establish a route by sea between England and Venice. They have a new kind of ship they call a merchant galley. It will sail farther in rougher weather with larger cargoes."

"Why Harfleur?" Tregloyne said. "Why not Calais? It's much closer."

"From everything I have heard so far, every power in this part of the world spends all their time either invading the Low Countries or planning to. Harfleur would be a much more peaceful port to cultivate. And they just started their own merchants association, which you should join immediately, captain."

She shook her head. "They won't let a woman join, ship-owner or not." She looked at Tregloyne.

He laughed, his great belly shaking. "It seems young Jaufre here is going to solve all our problems."

"Problems?"

Tregloyne leaned forward, his broad face intent. "Do you intend to settle here in Cornwall, Jaufre?"

Taken aback, Jaufre said, "I mean to start a business here, certainly."

Tregloyne shook his head. "Not what I asked you. Come with me."

He led the company down to the rock pier where the Faucon was docked, but turned left before the pier and followed a path around an outcropping. At first it looked as if they were heading straight into the rocky cliff, and then they saw that the cliff was made of two immense slabs of granite, one in front of the other. The path led around the first slab and between it and the second. There they halted and stood, gaping.

It was an enormous cavern, well above the tide line and remarkably dry. Over the years rows and rows of shelves had been laboriously chipped out the walls. In the center of the cavern, bundles, bags and boxes were stacked in orderly fashion, including, Jaufre noticed, a few bundles of fleeces. He rubbed one of them between his fingers. While not as fine or as well cured as those he had seen in Shropshire, they would still fetch a good price across the Channel. Tregloyne noticed what he was doing and said, "Yes, we farm a few sheep ourselves down here in Cornwall. If my people knew there was a market for more, they might improve their breeds."

Jaufre crossed his arms. "What are you proposing?"

"You don't have to build a house, or a warehouse," Tregloyne said with a wave of his hand. "You have all the storage space you need here, and all the living space you need in my keep."

"You want us to move in with you?"

Tregloyne laughed, the sound booming off the cavern walls. "Tempting as that sounds, no." He looked at Angelique. "I have longed to see what lays beyond my own shores for some time," he said, "but I could not leave my people." He looked back at Jaufre. "If we came to an agreement, you would be factor here, and responsible for the care of the people of Glynnow."

"Making sure they don't starve, is that what you mean?" Johanna said.

"That and more. You will look after their interests, represent any of them if they run into trouble with the sheriff in Launceston, which does happen now and then, or if someone takes it into their heads to encroach on any of their lands. They would look to you, and tithe to you. You would be, in effect, their lord."

Daunted, Jaufre said, "I don't know, Tregloyne. How many people look to Glynnow?"

"A hundred and three," Tregloyne said promptly.

"A hundred and three!" Jaufre looked at Johanna, at Shasha, at the rest of Wu Company. There were only nine of them, and that many had on occasion felt more than enough. And they were all pretty self-sufficient, too, if it came to that. The prospect of having a hundred and three people dependent on him was daunting in the extreme.

"Possibly a hundred and four, if Mistress Melwyn has finally given birth to her first. She's been in labor for a full day and night, poor lady."

Jaufre was speechless.

Tregloyne nodded placidly, as if that was what he had expected. "I can see you're a bit overwhelmed. Let's go back to the house and have some cider. Fresh pressed, from our own trees. You won't have seen them, they're farther inland than the village, in a little valley that protects them from the wind."

When they would have turned to leave the way they had come, Tregloyne said, "No. This way."

He walked back into the cave where the shadows were darkest and seemed to disappear. Jaufre, approaching, put out his hand and where there should have been rock wall there was nothing.

Tregloyne's voice came out of the darkness. "There is nothing to fear." A scrape of flint and a spark, and the master of Glynnow was seen to be holding a torch now ablaze, looking at them with a grin on his face.

"Where does this lead?" Johanna said.

"Follow me and find out," Tregloyne said.

The tunnel was long and narrow and so dark that Tregloyne's torch did not reach very far. Jaufre heard Alma say something, sounding a little panicky, and heard Hayat reply in a soothing murmur. The tunnel ended in a flight of narrow, lumpy steps carved from the rock. They went up, and up, and up some more, until they finally emerged on the cliff above the house, blinking in the light. The exit was concealed by a hawthorn bush that had been allowed to run wild, and they were all scratched and a few of them bleeding by the time they were aboveground again.

The exit wasn't far from where Jaufre and Johanna had come together the first time, and he looked at her to see her smiling at him.

"The Romans mined tin and silver all up and down the coast in these parts," Tregloyne said. "This tunnel was part of one such. We, ah, repurposed it to our own uses. There is another exit halfway up the cliff, nearer the house. I will show it to you later."

He led the way back to the house. As they neared the door, Shasha said, "I know something of the healing arts, sir. Might I offer my help to Mistress Melwyn?"

"We would take it most kind in you," Tregloyne said. "Hicca!" A young boy came trotting up. "Show Mistress Shasha to Mistress Melwyn's cottage, and fetch anything she needs."

"Yes, Tregloyne."

Shasha took her pack and she and the boy vanished up the path next to the stream.

The rest of them followed Tregloyne inside and sat down to pitchers of cider and a dinner of whole roast pig and a vast bowl of mashed turnips. "Here it is, Jaufre," Tregloyne said, as the table was cleared. "You have to belong somewhere. You may have already noticed that our island is a contentious and violent place, and one needs to know who one's friends are. Jaufre of Glynnow has a much better chance to form friendships and associations and partnerships with the English than does Jaufre of Nowhere in Particular. Jaufre of Nowhere in Particular, especially if he is going into competition with the local merchants, will carry no weight with the authorities who are, inevitably, bought and paid for by those same merchants."

"You barely know me," Jaufre said feebly. "Why would you trust me with the care of your people?"

"I'm used to summing up men and women pretty quickly," Tregloyne said, with a sidelong glance at the captain. "It comes of living on such a chancy place as the Cornish coast." He smiled. "I like you. I like your friends. I especially like how your plans will bring prosperity to my people. They could use some." He held up a hand. "Don't worry, I'll spend this winter with you, to make you known to Glynnow and to see you into the way of things. But next fall—" he looked at Angelique "—next fall it is my wish to leave with Angelique on her last trip of the season."

He drained his cup and pushed himself to his feet. "I will leave you to discuss this. It's not a decision to be made without due consideration, and you will have more questions. We will talk again in the morning."

He and Angelique ascended the stairs, and the company gathered around the hearth. Jaufre's head, for one, was whirling. "Well," he said. "What do you think?" He looked at Johanna.

"I think I like it here," Johanna said. "I think you do, too." She jerked her head in the direction of the dock. "And I think here we have easy access to a ship if we need to feel the Road beneath our feet again."

"What if they sail away and we never see them again?" Tiphaine said in a small voice.

"They won't," Jaufre said, tousling her hair. "Tregloyne will want to check up on how I am doing my job, and Angelique makes her living on the freight she ships in and out of Glynnow. But even if they did, why…" He smiled. "We'd build our own ship. Or have Ser Gradenigo build one for us." He looked around the circle, every face dear to him. "What you think?"

Hayat frowned. "I think I spent too many years locked up in a harem. I've only had a taste of freedom. I don't think I'm ready to settle down."

"Or me," Alma said.

"Or me," said Hari, not unexpectedly.

"But this could be home for you," Johanna said. "You could come back whenever you wanted, stay as long as you wanted."

"I like the sound of that," Alma said, smiling at her.

"I wasn't intending on leaving forever," Hayat said.

Hari bowed his head. "There is much still to be learned here."

"Angelique will have to build a warehouse on her side," Jaufre said, thinking. "And I must write to Gradenigo immediately. Perhaps I should even go to him myself."

"I will take your letter to him," Firas said. "Shasha will want seeds to grow her own herbs, and a larger supply of spices if she's going to be ministering to the needs and ailments of an entire village."

"You're staying, then?" Jaufre said.

Firas nodded. "If Johanna is staying, Shasha is staying, and if Shasha is staying, so am I." He smiled. "I'm already half a merchant. I might as well become a whole one."

· Nineteen ·

Winter, 1326-1327 A.D.
England

———

Firas, Alma, Hayat and Hari departed with Angelique two days after Tregloyne had made his offer. Alma, Hayat and Hari were bound for Paris. Firas would accompany them that far before moving on to Lyon and then Venice if the mountain passes were open to travel.

"Ask Imbert if Laloun ever showed up," Johanna said. At Firas' blank look she said, "Félicien's maid?"

Firas' face cleared. "And if she has?"

"Make an offer of employment. Alma and Hayat could use a maid." At his expression she said impatiently, "Fine, if they don't want her bring her here, we'll find a job for her."

Firas salaamed deeply, hand to heart, lips and head. "All shall be as you desire, mistress."

She picked up a roll and made as if to shy it at him. He went out, laughing.

Jaufre, Johanna, and Shasha settled in to plan an English extension of the Road, and Jaufre began his study of how to be a lord under the tutelage of Tregloyne. "Not a lord," Tregloyne told him, "God's teeth, save me from that, I'd be taxed to death and have to take up arms at the king's behest to boot. Master of Glynnow is what they call me, and what they'll call you."

At first Jaufre was certain they wouldn't. They were a taciturn bunch, these Cornishmen, and unwilling to put their trust in strangers, no matter whether Tregloyne vouched for him or not. Grunts were the usual response to his attempts at conversation, and when it wasn't grunts it was Cornish, which was worse.

He didn't force things, and instead let his company speak for him. Shasha spent part of every day in the village, administering tonics and tinctures and dressing wounds and splinting the occasional broken limb. Alaric had hired two of the more likely Glynnow lads to help him maintain their small armory, and had begun to teach them how to use a small sword, which, when they went back to the village and told the tale, had the entire male population of the village there the next day. Tiphaine was ever attended by a covey of small children who wanted to learn to juggle, and after a while she started teaching them songs from Wu Company's repertoire.

Johanna kept herself busy with North Wind and the rest of their string. This was a good land for horses, covered in rich sweet grass, and as the summer's travels had taught her horses were highly valued in England not just for transportation and war but for entertainment. She broached the notion of planting more oats and lucerne with the villagers, and was met with a receptive ear. She brought the men of the village into the stables a few at a time to introduce them to North Wind and to discover if there might be some among them with the gift for horses. She found a boy, Talan, who could be relied on to muck out stalls and replenish feeding troughs when he was supposed to. Then one day she found Talan's younger sister, Kerra, in North Wind's stall, currying him with long, slow strokes. North Wind was so annoyed by this invasion of his personal space that he was sound asleep. Johanna engaged brother and sister as permanent stablehands on the spot.

When they discovered that Cornishmen were natural stonemasons Johanna hired some to expand the stable. When the Arabian mare who had traveled with them all the way from Talikan came into season she planned to put North Wind to her. The resulting foal would be the beginning of their own breeding stock.

Shasha hired more men to build a high-walled garden in which to plant her garden, aided in its design by Jaufre, who remembered the walled garden at Sant' Alberto. She hired boys to bring in topsoil for the garden by the basket, hauled on their shoulders from a vacant farm inland, and then set them to working seaweed harvested from the beach into the soil.

Johanna got wind of the vacant farm and went to look for herself. She came back full of plans for a practice track and badgered Tregloyne to seek out the holder of the title to see if he would sell. He did, he would and for a pretty cheap price, too, and Johanna found herself in possession of a nice piece of flat land where most of the rocks had long since been harvested for fences. She got two men from the village to clear the undergrowth that had begun to creep back in after the farm had been abandoned and then set them to building a dirt oval from one corner of the lot to the opposite corner. The village carpenter built a wide, wooden rake according to her specifications and each morning the dirt of the track was groomed. While the weather held she was out there every day, exercising each horse in turn and when he insisted North Wind twice a day.

Before midwinter the horses were snugly housed and the walled garden was ready for planting in the spring. Improvements to the house were in the planning stages because, Johanna told Jaufre, she was not prepared to spend their lives sleeping in the same room as the rest of Wu Company.

"Or not sleeping," he said, sliding his hands around her waist and kissing her.

When she could speak again she said, "Oh well, there are always the stables."

"So there are," he said, and tossed her up in his arms and carried her out the door.

Tregloyne, accompanied by Alaric, disappeared inland for a month, and returned in time for Christmas, barely beating the first winter storm to the door. He handed Jaufre a scroll tied with a red ribbon.

"What's this, then?" Jaufre said. It was a long document, written in Latin side by side with a French translation. His eyes ran down the document, and his jaw dropped. He read it a second time, and a third, before he looked up, dazed. "You adopted me?"

"All legal according to the laws of the land. Keep that in a safe place and should someone try to come the lord over you, pull it out. It was the best thing I could think of to keep you and this place safe."

Jaufre carefully rolled the document back up and retied the ribbon. Johanna, watching, smiled to herself. Jaufre liked Tregloyne a great deal. It was warming to know that that feeling was returned.

Alaric had brought back news of the wider world. "Edward and the few followers he had left fled into Wales. The queen said that since he'd left the country their son should take the throne, and he did so on October twenty-sixth."

"He was right then," Johanna said. "The queen didn't have to bring anyone with her. All her supporters were already here."

"Waste no sympathy on Edward of Caernarfon, as he is now to be styled," Tregloyne said. "Twenty years we had of him, and in twenty years there was neither peace nor prosperity in the land. He had a positive genius for befriending the one person who was most guaranteed to inflame the nobles into rebellion, and to inflict more suffering on humbler folk than they have any right to bear."

"He looked tired, when we sang for him in September. Maybe he's glad to be rid of the crown. What have they done with him?"

"He's at Kenilworth, they say."

"And the men who were with him?"

"The younger Despenser was dragged through the streets of Hereford by four horses, and then hanged from a fifty-foot scaffold so everyone could see, and so could he, because he was not quite dead as they cut off his cock and balls and threw them into a fire burning below." Alaric's voice was flat and even. "His entrails and heart were pulled out and also thrown into the fire. One hopes he was dead by the time his body was lowered to the ground to be butchered into quarters." He paused. "It is said that the crowd whooped for joy during the entire display."

Even Tregloyne looked a little ill at this.

"His head hangs now in London. The elder Despenser was likewise disposed of in Bristol, the day after the new king was proclaimed. They sent his head to hang on the walls of Winchester."

Johanna shuddered, and thought of Gokudo before the walls of Talikan. "And Wilmot?"

"I can discover no news of him." Alaric looked drawn. "It may be that he held so minor a post in the king's household that he escaped punishment. After all, they couldn't kill them all."

Tregloyne snorted.

At Christmas they held a celebration at the house for the entire village, and put on a performance for which Johanna brought out the Robe of a Thousand Larks, which alone elevated her to the role of goddess in the dazzled eyes of the villagers. Who were then doubly astonished when their new master stepped up with a tambour and joined his pleasant baritone to her smoky contralto. Shasha and Tiphaine provided an admittedly high baseline that nevertheless had everyone tapping their feet. These Cornish could dance, too, as they discovered in short order, and it was a merry evening that ended in gifts for all that Tregloyne had brought back with him from his trip to Launceston. They roasted a whole beef and a whole sheep and Tregloyne had brought sugar back from the Launceston shops for the baker to make iced cakes. There was a barrel of hard cider, but only one, and it wasn't enough for anyone to become too jolly.

Jaufre watched everything Tregloyne did very carefully, storing away information against the next Christmas celebration, when Tregloyne would be gone and Jaufre would be expected to host his own feast. Tregloyne read his intent expression correctly and roared with laughter. "You will make a fine Master of Glynnow, my boy, never fear!"

After the new year Johanna called for the carpenter, this time to remodel the first floor of the house. As it existed it was little more than a copy of the great room below, with the addition of a garderobe, which at least obviated the necessity of chamberpots. There was one bed and one clothes press and one stool and one fireplace that was built into the existing chimney. The roof of the first floor was much lower than that of the great hall and therefore more amenable to walls, as well as much easier to heat. She was able to create eight rooms separated by walls made of woven lathes and a plaster compounded of sand, straw and clay found in deposits along the coast which the local people used for pottery. She set the carpenters to making beds, and found a local woman to sew mattresses and fill them with straw and sweet smelling herbs. She was determined to have their own weavers in Glynnow as soon as possible, but for now most of the beds were without blankets.

The rooms smelled of sawdust and lavender when they were done. There was room and beds enough to house all of Wu Company when they were all at home.

When they were all at home. Johanna wondered what it would be like, to live in one place all the rest of their lives, and knew a cold feeling in the pit of her stomach. She took the feeling to Jaufre. "We must find another Jaufre," she said.

"What?" Jaufre was hunched over Wu Li's book, calculating from Johanna's drawings of the past summer's journey through England where they should be and when during the following summer's buying trip, so as to produce some kind of schedule for Captain Angelique.

"We've spent our whole lives on the Road, Jaufre," she said.

"What?" He looked up.

"We've spent our whole lives on the Road," she said. "We don't know how to live in one place."

He closed Wu Li's book and put it down carefully. "I thought you liked it here."

"I love it here," she said. "I'm coming to love the people here, too, and the land is beautiful. But it won't be enough to satisfy me my whole life long, or you, either." She laid a hand on his arm. "You need to find another Jaufre, and train him up as you are being trained. A trustworthy man from the village, known to the people here."

"Another Jaufre," he said. "To take the reins when we are gone away for a time."

She grinned. "Someone, preferably, who won't usurp us in our absence."

He took it to Tregloyne, who saw the sense of it at once. "You'll be gone every summer on buying trips. You'll need someone sensible in authority while you're gone then, too. Let me think on it."

Shortly thereafter Shasha announced, "No one in Glynnow can read or write."

She looked at Tregloyne, who raised his hands. "And for what would they be needing that, lady?"

"They at least need to know how to sign their names," Shasha said severely.

"They can make their mark like everyone else," Tregloyne said.

So Shasha started a school for the children at the house most afternoons, beginning with writing their names. She taught them in French, because it was the language of trade from Ludlow to Venice. Some of the children were very quick to learn their letters, some not so. The quicker ones she began to teach their numbers, too. If they were going to be members of a merchant's company, they would be that much harder to cheat if they were in possession of both skills.

During a spell of fine weather in February Alaric made another trip to Launceston, for salt for the kitchen, he said, but really for news, as they all well knew.

While he was gone Angelique took advantage of that same fine weather to make a quick trip from Harfleur, carrying spices, dried fruits, bales of linen, wool and silk, and Firas.

Shasha stood at the top of the path, watching the assassin take long strides toward her. They disappeared into their new room and were not seen again until the following morning, both ravenous with hunger. Alma and Hayat and Hari sent their regards from Paris, where Alma had discovered the existence of a library even larger than the one in Venice and had, according to Firas, been translated straight to heaven. Hayat had found a swordsman who didn't disdain teaching a woman and a weaver of silk who was willing to take her on as a paying apprentice. Hari had disappeared inside the cathedral of Notre Dame, which in Firas' opinion while magnificent did not hold a candle to Chartres.

The Alps having proved passable, Firas continued on to Venice. "I found Ser Gradenigo at home," he said, "and he is very excited about this venture of ours. His new ship is scheduled to be launched in May. He had me meet with the weavers' guild, and they, too, are very excited at the prospect of getting their hands on English fleeces without having to pay excise taxes on them from Dortend to Cenis to Ravenna."

"Did you see Moreta?"

Firas inclined his head. "One gets the impression that Ca' Polo resembles something of a hostile frontier these days, with Serra Polo on one side and the lady Moreta on the other, but she looks well. She wrote, so you may judge for yourself."

"And Laloun?" Johanna said. "Did Sieur Imbert have any word of her?"

Firas smiled at her. "He did. She is working in his house. I spoke with her, and she is happy there." HIs smile faded. "She was very sorry to hear of her mistress' death, but she told me to say that she was glad she did not have to die in L'Aréte."

"Any news of L'Arête?" Jaufre said.

"There is rumored to be a new lord of L'Arête," Firas said, "but nothing more than that. Except—"

"Yes?"

Firas toyed with his mug, making them wait. "This new lord seems less inclined to teach his tenants how to fly." He looked up, smiling beneath his beard.

"Do you think the new lord is Florian?" Johanna said.

"Who knows?" Jaufre said, pushing himself to his feet. "And who cares?" He gave Firas a brief smile and went out. Johanna watched him leave but stayed where she was.

Alaric returned home a few days later with a long face. "Parliament assembled at Westminster after Christmas, and insisted that Edward be replaced by the Duke of Aquitaine. It was done on January twenty-fourth, and the new king crowned on February first." He shook his head.

"The old king was a bad king, and bad for England," Tregloyne said.

"Perhaps," Alaric said, "but the new king is barely fourteen years old. It is Isabella who rules England now, with her lover Mortimer at her side."

"What have they done with the old king?"

"He is imprisoned in Berkeley Castle, under the closest watch."

"They should kill him and be done with it," Tregloyne said.

Alaric was shocked. "He was anointed by God!"

"Proof positive that even God can make a mistake. He's a constant danger to the new king, a point of rebellion for every noble who lost out in the new order. There are always some who back the wrong horse and are then aggrieved and scheming for revenge and redress. Pah."

"Tregloyne," Johanna said, "I have often wondered why there is no priest in Glynnow."

Tregloyne's smile was broad and sharp. "Why, lady," he purred, "it is simple. There is no priest in Glynnow because there is no church in Glynnow."

Johanna laughed. Alaric looked perfectly appalled.

Spring arrived like an invading army, if possible even more aggressively than the previous year, pushing aside the melting snow with vigorous shoots of green grass and brightly-colored wildflowers. Brambles sprouted a profusion of roses red, pink and white, swarmed over by bees drunk on nectar. Hawthorns budded in the hedges and the blooms perfumed the air with an aroma that was said to smell like a woman in need. Shasha harvested the flowers and the berries from one tree for the distillation of an excellent tonic for an unsteady heart, and then allowed herself to be seduced beneath it, all in the name of the study of medicine, she assured Johanna, who noticed that Shasha had had recourse to her special tea herself.

Johanna and North Wind spent most of the daylight hours together and Glynnow became accustomed to the sight of the bronze-haired young woman clinging to the back of the great white stallion, the two of them galloping at full speed across the grass-topped cliffs of the coast. It was scandalous, to be sure, a woman on a stallion and that woman in trousers besides, but the people of Glynnow were learning to take a certain pride in the eccentricities of their new master and his woman. They certainly weren't ordinary.

Captain Angelique returned with the *Faucon*, and they gathered at dinner that evening to set out the details of the summer's buying trip and fix dates for *Faucon's* departures, hopefully with a hold full of high grade fleeces.

"I know there is an excellent livestock fair at Launceston," Jaufre said, "but then we'll have to feed the pack animals all the way to Ludlow. I think we should wait and buy our pack animals there."

"You know what they'll cost in Launceston," Tregloyne said. "You have no idea what the prices will be in Ludlow."

"Even if they're high, we'll have saved on feed and pasturage en route."

"And we'll be able to travel faster going north," Johanna said.

"Are we Wu Company, or Jerome's Jongleurs?" Tiphaine said.

"Wu Company," Jaufre said firmly, and relented a little when the girl looked disappointed. "We can perform if the price is right, but we pick and choose and we don't wear ourselves out singing. We're traders first."

Tiphaine sighed.

"Who runs things here?" Firas said.

"Ah," said Tregloyne, and beckoned to a small man with dark hair and eyes, calloused hands and an air of quiet authority. "This is Kevern. He is the headman of the village, and a carpenter by trade."

Johanna nodded. Kevern was responsible for most of the work done on the first floor of the house.

"He's a Glynnow man back ten generations. Everyone knows him and everyone trusts him, including me. And—" Tregloyne winked "—he has a large enough family that he's happy for the extra income."

"How big?" Shasha said.

"Thirteen," Kevern said, not without pride.

"Talan and Kerra among them?" Johanna said, Talan having said that his father worked with wood.

He nodded

"And Cador, I believe," Shasha said. "He's one of my best students."

"So we leave Glynnow in good hands," Tregloyne said, rubbing his own together. "How soon can we be off?"

"The sooner the better," Captain Angelique said.

"The merchants of Harfleur anxious for our wool?" Alaric said, almost genially.

"Better," she said, and produced documents that guaranteed sales at a set price per bale that made Jaufre smile. "No limit on amount," she said, pointing.

"Well done, sister," Alaric said, sounding almost respectful.

Captain Angelique actually smiled.

It seemed spring in England could cure anyone of anything.

"Do we take North Wind?" Shasha said.

"Can anyone stop him from coming?" Jaufre said.

Johanna laughed.

They set forth the first week of June, this time with Tregloyne in tow, who, having seen little of his native land beyond Exeter was anxious to see more of it before he set off with Captain Angelique to explore foreign lands. They performed as minstrels when the purse was right, and accepted those races for North Wind when those requests were made by those too powerful to refuse, but otherwise Jaufre was insistent that they move up the road with all dispatch. They took one detour for Alaric, passing near Berkeley Castle, where Edward of Caernarfon was imprisoned, and where they asked as many questions as they dared. Most were too wise to say anything, but one older farmer did say, "Oh, aye, they have the old poofter locked away up there. No one has seen him since they brought him in, but there is talk he won't be there long." He gave them a significant wink, downed his mead and went on his way.

"A rescue attempt?" Jaufre said in a low voice.

"Not much of one if the local people are already talking about it," Alaric said, looking disgusted, and went off to find the tavern where the castle guards drank, because there was always that tavern in a fortified town. It was the one nearest the gate, called, imaginatively, the Crown and Castle. He returned late that evening to their campsite after they were all asleep.

"No news of Wilmot, then?" Johanna said tentatively the next morning.

Alaric shook his head.

They hastened up the road to Worcester, where there was a fine livestock fair that was able to supply all their needs. They led this much longer caravan to Ludlow and environs—"Now it feels like we're back on the Road," Jaufre said, grinning—and spent the next eight weeks going from grazier to grazier, collecting fleeces as they went. They prospered so well that Jaufre began to wish they'd bought twice as many pack animals, but Johanna overruled him. "Better to sell all we have than have more sitting around mouldering in the cave," she said. "Besides, we don't know how many donkeys the Launceston livestock fair can absorb."

As it happened, the Cornish tin mines further west were always in need of more donkeys and they were able to dispose of their stock for a penny more per head, which even Johanna admitted was a triumph. They reappeared in Glynnow on the first of September to find that nothing had burned down and no landless lord had appeared to seize the estate by force. Kevern's chest swelled when he reported the size of the harvest, and animals and villagers alike were healthy. Everyone fell to with a will to transport the bundles of fleeces to the cavern below, there to await shipment to Harfleur and, possibly even trans-shipment to Venice, if Gradenigo had managed to find his way up the coasts of Spain and France to the correct port.

Jaufre, without prompting from Tregloyne, declared a holiday and held a harvest festival. Mead, wine and small beer ran like water and there was a whole roast pig and small mountains of fruit pasties. The company sang songs not yet heard by the villagers and Tiphaine startled them all by conducting a choir of village children performing "O Wandering Clerks." Hearing those shrill young voices raised in that particular song took Johanna straight back to Kashgar and the first time she had heard Félicien sing it, dressed in her black robe and cap, her head thrown back, her high, pure voice rising up and reaching out and enveloping them all in song. She had to close her eyes against sudden tears. She felt Jaufre's arm come around her and opened her eyes to see that his were wet, too. "We will not forget her," he said.

That night Jaufre said, "I love being on the Road, wherever it leads us, but it's good to come home, too. For one thing, we don't have to work so hard to find a place where we can be alone." He closed the door of their own room firmly behind them, and dropped the bar into the brackets.

Johanna reached for her braid and began to loosen her hair, her heart beating high in her throat. Was it like this for every woman and every man who came together? Perhaps she should ask Shasha.

He walked toward her, pulling his tunic over his head, pushing his trousers down and kicking them to one side.

Perhaps not.

He reached up and replaced her hands with his own, unplaiting her braid and tousling the bronze-streaked hair into a wild mane. She shook it back from her face and raised an eyebrow, waiting. He smiled and reached beneath her tunic to yank her trousers down and pushed her on the bed. He thrust into her without waiting and she cried out at the shock, but she was ready for him. He reached between them and rubbed and she made a sound deep in her throat and tried to move her hips. He wouldn't let her, holding her down, rubbing that place where all the pleasure came from. She whimpered. She begged. She pleaded. "Jaufre. Move. Please. Move."

"No," he said, his voice a deep growl, and he shoved her tunic up and sucked a nipple hard into his mouth, and all the while he was this hard, hot, unmoving presence within her and all the while his thumb was rubbing, rubbing and she tried to move and couldn't. She reached up and caught the hair at the nape of his neck in her hand, forcing him to look at her. His eyes were slits, his lips drawn back, his neck corded. She smiled, a feral, predatory smile, and contracted her muscles around him.

He very nearly shouted. "Ah! Johanna! That's not fair!"

"Move," she said, her turn to growl, and he did then.

They lay together in an exhausted tangle, watching the last of the light leave through the tiny window in the thick stone wall. "Yes," she said, her voice slurred from pleasure, "it is nice to come home."

He laughed and nuzzled her neck. "It almost doesn't feel real." When she raised her head and looked at him, he said, "I've thought of this, of us like this, for so long." He traced the line of her spine. She arched involuntarily, and he smiled. "It's still hard for me to believe this is real."

"Some people take a lot of convincing." She touched his face, tracing his eyes, his nose, his lips, threading her fingers into his hair to pull him back to her. "So was it worth the wait?" she said against his mouth. When he didn't answer at once she rolled on top of him, caging his hips in her thighs and shoving his arms back against the bed. His sex stirred against her and she smiled. "You are at my mercy," she said. "Answer me, or be destroyed."

She looked flushed and triumphant and rumpled and he'd never seen anything so beautiful in his life. Best of all she was naked and in his bed, and so was he. "I don't know," he said. "Maybe I'll take destruction."

A thunderous knocking woke them well before dawn. "What?" Jaufre said, feeling for the sword that hung always within reach before his eyes were half open.

"Who is it?" Johanna said, awake and alert in an instant and already pulling on her clothes. She heard doors opening and other voices, and when she had their door open everyone else was already in the hall and making for the stairs, and everyone was armed. "I knew things were going too well," she said to Jaufre in an undertone.

"Nonsense," he said, stealing a quick kiss before leaping the last three steps into the great hall. He strode to the door and said in a loud voice, "This is Jaufre, master of Glynnow. Who disturbs our rest at this hour?"

Tregloyne, last down the stairs, smiled.

"Wilmot, friend to Alaric de Claret. I must speak with him."

Jaufre looked at Alaric, who stood next to him with his sword drawn.

"Is that his voice?" Alaric nodded.

They unbarred the door and Wilmot stumbled in. He was alone and distraught, and they immediately barred the door again behind him. Shasha stirred up the fire on the hearth and heated some wine and Wilmot drank it gratefully. He looked thinner than when they'd seen him last, and his clothes were worn and shabby. "What's amiss, Wilmot?" Alaric said. "Is it the king?"

Wilmot nodded as Shasha refilled his cup. "They're going to kill him."

"Good," Tregloyne said, but he said it beneath his breath and only Shasha heard him. She gave him a speaking glance.

"There have been three attempts to free him," Wilmot said, "one in April, one in July, and one just this month that nearly succeeded. Isabella and Mortimer will no longer tolerate his presence. It is too dangerous to them."

"What are you going to do?"

"I'm going to get him out of Berkeley and across the Channel to the continent. You said you had a ship. Do you know when it will call here next?"

"No, but soon," Jaufre said. "The captain knows we have goods to carry to Harfleur at this time of year."

"Harfleur?"

"It is the *Faucon's* home port."

Wilmot brightened a little. "Harfleur is still small enough that we may escape notice. Will you arrange passage for us?"

"How many?"

"The king and one attendant."

"Is there money?"

"There is, more than enough. I'll explain later." He looked at Alaric. "I'm sorry, Alaric, but there is no one else to ask. I need your help to get him away."

"There was no need to ask, Wilmot." Alaric stood up, his shoulders squared, his chin high, his expression that of one who had heard the trumpets sound one more time. "Of course I will go with you."

"So will I," Jaufre said.

"What?" Tregloyne said.

"What!" Johanna said.

"It's forty-five leagues to Berkeley," Jaufre said, thinking out loud. "Four to five days—"

"If we can get there in four," Wilmot said, "the king's keepers will be away overnight in Bristol."

Tregloyne regarded Wilmot, clearly wondering how Wilmot had arranged that.

"Four days," Jaufre said, "provided we camp and carry our own food. We'll take the Arabians. They're the best over distance and God knows they're used to a hard pace."

"Jaufre!"

"You heard what was done to the Despensers, Johanna. Can we really leave that man, that tired old man who listened to us sing with so much pleasure, who rewarded us so handsomely, to that kind of end? When we could have helped to prevent it?"

"You can't be serious," Shasha said flatly, and next to her Tregloyne, arms crossed over his chest and a glower on his face, gave a most emphatic nod.

"Shasha, listen—"

"No, Jaufre. You listen to me. I have followed the two of you halfway around the world, and make no mistake, I don't regret a moment of it, but after five years we have finally come to rest. I can plant a garden and begin my book of herbal remedies, and—and perhaps begin a family."

She glanced at Firas. He smiled at her. Visibly heartened, she turned back to Jaufre. "You can build your wool business. Johanna can start her breeding stable. For a full year we have been making a home for ourselves here in Glynnow, and now you want to hare off on some idiot mission to rescue a man whose rule, by every report we have ever heard, this adopted country of ours is well rid of? You want us to think of what happened to the Despensers? Let's think for just a moment of what they will do to you if they catch you!"

She had been gaining in volume as she spoke and by the end she was standing on her feet with her voice ringing off the stone walls. She paused, breathing heavily and glaring at Jaufre.

"Besides," Tregloyne said, leaning forward, "you are the new master of Glynnow, or had you forgot? You have responsibilities here, people depending on you here. Or did I go through all that legal nonsense for nothing?"

"I don't take up those responsibilities in full until you leave," Jaufre said.

"And if you are killed during this ridiculous rescue attempt? If you don't return?"

"Then you'll have to find another Jaufre."

Tregloyne's face a turned a dark red. "God's nightgown, mayhap I should find another Jaufre now, if the one I have is determined to risk his life on such a foolish and dangerous and useless mission!" His voice boomed so loudly it created its own echo.

For the first time since she'd known her, Johanna saw that Tiphaine was afraid, and tried to give her a reassuring smile. It wasn't much of a success, because Tiphaine flinched away from it and went to curl up in a ball next to the hearth, studiously ignoring the ongoing argument.

"That is of course your choice, Tregloyne," Jaufre said, so politely and in so comparatively calm a voice that Johanna for one realized there was no moving him from his purpose. Her mind raced for a solution, and found only one.

Into the fraught silence Wilmot, who was looking at Jaufre with an expression Johanna could not quite interpret, said softly, "There is much of your father in you, boy."

"The name's Jaufre, not boy," Jaufre said curtly, and turned back to Shasha. "Alaric and Wilmot were friends of my father's. My father can't help them. I can."

Shasha gave a sound very much like an infuriated cat. Tregloyne growled.

"Very well," Johanna said. "If you're going, I'm going, too."

As one, all the men turned to gape at her. "Oh, of course," Jaufre said scathingly. "On North Wind, I suppose. Whom no one will notice as we gallop over the countryside, or recognize as the reigning racing champion of all England!"

"I'll darken his hide with dirt, and need I remind you that North Wind is an army in and of himself?" Johanna said. Her voice was as calm as his had been when he faced down Tregloyne. "Jaufre, if you thought being together meant I stay at home like a good little girl while you ride off on some Sir Gawainish quest, you much mistake the matter. Being together means being together, no matter the journey or the destination or the danger." She crossed her arms. "We are together, truly together, sharing everything, going forward from this moment. Or we are apart. Choose."

She stood before the fire on the hearth, slim, vibrant, willful, determined. He knew her well enough to know that she meant exactly and precisely what she said.

"You can't bring a woman," Wilmot said, who looked horrified at the prospect. "We have to move fast. She'll slow us down, and if there's a fight we'll have to protect her."

Alaric cleared his throat. "I'm sorry, Wilmot, but I'm afraid they come as a set." And he smiled at Johanna, the first time in all their acquaintance he had ever done so. "And I promise you, she won't slow us down, and you will not have to protect her in a fight."

Jaufre couldn't help it. He laughed out loud.

Johanna laughed, too, and ran upstairs to get her belt, boots and short sword.

They rode by day and by night, stopping only to rest the horses before pressing on again. Alaric was reminded of the ride from Sant' Alberto to Milano and over the mountains into Lyon, with Jaufre nagging them on every step of the way. This time it was Wilmot pushing them, but there was no need because everyone was in a hurry for different reasons. "For one thing, the Faucon is expected any day," Jaufre said, "and I don't want Edward sitting around Glynnow waiting to be discovered while he waits for transportation."

They went around Launceston at night and avoided Exeter altogether, eating dried meat and fruit and feeding the horses on oats they had brought with them. Covered with dirt to color his white hide, North Wind was in excellent form, nipping at the rumps of the others when he felt they were going too slow. "By Christ's holy bones," Wilmot said on the second day, "he can practically talk," and there was no further grumbling about women slowing them down.

The fourth day they passed Bristol near enough to see the castle on the hill and the glitter of sunlight on the Avon. When they approached Berkeley it was coming on sunset. Wilmot led them to a thicket of trees clustered below the high walls far enough out of earshot of any guards patrolling the crenelated wall. There was a large round tower, looking solid and impenetrable. "That is where he is being held," Wilmot said, pointing.

"Is the front door the only way in?"

"No." Wilmot hesitated. "Jaufre, if you and Johanna could provide a diversion, Alaric and I can get the king out of his cell and outside the walls."

"What kind of diversion?"

"Draw the attention of the guards to the front gate."

"How?" Jaufre said.

Wilmot smiled. "You had no problem getting and holding the attention of the king the last time you met."

Johanna looked at Jaufre and smiled. "Well," she said. "It worked at L'Arête."

"Did you hear that?"

"Hear what?"

"I could swear I heard someone singing." The guard peered over the wall.

A woman strolled up the road to the front gate like she owned it.

I came riding into a land on a blue goose
There I found marvels
A crow and a hawk catching pigs
A bear hunting a falcon and flies playing chess
A stag spinning silk and if this is true
A donkey makes hats

Her voice was a fine, warm, contralto. She looked up to see them peering down at her, and smiled at them. "Ho, my fine gentlemen," she said, "have you a few coins for a hungry minstrel? I promise to sing for my supper, and sing well, too."

They came through the small door cut into the larger one and gathered round to hear her sing. What was the harm, after all? Their lords and masters were away and their prisoner was safely tucked away. They might have hoped for other favors in addition to the serenade, but Jaufre put paid to that notion. He looked muscular, protective and like he knew how to use the short sword at his side.

He was also her accompanist, keeping time on two sticks he'd picked up in the forest. They could have taken him at a rush but some of them would have been hurt in the process, and besides, she sang so prettily, they just wanted to listen to her. She sang the drinking song, and the song of wandering clerks, and the song about the farmer's wife and the traveling tinker, and a Mongol marching song, and a song about a knight and his lady love. She sang for what felt like hours but was probably only one and perhaps a little more, before Jaufre heard an owl hoot three times from the trees to their left and poked Johanna in the back with one of the sticks. She finished the verse of the current song with a little trill and a bow and a beaming smile that set all of them aglow. "Thank you for your kind attention, good sirs. Your generosity will make the difference between my husband and I going to bed hungry or not this eve."

Jaufre doffed his cap and passed it around. The guards were generous within their means, and Johanna felt badly for fooling them, and for the punishment that would undoubtedly be coming to them in the morning. Jaufre returned with a respectable clank of coin and she thanked them warmly again, and sang her way down the road and out of sight.

She looked at Jaufre. "It can't be that easy."

A shout was heard behind them.

"No," he said, and hustled her toward the thicket, where North Wind stamped his impatience and where they found Wilmot and Alaric with a man they scarce recognized as the king who had commanded their performance. Gaunt, almost bald, he managed a smile that only made him look more like a death's head. "Good people, I thank you for the timely rescue."

"You got yourself out, sire," Wilmot said, "now we have to get you away."

Edward of Caernarfon cocked his head at the steadily rising clamor coming from behind the castle walls. "Indeed."

Jaufre unbuckled Johanna's sword and handed it back to her. She put it on while he untied his father's sword from North Wind's saddle and slung it over his shoulders. It wasn't a sword a poor minstrel would wear, and it would have been a curiosity and possibly a temptation to the castle guards.

They mounted without further ado, the king behind Wilmot for the first leg of the journey. Wilmot and Alaric had wrapped their horses' hooves in rags to muffle the sounds of their passage. The horses sensed the urgency of their riders, especially North Wind, who snorted and sidled impatiently, but Johanna kept him on a short rein, patting his neck and whispering soothingly into his ears. They moved at a forced walk, ignoring every instinct to break into a mad gallop, picking their way downstream through the forest, letting the trees hide them as long as possible.

"The king got himself out?" Jaufre said to Wilmot.

"Indeed, and slew the porter at the door who would bar his way," Wilmot said.

Jaufre and Johanna exchanged a glance. The death of one of the castle's men would make a hot pursuit that much more certain, particularly if the porter had friends among the guards. North Wind's pace quickened, and the other horses followed suit.

It had taken them four days to get from Glynnow to Berkeley. It took them nine days to return, with Jaufre fretting and swearing beneath his breath every day they had to remain hidden in dense thickets and rocky caves and one memorable evening in the middle of a moor that on every side threatened to suck them down to their deaths. The king took turns riding with Wilmot, Alaric and himself. Johanna brushed dirt into the stallion's hide every morning after they made camp, and every evening he ghosted his way over the countryside. The only people they saw were two young lovers trysting in a hay stack, who took one look at North Wind and ran screaming into the night.

For his part Jaufre lived every moment of the journey in the fear that Angelique would have come and gone before they got home. It had been easy to be caught up in the excitement of the rescue, but in the aftermath he was very much afraid that Tregloyne had been right, that his action had been foolish beyond permission and that he had risked the lives not only of every member of Wu Company but of Tregloyne, too, and everyone else in Glynnow for that matter. The farther south they traveled, the less triumphant he felt. Shasha had been right, and he had known it when they quarreled that last evening. After all, he had said the same many times himself. He was a trader, not a warrior.

He compensated by sleeping very little during that fraught journey, remaining awake no matter who was on watch, doggedly seeking out the least-traveled paths with the most cover, constantly alert to the possibility of anyone picking up their trail. He took it upon himself to check the horses at the beginning and end of every day, for fear that one would pick up a stone or cast a shoe or suddenly go lame. Days he sat with his father's sword drawn, laying across his lap, ready at need to defend himself and Johanna to the last drop of blood in his veins. Which it might come to, he thought bleakly.

But either they were very clever or very lucky, for they saw no one who looked like they might be interested in the king's whereabouts. Alaric in particular could not account for it, and was inclined to be indignant. "A royal prisoner escaped, and no hue and cry?"

"Under the circumstances," the king said dryly, "I will forgo the honor." He had held up remarkably well on the journey, unflagging and uncomplaining, although it was evident that he was unused to rough travel and was exhausted and half faint from hunger, as indeed they all were.

They reached Launceston at last. They stopped well out of town and Alaric went in on foot for food. He came out without food, stumbling in his haste to impart the news. "They are saying that you are dead of an accident, majesty," he told the king. "They say the warders cut your heart out and sent it to the queen as proof. Your body is to be buried in Gloucester Cathedral."

"What?"

"What!"

"But—"

"They lied," Johanna said. She looked at Jaufre, a smile spreading across her face. "The guards. They lied."

"Very probably at Maltravers' instigation," Wilmot said, thinking out loud.

"Maltravers?"

"The queen made him responsible for the king's person," Wilmot said. His mouth curved into a small, satisfied smile. "He is even now undoubtedly shaking in his boots imagining what Isabella and Mortimer would do to him if it became known the king had escaped his custody while Maltravers was off whoring in Bristol, never mind while guards under his command were humming along to an itinerant minstrel."

"Whoring?" Alaric said.

Wilmot shrugged. "One of his mistresses lives in Bristol. Maltravers is the veriest of dogs. It was easy enough to arrange."

"That's why no one is looking for him," Jaufre said," Or for us." He felt dizzy, and held a hand out to lean on a tree that was across the clearing, and then Johanna was there beside him, warm and solid. He looked up to see her grinning at him.

"Not yet," she whispered in his ear. "Wait to faint until we get home."

He let out a short laugh and pulled his scattered senses together.

"They took the porter's heart and sent it to the queen as proof," Alaric said in an almost awed voice. "And the porter will be buried in Gloucester Cathedral."

The king started to laugh. He laughed until he could no longer stand and Wilmot helped him to a seat on a fallen tree, where he laughed still more, clutching his belly and rocking back and forth.

Wilmot was distressed. "Majesty. Majesty, please, be calm. Be calm, sire."

Johanna thought His Majesty was in the first stages of hysteria, aggravated by hunger and fatigue, and wondered what the protocol was for slapping a king. Edward did calm, eventually, although occasional chuckles erupted like hiccups as they remounted and left Launceston behind. He was in much better spirits during the last leagues to Glynnow. They detoured around the village, wanting as few witnesses as possible. Along the cliff they rode and down the path to Tregloyne, where Tregloyne himself waited with a scowl on his face. The king dismounted. He was moving a little stiffly, but he looked less like a death's head and more like a man who might live to see the next day.

"Has Angelique been and gone?" Jaufre said.

"Once," Tregloyne said. "She should return shortly."

Jaufre went limp with relief.

"I tell you, Jaufre, I did not look to see you again alive," Tregloyne said. "And now that I do, I am not sure that I rejoice in the sight of you."

Jaufre held up a hand. "Peace, I beg you, Tregloyne. You cannot damn me any more than I damned myself all the way here from Berkeley."

Before Tregloyne could start in on him, Johanna said, "Have you heard the news, Tregloyne? Edward of Caernarfon is dead. They have sent his heart to the queen as proof."

Tregloyne scowled, looking from her to the king and back again. "What is this nonsense then, mistress Johanna?"

So they told him, and Tregloyne stared, dumbfounded, and then a rumble began in his chest that erupted in a braying laugh. He laughed until tears started from his eyes and then he laughed some more. They watched him, grinning, not least the king.

"Well," Tregloyne said, wiping away tears, "if I am to entertain royalty uninvited, I'd best get on with it. This way, sire."

He bowed the king into his house and gave him the spot closest to the fire and called for a blanket to wrap around his shoulders, and mulled wine and the inevitable pasties from the kitchen. Johanna returned from stabling the horses in time to polish off the dregs in the pitcher and the crumbs on the tray.

"Why, I know you," the king said to her, as one coming awake after a long sleep. "You sang for me. In Bristol, wasn't it?" He looked at Jaufre. "And you, too. And you, Alaric—Alaric de Claret, isn't it?"

Alaric bowed.

The king stared from one face to another. "You're not even English," Edward of Caernarfon said at last. "Not even Wilmot. Why would you do this for me?"

"Good question," Tregloyne said to Shasha, but he said it in a low voice that only she could hear.

"I did it because I took an oath to serve you, majesty," Wilmot said.

Jaufre glanced at Johanna. "We did it because Wilmot said they were going to kill you, and we could not bear to have someone who was so kind to us so unkindly used, if we could help it."

"I did it because my friend asked for my help," Alaric said. "And because my father was your liege man, which means I am, too."

The king smiled and shook his head. "You ran a dreadful risk."

"God's balls and that they did," Tregloyne said to Shasha, angry all over again.

"There is something you should know, sire," Wilmot said "Something we have not had the time to discuss."

"What is it, good Wilmot?"

"Your escape was arranged by your son, sire."

There was dead silence. "My son?" Edward said at last.

"Your son, majesty. He had me brought to him after you were taken in Wales, and bade me watch you wherever you were taken and report back to him on your condition and the manner of your keepers. When I heard of Mortimer's plot to murder your majesty, I rode to him and told him. He bid me arrange for de Berkeley and Maltravers to be called away to Bristol that night. Any guard is always lax absent supervision, no matter how well trained they are. You found it easy to get to the postern unobserved, I imagine."

Edward looked a little deflated at the thought that he might not have escaped under his own power after all.

"Majesty, forgive me for speaking so frankly, but your son bade me tell you he cannot guarantee your safety. His mother and Mortimer rule all. Later, when he gains full power, it may be safe for you to return."

Edward waved a hand and leaned against the warm stones next to the hearth, pulling the blanket more fully around his shoulders. "He won't ever want me back here," he said. "I am a danger to whoever rules England."

"That you are, old man," Tregloyne said. "I'm glad you finally recognize it." This time he didn't bother to lower his voice.

Edward either didn't hear him or pretended he didn't. "I am tired," he said. "I don't want to stay in England."

Wilmot said softly, "What do you want to do, majesty?"

The king's eyes were drooping. "I want quiet and safety. I want time, to confess, to repent, to make my peace with God. I have had enough of trying to rule an ungrateful people who so resent my friends that they rise up in rebellion against me." He opened one eye. "And I have had more than enough of Isabella. Tell my son I thank him for his timely rescue, and that I wish him well."

"But where do you want to go, majesty?" Wilmot said.

But the king was asleep.

"I know where he wants to go," Alaric said.

Jaufre understood immediately. "Can you get him there?"

Alaric looked almost beatific. "No one is looking for him. He's already dead."

"Oh," Wilmot said. "Alaric, of course. It would be the perfect place for him." He hesitated. "He cannot go alone, and I must return to the king."

"I will go with him," Alaric said, "and I will stay with him as long as he needs me." He paused, and said in a lower voice, "I have sins to repent me of, too."

Jaufre looked at Wilmot, and something in the other man's expression told Jaufre that that had been the plan all along.

The next morning they put it to Edward as they watched for a sail. "A monastery," he said. "In Lombardy, you say?"

"Yes, sire. It is a good place, beautiful and peaceful. Wilmot says your son has provided sufficient coin so that we may travel in comfort. I will guide you there, and stay with you as long as you wish."

The king smiled. "It seems I have my freedom, and a place to go. Now all we need is a ship."

But the ship did not come that day. That evening, Tregloyne took Alaric aside and said, "Are you going to tell him? Are you going to tell either one of them?"

"Tell them what?" Alaric said.

"Jaufre told me that Edward recognized Robert's family name, but Edward couldn't remember why. You know why, don't you?"

Alaric's face was a perfect blank. "Do I?"

"The reason Edward knows the name of de Beauville is that he has heard the story of the lovely Ailene de Beauville," Tregloyne said, "who caught his father's eye and whom his father then caught with child. Unfortunately, she was married to one of his own knights, who couldn't bear the sight of his fourth child, so unlike his other three, and so packed him off to the Knights Templar as soon as he was old enough to hold a sword. The sword, I am betting, that was given to Robert de Beauville by Longshanks himself before he left Outremer. The sword Jaufre of Cambaluc carries to this day." He paused. "Edward of Caernarfon and Robert de Beauville were half-brothers. Jaufre is Edward's nephew."

"You have no proof of any of this," Alaric said.

"I don't need it. All I have to do is look at them. Jaufre is Edward in another thirty years, or would be if Edward's recent time had not worn on him so. Why not tell them?"

"What good would it do?" Alaric said.

Tregloyne, goaded, said, "Why, then, bring Jaufre to the king's attention in the first place?"

Alaric folded his arms and sighed. "I owed his father my life. It is a debt even yet unpaid. I had hoped—but Gilbert had already spent what we took from Ruad. There was none left to benefit Jaufre. So then I thought that if I brought Jaufre to Edward's attention, that perhaps Edward would show the boy some favor, a knighthood, some land perhaps. Royal bastards never starve."

Tregloyne snorted. "Jaufre's not the starving type."

Alaric's mouth twisted up in a half smile. "No. No, he isn't."

"Does Wilmot know?"

"Like you, Wilmot knew the moment he set eyes on Jaufre." He looked at Tregloyne, very stern. "We will leave it to him to tell the new king. If he does, then Jaufre will have to be told, I suppose, but that, too, I leave to Wilmot." He looked across the room at the man dozing in Tregloyne's chair. "As for Edward of Caernarfon, you heard him yourself. He only wants peace."

The next day the *Faucon* came, and loaded a hold full of good English fleeces, one ex-Master of Glynnow, one ex-Knight Templar, and one ex-king, and set sail for Harfleur on the evening tide.

"Will we ever see Alaric again, do you think?" Johanna said.

They were standing at the top of the cliff, watching the ship sink below the horizon.

"I don't know," he said. He looked down at her and grinned. "We could always go visit him," he said.

She smiled. "We could," she said. "He's still a member of Wu Company, after all."

Hand in hand they walked home down the narrow cliff path.

· Twenty ·

December, 1327 A.D.
London

┝━━━┥

Woman should gather roses ere
    Time's ceasless foot o'ertaketh her,
    For if too long she make delay,
    Her chance of love may pass away.

A few ladies looked askance but Johanna proved she knew her audience well when the opening verse was greeted with a roar of male approval. Well, and wasn't it a man's world? Certainly it was best to let them think so. Smiling, she continued.

And well it is she seek it while
Health, strength, and youth around her smile.
To pluck the fruits of love in youth
Is each wise woman's rule forsooth,
For when age creepeth o'er us, hence
Go also the sweet joys of sense,
And ill doth she her days employ
Who lets life pass without love's joy.

Johanna's eyes met Jaufre's and she sang the last verse directly to him.

And if my counsel she despise,
Not knowing how 'tis just and wise,

Too late, alas! will she repent
When age is come, and beauty spent.

There was thunderous applause from the men, tepid applause from
the women, and Johanna took the moment to wink surreptitiously at
Edward's young queen, whose polite blankness eased into a brief but
genuine smile. Nearby, Wilmot, dressed now in the livery of Edward III,
gave Johanna a wry smile and a slight bow.

The full complement of Wu Company stood at her back, absent one.
Alma, Hayat and Hari had returned for a long visit on Angelique's
last trip to Glynnow for the year. Tiphaine had acquired a timbrel and
had worked up a flourish of different accompaniments to their most
requested songs. She stood very proud in her new blue robes, a red
ribbon tying back her black curls. Hari hummed as well as ever, and
Shasha, Firas and Jaufre gave body and soul to every chorus.

For an encore, Johanna sang of the village of Ferlec, where whatever you
saw first upon waking was what you worshipped for the rest of the day,
be it your wife, the rising sun, or your neighbor's pig. Always leave them
laughing, she thought, and struck the final chord with a flourish as she
laughed along with them.

Edward himself led the applause, and came forward to take her hands
and raise her to her feet. "And what will you do to keep yourself
occupied between songs, hmm?" he asked her, his brilliant blue eyes
caressing the curves beneath the embroidery of her robe.

"Why, I believe I would like to raise horses, sire," Johanna said demurely.

"Then so you shall, my dear," Edward said, dropping a kiss on the
back of the hand he still held. "So long as you pay me in song every
Christmas. It is agreed?"

"It is, sire."

"Good." And then, because even at fifteen Edward Plantagenet was as
much man as king, he turned Johanna's hand up and placed another
kiss on the inside of her wrist. He raised his head and looked at her with
a smile and a query in his eyes.

She met his smile with one of her own, and withdrew her hand gently from his to place it on Jaufre's wrist.

Edward gave up her hand with good grace, flicked Tiphaine's nose with a finger, and clapped his unacknowledged cousin on the back. "Congratulations, Jaufre, Master of Glynnow. You have won name, hearth and hand this day."

Edward had done his level best to make Jaufre accept a title. Jaufre had remained steadfast in his refusal, and when Wilmot reported that Jaufre and Wu Company were going to single-handedly double the tax revenue from that part of Cornwall, Edward desisted. All it cost him was an exclusive royal charter to buy and ship good English wool between Tregloyne and Harfleur.

Jaufre, whose eyes had darkened when Edward kissed Johanna's hand, responded to the death grip on his wrist and managed to reply to Edward's pleasantries with a reasonable amount of civility. Edward laughed out loud, interpreting the stilted phrases with no difficulty, and moved on.

Johanna sighed, and felt her body relax with the release of tension. "I was afraid you were going to hit him," she murmured.

Jaufre looked down at her, at the changeable gray eyes, at the pure texture of her skin, at the unbound chestnut hair tumbling from brow to breast, at the lithe curves beneath the Robe of a Thousand Larks. It was five years since they had left Cambaluc, to begin the long journey that would bring them adventure and sorrow, new friends as well as new enemies, and, at long last, a home.

He said, the warmth of a smile in his voice, "So was I. But how can I blame him? I want to take you to bed, too."

And they laughed, their voices blending together as they did in song, as their lives would down the long years at Glynnow. Wu Company laughed with them, and irresistibly so did the members of the court, even if they didn't know why.

And if they did not live happily ever after, well, that is only to be expected. There would be children, who bring their own heartaches with them into this world, and there would be prosperity, but only after great toil, and there would be safety, although it would be paid for with precious blood.

But let it here be said that Jaufre of Glynnow and Johanna his wife lived longer, laughed louder, and loved better than many of that time, and they would not have changed their place with kings.

Timeline

Fictional events in italics.

1215

Kublai Khan born

1254

Marco Polo born

1270

Edward I of England joins French King Louis IX on Crusade

1271

The Polos depart Venice for Chandu

The beginning of the Ninth (and last) Crusade

1272

The end of the Ninth Crusade

1275

The Polos arrive in Chandu

1280

Alaric the Templar born in Languedoc

1281

Robert de Beauville born in England

1285

Marco Polo given a concubine by Kublai Khan, the beautiful Shu Lin

1289

Marco Polo and Shu Lin have a daughter, Shu Ming

1291

Acre falls to the Mameluks

1292

The Polos leave China

Kublai Khan holds Shu Lin and Shu Ming hostage against Marco Polo's return

Marco commits them to the care of his merchant friend, Wu Hai

Ogodei born to Daiyin

1294

Kublai Khan dies

Shu Lin dies

Wu Hai marries Shu Ming, age 5, to his son, Wu Li, age 9

1296

Robert de Beauville joins the Knights Templar

1302

The Templars lose Ruad

1306

Agalia, a Greek merchant's daughter, marries Robert de Beauville, ex-Templar, in Antioch

Jaufre, their son, born

Johanna born to Wu Li and Shu Ming

Shu Shao, 12, becomes her foster sister

1307

Wu Hai dies, Wu Li inherits all

Philip IV arrests all Knights Templar in France

July—Edward I dies

1308

February 25—Edward II crowned at Westminster

1309

March Pope Clement VI moves papacy to Avignon

Papal bull dissolving the Knights Templar

Giovanni Soranzo elected Doge of Venice

November—Edward III born at Windsor

1312

Wu Li, Shu Ming, and Johanna find Jaufre east of Kashgar, the lone survivor of a caravan attacked by bandits

1314

March 18—Knight Templar masters Jacques de Molay and Geoffroi de Charney burned at the stake in Paris by Philip IV

Philip IV of France dies

Battle of Bannockburn

1314-1317

Hard winter and wet summers

Crops fail, Europeans starve and some resort to cannibalism

1316

August 7—Pope John XXII crowned in Avignon

1320

November—Shu Ming dies

1321

July—Wu Li marries Dai Fang

1322

Wu Li dies

April—Johanna, Jaufre and Shu Shao leave Cambaluc

June—Arrive Kashgar

Firas, Hari and Félicien join the company

August—The company crosses Terak Pass

1323

Ogodei arrives at Talikan

Alaric joins the company

October—Arrive Gaza

November—Arrive Venice

1324

January 8—Marco Polo dies

January—Tiphaine joins the company

May—The wedding to the sea

Summer—Wu Company travels and trades through Lombardy

September—Wu Company travels to Avignon

October—Wu Company travels to Chartres

1325

April—Wu Company travels to England

1326

September—Isabella, Mortimer and Edward III cross the channel and land in Suffolk

October—Edward III assumes his duties as heir

November—Edward II captured by Isabella's forces

1327

January 24—Edward II of England deposed in favor of Edward III with his mother as regent

February 1 Edward III crowned at Westminster

April, July, September—Plots discovered to free Edward II

September 21—Edward II dies in Berkeley Castle

Supplemental

Including cast of characters, place names, historical notes, and the Silk and Song Bureau of Weights and Measures.

Abraham of Acre Wu Li's agent in Gaza.

Agalia Jaufre's mother, Robert de Beauville's wife. Sold to Sheik Saghir bin Nazari as the Lycian Lotus.

Alaric de Claret Knight Templar.

Al-Idrisi A Persian mapmaker of great renown.

Alma An inmate of Sheik Mohammed's harem, a scholar.

Ambroise de L'Arête Also known as The Blade. Lord of L'Arête by marriage.

Audouard Second in command to Florian.

Angelique Ship owner and captain, smuggler, sister to Alaric de Claret.

Anwar the Egyptian Slave dealer in Kashgar.

Balasaga An historical province of Persia, now Iran.

Bao A personal seal. Chinese.

Basil the Frank Wu Li's agent in Baghdad.

Bastak A small town in central Persia, ten days' ride west of Kerman.

Bayan Genghis Khan's favorite general. Friend to Marco Polo.

Beda Bedouin.

Bernart Page to Ambroise de l'Arête.

Bible All verses quoted are from the Vulgate Bible, English translation via the website vulgate.org. The King James version was three hundred years down the road.

Biblioteca Nazionale Marciana The National Library of St. Mark's, in Venice. I have advanced its existence by several centuries so Alma wouldn't drive everyone crazy that winter in Venice.

Blister Foot-and-mouth disease, which produces blisters on cows and camels and anything with a split hoof. It is highly contagious and was indeed used as a bioweapon.

Bo He Dai Fang's doorman.

Brescia Then a city-state in Lombardy, Italy. Now just a city.

The *Silk and Song* Bureau of Weights and Measures No two nations back in 1322 measured anything the same way, so here for the sake of narrative clarity and my sanity time is measured in minutes, hours, days, weeks, months and years, and no notice is taken of that error in Julius Caesar's 45 BC calendar that wouldn't be corrected until 1582 AD by Pope Gregory XIII.

Length is measured in fingers (about an inch), hands (about 4 inches), rods (16.5 feet) and leagues (3 miles).

Travel is measured in leagues, about three miles or the distance a man could walk in an hour.

Fabric is measured in ells from China to England. Smaller lengths are fingers (three-quarters of an inch) and hands (three to four inches).

Google "weights in the Middle Ages" and you get over 8 million hits. Here, I use drams (one ounce), gills (four ounces), cups (eight ounces), pints (16 ounces), quarts (32 ounces) and gallons (124 ounces) in ascending order of liquid measurement.

Dry weight pounds then ranged from 300 grams to 508 grams, so the hell with it, here it's 16 ounces or about 453 grams. Ten pounds is a tenweight, and yes, I just made that right up. A hundredweight is a hundred pounds.

Caffa Now Feodosia, Crimea.

Calicut Now Kozhikode, India.

Cambaluc Built by Kublai Khan. Became the basis for what is now the Forbidden City in Beijing, China.

Ceylon Today, Sri Lanka.

Chang'an Now Xi'an, China.

Cheche Pronounced "shesh." A long scarf, usually indigo-dyed blue, worn by Tuaregs. It can be knotted many different ways to keep the sun out of the eyes and protect the neck and face from sunburn. The indigo leeched onto the face and hands of the wearer. Or, alternatively, depending on which story you believe, Tuaregs deliberately dyed their face and hands blue to protect themselves from the sun. I heard both in Morocco.

Chi Yuan A powerful Mandarin at the court of the Great Khan, and Dai Fang's uncle.

Chiang Edyk the Portuguese's manservant.

Cipangu Now Japan.

Countries France wasn't France as we know it in 1322, and thanks to Henry II of England's heritage and marriage they would be disputing boundaries with England for for a Hundred Years' War. Italy certainly wasn't Italy, being a haphazard collection of city-states like Venice that spent most of their time making bloody war on one another and who suffered greatly during the Hundred Years War at the hands of condottiere like John Hawkwood. Fortunately, my characters don't go to Germany so I don't have to try to explain the Holy Roman Empire or even mention Charlemagne, except here. I am relieved to report that England really was England. For convenience I refer to each by its modern name, and again I have moved up, pushed back and eliminated events to suit my plot. My book, my rules.

Currency Tael: China. Bezants: Byzantium. Drachma: Arabic. England: Silver penny. France: Livre, and I cannot tell you how much it delights me that today this word in French means "book."

Now that's currency. Florence: Florins. Venice: Accommodate all currencies but rely on gemstones. In *A Distant Mirror: The Calamitous 14th Century*, Barbara Tuchman writes, "...the non-specialist reader would be well advised not to worry about it, because the names of coins and currency mean nothing anyway except in terms of purchasing power." Surely a bargain in Baghdad that begins with a search for bezants to buy malachite beads which is concluded with a horse race sufficiently illuminates her statement.

Curzola Now Korkula, an island in Croatia.

Dai Fang Wu Li's second wife. Johanna's step-mother. Gokudo's lover.

Dayir Aide to Bayan. Friend of Marco Polo. Ogodei's father.

Ambroise De L'Arête Lord of Château L'Arête by marriage.

Deshi the Scout Caravan master to Wu Li.

Edward I of England King of England, 1272–1307. Known also as Longshanks. Yes, he was in Acre in 1271 at the same time as the Polos, and as fellow strangers in a strange land are surely drawn together in faraway places even today, Edward and the Polos could have met. Maffeo and Niccolo had already been to the court of the Khan and they could have dined out forever on tales of Cathay. Why not at table with kings? Marco Polo certainly did after he got home.

Edward II of England King of England, 1307–1237. Oh my yes, lots of competing stories here. When you tour Nottingham Castle, the guide will tell you definitively that Edward II was killed in September 1327 by having a red-hot poker shoved up his rectum. Barbarity in the Middle Ages was not reserved to Mongols. But! In the 1800s a letter written to Edward III from a papal prelate was found, telling of Edward III's father killing his jailer and escaping into the night, eventually ending his days as a monk in Italy. It is even rumored that Edward III met with Edward II in Koblenz in 1338. Note: He was imprisoned by Isabella and Mortimer first in Kenilworth and then in Berkeley, but for the purposes of my plot I have imprisoned him only in Berkeley.

Edward III of England King of England, 1327–1377. True, he was only fourteen in 1327, but fourteen then and fourteen now are two very different things. He was the heir to a throne and had his share of the Plantagenet good looks. Very little would have been denied him. He could have had Johanna on the nearest flat surface in five minutes and no one would have lifted a finger to stop him. But he was also a lover of all things Arthurian and the creator of the Order of the Garter in the Round Table's image, and I have chosen to imagine him as being amused by and respectful of Jaufre's prior claim.

Edyk the Portuguese Trader residing in Cambaluc.

Ell See Bureau of Weights and Measures above. The distance from a man's elbow to the tip of his middle finger, or about 18 inches. A standard unit of measurement for textiles in the Middle Ages, and never mind the differences between Scots, English, Flemish, Polish, German and French ells.

Europe A name I did not discover has been in use since Anaximander until I was writing Book III. What a futile thing is research.

Fatima Daughter of Malala and Ahmed, betrothed of Azar, friend to Johanna.

Félicien Old lord of L'Arête.

Félicien Goliard.

Félicienne Daughter to the lord of L'Arête.

Firas A Nazari Ismaili from Alamut, the hereditary home of the Old Man of the Mountain, leader of the Assassins.

Florian Lieutenant for Ambroise de L'Arête.

Gokudo Samurai, now ronin. Dai Fang's lover and hatchet man.

Giovanni Gradenigo Ship's captain, and member of a powerful Venetian shipping family.

Grigori the Tatar Wu Li's agent in Kabul.

Guilham Page to Ambroise de L'Arête.

Gujarat Now a province in northwest India.

Hari Chughi monk, itinerant preacher, self-styled priest.

Hayat An inmate of Sheik Mohammed's harem. A weaver.

Hicca A boy of Glynnow.

Hilde Servant of L'Arête.

Ibn Battuta Berber slave trader, 1304-1369, known for writing *The Rihla (The Journey)*, an account of his extensive travels throughout the medieval, mostly Muslim world. I have advanced his first visit to Kabul purely for the convenience of my plot.

Ibn Tabib Doctor in Kabul.

Philippe Imbert Agent for the Gradenigo interests in Lyon.

Ishan Stablemaster to Sheik Mohammed of Talikan.

Jaufre of Cambaluc Son of Agalia and Robert de Beauville. Orphaned on the Silk Road, rescued by Wu Li, raised as Johanna's foster brother.

Jibran Headman of the village of Aab.

Joan Burgh English pilgrim on the Jerusalem Journey. Based on the real life Margery Kempe.

Johanna of Cambaluc Daughter of Wu Li and Shu Ming, granddaughter of Marco Polo and Shu Lin. Known in Sheik Mohammed's harem as Nazirah.

John XXII Pope in Avignon from 1316–1334.

Kabul Now the capital of Afghanistan. Holdout against attack from every invading force from Alexander the Great on, including Genghis Khan, the USSR and the USA.

Kadar The chief eunuch in Sheik Mohammed's harem.

Kerra A girl of Glynnow, Johanna's stablehand.

Khuree The summer capital of the Mongols. Now Ulan Bator, Mongolia.

Kinsai Now Hangzhou, or Hangchow, China.

Koran Or Quran. All quotations from quran.com.

Lanchow Now Lanzhou, China.

League The distance one person could walk in an hour, also defined as about three miles. I have rounded up and down. The Khan's yambs were built every 25 miles, therefore in Silk and Song every eight leagues. The Khan's imperial mailmen rode 200 miles daily, hence sixty leagues. Close enough for government work and fiction.

The Levant From Wikipedia: "A geographic and cultural region consisting of the eastern Mediterranean between Anatolia and Egypt...The Levant consists today of Lebanon, Syria, Jordan, Israel, Palestine, Cyprus and parts of southern Turkey. Iraq and the Sinai Peninsula are also sometimes included."

Mangu Cook in Wu Li's caravan.

Marco Polo Venetian merchant, c.1254–1324. Traveled to China with his father and uncle where they spent twenty years working for Kublai Khan. He did say upon his deathbed, "I did not tell half of what I saw."

Did Marco leave a daughter behind when he finally went home? I'd be surprised if he didn't leave a dozen. In any edition of his memoir, no matter how bowdlerized, it is clear that he loved the ladies, and during the twenty years he was from home he must have gotten lucky at least a couple of times. If he didn't, yes, by Marco's own account Kublai Khan did in fact exact tributes of nubile young women from his various suzerainties, enjoy their company, and then award them as gifts to his vassals. This was deemed to be the highest honor. Marco was a personable and capable young man, high in the Khan's favor. It is reasonable to suppose he might have been so rewarded, so I have the taken the liberty to suppose it here.

The Travels of Marco Polo Published as *Il Milione* in 1300, and Marco himself was nicknamed "Marco Milione" because of the exaggerated figures he used in description. His stories were at first disbelieved and derided, especially by comparison to Sir John Mandeville's book, which was of course the truth, the whole truth and nothing but the truth itself. Much later, when advanced scholarship discredited Mandeville as a fabulist and a plagiarist, Marco's far better informed star (and story) rose by comparison. You can see Christopher Columbus' copy, with marginalia by Columbus himself, in the Biblioteca Columbina in Seville.

Donata Polo Marco Polo's second wife. Mother of Fantina, Bellela, and Moreta.

Moreta Polo Daughter of Marco and Donata Polo.

Middle Sea The Mediterranean. Also called the Western Sea.

Mien Now Myanmar, or Burma.

Mintan A short-waisted, long-sleeved coat. Ottoman.

Mohammed Sheik of Talikan. Father of Sabir.

Mongol battle tactics and strategy Surrender or die. If you surrendered, you would continue to live, albeit under Mongol rule, which was, amazingly, pretty reasonable. If you fought, if you crossed them or betrayed them in any way, they would annihilate you with whatever means they had to hand. They mounted hundreds of thousands of soldiers with extensive training. Their engineers were superb. They didn't travel with siege engines, they built them from available materials when it came time to use them. They'd catapult anything into a city they thought would kill and spread terror, naphtha bombs, stoppered urns filled with poisonous snakes and spiders that burst upon impact, bodies dead from the plague (weapons that stretch back to antiquity, FYI, the Mongols didn't have to invent them). When the city fell, as it almost invariably did, the Mongols would send in execution squads to kill off any remaining survivors, including women and children. Sometimes they'd save the soldiers and the engineers and put them to work. Sometimes the conquered soldiers would be placed in front in the attack on the next target, keeping the Mongols' own soldiers in reserve until the besieged ran out of ammunition. You really, really didn't want to get on their bad side, and it astonishes me how many cities didn't just strike their colors at the first hint of a Mongol flag on the horizon.

Mongols and torture Yes, they did those things. Those exact things. And more.

Mysore Then as now, a city in northwest India.

Ogodei Son of Dayir. One of the twelve barons of the Shiang. Named for Ghengis Khan's successor.

Paiza The royal Mongol passport. The Mongols called it a gerrega. Also a yarlik.

Pascau A boatman of Avignon.

Peter Marco Polo's Mongol servant.

Philosophy The words "science" and "scientists" would not be invented for another five hundred years. I have used "philosopher" here as a catch-all for anyone studying the hard sciences.

Rambahadur Raj Havildar of the first caravan into Kabul in 1323.

Robert de Beauville Knight Templar, Jaufre's father, Agalia's husband.

Messire Roland A fencing master in Venice.

Roubin Page to Ambroise de l'Aréte.

Sabir Sheik Mohammed's son and heir.

Eremo di Sant' Alberto The Hermitage of St. Albert in Pavia, Italy. A real place I shanghaied for my own fell purpose.

Shang-tu The summer capital of the Mongols. Now Ulan Bator, Mongolia. Also called Khuree.

Shensi Now Shaanxi, China.

Shidibala Gegeen Khan The Khan in Cambulac when Johanna and company departed. I have waved my authorial wand and made his tenure in office even shorter than it actually was.

Shu Lin Shu Ming's mother, Marco Polo's concubine, the Khan's gift to Marco Polo, Johanna's grandmother.

Shu Ming Johanna's mother, Wu Li's wife, Shu Lin's daughter, Marco Polo's daughter.

Shu Shao Also called "Shasha." Johanna's foster sister, wise woman.

Silk Road The trade route(s) between Europe and China. "Silk Road" is a term that did not come into common use until the twentieth century. Here I use the more generic Road.

Giovanni Soranzo Doge of Venice 1312–1328.

Talan A boy of Glynnow, Johanna's stablehand.

Talikan I have appropriated the name of today's tiny (pop. 43) village in northeast Iran for Sheik Mohammed's great walled city of 1323, which exists somewhere in Dana World south and west of the Terak Pass and south and east of the Caspian Sea.

Templars Their order existed for nearly 200 years, from between the First and Second Crusades until their dissolution in 1307 (or 1312 or 1314, take your pick). They weren't all slaughtered, contrary to the fervent wishes of Philip the Fair of France, and after the dissolution many were allowed to join the Knights of the Hospital and other orders. As late as 1338, former Templars were still drawing pensions in England. Surely others, perhaps those who felt themselves more at risk, must have seen the writing on the wall and decamped early enough to escape the coming purge. It isn't much of a stretch to imagine them hiring their experienced swords as caravan guards after their Templar gig fell through. It is no stretch at all to imagine some of them absconding with whatever treasure was near to hand on their way out the door.

Tiphaine Venetian street kid.

Time See Bureau of Weights and Measures above. In Europe: divided into times for prayer. Matins: midnight. Lauds: 3am. Prime: Sunrise. Terce: Mid-morning. Sext: Noon. None: Mid-afternoon. Vespers: Sunset. Compline: Bedtime.

Tregloyne Master of Glynnow in Cornwall, England.

Turgesh, or Turkic Turkey, or Turkish.

Umar al-Khayyam Omar Khayyám, author of the Rubáiyát of Omar Khayyám, a verse of which Johanna translates so ably under Alma's direction.

Wilmot of Bavaria Knight Templar.

Wu Cheng Wu Li's brother. A eunuch who was gelded by his parents for advancement at court. Fell out of favor when the old Khan died and with the help of his brother went into business as a trader on the Road.

Wu Hai Marco Polo's friend and Wu Li's father.

Wu Li Johanna's father, Shu Ming's husband, and later Dai Fang's husband.

Bibliography

Silk and Song was influenced by the work of many scholars, without whose heavy lifting this by comparison light-hearted romp would not have been possible. Here is a list of just a few of the books that helped Johanna and Jaufre on their way.

Ackroyd, Peter. *Foundation: The history of England from its earliest beginnings to the Tudors.*

Bergreen, Laurence. *Marco Polo, From Venice to Xanadu.*

Bonavia, Judy. *The Silk Road.*

Boorstin, Daniel. J. *The Discoverers: A History of Man's Search to Know His World and Himself.*

Brown, Lloyd A. *The Story of Maps.*

Brown, Michelle. *The World of the Luttrell Psalter.*

Burman, Edward. *The Assassins.*

—. *The World before Columbus, 1100-1492.*

Cahill, Thomas. *Mysteries of the Middle Ages: The Rise of Feminism, Science and Art from the Cults of Catholic Europe.*

Cantor, Norman. *The Medieval Reader.*

Caro, Ina. *Paris to the Past: Traveling through French History by Train.*

Chareyron, Nicole. *Pilgrims to Jerusalem in the Middle Ages.*

Collis, Louise. *Memoirs of a Medieval Woman: the Life and Times of Margery Kempe.*

Costain, Thomas. *The Three Edwards.*

Coss, Peter. *The Lady in Medieval England, 1000-1500.*

Croutier, Alev Lytle. *Harem, The World Behind the Veil.*

Crowley, Roger. *City of Fortune.*

Dalrymple, William. *In Xanadu.*

Dougherty, Martin. *Weapons & Fighting Techniques of the Medieval Warrior.*

Evangelisti, Silvia. *Nuns: A History of Convent Life.*

Foltz, Richard C. *Religions of the Silk Road.*

Fox, Sally, researched and edited by. *The Medieval Woman: An Illuminated Book of Days.*

Freeman, Margaret B. *Herbs For The Medieval Household For Cooking, Healing And Divers Uses.*

Gies, Frances and Joseph. *Cathedral, Forge, and Waterwheel: Technology and Invention in the Middle Ages.*

—. *Life in a Medieval City.*

—. *Marriage and the Family in the Middle Ages.*

Gillman, Ian, and Hans-Joachim Klimkett. *Christians in Asia before 1500.*

Grotenhuis, Elizabeth Ten, editor. *Along the Silk Road.*

Hansen, Valerie. *Silk Road, A New History.*

Hollister, C. Warren. *Medieval Europe.*

Hutton, Alfred. *The Sword and the Centuries.*

Jones, Dan. *The Plantagenets.*

Jones, Terry. *Medieval Lives.*

Lacey, Robert & Danny Danzier. *The Year 1000, What Life was Like at the Turn of the First Millennium.*

Leon, Vicky. *Uppity Women of Medieval Times.*

Lewis, Raphael. *Everyday Life in Ottoman Turkey.*

Manchester, William. *A World Lit Only by Fire.*

Mayor, Adrienne. *Greek Fire, Poison Arrows & Scorpion Bombs: Biological and Chemical Warfare in the Ancient World.*

Miller, Malcolm. *Chartres Cathedral.*

Mortimer, Ian. *Medieval Intrigue.*

—. *The Time Traveler's Guide to Medieval England.*

Newman, Sharan. *The Real History Behind the Templars.*

Norwich, John Julius. *A History of Venice.*

Polo, Marco. *The Adventures of Marco Polo.* Multiple editions.

Rowling, Marjorie. *Everyday Life of Medieval Travelers.*

—. *Life in Medieval Times.*

Stark, Freya. *The Valleys of the Assassins.*

Starr, S. Frederick. *Lost Enlightenment: Central Asia's Golden Age from the Arab Conquest to Tamerlane.*

Tooley, Ronald Vere. *Maps and Map-Makers.*

Trask, Willard R. *Medieval Lyrics of Europe.*

Tuchman, Barbara. *A Distant Mirror, The Calamitous 14th Century.*

Turner, Jack. *Spice: The History of a Temptation.*

Weatherford, Jack. *Genghis Khan and the Making of the Modern World.*

Whitfield, Susan. *Life Along the Silk Road.*

Wood, Frances. *The Silk Road, Two Thousand Years in the Heart of Asia.*

The first historical novels I read were bestsellers in the '50s and as such available in the '60s as tattered paperbacks in boat cubbies all over southcentral Alaska, which was how they swam into my ken. They include but are not limited to Anya Seton, Thomas B. Costain, Norah Lofts, Samuel Shellabarger, Georgette Heyer, Frank G. Slaughter, Grace Ingram, C. S. Forester, and Rosemary Sutcliff.

Nowadays I read Diana Gabaldon (*Outlander*), Sharon Kay Penman (*Princes of Gwynedd*), Sharan Newman (*Catherine LeVendeur*), Francine Matthews (aka Stephanie Barron and the Jane Austen history mysteries), C.J. Sansom (*Matthew Shardlake*), Imogen Robertson (*Westerman and Crowther*) and P. F. Chisholm (*Sir Robert Carey*), as well as the late Ariana Franklin (*Adelia Aguilar*), Ellis Peters (*Brother Cadfael*) and Elizabeth Peters (*Amelia Peabody*).

For a lifetime of enjoyment and for the inspiration to write my own, my heartfelt thanks to you all.

├──────┤

This book was designed, edited and set by Gere Donovan Press
in Vancouver, WA and printed by CreateSpace in the USA.

The text face is Minion Pro, designed by Robert Slimbach.
An enlargement and revision of Slimbach's original Minion
type (Adobe, 1989), it was inspired by the elegant faces of the
late Renaissance.

The cover and interior title are set in Neris, designed by
Eimantas Paškonis. It takes its name from the river Neris that
flows through the designer's hometown of Vilnius, Lithuania.

├──────┤